Jane Harper is the author of the international bestsellers *The Dry* and *Force of Nature*. Her books are published in more than thirty-six territories worldwide, with film rights sold to Reese Witherspoon and Bruna Papandrea. Jane has won numerous top awards including the Australian Book Industry Awards Book of the Year, the Australian Indie Awards Book of the Year, the CWA Gold Dagger Award for Best Crime Novel and the British Book Awards Crime and Thriller Book of the Year. Jane was born in the UK and worked as a print journalist for thirteen years both in the UK and Australia. She now lives in Melbourne with her husband and daughter.

Also by Jane Harper

The Dry
Force of Nature

JANE HARPER

THE

LOST MAN

ABACUS

ABACUS

First published in Australia in 2018 by Pan Macmillan Australia Pty Ltd
First published in Great Britain in 2019 by Little, Brown
This paperback edition published in 2019 by Abacus

1 3 5 7 9 10 8 6 4 2

A CIP catalogue record for this book
is available from the British Library.

ISBN 978-0-349-14213-5

Typeset in Bembo by M Rules
Printed and bound in Great Britain by
Clays Ltd, Elcograf S.p.A.

Papers used by Abacus are from well-managed forests
and other responsible sources.

Abacus
An imprint of
Little, Brown Book Group
Carmelite House
50 Victoria Embankment
London EC4Y 0DZ

An Hachette UK Company
www.hachette.co.uk

www.littlebrown.co.uk

For Pete and Charlotte, with love

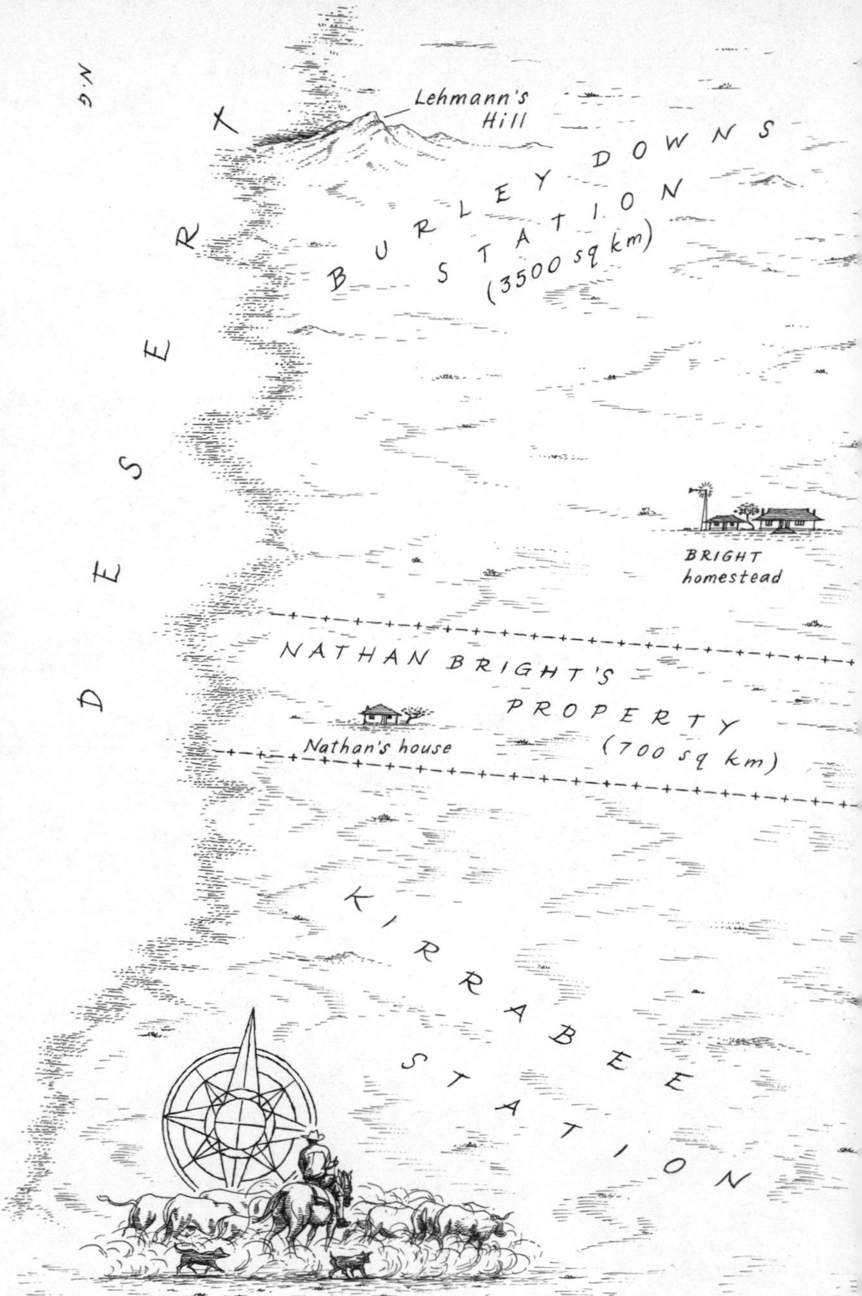
DESERT
Lehmann's Hill
BURLEY DOWNS STATION
(3500 sq km)
BRIGHT homestead
NATHAN BRIGHT'S PROPERTY
(700 sq km)
Nathan's house
KIRRABEE STATION

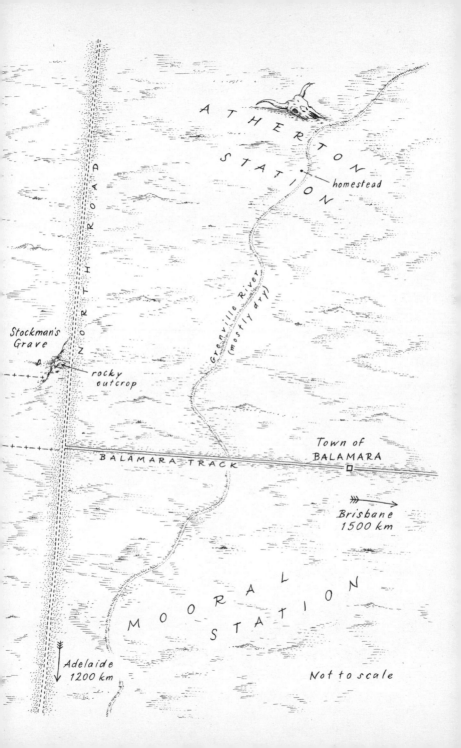

Prologue

From above, from a distance, the marks in the dust formed a tight circle. The circle was far from perfect, with a distorted edge that grew thick, then thin and broke completely in places. It also wasn't empty.

In the centre was a headstone, blasted smooth by a hundred-year assault from sand, wind and sun. The headstone stood a metre tall and was still perfectly straight. It faced west, towards the desert, which was unusual out there. West was rarely anyone's first choice.

The name of the man buried beneath had long since vanished and the landmark was known to locals – all sixty-five of them, plus 100,000 head of cattle – simply as the stockman's grave. That piece of land had never been a cemetery; the stockman had been put into the ground where he had died, and in more than a century no-one had joined him.

If a visitor were to run their hands over the worn stone, a partial date could be detected in the indentations. A one and an eight and a nine, maybe – 1890-something. Only three words were still visible. They had been carved lower down, where they had better shelter from the elements. Or perhaps they had been chiselled more deeply to start with; the message deemed more important than the man. They read:

who went astray

Months, up to a year even, could slip away without a single visitor passing by, let alone stopping to read the faded inscription or squint west into the afternoon sun. Even the cattle didn't linger. The ground was typically sandy and sparse for eleven months of the year and hidden under murky floodwater for the rest. The cows preferred to wander north, where the pickings were better and trees offered shade.

So the grave stood mostly alone, next to a thin three-wire cattle fence. The fence stretched a dozen kilometres east to a road and a few hundred west to the desert, where the horizon was so flat it seemed possible to detect the curvature of the earth. It was a land of mirages, where the few tiny trees in the far distance shimmered and floated on non-existent lakes.

There was a single homestead somewhere to the north of the fence, and another to the south. Next-door neighbours, three hours apart. The road to the east was invisible from the grave itself. And road was a generous description. The wide dirt track could sit silent for days without being troubled by a vehicle.

The track eventually led to the town of Balamara – a single street, really – which catered loosely for a scattered population that could almost fit into one large room when gathered together. Fifteen hundred kilometres further east lay Brisbane and the coast.

At scheduled times during the year, the sky above the stockman's grave would vibrate with the roar of a helicopter. The pilots worked the land from the air, using noise and movement to herd cattle over distances the size of small European countries. For now, though, the sky loomed empty and large.

Later – too late – a helicopter would fly over, deliberately low and slow. The pilot would spot the car first, with its hot metal winking. The grave, some distance away, would draw his attention only by chance as he circled around and back in search of a suitable landing site.

The pilot would not see the dust circle. It was the flash of blue material against the red ground that would catch his eye. A work shirt, unbuttoned and partially removed. The temperature the past few days had hit forty-five degrees at the afternoon peak. The exposed skin was sun-cracked.

Later, those on the ground would see the thick and thin marks in the dust and would fix their eyes on the distant horizon, trying not to think about how they had been made.

The headstone threw a small shadow. It was the only shade in sight and its blackness was slippery, swelling and shrinking as it ticked around like a sundial. The man had crawled, then dragged himself as it moved. He had squeezed into that shade, contorting his body into desperate shapes, kicking and scuffing the ground as fear and thirst took hold.

He had a brief respite as night fell, before the sun rose and the terrible rotation started again. It didn't last as long on the second day, as the sun moved higher in the sky. The man had tried though. He had chased the shade until he couldn't anymore.

The circle in the dust fell just short of one full revolution. Just short of twenty-four hours. And then, at last, the stockman finally had company, as the earth turned and the shadow moved on alone, and the man lay still in the centre of a dusty grave under a monstrous sky.

Chapter 1

Nathan Bright could see nothing, and then everything all at once.

He had crested the rise, gripping the steering wheel as the off-road terrain tried to snatch control from his hands, and suddenly it was all there in front of him. Visible, but still miles away, giving him too many minutes to absorb the scene as it loomed larger. He glanced over at the passenger seat.

'Don't look,' he was tempted to say, but didn't bother. There was no point. The sight dragged the gaze.

Still, he stopped the car further from the fence than he needed to. He pulled on the handbrake, leaving the engine and the air conditioner running. Both protested the Queensland December heat with discordant squeals.

'Stay in the car,' he said.

'But —'

Nathan slammed the door before he heard the rest. He walked to the fence line, pulled the top wires apart and climbed through from his side to his brothers'.

A four-wheel drive was parked near the stockman's grave, its own engine still running and its air conditioner also spinning full pelt, no doubt. Nathan cleared the fence as the driver's door opened and his youngest brother stepped out.

'G'day,' Bub called, when Nathan was close enough to hear.

'G'day.'

They met by the headstone. Nathan knew he would have to look down at some point. He delayed the moment by opening his mouth.

'When did you —' He heard movement behind him and pointed. 'Oi! Stay in the bloody car!' He had to shout to cover the distance and it came out more harshly than he'd intended. He tried again. 'Stay in the car.'

Not much better, but at least his son listened.

'I forgot you had Xander with you,' Bub said.

'Yeah.' Nathan waited until the car door clicked shut. He could see Xander's outline through the windshield; at sixteen, more man than boy these days. He turned back to his brother. The one standing in front of him, at least. Their third sibling, middle-born Cameron Bright, lay at their feet at the base of the headstone. He had been covered, thank God, by a faded tarp.

Nathan tried again. 'How long have you been here?'

Bub thought for a moment, the way he often did, before answering. His eyes were slightly hooded under the brim of his hat, and his words fell a fraction of a beat slower than average speaking pace. 'Since last night, just before dark.'

'Uncle Harry's not coming?'

Another beat, then a shake of the head.

'Where is he? Back home with Mum?'

'And Ilse and the girls,' Bub said. 'He offered, but I said you were on your way.'

'Probably better someone's with Mum. You have any trouble?' Nathan finally looked at the bundle at his feet. Something like that would draw out the scavengers.

'You mean dingoes?'

'Yeah, mate.' Of course. What else? There wasn't a huge amount of choice out there.

'Had to take a couple of shots.' Bub scratched his collarbone and Nathan could see the edge of the western star of his Southern Cross tattoo. 'But it was okay.'

'Good. All right.' Nathan recognised the familiar frustration that came with talking to Bub. He wished Cameron were there to smooth the waters and felt a sudden sharp jab of realisation under his ribs. He made himself take a deep breath, the air hot in his throat and lungs. This was difficult for everyone.

Bub's eyes were red and his face unshaven and heavy with shock, as was Nathan's own, he imagined. They looked a bit, but not a lot, alike. The sibling relationship was clearer with Cameron in the middle, bridging the gap in more ways than one. Bub looked tired and, as always these days, older than Nathan remembered. With twelve years between them, Nathan still found himself faintly surprised to see his brother edging into his thirties rather than still in nappies.

Nathan crouched beside the tarp. It was weather-bleached and had been tucked tight in places, like a bedsheet.

7

'Have you looked?'

'No. I was told not to touch anything.'

Nathan instantly disbelieved him. It was his tone, or perhaps the way the sheet lay at the top end. Sure enough, as he reached out, Bub made a noise in his throat.

'Don't, Nate. It's not good.'

Bub had never been good at lying. Nathan withdrew his hand and stood. 'What happened to him?'

'I don't know. Just what was said on the radio.'

'Yeah, I missed a lot of it.' Nathan didn't quite meet Bub's eye.

Bub shifted. 'Thought you promised Mum you'd keep it on, mate.'

Nathan didn't reply and Bub didn't push it. Nathan looked back across the fence to his own land. He could see Xander, restless, in the passenger seat. They'd spent the past week moving along the southern boundary, working by day, camping by night. They had been on the brink of downing tools the previous evening when the air around had vibrated as a helicopter swooped overhead. A black bird against the indigo death throes of the day.

'Why is he flying so late?' Xander had said, squinting upwards. Nathan hadn't answered. Night flying. A dangerous choice and an ominous sign. Something was wrong. They'd turned on the radio, but by then it was already too late.

Nathan looked now at Bub. 'Look, I heard enough. Doesn't mean I understand it.'

Bub's unshaven jaw twitched. *Join the club.* 'I don't know what happened, mate,' he said again.

'That's okay, tell me what you do know.'

Nathan tried to tone down his impatience. He'd spoken to Bub on the radio briefly the previous evening, as dark fell, to say he would drive over at first light. He'd had a hundred more questions, but hadn't asked any of them. Not on an open frequency where anyone who wanted to listen could tune in.

'When did Cam head out from home?' Nathan prompted when Bub seemed at a loss as to where to start.

'Morning the day before yesterday, Harry said. Around eight.'

'So, Wednesday.'

'Yeah, I guess. But I didn't see him 'cause I'd headed out myself on Tuesday.'

'Where to?'

'Check a couple of those water bores way up in the north paddock. Plan was for me to camp up there, then drive over to Lehmann's Hill on Wednesday and meet Cam.'

'What for?'

'Fix the repeater mast.'

Well, so Cam could fix it, Nathan thought. Bub would mostly have been there to pass the spanner. And for safety in numbers. Lehmann's Hill was on the western edge of the property, a four-hour drive from home. If the repeater mast was out in that area, so was long-range radio contact.

'What went wrong?' Nathan said.

Bub was staring at the tarp. 'I got there late. We were supposed to meet at around one but I got stuck on the way. Didn't get to Lehmann's until a couple of hours later.'

Nathan waited.

'Cam wasn't there,' Bub went on. 'Wondered if he'd been and gone but the mast was still out so I thought probably not. Tried the radio but he never came into range. So I waited a bit, then headed towards the track. Thinking I'd run into him.'

'But you didn't.'

'Nup. I kept trying the radio but no sign of him.' Bub frowned. 'Drove for about an hour but I still hadn't made the track so I had to stop. Getting dark, you know?'

Under the brim of his hat, his eyes looked for reassurance and Nathan nodded.

'Not much else you could do.' It was true. The night was a perfect shroud of black out at Lehmann's Hill. Driving in the dark, it was only a question of whether the car would crash into a rock or a cow or roll off the road. And then Nathan would have had two brothers covered by a tarp.

'But you were getting worried?' Nathan said, although he could guess the answer.

Bub shrugged. 'Yeah and no. You know how it is.'

'Yeah.' Nathan did. They lived in a land of extremes in more ways than one. People were either completely fine, or very not. There was little middle ground. And Cam wasn't some tourist. He knew how to handle himself, and that meant he could well have been half an hour up the road, slowed down by the dark and out of range, but snug in his swag with a cool beer from the fridge in his boot. Or he might not.

'No-one was picking up the radio,' Bub was saying. 'No-one's ever bloody up there this time of year, and with the tower out –' He gave a grunt of frustration.

'So what did you do?'

'Started driving in at dawn, but it still took ages before anyone picked up.'

'How long?'

'I dunno.' Bub hesitated. 'Probably a half-hour to get to the track, then another hour after that. Even then, it was only a couple of those idiot jackaroos over at Atherton. Took them bloody ages to get hold of the manager.'

'They always hire dickheads at Atherton,' Nathan said, thinking of the neighbouring property to the north-east. It sprawled over an area the size of Sydney. It was, as he'd said, staffed by dickheads, but was still the best chance around there of connecting with anyone. 'So they raised the alarm?'

'Yeah, but by then . . . ' Bub stopped.

By then no-one had seen or heard from their brother for about twenty-four hours, Nathan calculated. The search was well into the urgent phase before it had even started. As per protocol, every surrounding property would be informed and it was all hands on deck, for what it was worth. Over those distances, hands were few and far between and it could take a long time to reach the deck.

'The pilot spotted him?'

'Yeah,' Bub said. 'Eventually.'

'Anyone you know?'

'Nah, contractor based down near Adelaide. Been working on Atherton for the season. Some cop got him on the flight comms, told him to do a flyover and check the roads.'

'Glenn?'

'No. Someone else. From police dispatch or something.'

'Right,' Nathan said. It was lucky the pilot had seen

11

Cameron at all. The stockman's grave was two hundred kilometres from Lehmann's Hill and the main search area. 'When did he call it in?'

'Mid-arvo, so most people hadn't even made it to Lehmann's by then. It was pretty much only me and Harry out there still, but I was about an hour closer so I said I'd drive over.'

'And Cam was definitely dead?'

'That's what the pilot said. Had been for a few hours, by the sound of it. Cop still got on the radio and made him do all these checks.' Bub grimaced. 'I got here near sunset. The bloke had covered Cam over like he was told to but he was pretty keen to get going. Didn't want to lose the light and get stuck here.'

Fair enough, Nathan thought. He wouldn't have wanted to stay either. He felt bad that the task had fallen to Bub.

'If Cam was supposed to be meeting you at Lehmann's Hill, what was he doing out here?'

'Don't know. Harry said he'd written in the planner that he was heading out to Lehmann's.'

'Nothing else?'

'Not that Harry said.'

Nathan thought about that planner. He knew where it was kept, next to the phone, inside the back door of the house that had once been their dad's and had then become Cameron's. Nathan had written in it himself plenty of times growing up. He'd also not written in it plenty of times, when he'd forgotten or couldn't be bothered, or didn't want anyone to know where he was going, or couldn't find a pen.

He could feel the heat bearing down on his neck and he

looked at his watch. The digital numbers were covered in fine red dust and he wiped his thumb across them.

'What time are they due?' *They* meaning police and medical. *They* also meaning two people. One of each. Not a team, not out there.

'Not sure. They're on their way.'

That didn't mean it would be soon, though. Nathan looked down at the tarp again. The marks in the dust.

'Did he look injured?'

'Don't think so. Not that I could see. Just hot and thirsty.' Bub's face was tilted down as he touched the edge of the dust circle with the toe of his boot. Neither brother mentioned it. They both knew what it meant. They had seen similar patterns made by dying animals. A thought struck Nathan and he looked around.

'Where's all his stuff?'

'His hat's under the tarp. He didn't have anything else.'

'What, nothing?'

'Pilot said not. He was told to check, take some pics. Reckoned he couldn't see anything else.'

'But –' Nathan scanned the ground again. 'Not *anything*? Not even an empty water bottle?'

'Don't think so.'

'Did you have a proper look?'

'You can see for yourself, mate. You've got eyes.'

'But –'

'I don't know, all right? I don't have any answers. Stop asking me.'

'Yeah, okay.' Nathan took a deep breath. 'But I thought the pilot found the car?'

13

'He did.'

'So where is it?' He didn't bother to hide his frustration now. *Get more sense from the cows than from bloody Bub*, as their dad used to say.

'Near the road.'

Nathan stared at him. 'Which road?'

'How many roads are there? Our one. This side of the boundary, a bit north of your cattle grid. Jesus, this was all on the radio, mate.'

'It can't be. That's ten kilometres away.'

'Eight, I reckon, but yeah.'

There was a long silence. The sun was high and the slice of shade thrown by the headstone had shrunk to almost nothing.

'So Cam left his car?' Beneath Nathan's feet, the earth tilted very slightly on its axis. He saw the look on his younger brother's face and shook his head. 'Sorry, I know you don't know, it's just –'

He looked past his brother, to where the horizon lay long and still. The only movement he could see was Bub's chest, expanding in and out as he breathed.

'Have you been out to the car?' Nathan said, finally.

'No.'

Telling the truth this time, Nathan thought. He glanced over his shoulder. Xander was a dark shape hunched forward in his seat.

'Let's go.'

Chapter 2

It was nine kilometres in the end.

Nathan's own four-wheel drive was on the wrong side of the fence, so he'd climbed back through the wire and pulled open the passenger door. Xander had looked up, questions already forming on his lips. Nathan held up a hand.

'I'll tell you later. Come on. We're going to find Uncle Cam's car.'

'Find it? Where is it?' Xander frowned. His private schoolboy haircut was looking a little shaggy around the edges after the past week and the stubble on his chin made him look older.

'Somewhere near the road. Bub's driving.'

'Sorry, all the way out at *your* road?'

'Yeah, apparently.'

'But –? What?'

'I don't know, mate. We'll see.'

Xander opened his mouth, then shut it again, and climbed out of the four-wheel drive without further comment. The kid followed him through the fence, glancing once at the tarp and giving the grave a respectfully wide berth as he walked to Bub's car.

'Hi, Bub.'

'G'day, little mate. Not so little now, hey?'

'No, I suppose not.'

'How's Brisbane?'

Nathan saw his son pause. *Better than here*, was clearly the answer.

'It's fine, thank you,' he settled for instead. 'I'm sorry about Cameron.'

'Yeah, well, not your fault, mate.' Bub opened his car door. 'Jump in.'

Xander's eyes were on the grave. 'Do we just –?'

'What?' Bub was already behind the wheel.

'Leave him here like this?'

'They said not to touch it.'

Xander looked appalled. 'I wasn't going to touch it. Him. I was just wondering if one of us should –' He faltered under Bub's blank gaze. 'Never mind.'

Nathan could see Xander's city softness exposed like a layer of new skin. His edges had been gently rounded by nuanced debate and foreign coffee and morning news. They had not been chipped away and sanded down to a hard callus. Xander thought before he spoke, and he weighed up the consequences of his actions before he did anything. Mostly, Nathan thought, that was no bad thing. But it depended where you were. Nathan opened the car door.

'I think we'll be right, mate.' He climbed in. 'Let's get going.'

16

Xander didn't look convinced, but got in the back without argument. Inside, the car was cool and dark. The radio lay silent in its cradle.

Nathan looked over at his brother. 'You going to follow the fence line?'

'Yeah, reckon that'd be quickest.' Bub squinted in the rear-view mirror at Xander. 'Hold on back there, I'll do my best but it's looking pretty bumpy.'

'Okay.'

They drove without speaking as Bub focused on the ground in front of his wheels, wrestling control back from dips and hidden soft earth. The grave quickly disappeared in the rear window as they went over a rise, and Nathan saw Xander's grip tighten on the back seat. Nathan turned to stare out at the fence line separating his property from his brothers'. The wire vanished into the distance in both directions. He could see no end. As they passed a section where the fence posts looked loose, Nathan made a mental note to mention it to Cam. He caught himself. Another sharp jolt of realisation.

Bub started to slow as they reached the edge of Cameron's land. The main road up ahead was hidden by a natural rise that ran along the eastern border of both Cameron's and Nathan's properties. On Nathan's side it was mostly a dirt dune; on Cameron's there was a rocky outcrop that had managed to weather a few thousand years. In the sunset, it glowed red as though lit from within. At that moment, it was a dull brown.

'Where's the car?' Nathan said.

Bub had come almost to a halt and was peering through

17

the windscreen. Xander twisted around, looking back the way they had come.

'Nothing out this side.' Nathan squinted through the dusty glass. 'What exactly did the pilot say?'

'He was going off the GPS, so –' Bub shrugged. Not much help there. 'But he said somewhere on the rocks, north of the grid.' Bub changed gears. 'I'll drive onto the road. See what we can see.'

Bub kept close to the fence line, following the thin unofficial track that linked paddock to road. He cut through a gap in the rocks and with a jolt and a squeal from the engine, they found themselves on the other side of the outcrop. The unsealed road was deserted.

'So, north, you reckon?' Nathan said, and Bub nodded. The wheels whipped up a cloud of dust, and Nathan could hear the *ping* of stones chipping off the bodywork as they picked up speed. The road lay ahead like a dirty ribbon as the rock face loomed along their left side. In a few hours, it would block out the westerly sun.

They drove for a minute, then Bub slowed in front of an almost invisible break in the outcrop. There were no signposts. The few locals knew most of the off-road tracks and the occasional tourist was not encouraged to explore them. Bub turned the car into the gap between the high rocks and through to the paddock on the other side. From this vantage point, the outcrop was a gentle slope leading to the highest point before dropping sharply to the road.

Bub stopped, the engine still running, and Nathan opened his door and stepped out. The wind had picked up and he felt the grit cling to his skin and eyelashes.

He turned in a slow, full circle. He could see rock, and the fence, now small in the distance. And the horizon. Nothing else. He got back in.

'Try further up.'

They rejoined the road and a few moments later, Bub pulled in again through a different gap. They repeated the procedure. Stop, circle. Nothing but more of the same. Nathan was losing hope and had opened the passenger door to climb back in when he heard a soft tapping on the window. Xander was pointing and saying something.

'What's that?' Nathan leaned in.

'Over there.' Xander was pointing up the slope, back towards the road. 'In the light.'

Nathan could make out nothing as he squinted against the sun. He bent down, aligning his view with his son's. He followed his line of sight until, at last, he could see. On a distant outcrop, on its rocky peak, there was the dull glint of dirty metal.

The driver's door stood open. Not thrown wide, and not just a crack. Part-way ajar, the perfect distance for a man to simply step out.

After Xander had spotted the faraway sheen of the car, Bub had rejoined the road and driven them up to the next hidden track. He'd pulled in once again and this time, the Land Cruiser was impossible to miss. It was parked on the flat peak of the rocky slope, its nose facing the sheer drop to the road.

By unspoken agreement, Bub parked at the bottom and

they walked up. At the top, the three of them stood beside Cameron's car as the air current snatched at their clothes.

Nathan walked around the four-wheel drive and for the second time that day felt something shift and tilt off-centre. The exterior was completely unremarkable. It was dirty and stone-chipped, but he could see nothing wrong with it. He felt an unpleasant cool prickle at the base of his neck.

Nothing was wrong, and that in itself felt very wrong indeed. Nathan had expected, he realised, at the very least to find the car bogged, or rolled, or smashed into a rock or crumpled into a jagged metal ball. He had expected hissing steam or leaking oil or flames, or for the bonnet to be propped open, or all four tyres to be deflated rubber sacks. Nathan wasn't sure what, but he had expected something. Something more than this, at least. Something like an explanation.

He crouched and checked the wheels. Four good tyres stood firm on solid rock. He opened the bonnet and ran his hands over the key components. Nothing out of place, as far as he could see. Through the window, the gauges on the dashboard indicated both fuel tanks – primary and reserve – were full or close to. Nathan heard a sound and looked up to see Bub opening the rear doors of the Land Cruiser. He and Xander were both staring into the large haulage area with strange expressions on their faces. Nathan walked around and joined them.

The vehicle was fully stocked. Litres of fresh water sloshed gently in sealed bottles next to cans filled with tuna and beans. A good collection. Enough to keep a man alive for a week or more. Nathan used one finger to open the mini fridge that could be hooked up to the car's power. More filled water bottles were stacked inside, along with wrapped sandwiches now curling at the edges, and a six-pack of mid-strength beer. There was other stuff too. Extra fuel in a jerry can, two spare tyres strapped down, a shovel, a first aid kit. In short: the usual. Nathan knew he could have opened his own vehicle and found exactly the same. Bub's too, he guessed. A basic survival kit for life in the harshest climate in Australia. Don't leave home without it.

'His keys are here.'

Xander was peering into the open driver's door and Nathan joined him. Side by side, their shoulders were the same height now, he noticed vaguely.

A light coat of red dust had floated in and settled on every surface. Beneath the veneer, Nathan could see the keys clipped to a black lanyard, which was neatly coiled into a loop and placed on the car seat.

That was a little unusual, a small voice whispered. Not so much leaving the keys in the car. Nathan didn't know anyone in the whole district who did anything else. He could picture his own keys now, tossed into the footwell of his car back at the gravesite. Bub's were dangling from the indicator lever in the car at the bottom of the slope. Nathan couldn't remember ever in his life seeing Cameron remove car keys from a vehicle. He also couldn't remember ever seeing him coil and place them quite so precisely.

'Maybe he broke down?' Bub sounded unconvinced.

Nathan didn't reply. He looked at those keys and all of a sudden, his hand was reaching out.

21

'Dad, no, we shouldn't touch –'

He ignored Xander, the movement of his arm sending delicate dust patterns swirling into the air. As his hand closed around the keys, Nathan knew with cold certainty what would happen next.

He climbed into the seat, put the key in the ignition and turned it. The movement was smooth and the metal slid easily. He felt the vibrations as the engine started with a roar, then settled to a rumble. It sounded loud in the silence.

Nathan shot a look at Xander, but his son wasn't watching him anymore. Instead, he was gazing beyond the car and into the distance. He was shielding his eyes and frowning. Nathan turned to look himself. Far away, a single tight cloud of dust was moving in the south. Someone was coming.

Chapter 3

Nathan stood beside the stockman's grave for the second time that day and watched as the new vehicle approached. It slowed as it drew near.

It was a four-wheel drive with industrial tyres and a bullbar at the front, the same as almost every other car in the area, but this one had a stretcher in the back. Reflective ambulance branding on the front and sides caught the sun.

Nathan, Bub and Xander had remained on top of the outcrop next to Cameron's Land Cruiser until the dust haze from the south took shape. Then, wordlessly, they had walked down the rise and driven back to the grave-side to wait.

For the first time all morning, Nathan felt a stirring of relief as the ambulance came to a stop and the nurse raised his hand. Some help, at last.

Steve Fitzgerald was a wiry man in his early fifties who occasionally shared stories of his tours with the Red Cross. He spent half his year in Afghanistan, Syria, Rwanda, wherever, and the other half on call in a single-staffed medical clinic in outback Balamara. He enjoyed a challenge, he'd once said, which struck Nathan as an understatement. Steve emerged from the ambulance with a police officer Nathan had never seen before.

'Where's Glenn?' Nathan said immediately, and the cop frowned.

Steve didn't answer straight away. He took in the grave and the tarp and shook his head.

'Jesus. Poor Cameron.' He crouched down but didn't touch anything. 'Glenn's been stuck out at Haddon Corner since yesterday. Got a family with young kids bogged their hire car in the sand, but weren't sure where they were. He's found them now, but won't get out here until tomorrow.'

'Tomorrow?'

'He's only got one pair of hands, mate.'

'Shit.' It was true, Sergeant Glenn McKenna single-handedly policed an area the size of Victoria. Sometimes he was nearby, sometimes he wasn't, but at least he knew the lie of the land. Nathan eyeballed the new cop. He was already sunburned and looked barely older than Xander. 'Where've they flown you in from?'

'St Helens. This morning. Sergeant Ludlow.'

'You do your training up there?'

'No.' Ludlow hesitated. 'Brisbane.'

'Christ. The city?' Nathan knew he was being rude but he didn't care. 'How long've you been at St Helens for?'

'A month.'

'Great.' Nathan heard even Bub sigh this time. He looked at Steve, who was unpacking his medical kit. 'Maybe we should wait for Glenn to get back.'

24

'You can wait out here as long as you like, fellas,' Steve said, not unkindly, 'but Sergeant Ludlow and I are dealing with this now.'

Nathan met Bub's eye. No reaction. 'Yeah, all right,' he said. 'Sorry, mate, it's not you, it's –'

'I understand,' Ludlow said. 'I'm afraid it was me or nothing.'

There was an awkward silence as the choice was considered.

'But I'll obviously do my very best for your brother,' he added.

Nathan suddenly felt like a bit of an arsehole. 'Yeah. Right. Thanks for coming all the way out.' Nathan saw a hint of relief in the guy's face and felt even worse. He introduced them all properly, then waited while the cop extracted a camera from his bag.

'I'm going to . . .' Ludlow pointed at his lens and at the grave and they all stood back while he prowled around, taking shots of the tarp and surroundings from every angle. Finally, after his knees and shirt were covered in dust, he stood up.

'All yours,' he said to the nurse.

Steve knelt by the grave and folded the edge of the tarp back in such a way that Nathan couldn't see underneath. He felt a flash of gratitude. Bub wandered away, leaning on the shady side of his car and looking at the ground, while the sergeant squinted at his digital photos.

Nathan and Xander stood a short distance apart and watched the nurse work. Cam wouldn't have been too happy, Nathan caught himself thinking. Cameron and

Steve Fitzgerald had never quite seen eye to eye. As though his ears were burning, Steve looked up at Nathan.

'How are you going these days, mate?'

'Okay.'

'Yeah? Things all right? Other than this, obviously.' Steve's voice was friendly but his tone had a professional note. A question, not a pleasantry.

'I'm fine. It's Bub who was here all night.'

'I know. Just haven't seen you in a while.' Still not a pleasantry. 'You missed the appointment I made at the clinic.'

'I called.'

'Point was for you to come in, though.'

'Sorry.' Nathan shrugged. 'Been busy.'

'But, you're good?'

'Yes. I said.' Nathan gave Steve a look. *Not in front of the kid.* It was too late, and he caught Xander glance at him then look away. After what seemed like a long time, Steve dusted his hands and sat back on his heels.

'Well –' He signalled for the sergeant and Bub to rejoin them. 'I had a chat with the pilot yesterday and no real surprises here today. Dehydration, I'd say. We'll have to send him up to St Helens for an autopsy to be sure – youngish healthy guy, unexpected death, they'll want to take a look – but he's showing all the signs.' Steve looked up. 'What was he was doing out here?'

'We're not sure,' Nathan said.

Sergeant Ludlow was flipping through a notebook. 'So, er . . .' He looked at Bub. 'You and he were supposed to meet on Wednesday, is that right?'

'Yeah.'

26

The sergeant waited, his sunburn turning a deeper shade of red as Bub stared back. 'Could you tell me about that?'

Bub looked a little surprised but, haltingly and with plenty of prompting, recounted the same story he'd told Nathan earlier. It was disjointed in the retelling, and even Nathan found himself frowning in confusion in places. Sergeant Ludlow scribbled furiously long after Bub had finished, then flipped back a page, his eyes moving across the words.

'Why were you late?' He spoke lightly, as though the thought had just occurred to him, but Nathan felt sure the question had been brewing for minutes. He looked at the cop, with his burned skin and wide eyes, and suddenly wondered if he'd misjudged him.

'What?' Bub blinked.

'Why were you late to meet your brother as arranged at Lehmann's Hill?'

'Oh. I got two flats.'

'Tyres?'

'Yeah.'

'*Two* flat tyres?'

'Yeah.'

'That's pretty unlucky.' The sergeant was smiling, but there was something new in his tone.

'It's happens,' Nathan said quickly, and he was relieved to see Steve nodding in agreement. 'It's not unusual, with the heat and the rocks. You wreck one tyre, quite often you wreck two. And it'll take you forty-five minutes to change a flat this time of year, an hour even.' He could feel himself rambling, and stopped.

Sergeant Ludlow was still looking at Bub. 'That's what happened?'

To Nathan's relief, Bub kept his mouth shut and nodded. The sergeant regarded him over his notebook, then scratched a few words. His expression was open, but again Nathan had the sensation of something lurking beneath. Nathan flicked his eyes towards Bub's car. The front two tyres did look newer. He caught Xander doing the same thing and they both immediately looked away.

The sergeant at last turned his attention from Bub to Steve. 'Do you have any thoughts on time of death?'

'Probably sometime yesterday morning, at a guess. Given the temperature and the lack of shade or water, I'd be very surprised if he lasted beyond twenty-four hours. The autopsy should tell us more.'

'That doesn't sound like long.' Sergeant Ludlow frowned. 'What was he, late thirties?'

'Forty,' Nathan said.

'He did better than some would've,' Steve said. 'Twenty-four hours might even be a bit optimistic.'

'How far are we from Cameron's home?' Ludlow looked at the brothers again.

'On foot, it's about fifteen kilometres in a straight line north-west,' Nathan said. 'Driving from here, you have to follow the dirt track west then north if you don't want to get sand-bogged, so that route's probably over thirty. Safest way is another ten kilometres on top of that – east from here to the rocks, then north along the road.'

The rocks and road where they had found Cam's car. Nathan exchanged a glance with Bub and Ludlow caught it.

'So even the shortest distance, you're looking at a few hours' walk home?' Ludlow said.

'You can't walk it, not in this weather,' Steve said, his voice muffled. He was looking under the tarp again. 'That's what went wrong with those three contractors sand-bogged out at Atherton a few years ago. You remember, Bub? You were on that search, weren't you?'

Bub nodded.

'They were, what? Mid-twenties?' Steve said. 'Tried to walk back. Got about seven kilometres, if that. Two were dead within six hours.'

'What else is around here?' Ludlow walked to the fence and rested his hands on the wire. 'That's your land on the other side?' he said to Nathan.

'Yeah.'

'Could your brother have been hoping to find you?'

Nathan saw Bub and Steve both look over. 'No.'

'You sound sure.'

'I am.'

'But —' Ludlow opened his notebook again. 'Cameron knew you and your son were out doing a fence check?'

'Yeah, I always do this time of year. But we weren't around here.'

'Did Cameron know that for certain?'

There was a long silence. 'No.'

Ludlow ran a hand along the top wire then opened his palm and looked at the dust. 'Can you think of a reason why your brother might have needed to come to this spot?'

'I don't know why he would have needed to,' Nathan said finally. 'But he knew it well.'

'Was he out here often?'

'I don't think so anymore.' Nathan glanced at Bub, who shrugged. 'But he used to.'

'This is also the only bit of shade for miles,' Steve said. 'It might have been instinct to seek it out.'

Sergeant Ludlow contemplated that as he looked at the shape on the ground. Even beneath the tarp, it was unmistakably human.

'How was your brother's state of mind these past few weeks?'

The question was delivered gently, and it took Nathan a moment to realise it was aimed at him.

'I don't know. I hadn't seen him in a few months.'

'How many?'

'Four, maybe? When were we all doing that track work, Bub?' It had been the last time Nathan had seen either of his brothers, he realised now. Bub looked blank.

'Four months,' Ludlow said. 'So August, September time?'

'Probably a bit earlier.' Nathan tried to think. 'Actually, wait. It was around the first State of Origin match. Because we talked about that.'

'June,' Ludlow and Bub said in unison.

'Yeah, I suppose.'

'So six months,' Ludlow said.

'Yeah, must be then. We spoke on the radio sometimes.'

'Often?'

'Often enough.'

'Was there a reason you hadn't seen each other?'

'No. No reason. I live nearly three hours away door to door. We're all busy.' He turned to Bub for help, and was

30

rewarded with nothing. 'You see him every day at home, what did you think?'

Nathan expected a shrug, but instead, Bub seemed to be thinking. Finally he took a breath. 'Cam was a bit wound up lately.'

Nathan stared at him in astonishment. How bad had things been if even Bub had noticed?

'Wound up in what way?' Ludlow asked.

Bub did shrug this time. He looked a little edgy. 'Dunno. The usual way.'

They all waited, but he apparently had nothing further to add on the subject.

Ludlow checked his notes. 'Cameron lived on this property with who else?'

'Me,' Bub said, counting on his fingers. 'Mum, Ilse – that's Cam's missus – and their two girls, Uncle Harry –'

'Harry Bledsoe,' Nathan cut in. 'He's not actually our uncle, he's a family friend. He's worked on the property since before we were all born.'

'So technically an employee?' Ludlow asked.

'Technically, but no-one thinks of him like that,' Nathan said.

Bub nodded. 'We've got a couple of backpackers at the moment too.'

'Doing what?' Ludlow said.

'Usual. Labouring, work around the house. Whatever. Cam hired them a few months ago.'

'Would he hire in people often?'

'Whenever he needed,' Nathan said. 'There'd be contractors and labourers coming and going during the

31

year, depending on what's going on. Glenn – Sergeant McKenna – he knows all this.'

Ludlow just wrote something in his notebook.

Steve stood up and dusted his knees. 'All right. I'd like to get him into the ambulance now. The sergeant and I can manage the stretcher unless either of you particularly wants to help?'

Nathan and Bub both shook their heads. Nathan was relieved. He suspected he would have felt the weight of that bundle for the rest of his life.

Steve crouched down again. 'I'm going to completely remove the tarp now, if you want to look somewhere else.'

Nathan started to say something to Xander but the kid was already turning away. City softness, he thought, but was glad. Bub's eyes were fixed on the horizon.

Nathan debated too long and the decision was made for him. The tarp slipped loose as Cameron's limp form was lifted onto the stretcher. Bub had been right. Their brother didn't look injured, at least not in the traditional sense. But heat and thirst did terrible things to a person. He had started to remove his clothes as logic had deserted him, and his skin was cracked. Whatever had been going through Cameron's mind when he was alive, he didn't look peaceful in death.

Nathan was still staring at the stretcher long after it had been placed in the ambulance. Sergeant Ludlow turned back to the grave, unconsciously dusting his hands on the side of his trousers. He suddenly stopped mid-motion, then took a step forward, studying the space where Cameron had lain. The exposed earth was sandy and studded with poor tufts of grass. The sergeant bent closer.

'What is this?'

Nathan felt Bub come up behind him on one side and Xander on the other. They all looked to where Ludlow was pointing.

Near the base of the headstone, where Cameron's back had pressed against the ground, was a shallow hole.

Chapter 4

The hole was about the size of three fists, and it was empty.

Ludlow took a string of photos, then Nathan watched as he put a single gloved finger into the gap. The side immediately began to collapse as the soft ground trickled in. The land behaved like a living thing and Nathan knew that in a day or two, the area would have repaired itself seamlessly. Ludlow scrabbled deeper into the space and Nathan wondered vaguely how far down the stockman had actually been buried.

'I can't see anything in there.' Ludlow wiped his palms on his trousers and frowned up at Steve. 'Have you checked his hands?'

Steve disappeared around the back of the ambulance, re-emerging a minute later. 'Nails are broken and there's some sand and grit clogged underneath. He could have dug it by hand, if that's what you're asking.'

'Why would he waste energy doing that?'

'Because his bloody brain was fried, wasn't it?'

They all turned at Bub's voice. He was watching with his shoulders hunched and his arms folded across his chest.

'What?' He gave a shrug. 'It's obvious, isn't it? It was forty-five degrees yesterday. I dunno why Cam left his car, but the minute he did that, he was fucked. End of story.'

Ludlow looked at Steve, who gave a tight nod. 'Look, he's not wrong. Dehydration leads to confusion very quickly.'

They all stared into the scrabbled hole for a long time. Ludlow was the first to look up.

'I'd like to see his car now.'

Nathan offered to drive the sergeant and Bub didn't argue. He looked relieved to be staying behind with Steve, who wanted to draw samples and get them in the coolbox before they were completely worthless.

Nathan climbed through the fence with Ludlow and Xander and they got into his Land Cruiser. It felt better for once, being back on his own side of the fence. The unnatural sight of Cameron laid out on the land he loved had upset the balance of the place somehow, as though there was a pollutant in the air.

Nathan's hands were not quite steady on the steering wheel as he tried to remember that last time he had seen Cam, back in June or whenever. Cam had probably been smiling, because he usually was. Nathan flexed his hands one at a time. He could only picture the face under the tarp. He was already wishing he'd looked away. As he started the car and pulled away from the grave, he realised Ludlow was saying something.

'Sorry?'

'I was asking if you and your brother deliberately bought land next to each other?'

'Oh. No. Burley Downs Station was our dad's, so me, Cam and Bub grew up there. Then I got given some land on this side of the fence when I – ah – when I was married –' In the rear-view mirror he could see Xander was looking out of the window, pretending not to listen. 'That was about twenty years ago. Our dad died around then and eventually Cam took over Burley Downs.'

'So Cameron owned it?'

'He runs it. And he has a majority stake now.'

'Oh yeah?'

'Yeah, but you don't have to look so interested. It's been like that for years. We all got a third when Dad died, so it was nice and fair. I sold half of mine to Cam pretty soon afterwards, and he manages the place. Organises all the daily running and does most of the long-term planning. Bub has a third and I've still got a sixth.'

Ludlow made a note. 'And how big is Burley Downs?'

'Three and a half thousand square kilometres, with about three thousand Herefords.'

'And the family looks after all that themselves?'

Something felt very strange about the way Ludlow was speaking. It was only when Nathan opened his mouth to reply that it hit him. The man was speaking to him completely normally. Nothing overt, or implied, or threatening or, very occasionally, concerned. Nathan wondered how soon Steve would fill him in. Probably in the ambulance on the drive back to town. The story was decent small talk filler, and wasn't like it was confidential. If anything, it was entrenched in local lore now, from what Nathan could tell.

Ludlow shifted in his seat and Nathan realised he was still waiting for a reply.

'They hire in help when they need it, like I said. Mustering, you always need it, but there are contract firms so you can call up and book the teams. It's pretty much all done by helicopter and motorbike now. Cam'd get in contractors when he needed help with engineering stuff or laying fences or whatever. But day-to-day stuff is mostly the family. Especially when it's quiet. Like, there's nothing happening now because the markets and meat plants are all closed for Christmas.'

'You don't need help milking all those cows?'

In the mirror, Nathan saw Xander bite back a smile. 'It's beef around here, not dairy.'

'So, what, your fridges are full of steak?'

'And long-life milk. But, no, it's not the same as with cattle on farms. Properties this size, the cattle mostly wander. Drink from the bores, graze, get rounded up when it's their time.' They were almost wild in a lot of ways. Some of them barely saw a human from birth to slaughter.

'And how big is your place?'

'About seven hundred square kilometres.'

'A fair bit smaller than Burley Downs.'

'Yep.'

'Why is that?'

Nathan hesitated. Xander had gone back to staring out of the window. 'Long story. Messy divorce is the short version.'

Ludlow seemed to accept that without question, for once, and Nathan wondered if there was a similar explanation for the cop finding himself stationed fifteen hundred kilometres from Brisbane.

'Who else lives at your place?' Ludlow said.

Nathan didn't answer straight away. 'No-one else full-time. I'm there on my own.'

Ludlow turned his head and stared. 'Just you?'

'Yup. One-man show. I mean, contractors and people when I need them.' And could afford them.

The sergeant was openly gaping. 'And your place was what, seven hundred square kilometres? And how many cattle?'

'Probably five or six hundred.'

'Christ, that still sounds like a lot.'

Nathan didn't reply immediately. It was and it wasn't. It was enough to overwork his crappy strip of land until it became a sandpit. It wasn't enough to help him break anything like even.

'But –' Ludlow scanned the extensive horizon all the way from one empty side to the other. 'Don't you get lonely?'

'No.' Another quick glance in the mirror. Xander was watching now. 'No, I'm good. I don't mind it. And as long as there's enough water, the cattle pretty much look after themselves.'

'Not completely, though.'

'No, not completely, but we've been lucky with the Grenville the last couple of years,' Nathan said, keen to change the subject.

'What's that, the river?'

'Yeah. It picks up all the nutrients from the rainwater so it's good for the ground when it floods. Flooded last year, then a couple of years before that.'

Ludlow squinted at the sun.

'How much rain does that take?'

'It floods around here without rain,' Xander said from the back seat, and Ludlow twisted around.

'Really?'

Nathan nodded. It was a strange sight, even after forty-two years, to watch the water rise, silent and stealthy, under a cloudless blue sky. The river would lap at its banks, swollen with rain that had fallen days before and a thousand kilometres north. He pointed outside.

'When it floods, most of this is under water. The river gets ten kilometres wide in places. You can't get over without a boat. The houses and the town are all built on high ground but the road disappears.'

Ludlow looked amazed. 'How do you get out?'

Nathan heard Xander laugh. 'You don't. A lot of properties become islands. I was stuck out at my place for five weeks once.'

'Alone?'

'Yeah,' Nathan said. 'It's all right though. You just have to be prepared. No choice, it's the geography.'

He looked out at the red earth stretching around them.

It was hard to imagine, but millions of years ago this had been the bottom of a massive inland sea. Aquatic dinosaur bones had been dug up under this soil and there were still places in the desert where mounds of fossilised seashells baked under the sun. Nathan suddenly remembered how he and Cameron had used to go dinosaur hunting when they were young, shovels in hand and bags ready to bring home the bones. Years later, it had been Xander's turn and Nathan's pockets had bulged with plastic dinosaurs to bury when the real ones inevitably didn't come out to play.

The sergeant was writing in his notebook again.

'Who are the neighbours?' he said.

'Nearest property is Atherton.' Nathan pointed north-east. 'The town's south of that, then you've got another couple of properties east of there. The second biggest one around here is Kirrabee Station, and that shares a border with me. It's owned by a company now.'

It had previously been family owned, though. Specifically by Nathan's father-in-law. *Ex*-father-in-law, Nathan reminded himself, because he preferred the sound of it. He put his foot on the brake as they approached a spot in the fence line where he could pass. Xander jumped out and opened the gate, and they bumped through, and were once again on Cameron's land.

'Not far now,' he said to Ludlow.

'What were you saying earlier about your brother knowing the grave area well?' The sergeant looked over. 'Seems like a strange place to want to spend any time.'

'Uncle Cam painted a picture of it,' Xander said, climbing back in. 'He made it famous. For around here, anyway.'

'Oh yeah?'

Nathan nodded. 'He's only an amateur – was an amateur – but he was pretty good. He kind of got into painting when we were kids. There wasn't a lot to do for fun, so we did all this weird old-lady stuff. Stamp collecting and things. I couldn't paint for shit, but Cam was all right. He kept doing it, on and off I think, but he did this picture of the stockman's grave about five years ago.'

One of the seasonal workers at the time had taken a photo of it and put it online when she'd got home to France or Canada or wherever she was from. Cameron had suddenly got calls from people trying to order prints. Eventually, at the suggestion of his mother, he'd entered the painting in a competition and won a state-wide prize.

'You can buy postcards of it at the shop in town,' Nathan said.

'So the grave meant a lot to your brother?' Ludlow said, in a voice that suggested he found that significant.

'I wouldn't say that exactly,' Nathan said. 'I think he liked the painting more than the place. He just got lucky one day with the way the light fell.'

'It's quite strange out there,' Ludlow said. 'A grave on its own in the middle of nowhere. I've never seen that before.'

'There are a few around here.' Xander leaned forward. 'From the old days, when a person died suddenly. They'd get buried on site and later the family or someone might come along and put a headstone up. There are maps and photos and things online for the tourists.'

'Who would come all the way out here for that?'

41

Nathan shrugged. 'You'd be surprised.'

'They visit the stockman?'

'Sometimes. Used to get a few a year when Cam's picture was big. Not many now. There's a more popular one past Atherton.'

'What's the draw with that one?'

'Sadder, I think. It's a kid. Little boy. 1900s.'

Ludlow looked unsettled and Nathan wondered if he had children. 'What happened to him?'

'Usual story out here.' Nathan made himself keep his voice even. 'Wandered the wrong way and got lost.'

Out on the road, Nathan overshot the break in the rocks on the first attempt. He swore and reversed, then threaded his four-wheel drive through the hidden gap in the outcrop. On the other side, he looked around in bewilderment. Cameron's car was nowhere in sight. For a bizarre moment, he thought the car was actually gone. Xander tapped the dusty window.

'We've gone too far,' he said, pointing behind them.

Nathan returned to the road and tried again. The correct track was almost identical. He parked in the same spot as Bub had earlier, and they all walked up the slope. At the top, he and Xander hung back while Ludlow put on his gloves. He circled Cameron's car, taking even more photographs. He paused at the open driver's door.

Nathan cleared his throat. 'The door was open like that but the keys were on the seat when we arrived. I tried the engine.'

'You shouldn't have touched anything.'

'Sorry.'

'And what happened when you tried it?'

'It worked.'

Ludlow climbed in and turned the key for himself. He let the engine roar for a few seconds then switched it off.

'Was the car generally reliable?' he asked. 'It's a pretty old model.'

Eighteen years old, Nathan knew. Around the same age as his own.

'The older ones work better out here. New models all have electronic displays and things that can't cope with the dust. It gets in the cracks and stuffs the whole system. Cam looked after this one well.'

'What about the radio?' Ludlow pointed to the cradle on the dashboard.

Nathan showed him how to work through the frequencies. 'Sounds okay to me. His EPIRB's probably under the passenger seat as well.'

Ludlow reached down and pulled out the personal distress beacon. It was still in its box, and had not been activated.

'You don't use handheld radios?' he said.

'No. They're all connected to the cars.'

'So if you leave your vehicle, you're without comms?'

'Yeah.'

'What's the range?'

'Depends. You can get twenty kilometres straight, further with the repeater masts, but there are black spots,' Nathan said. 'It's line of sight, basically.'

The sergeant continued working his way through the car, running his gloved hands over the interior. He checked behind the visors, in the glove box, under the seats, then checked again.

'I think his wallet's missing.' Ludlow raised his head. 'It wasn't in his pockets either.'

'No. It'll be at home.'

'He wouldn't carry it?'

Nathan, whose own wallet was on his kitchen table in his unlocked house a couple of hundred kilometres away, waved a hand at their surroundings. Why bother?

A hint of embarrassment flitted across Ludlow's face. He opened a repair manual and flicked through the pages.

'What are you looking for?' Nathan asked eventually.

Ludlow hesitated. 'Anything.'

He doesn't know, Nathan thought. *He has no idea what to make of any of this.* He saw Xander frown. Probably thinking the same thing.

'Are you going to dust for fingerprints or something?' Xander said.

'The Criminal Investigation Branch would need to fly out for that.'

'And will they fly out?'

'Only if there are signs of violence.'

They all turned their eyes to the car. The windows were not cracked, the seats had seen nothing worse than general grime and the mirrors were positioned at the correct angles.

Ludlow looked back at Xander. 'I'm sorry.'

He worked on methodically, stopping short only when

he opened the rear doors. He stood, as they had, staring at the water and food stacked neatly in front of him.

'He left all this?'

Nathan didn't have an answer. *That's supposed to be your job to work out*, he thought.

Ludlow looked over. 'Is there any practical explanation you can think of?'

'I've heard of people –' Nathan sounded desperate even to his own ears. 'Sometimes people leave their vehicle for some reason – chase down a stray calf or something – and go further than they meant to. They start running and they don't realise how far they've gone and suddenly they're disoriented.'

Ludlow peeled off his gloves. 'Do you think that's what might have happened?'

'No. I don't know, I'm just saying. But I don't think Cam would have got lost around here.'

'Right,' Ludlow said. 'The car looks in good shape to me, but let's say there was something wrong with it. The break-down advice is to stay with your vehicle, isn't it? Golden rule, I was told.'

'Yeah.' The sergeant caught the note in Nathan's voice and looked up. Definitely more switched-on than he'd seemed at first, Nathan thought.

'Yeah but what?' Ludlow said.

'Nothing. Just, you use your common sense as well. And Cam knew that. I mean, there's a bloody road right there. He had plenty of water. If the car wasn't working and he had to walk anywhere, it would have been to the road, no question. And he would have taken water.'

'So why –?'

'I dunno why.' Nathan could hear his voice rising. 'I'm just saying. That's what he would have done. But first choice by an absolute bloody mile, he would have stayed with the car and kept the air con running and got on the radio for help. And if he absolutely had to leave it, he would have walked to the road, not the middle of nowhere.'

'That's what Cameron would have done,' Ludlow said.

'Yeah.'

'If he'd wanted to be found?'

Ludlow's words hung in the air.

'Yeah, obviously, mate.' Nathan bristled. 'Look, I hear what you're getting at, you can come out and say it.'

To his credit, the cop just gave a small nod of assent. 'I'm just thinking about what your other brother said. About Cameron perhaps feeling under pressure.'

'He had access to guns.'

'Cameron did?'

'Yeah. Rifle cabinet at home, same as everyone.'

'There's no weapon in the car.'

'No, well, he didn't carry one around all the time. But at home, he wouldn't have had any trouble, you know? If he'd wanted to put his hands on one.'

'So, you think –'

'I don't think anything. I'm just saying. If that's what *you're* thinking, why wouldn't he –' Nathan stopped short. He didn't say it.

'It's a good point,' Ludlow nodded. 'But you would have seen what the damage from a gunshot looks like?'

'Of course. On animals,' he added.

'Your brother would be familiar with that too.'

'So?'

Ludlow's expression made his face looked strangely older. 'So maybe nothing. But sometimes people make the mistake of thinking a gun offers an easy way out, and it doesn't. Mentally, it's a huge hurdle. An impossible step for some people. Sometimes –' Ludlow stopped and frowned. He turned his head slowly, taking in the view on all sides. The land was enormous in every direction. 'Is this one of the highest points around here?'

'This outcrop is *the* highest point around here,' Nathan said. They used to call it the lookout, not entirely as a joke. 'Sometimes, what?'

Ludlow didn't answer as he took a few steps to the rocky edge. He leaned over. Nathan didn't need to follow him. He knew what was down there.

'Sometimes, what, mate?' he repeated. 'What were you going to say?'

'Just that sometimes people simply need a way out. And the direct approach isn't for everybody.'

Nathan took a few steps and joined him on the edge of the lookout. He could feel Xander watching him. Below was a five-metre drop onto a pillow of sand. You'd be lucky to break your ankle, let alone your neck, he knew. It was nowhere near high enough to offer a desperate man a certain escape.

The other direction, though. Nathan turned and looked past his son. To the west. As far as he could see, the land stretched out, deep and open, all the way to the desert. A perfect sea of nothingness. If someone was looking for oblivion, that was the place to find it.

Chapter 5

Nathan gripped the steering wheel. In the passenger seat, Xander sat with his arms crossed and his shoulders hunched. They both stared at the road ahead.

They hadn't spoken in twenty minutes, and it suddenly hit Nathan that his son was on the verge of tears. He was holding them back as hard as only teenage boys can – pale and tight-faced with the effort of shoring up the dam – but the grief was lapping at the edges. Xander had always looked up to Cameron, Nathan knew, and as he sat there, fully alive himself, he felt a brief stab of envy for his brother under a tarp.

Before they'd left Cameron's Land Cruiser, Ludlow had produced a roll of crime scene tape from his bag and looked for a way to surround the vehicle. There were no trees, or even any sticks he could use as stakes in the ground. In the end, he'd cut strips of tape and tied them to the door handles.

'I don't think you need to be too worried, mate,'

Nathan had said, but Ludlow had still locked the driver's door and handed the keys to Nathan.

'You okay holding on to these? Your own sergeant wants to see all this tomorrow.'

Nathan had put the keys in his pocket, where he could still feel them now as he drove. They pressed heavy and uncomfortable against his hip. He and Xander had driven the sergeant back to the gravesite in silence, where Steve had thankfully finished his immediate duties. The rear door of the ambulance was shut now and Nathan was glad Cameron was no longer in sight.

Steve had eyeballed them. 'Are you blokes all right to drive home?'

Nathan realised they all looked terrible, but they'd nodded anyway.

'Maybe we should camp?' he'd suggested half-heartedly as the ambulance drove away. 'Save driving out here again tomorrow.'

'No way. I had enough last night, thanks.' Bub was already halfway into the driver's seat. 'You both coming back to ours?'

Nathan nodded. 'Yeah, we will. Mum's expecting us tomorrow anyway. For Christmas on Thursday?' he added, when Bub looked surprised.

'Oh, yeah. Righto.' Bub started his engine. 'See you at home, then.'

'Which way do you want to go?'

'Road,' Bub said. 'Back route'll take longer if we get bogged. Dunno about you, but I can't be arsed digging my way out today.' He slammed his door.

49

Nathan could see Bub's car a short way ahead on the road now. The dust billowing from under his wheels stopped for a few hundred metres as the unpaved road suddenly switched to seamless bitumen, well maintained and clearly marked with white paint. An emergency landing strip for the Flying Doctor. The smoothness lasted barely a minute before they were jolted back onto gravel.

Xander leaned forward in the passenger seat. In the distance was a rare flicker of movement. A car was approaching, still too far away to see properly.

'All the Christmas presents are still at your place,' Xander said, sitting back heavily.

'Shit. Sorry, I thought we'd be going home before heading to Grandma's.' Nathan had planned to get back to his own house today, where they could scrub a week's worth of dust from themselves and their clothes ahead of the family Christmas reunion.

'It doesn't matter,' Xander said. 'No-one will care after this.'

No, Nathan thought. But he was annoyed with himself. He'd wanted to make this Christmas a good one for Xander, even if that was already turning into a pretty big ask.

The approaching car was still small but growing more visible ahead. Nathan recognised it as belonging to a long-term jackaroo from Atherton. The guy must be heading into town, there was nowhere else to go. The car grew closer, slowly. It felt like it took an age. There was time to consider the slight bend in the guy's bullbar and the scraped paintwork on the hood.

The jackaroo reduced his speed a touch as he drew level with Bub, raising his hand in a wave. The greeting froze mid-air when he clocked Nathan driving behind. Nathan couldn't make out the man's eyes behind the windscreen but he could see the swivel of his wrist. Firmly and deliberately, the wave turned into the finger.

It was nothing less than Nathan had expected from the first sight of the dust in the distance. He stole a glance sideways. Xander was staring out of the passenger seat window, pretending, as always, not to have noticed.

Nathan sometimes thought he could see his childhood homestead appear a thousand times, and a thousand times find it surprising.

The house stood on a slight rise at the end of a driveway that stretched for more than twenty kilometres. The homestead glowed like an oasis as the red desert gave way to a lush lawn and well-tended garden, kept green by bore water. The house itself, with its sweeping verandah, looked plucked from a country street in a time when homes were still generous and sprawling. The large industrial sheds dotted around spoiled the illusion a little, as did the staff accommodation cabins. They looked deserted to Nathan's eye, but a caravan he hadn't seen before was parked in the yard beside a dusty four-wheel drive.

As he drove up to the house, he kept his eyes peeled for signs of decay or disrepair. He could see none. The house, like the property and the well-fed cattle they'd passed on the journey, appeared to be doing well. Better than

Nathan's own place at any rate, he couldn't help thinking as he parked next to Bub. Strings of tinsel and Christmas lights had been wound along the verandah. They had been put up with care, but already looked tatty as they flapped in the hot wind.

Harry was waiting, leaning on the wooden railings. He straightened as the three of them got out of the cars. Harry had skin like a leather bag and an expression that barely changed, making it hard to guess what he was thinking. Balamara born and bred, he had started working on stations at an age when he should have still been in school. He had come to Burley Downs before Nathan was born, and he was still there, after Nathan had left.

'Good to see you both,' Harry said, shaking Nathan's hand and giving Xander a gentle slap on the shoulder. Bub was engulfed in a slobbery reunion with his dog. Nathan saw Cameron's cattle dog, Duffy, hanging back and watching the empty road. He reached out a hand and she came to him reluctantly.

Strains of music floated from somewhere in the house as a recorded voice sang about snow and sleighbells. Coming from his nieces' rooms, Nathan guessed. It had been a year since he had seen Cameron's daughters and he wondered how they would cope with the news about their dad. The festive music sounded strangely grotesque, but the girls were only eight and five, he thought. Whatever helped.

The front door opened and Nathan felt a jolt of horror at the sight of his mother. Her cheeks were pale and sunken beneath bloodshot eyes and her shoulders were hunched as though it was taking all her effort simply to be upright.

'I thought you were trying to sleep,' Harry said.

Liz Bright didn't bother answering as she blinked into the light through slitted swollen lids. Nathan could see fresh tears forming as she looked at them. Neither he nor Bub was the son she wanted to see, Nathan knew, then immediately felt guilty for thinking it. Liz had always tried hard not to play favourites, but Cameron's ready smile, quick mind and well-run property hadn't made it easy. Bub, unshaven and dust-streaked, was rubbing his eye with a dirty finger. Nathan knew he looked no better.

Liz brightened a touch at the sight of Xander, and she pulled him close, holding him fiercely. When she let him go, she reached up and put her arms around Nathan too. He hugged her back. The movement had the rusty edge of underuse.

Liz took a deep breath. 'Tell me.'

'Maybe we should go inside –' Harry started, but she cut him off.

'No. The girls are inside. Tell me here.'

Nathan found himself once again wishing that Cameron were there. He would handle this properly. Bub, who was crouched down whispering to his dog, offered no help.

'It was quite strange,' Nathan started, then stopped. He tried again, doing his best to explain as Liz began to pace up and down the verandah. She only went a short way, as though torn between wanting to hear but unable to bear it. 'We're not sure,' he found himself repeating. 'I don't know.'

'His car worked,' Bub interjected at one point, sending Liz shuffling to the far end of the floorboards. 'We tried it.'

'Not bogged?' Harry said, looking from one brother to the other. 'No flats?'

They shook their heads.

'Any idea what Cam was doing out there?' Nathan asked.

'Didn't mention any work in that area,' Harry said. 'He wrote in the book that he was going to Lehmann's Hill.'

'Bub said he seemed a bit stressed lately,' Nathan said.

He saw Harry glance at Liz and wondered if he was reluctant to talk in front of their mum. Harry nodded. 'I reckon that's fair to say, yeah.'

'How bad was it?'

'Hard to tell.' Harry's face moved a fraction. It was still impossible to read. 'He hadn't been himself for a few weeks, looking back. Maybe a month, would you say?' He looked to Liz, who gave a tight nod, staring past the lush garden to the barren brown land beyond.

'It didn't seem like anything too serious though,' Harry went on. 'Obviously. Or we would have done something.'

'What do you mean by not himself?' Nathan said.

'Didn't have his eye on the ball around here as much as usual, but nothing we couldn't handle. He said he was tired a few times. I got the idea he maybe hadn't been sleeping that well.'

'He hadn't,' Liz said quietly. 'I heard him sometimes in the night.'

'And he was touchy,' Harry said. 'Sometimes looked a bit rough around the edges.'

No, that definitely didn't sound like Cameron, Nathan thought.

'Had something happened?' he asked. 'You been having any problems here?'

Harry shook his head. 'Property's been good. Going well. We've had a strong year.'

'Great. Good to hear,' said Nathan, whose own bottom line had once again been written in red rather than black. The children's decorations shimmered in the wind and he thought of his nieces. 'Do Sophie and Lo know yet?'

'Ilse's in there telling them now,' Harry said, and Nathan automatically glanced towards the door. It was empty. He missed what Harry was saying. 'Sorry?'

'Glenn called.'

'Oh.' The regular sergeant. 'He's back in town, is he?'

'Not yet, he wants someone to meet him at Cam's car tomorrow.'

Nathan could feel Cameron's keys in his pocket. 'I'll go.'

'I already told him I would,' Harry said.

'Still, I'll come with you.'

'Me too,' said Xander and Bub, almost in unison.

Liz, who had been staring at nothing, dragged her eyes back and frowned. 'Bub, take Xander inside and show him where he's sleeping.'

'He knows. Same as always,' Bub said.

She closed her eyes and took a breath. 'Take him anyway.' When the screen door slammed behind them, she turned to Nathan. 'How's Xander coping?'

'Okay, considering.'

'How long have you got him for?'

'He's getting the plane on the twenty-seventh.'

'Oh.' She looked disappointed. 'He can't get the next week's flight? I thought it was your turn for New Year?'

'It is, but no.' Xander would be leaving a week before the court-ordered date. Nathan could have insisted. It was his legal right, secured and well and truly paid for, but he hadn't. 'He wants to go to a party in Brisbane with his mates.'

'How long until he's back again?'

'I don't know.' Nathan tried to keep his voice light but could feel Liz watching him. 'He's got some big exams starting this year.'

Two years of revision schedules and standardised testing and university entrance marks lay ahead, Nathan had been warned, via his ex-wife's lawyer. Xander would need focus and stability for these two years. He needed time at home to study. Could Nathan please acknowledge that he understood that?

In fact, Nathan could understand that. He could also understand that in less than two years' time, his son would be eighteen years old. Court-ordered visitations would be among the many relics of Xander's childhood left behind at that juncture.

The Christmas carols had stopped, Nathan realised, and in the vacuum, he could hear a child crying. He wished the music would start again. Liz turned towards the sound and, without a word, walked to the door and disappeared inside.

Nathan and Harry were alone on the verandah. In the west, the sun was a burning yellow blaze as it crept lower.

'Between us,' Nathan said. 'Have you ever seen anything like this?'

'I've seen tourists do some bloody stupid things,' Harry said. 'But I knew Cam hadn't just broken down, soon as I heard. If that had happened, he'd still be in that car with the air con on, complaining all about it on the radio. Everyone knows that. When Ilse broke down earlier this year, she did the right thing. Sat tight in her car on the north road for four hours until Cam could get to her.'

'That's what I told the St Helens cop,' Nathan said.

'What does he reckon?'

'He doesn't know anything. He wasn't even trained there.'

'But he thinks Cam walked away on purpose?'

'I think so,' Nathan said. 'You saw Cam most recently, though. You tell me.'

'I can tell you there are easier ways to do it. But –' A long pause. 'People have done some strange things around here over the years.'

'You'd just shoot yourself, wouldn't you?'

Harry's eyes flicked over. 'Would you?'

'Well, I would.' Nathan had meant to sound factual but it came out wrong. Too definitive. It implied a level of thought had gone into it. Harry was still looking at him, closely now, and neither spoke again for a while. The crying inside the house had stopped, audibly at least. The Christmas carols had not restarted, though. No tidings of comfort and joy here.

'What do you think was worrying Cam?' Nathan said eventually.

'I don't know. Like I said, we've had a good season. If

it was something work-related, it's news to me.' Harry leaned heavily against railing. 'I suppose he turned forty this year.'

'Did that bother him?'

'He never mentioned it, but it's a milestone, isn't it? Bothers some people.'

Nathan tried to think back to his own milestone birthday two years earlier. Other than a card from Xander and a phone call from Liz, it had passed as a completely unremarkable day.

Above him, the decorations fluttered, shedding dust to the wind.

'Kerry McGrath killed himself around Christmas,' Harry said.

'I suppose.'

Although that was different, Nathan thought. Kerry had swallowed every pill in his Flying Doctor supply box after his wife left him. He'd opened the compartments you weren't supposed to open without explicit instructions from the doc on the other end of the phone, and he'd taken everything from paracetamol to morphine in one go. It had been neither quick nor painless, apparently. At least that was what Steve Fitzgerald at the clinic had told everyone, probably as a deterrent as much as anything, Nathan suspected. He remembered hearing about Kerry. Nathan's own box was now at the back of a high cupboard, out of sight.

He cleared his throat. 'There was Bryan Taylor. He wandered off.'

Harry made a noise. 'He wandered from the pub to his

58

car and drowned drunk in the river. Speaking of, you all set for supplies down at your place?'

'Yeah. Mostly.'

'Well, make sure you are. I reckon the water's coming.'

'Again?'

'I think so. There'll be rain up north, I reckon.'

Nathan nodded. When Harry made a prediction, it was worth paying attention.

'There was also your dad,' Harry said out of nowhere and Nathan looked over in surprise. 'That was around this time of year.'

'February. And he didn't kill himself.'

'I know.' Harry was thoughtful. 'Just wondered if something might have been going through Cameron's head. Out there on his own. Maybe it triggered something.'

'Dad wasn't on his own when he died.'

'No. I know that, I meant —'

'What?'

'Nothing. Sometimes people do strange things.'

They were cut off by the squeal of the screen door. Xander looked out. 'Grandma says dinner's ready.'

'Thanks, mate,' Harry said as Xander disappeared back inside. 'You coming?'

'In a sec. You go.'

Nathan waited until he heard the door slam and he was alone. He walked down the wooden steps and across the springy green lawn, a tangy citrus scent coming from the trees. From the direction of the big shed, he could hear the hum of the generator, turning itself over to keep the property lights burning. He reached the fence designed to keep curious cattle off the lush lawn, and without quite knowing why, climbed over it and stood on the other side.

Nathan looked out. The sun seemed to be dropping fast in the west. In another hour the horizon would disappear into something even more endless. He heard a distant wistful howl. It was early in the evening for dingoes, but there was nothing else it could be. Nathan took a couple of steps through the dust, away from the fence and the house and its cultivated greenery. He stared out. It was vast, like looking down from the edge of a cliff, and he felt a rare hint of vertigo.

At night, when the sky felt even bigger, he could almost imagine it was a million years ago and he was walking on the bottom of the sea. A million years ago when a million natural events still needed to occur, one after the other, to form this land as it lay in front of him now. A place where rivers flooded without rain and seashells fossilised a thousand miles from water and men who left their cars found themselves walking to their deaths.

Sometimes, the space almost seemed to call to Nathan. Like a faint heartbeat, insistent and persuasive. He listened now, and took an experimental step, then another. Behind him, he heard the squeal of the screen door. Xander calling out.

'Dad?'

Nathan stopped walking. He raised a hand, then turned towards the sound of his son's voice and slowly made his way back to the house.

Chapter 6

The exhaustion didn't hit Nathan properly until he was back inside. Xander had gone ahead into the kitchen and Nathan lingered in the dim hallway, feeling hollow. He was used to starting his days in the early-morning dark, but the last few hours had drained him. There was a jolt at his elbow as Bub pushed past and disappeared into the kitchen. Bub looked just as tired.

Cameron's dog, Duffy, wandered up to him, still looking forlorn. She had come from the same litter as Nathan's own dog, Kelly, and now nuzzled his leg in the same way that Kelly once had. Nathan crouched down to Duffy and was immediately reminded of that bad morning last year. He'd woken up and known straight away that something was wrong. He'd eventually found Kelly hiding in one of the sheds, her eyes rolling around in her head, whining in pain. Nathan, who spent more time with that dog than any other living thing, had taken her in his arms and carried her to the house. She had died on the way. She'd been baited, Nathan had told Glenn when he'd calmed down enough to call the police station. His voice had cracked and he hadn't cared. Someone had come out to Nathan's place and poisoned her.

To the sergeant's credit, he'd driven out to Nathan's property and helped him look for signs. They'd found nothing. It must have been targeted, Nathan had insisted. 'I know what a baited dog looks like. Someone got her on purpose.'

Glenn had been sympathetic but sceptical. 'I've had no other reports. And it's a fair way for someone to come to do that.'

'You don't think they would? To get at me?'

Glenn had put a hand on his shoulder. 'I'm not saying they wouldn't, mate. I'm just not sure if they actually did.'

Nathan paused now in the dim hallway, one hand on Duffy's head, as he heard a whisper coming from around the corner.

' . . . but they'll have to come . . . '

A woman. He didn't recognise the voice.

'No, I don't think so. I'm telling you, it's not that kind of place. He was on the phone asking if anyone was coming here –' A man this time, also whispering.

'Here to the house?'

'Yeah, but I think the cop was saying no –'

The voices stopped abruptly as their owners rounded the corner and saw Nathan standing there in the hall. The man's jaw was still open with a half-formed word unspoken. He appeared to be in his late twenties, as was the woman next to him. And, judging by their accents, they were English. Nathan felt fractious. That was all he bloody needed. A pair of Pommy backpackers.

'God, you gave me a fright.' The man recovered first. 'You must be Nathan.'

'Yeah. Who were you talking about?'

'Who?'

'The person you heard on the phone. Talking to the police.'

'Oh.' The man hesitated, glancing past Nathan to the empty kitchen door. 'It was Harry. Sorry. I wasn't listening, I just . . . heard.'

'Right.' It was hard to see the pair properly in the low light. 'Who did you say you were again?'

'Simon and Katy.' The man pointed as he said their names, as though Nathan might need help working out who was who. 'We're no-one.'

'You must be someone if you're hanging around my dead brother's hallway listening in on phone calls.' It was unnecessary and Nathan knew it. He just couldn't help it.

The woman found her voice. 'Cameron hired us.'

'Yeah, Bub said. To do what?'

'Help your mum around the house, for one thing,' she said, nodding towards the kitchen. 'So, if it's all right with you . . . ?'

She'd stepped around Nathan before he could answer and he found himself trailing them into the kitchen. Harry and Bub were already seated at the large wooden table. Nathan pulled up a chair next to Xander and looked across at the English bloke – Simon, was it? He had pale eyes and a very straight nose and thick dark hair that shone in a way that seemed strangely unnatural. Nathan would have had trouble tearing his eyes away from it, if it hadn't been for the girl.

Katy was – and Nathan could think of no other word – a stunner. In the brightly lit kitchen, he could see how her skin and hair shone, and her t-shirt clung to her in all the right ways. As she smiled at something, a hint of a dimple appeared. She brushed behind Nathan, and he had the overwhelming urge to reach out and take her hand. He frowned and put his palms on the table.

Bub was watching with a look of slavish devotion as Katy moved from benchtop to table, carrying plates of beef and rice. Even Xander was introducing himself with an enthusiasm Nathan hadn't seen before and a glaze in his eyes that made him look a little like Bub. Only Harry seemed unmoved, his stony expression unaltered. Katy bent over to get something from a low drawer and Nathan wondered what Cameron's wife made of her.

'We're not waiting for Ilse?' he asked Liz, who was hovering in front of the open fridge door as though unable to remember why she was there.

'She's still with the girls,' Harry answered instead. 'She said to start.'

'Oh.'

Katy set the final plate down. 'One for you, Bob.'

'Thank you, Katy.'

'It's Bub,' Nathan said automatically.

'Sorry?'

'Just –' He could feel Bub glaring at him. 'With your accent it sounds like you're saying Bob.'

'I am.'

'It's Bub. 'Cause he's the baby.'

'Oh.' Katy's brow creased. She looked at Bub, who was shovelling food into his thirty-year-old mouth. 'I'm so sorry.'

'I don't mind,' said Bub, with feeling.

'That's so embarrassing.' Katy gave an awkward laugh. 'I've been calling you the wrong name this whole time.'

'Well, his real name's Lee,' Liz said with a sigh. She had finally shut the fridge and sat down. 'So you're not the only one.'

Bub gave Katy a smile that made her glance away, then turned to Harry. 'What did Glenn have to say about meeting tomorrow?'

Harry's eyes flicked towards Liz. 'Not now, mate.'

'I'm only asking.'

Bub had changed his clothes, Nathan realised. He looked down at himself and across at Xander. The red dust from the death site had crept into the creases of their shirts, and the colour suddenly made his skin crawl. He rubbed at another red patch on his jeans. It made his hands feel gritty.

'I'll put the washing machine on later,' Liz said quietly and Nathan realised she was looking at the dust as well.

'Thanks.'

No-one spoke and for a while the only sound was cutlery against plates. After a few minutes, Xander turned to the backpackers, as Nathan had known he would. The kid lived in a city. He couldn't cope with quiet like the rest of them.

'How long have you been out here travelling?' Xander

asked Simon, who also seemed relieved to have the silence broken.

'Nearly a year.'

'You're not heading home for Christmas?'

'No plans –' Simon started, as at the same time Katy said: 'It's too expensive.' Their eyes met and something passed between them that Nathan couldn't read.

'And Cam hired you?' Nathan said, and they looked over. 'Was that pre-arranged, or –?'

'No. Just lucky.' Simon swallowed and put his fork down. 'We were in the pub in town and got talking to him. I've worked in a few trades at home so I've been helping fix the fences, water bores, whatever.'

Harry's features moved a hair's breadth and Nathan wondered how much help the new guy had actually been.

Simon nodded at Katy. 'And she's a teacher, so it worked out well with the girls here. Doing their School of the Air lessons with them.'

Katy gave a small smile. She had put down her knife and was picking at her thumbnail.

'Do you like it out here?' Xander asked.

'Love it,' Simon said. Katy didn't reply.

'Must be a fair change of pace for you,' Nathan said.

'That's kind of the point,' Simon said, and Nathan had a vague sense he was being patronised. 'You don't get anything like this at home. We were blown away by how big these stations actually are when we first came out. We passed through one in WA which was half the size of Wales.'

'Oh.' Nathan had no idea how big Wales was, but it didn't surprise him. 'So you've worked at other stations?'

'Yeah, a couple.'

'Where?'

'Out west, mostly.'

'Yeah, you said. West is a bloody big place.'

'I don't think you would have heard of it.'

'Try me.'

'Armistead.'

Nathan hadn't heard of it, much to his irritation. 'Where's that exactly?'

'Kind of east of Perth.'

'Everything's bloody east –'

Liz dropped her fork on her plate with a clatter. 'Jesus, Nathan.'

'Why don't you let them eat in peace, mate?' Harry said.

'No, it's my fault,' Simon said. 'It's a crap description, I know. But it's so hard out here. There's nothing to help pinpoint things.'

That was only true, Nathan thought, if you were completely blind to the subtleties of the land.

Across the table, Xander swallowed his mouthful. 'What brought you over to Queensland?'

Simon had taken a sip of water and took his time swallowing. 'Weather.'

'Really?'

'Too bloody hot in WA.'

'You know this is officially the hottest part of Australia?'

'Oh. I didn't, actually. Still, better than the freezing fog at home, isn't it?' Simon looked to Katy, who blinked, distracted.

'Sorry. What?' She had been staring at something unseen out of the window. The sky was dusky as evening drew in.

'I was saying –'

He was interrupted by the landline jangling loudly from the hall. Word must be spreading, Nathan thought.

'I'll get it.' Harry started to stand, but Liz was already gone, leaving her plate practically untouched. Harry looked at the empty doorway for a moment, then shook his head.

'We're so sorry about Cameron,' Simon said, to no-one in particular. Katy was picking her nails again. 'He was a great guy. When we were in town looking for work, we heard a lot of nice things about him, and people were right. They all said we'd be lucky to work for him.'

That was probably true, Nathan thought. Cameron had a reputation for being a good boss.

'I hadn't actually realised at first that you still lived so close to town yourself, Nathan,' Simon was saying.

'Not that close, nearly three hours away.'

'Yeah, relatively speaking, though. I'd got the impression you'd moved further away.'

'Nope.'

Katy had looked up now as well, and both she and Simon were watching Nathan with curiosity. He wondered what else people had been saying in town while they were singing Cam's praises. Although he didn't need to wonder, really. He could guess. The atmosphere had grown awkward but Nathan did nothing to displace it. He simply stared back, impassive, until Simon dropped his eyes. The backpacker turned to Xander.

'You live with your dad?'

'No,' Xander said. 'I go to school in Brisbane.'

The eternal diplomat, Nathan thought, with a rush of something both sharp and sweet. Seven words that glossed over a decade-long tug of war between him, his ex-wife Jacqui and, now, her new husband as well. Fractious phone calls, lawyers' letters, court orders, visitation schedules and always, *always*, the legal bills. Xander flashed a half-smile at Nathan as though he knew what he was thinking.

'Will you go into property management as well, do you think?' Simon asked.

'Oh. No. I don't think so. It's not really –' Xander saw Nathan, Bub and Harry all watching him and he hesitated. 'I want to go to uni. I'm not too sure after that.'

He looked a little embarrassed but was saved by movement at the kitchen door. They all looked up. In the doorway stood Cameron's wife, turned freshly made widow. Ilse had one hand on the doorjamb and an unsteady air about her. Her light brown hair was unbrushed and had been pulled back hastily with an elastic band. Her face was flushed and shiny and it was clear she'd been crying.

Nathan didn't sit up in his chair. He didn't straighten his shoulders or run a hand through his hair or neaten his shirt. The urge was so instinctive, he found it a little uncomfortable to resist, like holding his breath. But still he didn't move. He just sat there, pushing back against involuntary reactions. Eventually, he counted to three and allowed himself to raise his eyes and glance at Ilse, just once.

She wasn't even looking at him.

Chapter 7

Ilse hovered in the doorway, looking very much like she wanted to turn and leave.

'Come and sit down.' Harry beckoned to her and she took a few steps in. 'Are the girls coming?'

'They're asleep. Lo's in Liz's room. She wouldn't settle in her own.'

Katy stood up. 'I'll get you something to eat.'

'It's fine. I'm not –' Ilse started, but Katy had already placed a plate in front of the remaining vacant spot next to Nathan.

The hesitation was so brief Nathan could almost tell himself he imagined it, then he felt the cotton of Ilse's shirt brush against his arm and heard the soft creak of the chair as she sat down beside him.

'Nice to see you, Nathan.'

'You too.'

He could still remember the first time he'd seen Ilse standing in this kitchen. It was nine years ago and only the fifth time he'd seen her at all. He had walked in and seen someone standing alone at the sink, re-filling a water jug. Nathan had registered her dress, her light brown hair, and the curve of her back before he fully realised who he was looking at.

She had turned and they'd both stopped and stood there wordlessly, each as surprised as the other. Nathan had taken a breath to say – what? To this day, he didn't know – when Cameron had swept into the room and up to Ilse. He'd put his palm against the small of her back and gently moved a stray strand of hair before kissing her cheek. Nathan had made his lungs release the air and, with effort, shut his mouth. Later, Ilse had caught him alone in the hall.

'I didn't expect to see you here,' she'd said.

No shit, he'd thought. *Same here.* 'Well, Cameron's my brother,' he said out loud.

'I didn't know that when I met him. I'm sorry.'

But she hadn't looked sorry, she'd looked happy. Ilse did not look happy now.

'How are the girls, Ilse?' Harry asked.

'Confused. Full of questions. Same as everyone. I have no idea how to explain it to them.' Her voice was tight and she looked across at Bub, who was busy clearing his plate. 'You were about their age when your dad died.'

Bub's fork slowed. 'I suppose.'

'Did anyone say anything that helped you understand what was going on?'

It was a sign of Ilse's desperation that she was even asking, Nathan thought. Bub started eating again.

'Dunno,' he said, still chewing. 'Not really. I was okay.'

71

That wasn't even close to true, Nathan knew. Nathan had been barely twenty-one when their dad died, with Cameron two years behind. But Bub had only been eight and there had been nightmares. Nathan had seen and heard them for himself when he'd come home, the whole house waking up to the sound of shrieks. Bub's face shiny with sweat and tears, saying that Dad was alive, but now bloodied and furious at what had happened to him. The nightmares had lasted for years apparently, Nathan wasn't sure exactly how long. There were plenty of things worse than bad dreams, but Bub had not been okay, not at all.

'Did anyone actually talk to Uncle Cam before he left on Wednesday?' Xander looked around the table.

Harry pointed his fork at Simon. 'We'd both already gone, but –' He gestured at Katy, who nodded.

'I saw him. Briefly. The girls and I were playing in the schoolroom – it's in that cabin near the stables?' she said. 'I went to get something from the house and saw Cameron heading to his car.'

'Did he say anything?' Nathan asked.

'Only that he was on his way to meet Bob – sorry, sorry, Bub – at Lehmann's Hill. I asked if they were both still planning to stay out overnight, so I didn't need to worry about them for dinner. He said yes, and they would be back the next day.'

'And how did he seem?' Nathan asked.

'I didn't really know him that well.'

'You can say what you think, though.'

She was still picking at her nails. Simon noticed and put his hand on hers.

'Honestly,' Katy said finally. 'He seemed quite agitated. And he was keen to get going, like he had something to do that he wanted to get out of the way. I assumed it was the Lehmann's Hill trip, though.'

'Did he say he didn't want to go?'

'No, nothing like that. Not to me at least. He got in his car and headed off and that's when –' Katy looked over at Ilse, attempting to pass the narrative along.

Ilse, who was sitting very still, did not take it up.

Nathan turned to her. 'You saw Cam too?'

'Yes,' she said at last. 'I was further along the driveway, bringing in one of the horses. He had to go past me to leave.'

'Did he stop and talk?' Bub said. He had stopped eating and started paying attention since Lehmann's Hill was mentioned, Nathan realised.

'Of course he did. He's my husband.' Ilse snapped. She took a breath. 'Sorry, Bub.'

'No worries. What did he say?'

Ilse's face tightened. Nathan could understand she might be reluctant to share her final personal exchange with her husband with the group but he was as keen to know as anybody.

'He said he would see me when he got back.'

'That's it?' Bub said. 'And what did you say?'

'To drive safe and I would see him then.'

'Oh.' Bub looked disappointed and Ilse's eyes were suddenly hard and shiny.

'Well, I'm sorry, but what did you expect? I didn't know –'. She fished a tissue out of her pocket and blew her nose.

Nathan turned to Bub. 'And Cam definitely told you he was going to meet you at Lehmann's?'

'Yeah. We spoke the day before on the radio.'

'But not on the Wednesday morning?'

'No. No need, mate. I knew what we were doing.'

Harry was watching Bub. 'How did he sound when you spoke?'

'I already said. He seemed fine.'

'Seeming fine isn't the same as being fine.' The voice came from the door and they all looked up to see Liz. She had been crying again. Nathan wondered how long she'd been standing there. She was still looking at Bub in mild despair, but he just shrugged, like he couldn't see the distinction in what she'd said.

'Did you see Uncle Cam before he left, Grandma?' Xander said.

'No.' The weight of regret seemed to make the air in the room grow heavier. 'But it was obvious something was wrong with him.'

Nathan saw Ilse's expression harden.

'Where were you? Out riding?' Nathan said, and was relieved when Liz nodded. His mum rode almost every morning of her life. Nathan privately used it as a bellwether for her health and knew Cameron had, too. He looked pointedly at the table where her plate was still waiting, but Liz shook her head.

'No. I'm going to bed.'

'Who was on the phone?' Harry asked.

'Caroline from the post office.'

'Word's hit town then.'

'Yes. Sounds like it.'

'What did she want?'

'Same as everyone else. She said she wanted to help.'
Liz shook her head. 'But all they really want to know is
what happened.'

Liz looked around the kitchen as though the answer
might materialise, but Nathan could see only baffled
faces staring back.

'What are you telling them?' he said finally.

'I don't know. I don't know what to tell them.' Her face
creased. 'I have to try to sleep, I'll see you all in the morning.'
She was gone and the doorway was empty once more. After
a moment, Katy stood up and started stacking the dishes.

'What were you and Simon doing, Uncle Harry?'
Xander asked.

'Checking a few of the north-eastern bores. Thanks,
Katy –' Harry passed his plate over. 'We were gone before
dawn so we missed Cam completely.'

'Big area,' Nathan said. 'You get them all done or do
you need some help?'

'I think we're mostly right,' Harry said. 'I did the eastern
side and Simon did the north.'

Splitting up was the way to do it, Nathan thought.
They'd cover an extra hundred kilometres that way, even
if it meant working alone. They probably hadn't seen each
other all day. He looked from Simon to Harry and wondered why the thought had occurred to him.

Bub drained his water glass. 'It's bloody weird Cam being
out there at the grave. It's a bit like that story about the real
stockman.'

'Bub, mate. For God's sake.' Harry made a noise in his throat.

Simon frowned and looked over at Bub. 'What's that?'

Harry shook his head. 'It's ridiculous.'

'It's not.' Bub nodded at Nathan. 'Go on, you tell it, you know how it goes. The one with the campfire and the travellers.'

'No,' Nathan said.

'But you know the one I mean. With the horses.'

'Yeah, I know.' He felt Ilse shift in her chair. 'But not now.'

'How does it start again? There was this group of blokes or something.' Bub groaned. 'I can never remember it properly. Just bloody do it, Nate. Go on, or I'll have to.'

The room was quiet and the backpackers were watching expectantly. Nathan sighed.

'It's just this stupid legend they tell kids around here,' he said. 'It's supposed to have happened back in the 1890s and the stockman wasn't actually a stockman, he was a cattle rustler.'

Katy had turned off the water in the sink and was paying attention.

'He was part of a gang,' Nathan went on. 'They saw all this space and all the absent property owners back then, and saw the chance to make a few bucks. It was nothing too flash, pretty much keeping off the main tracks, and rounding up any loose cattle that came their way. When they had as many as they could handle, they'd walk them down to Adelaide. Disguise the branding if they could, sell them cheap if they couldn't.'

He stopped.

'Then one day, the horses went nuts,' Bub prompted.

'Yeah, thanks, mate.' Nathan frowned. 'So yeah, one day they're up in these parts and they all start having trouble with the horses. Skittish, you know, difficult to control, like they were spooked. So the stockman's horse is the worst and it gets to the point where he can barely keep up. So he calls it a day and stays behind to set up the group camp while the others get the cattle sorted for the night.' Nathan paused. 'The story goes that he was alone for no more than an hour. When they got back, his swag was rolled out and a campfire had been lit.'

'The kettle was strung over but had boiled itself dry,' Bub jumped in. He lowered his voice meaningfully. 'But there was no sign of the stockman.'

The backpackers looked back to Nathan, who shrugged. 'Like Bub says. No sign of the bloke, no sign of a struggle. His horse was still tied up, but barely. She was pulling and thrashing, like they do when they want to run. So his mates split up, ride around, can't find him. They search until dark, but nothing. They wait the next day, but he never comes back and eventually they have to move on 'cause they've got all these cattle still. Anyway, two days later, they run into this family of travellers coming north up the track and ask if they've seen any sign of their mate. The family seems a bit uneasy, then takes them around to look in one of their carts. In the back, all wrapped up in a blanket, is the body of the stockman. The family reckons they found him dead by the side of the track three days earlier and a hundred kilometres further south. They were taking him to the nearest town to see if anyone knew who he was. Apparently, his body was lying by the side of the road, no injuries, no water or supplies or anything with him.'

'But if they were telling the truth, he was found dead the same day he disappeared.' Bub leaned back in his chair. 'And too far away for him to walk, or even ride, so how did he get there?'

Simon glanced up at Katy, who held out her rubber-gloved hands and shrugged. Simon shook his head. 'I don't know.'

'No, well, none of those guys knew either,' Nathan said. 'So they panicked a bit, buried him right there where they were, and that would have been the end of it. But there's always talk and suddenly there were all these sightings of the dead stockman up and down the track, people claiming they'd seen him walking at night and things. Eventually workers started refusing to come here, saying it was haunted. There were a few accidents. Serious ones, a couple of people died. Anyway, it got so bad that eventually the landowner here at the time was forced to put the headstone up, to try to lay the whole ghost thing to rest and put a stop to the rumours. Didn't really work though. The story goes that if you dig, there's nothing under that headstone. That the grave is empty.'

The only sound was kitchen clock ticking. Both the backpackers were staring at Nathan.

'Bullshit,' Simon whispered.

'Yeah, of course,' Nathan said. 'It's only a bloody story.'

'Still. That's quite weird. Him vanishing then appearing like that miles away.'

'Yeah. Well, don't lose any sleep, it's not true –' Nathan started to say, but his words were lost as Ilse stood up suddenly, her chair scraping against the floor. She opened her mouth as if to say something, then snapped it shut, turned and walked out of the room.

There was a silence.

Bub's chair creaked as he leaned back, shaking his head. 'Good one, Nathan.'

Chapter 8

Dinner was well and truly over after that. Simon got up to help Katy, the pair muttering to each other as the family dispersed. Nathan saw Simon whisper something to Katy and they both looked at him, then away.

'Your mum's put Xander in your old room again so I suppose it's up to you where you want to sleep,' Harry said to Nathan as he got up to leave. 'The staff block's empty but the air con's broken in there.'

The staff accommodation would be like being locked in a tin can. 'I'll take the couch.' Nathan peered into the fridge in search of a beer.

'There're some in the coolroom if they're not in there,' Harry said.

'Shit.' Nathan stood up and shut the fridge.

'What?'

'Nothing. I just remembered something.'

Nathan's own coolroom had been on the blink for a while, and after several weeks of waiting, the repair contractor was in the area. He'd been due, finally, at Nathan's place that day, Nathan remembered now as he pulled open the heavy door to the large family coolroom built off the kitchen. The contractor would have let himself in, no problem with that, but Nathan had expected to be there. He'd try to call him.

There was no problem with this coolroom at least, he thought as he walked in, goosebumps immediately rising on his skin. He stood for a minute among the industrial quantities of frozen food, enjoying the temperature, before extracting a beer from a tower of slabs.

Back in the kitchen, he poked his head into the storeroom next door. It was well stocked, he was relieved to see. Not that he'd expected anything less, but if Cameron had been distracted, supplies weren't something you wanted to let slide. Much like Nathan's own storeroom at home, it was like walking into a corner store. The shelves groaned with months' worth of rice and pasta and cans. Lists were pinned to the wall, keeping track of how many of each item was in stock. Everything was in double figures.

Nathan looked around and sipped his beer. He'd need to double check his own stores were in shape if Harry was right about the flood. He should be all right though. Like every other household in the region, Nathan placed his regular supermarket order in the nearest city, and every six weeks a huge refrigerated truck trundled the thousand-kilometre road north from Adelaide with the whole town's orders. Plan ahead, or pay the price. Nathan knew what he would be eating for every meal for the next six months. He always had enough to get through the floods, especially with it just being him, but if he was going to be trapped, he wanted to be prepared.

He closed the storeroom door behind him, and out in the hall he picked up the landline and called the cool-room contractor. Cameron's wallet was sitting on the hall table next to the phone, as he'd expected. He picked it up as the call went to voicemail and flicked through while he left a message. A couple of credit cards, some cash. One or two faded receipts from the service station in town. Nathan pulled out the driver's licence and looked at his brother's photo. Cameron was not smiling, which was unusual, and he had instead assumed a dutifully neutral look. He still had a hint of humour around the eyes though and Nathan could imagine he'd just finished sharing a laugh with the photographer. Nathan snapped the wallet shut.

He picked up his beer and wandered through to the lounge. The house barely changed from decade to decade. The couch was the same one they'd had since he was a kid and he'd slept on it many times before. It wasn't bad. He saw that Liz had left some clean clothes folded for him and picked them up. They had to be Cameron's. Practicality always won out over sentimentality, but it still felt strange to be holding his dead brother's shirt and jeans.

A plastic Christmas tree stood in the corner of the living room, its lights twinkling. There were already a few presents underneath. Nearby, in the centre of the wall and displayed in a heavy frame that Nathan knew had been expensive, hung Cameron's prize-winning painting of the stockman's grave.

It had been a while since Nathan had last seen it and he leaned in to take a closer look. The image caught the grave at sunrise – viewers sometimes mistook it for sunset but Nathan knew from the position that it was morning – with beams of light refracting out from the horizon. Cameron had paid a lot of attention to the way the light played through the sky, with tiny brushstrokes and a rich palette of colour that captured the detail.

The grave itself was almost an afterthought by comparison. Its dark tones loomed in the bottom half of the painting, and its shape was implied rather than explicit. Even Nathan, who knew exactly bugger-all about art, thought he could see why it was so popular. When it had won its prize, he'd read a couple of discussions and critiques online where people had attached all sorts of meaning to it. Light vanquishing darkness, and vice versa. Loneliness, grief, rebirth. Someone had said they could see the hint of the stockman standing in the muddy greys where the light met the dark.

Personally, Nathan had never liked the picture all that much. It was a pretty good painting, he could admit, but it didn't capture the landscape for him. The contrast between the dark and the light seemed a bit heavy-handed. Whenever he was out there, especially alone, it always felt much more fluid.

Nathan flopped down on the couch and looked again at the pile of his brother's clothes. They were almost exactly the same as his own – not surprising given that everyone he knew shopped at the same place – but were a size or two smaller. Nathan and Cameron had been the same height since they were seventeen but his brother was – had been – lean and athletic where Nathan was more broad and solid.

When Nathan had found himself alone – not the first time when Jacqui had left, but the second time, the real time – he had passed long hours working out feverishly with a dented old weights set in one of his sheds. After a while, it had dawned on him that no-one ever saw what he looked like, let alone cared. Overnight he had stopped lifting weights and spent the hours instead lying on his couch drinking beer. But it was hard enough to get up every morning in the dark even without a hangover, and the physical work around the property demanded a certain level of strength and fitness, so he'd had to rein that in too. He'd put down the beer and picked up the weights on and off, and had managed to land somewhere in the middle. But he'd never quite got back to what he was.

Nathan looked down at his own shirt, still red with dust, as a shadow passed by the window. Ilse. She was silhouetted in the twilight, reaching up to unpeg bedsheets from the washing line. They billowed and snapped around her in the wind as though someone was running through them. Nathan watched a moment more, then dropped his brother's shirt back on the couch and went outside to talk to his brother's wife.

Ilse's eyes went to the red dust on his clothes straight away. It seemed more obvious somehow out there in the open air than it had been in the kitchen. Nathan could see her considering its origin as her hand stilled on a peg.

'They're going in the wash.'

She didn't say anything, just turned back to the sheets.

'Listen, Ilse, sorry about that stupid stockman story at dinner. I didn't mean to upset you.'

She pushed a sheet aside to look at him. 'I'm not upset because of the story, Nathan.'

'No. I suppose not.'

She stretched up to grab a pillowcase. They belonged to the girls, judging by the pattern.

'Leave them,' Nathan said. 'You don't have to do that now.'

'I do. They're Lo's. They've been out since yesterday.'

'It's already too late then.' The bed linen would have been dry five minutes after it was put out. The cotton was now covered in two days' worth of grit. 'They'll have to get washed again anyway. Leave it for now.'

'No.'

'Then let me give you a hand.'

Ilse opened her mouth as though to protest, then gave a defeated shrug. 'Thanks.' She twisted a peg in her fingers. 'Nathan, what do you think happened to Cam?'

He pulled a sheet off the line and didn't reply straight away.

'Did he get separated from his car by accident?' She stared hard at the peg in her hands. 'Or did it look like he meant it?'

'I don't know.'

'But you were out there. What did you see?'

'There was a cop from St Helens, he could talk through everything –'

'I know that.' She stopped him. 'I'm asking you. Please.'

He sighed. The sheets rustled around them as he told

her what he could, seeing the small crease deepen between her eyes. She listened mostly without speaking, her eyes damp and her mouth tight. She interrupted only twice, first when he told her about the shallow hole at the base of the headstone and again when he mentioned the water and supplies abandoned in the back of Cameron's four-wheel drive. She made him explain that again. It made no more sense the second time.

He watched Ilse as he spoke. It had been ten years but sometimes, in the right light, she still looked like the girl he had met behind the bar that first night. He'd been different too then, back when he was a semi-regular at the town's lone pub. Making the long drive a bit too often, if he was honest, when the sting of his divorce had still been pretty raw.

His wife – *ex-wife*, the paperwork had finally come through – had driven away down the Balamara Track a year earlier with five-year-old Xander in tow and without a backwards glance. Without much intention of sticking to the child access arrangement they'd managed to agree on either, as it had turned out.

Nathan had promised Xander that he would phone him in Brisbane every day, but the line rang out too many times to be a coincidence. When he did get through, Xander was called away before they'd had a proper chance to talk, leaving Nathan listening to the dial tone. Jacqui had been impossible to pin down on the dates of a promised visit. Nathan had made himself give her long enough to settle into her new life, and then even a bit longer, but he had walked into the Balamara pub that particular night having transferred an eye-watering sum to retain a family lawyer.

The distance from his son made him feel sad and the lawyer's fee had made him feel poor, and Nathan had turned up that night not expecting that to change. There was only so much benefit a man could realistically get from nursing a beer in an empty pub.

Ilse had been there.

She was the only one behind the bar and he was the only one in front of it, so she'd served him with a smile and he had introduced himself. She sat across from him as they chatted. She had been working in the pub for exactly three weeks and one day, she told him, having arrived in town with her backpack exactly three weeks and two days earlier. She was Dutch, originally, but had been studying environmental science in Canada, and she leaned across the bar as she taught him how to pronounce her name in a soft melodic accent.

'*Eel-sa*,' he'd tried, and she'd smiled.

'Close enough.'

He'd kept trying until he got it right.

Her parents were divorced and her mum had died a year earlier from breast cancer – she had stopped talking and looked down at the bar for a very long time, and eventually Nathan had tentatively reached out and put a hand on her arm. She had smiled then, and he felt something dislodge inside him. Anyway, she had said, still smiling, that had given her the motivation to finally go travelling. Have an adventure and see the world a bit.

'What do you think of the outback?' he had asked, and she'd laughed.

'It's cool. It's like the edge of the earth.'

He bought them both a drink and they'd sat together in the empty bar as he'd filled her in on the local gossip. He'd had his acoustic guitar in his car and – he cringed at this later – he'd fetched it and played for her. But they had laughed as he played Australian songs she'd never come across and she called out requests for Dutch songs he'd never heard of.

'So what else do people do for fun around here?' she'd asked eventually, in a way that reminded him a bit of how Jacqui had used to speak to him. Back in the early days, when things were still good.

'Apart from come here?' Nathan had said. 'Let me think. Sometimes people enjoy punching on.' She'd rolled her eyes. 'It's true, don't underestimate it. A couple of cousins from Atherton brawled in the street for four hours last year. People brought chairs out and watched.'

'Four hours?' She had laughed. 'If that's true, and I don't believe it is, by the way, they're either really good at fighting or really bad at it.'

He had grinned back. There were other things that people sometimes did for fun out there. Like drive up on the sand dunes to watch the sun set over the desert with a bottle of wine. That could be a lot of fun with the right person.

He had looked at her and been pretty sure from the slight tilt of her head and the smile on her lips that her answer to the invitation would be yes. It didn't have to be a big deal – God knew, he was never planning to get married again – but he was officially free and single now. And it was only a drive out to the dunes with a backpacker.

There was a hell of a long way from that to a ring on any-one's finger. But – the bitterness had slid in without him even realising it – it wasn't so far from a ring to a four-figure invoice from the lawyers. So Nathan had shut his mouth again, and let the moment drift past.

Instead, they'd had another drink and a few more laughs and at the end of the night, when she was closing up, they had stood facing each other in the doorway, both suddenly a little awkward, and he'd asked when she was working next week. He'd camped out in the back of his car like usual, with the stars shining through the dirty windscreen, and driven home with a grin on his face for the first time in a while.

He'd gone back to the pub the next weekend, and the next. Not the one after that, though. By then, Nathan had found himself barred from the pub, the shop and everything else worth visiting within a six-hour radius. The length of his ban wasn't specified. Ongoing, he was told when he finally broke and asked. So far it had been nine years and four months and counting.

'Did Cam leave a note on him?' Ilse asked from under the washing line, bringing him back to the present. 'Or in his car?'

'No,' Nathan said. 'Nothing here?'

She shook her head. 'Was there anything in his pockets that might explain why he was there instead of Lehmann's Hill?'

'No. What about on the radio? Did he call in at all?'

'I was in the office all day, nothing came through. I would have heard.'

Nathan pictured the large study where the desk-bound work that kept the property ticking over took place. It was a seven-day-a-week operation: ordering supplies, booking contractors, checking the payroll and supplier invoices. It had been Liz's job when Nathan was younger; now it fell to Ilse.

'Bub and Harry both said Cam had seemed under a bit of pressure lately,' he said.

'What? Just lately?' Ilse sounded annoyed.

'Longer than that?'

'You know what it's like running this place. *They* know what it's like. There was always pressure on him, even when it's doing well.' She snatched a pillowcase from the line, folding it badly into a crumpled square. She took a breath and flapped it out, folding it more carefully this time. 'I think there was something wrong, though. Harry's right. Cam was stressed, and he was in a bad mood a lot of the time. And he was distracted, which wasn't like him. I hoped it would pass, but it had been at least six weeks, maybe longer. It was getting worse, if anything.'

'Did you ask him why?'

'Of course I did.' She was instantly defensive. 'And he told me he was fine. There's always something that needs attention around here. Just because Cameron was working hard, that didn't mean —'

She stopped as they both sensed movement across the yard and turned to look. The light was fading now as they watched Bub walking near the furthest corner of the fence, where the land rose higher. He stopped and looked down at a patch of earth. Even from that distance, Nathan knew where he was standing. Bub didn't look towards the washing line, and Nathan wasn't sure if he had seen them amid the sheets.

'What's he doing over there?' Ilse frowned.

'God knows.'

Bub was standing at the foot of their dad's grave and, overhead, Nathan could see the shape of the eucalyptus tree he had planted with his brothers after the funeral twenty years earlier. It had been a hot day and hard work, but it had been Liz's idea so they'd done it, digging a hole at the head of the plot. The tree was a decent size now and its branches swayed, black against the sky.

To the left of Carl Bright's grave was the ground earmarked for the rest of the family when their respective times came. The plot directly next to his dad's would probably have been Liz's under normal circumstances but now, Nathan realised with a jolt, it would be Cameron's.

'I need to get back inside.' Ilse straightened suddenly. From her expression, he suspected she'd been thinking the same thing as him. 'I want to check on the girls before the generator goes off.'

The generator was switched off each night to save fuel and money, cutting the electricity and plunging the property into a complete blackout overnight. Nathan was used to it. He had started switching off his own for longer and longer these days, lying alone in the seamless dark from sunset to sunrise.

'Go.' Nathan nodded at the washing line. 'I'll bring these in.'

'Thank you.' She seemed about to say something more,

then changed her mind. A sheet blew in front of Nathan, hiding her from sight as she walked away, and he pushed it aside in time to see her disappear into the house. He turned back to the washing line. The white linen was a dull red-grey in the deepening gloom.

Across the yard, Bub was still standing by the grave plots, only his back visible. Nathan reached up for the next sheet, then stopped as Bub took a final swig from the can in his hand, placed it on the ground and dropped a hand to his fly. A second later came the unmistakeable sound of a long stream of urine cascading onto the ground. Nathan stood completely still. The noise ran on, steady before at last trickling away to nothing. Finished, apparently, Bub zipped up and sauntered towards the house without glancing in Nathan's direction. A faint note in the air suggested he was whistling.

Nathan didn't move until he was gone. The family plot was shadowy as he walked over, taking care where he put his feet in the growing dark. He looked at the ground where his dad was buried and where Cameron soon would be, then crouched and touched the soil with his fingertips. It was already dry. The thirsty earth had drunk in the moisture. It was impossible to tell which plot Bub had pissed on.

Chapter 9

It was still early but Nathan could see the two little girls already out in the horse exercise yard. Cameron's daughters. He watched them for a minute before climbing into the passenger seat of Harry's four-wheel drive.

Liz had lost the will or energy to protest, so Bub and Xander had both insisted on coming to meet the town's sergeant out at Cameron's car. No-one said it, but Nathan suspected everyone secretly hoped that Glenn McKenna would have a proper look and be able to tell them exactly what was what.

Bub didn't speak to any of them as he climbed into the back seat next to Xander. Nathan had still been able to detect the faint whiff of urine when he'd left the graves the night before, but back at the house he'd found Bub already in his bedroom with the door shut. Nathan had been debating whether to knock when he'd heard Harry shout out the nightly warning call. The generator was going off. Nathan had lowered his hand. This was not a conversation to have in faceless pitch black. Instead, as the generator fell still and the property was plunged into darkness, he had lain on the couch rehearsing what he would say. By morning, though, he woke to find that his ideas had evaporated and what he'd thought he'd seen suddenly seemed a lot less clear.

Harry started the engine and set off down the driveway. As they passed the exercise yard, Nathan signalled.

'Pull over for a minute, Harry.'

The eight-year-old, Sophie, was in the middle of the yard, guiding a horse in a circle on a long lead with one hand. Her other arm was in a sling. Lo, now five, was sitting by the fence, her head down as she drew something on a pad of paper. They were bigger than Nathan remembered, but then again, it had been a year. Nathan could see Ilse watching her daughters from the verandah. Cameron's dog, Duffy, sat listlessly at her feet.

'Hi, girls.' Nathan leaned out of the window and waved to his nieces as Harry came to a stop. 'I didn't get a chance to say hello last night. How are you going? And you remember Xander, don't you?'

Sophie tied up her horse and the girls took their time walking over. Lo in particular looked at Nathan like he was a stranger.

'Come on, say g'day to your uncle,' Harry prompted when they stood unsmiling.

'Hi, Uncle Nathan,' Sophie intoned. Lo, half a step behind her, didn't say anything. They looked a lot like Cam, especially around the eyes, Nathan thought. Their matching dirty-blonde hair would probably go dark as they got older. Xander's had been the same.

Nathan looked at Sophie's sling. It was made from colourful fabric with ponies printed on it. 'What happened to you?'

'Fell off.'

'Geez, you okay?'

'Small fracture.'

'That's no good.'

'No.'

Was that a mild hint of sarcasm? Nathan couldn't be sure. She seemed a bit young for that. 'Well,' he said. 'Be careful. I guess we'll see you later.'

The girls nodded and, after a glance towards Harry, ran back to the exercise yard.

'They seem a bit stunned by everything,' Nathan said as Sophie picked up the horse's reins with her good hand. 'Her arm doesn't seem to have put her off, at least.'

'No.' Harry's eyes were on the driveway. 'Well, you know Sophie.'

He didn't really, Nathan thought as they pulled away. They passed Ilse and she raised her hand in a wave.

They drove in silence while the homestead fell behind them. Harry took the road route rather than cutting across the paddocks and Nathan could hear the stones pinging off the bodywork, louder and more frequently than yesterday. Harry drove faster than Nathan tended to, but then again, most people did.

Nathan had been barely twenty-one when his dad had had the crash. He'd been practically living with Jacqui by then, at her suggestion, in the same house he now called home. It had felt very different then, the novelty still shiny and new, and the sex still on tap. Jacqui was good to look at and even better in bed and for a long time he'd loved her for it. Cameron had been away studying an agribusiness course, and Bub was still a little kid.

It had been the completely unremarkable nature of the accident that had shaken Nathan as much as anything. Carl and Liz Bright had been driving back from town, like they had a hundred times. A cow had stepped onto the track and Carl had swerved, like he'd also done a hundred times.

This time, though, he'd been too slow, or the car had been moving too fast, or he'd been too sharp with the wheel, or not sharp enough, and he'd clipped it. The car had rolled and come to rest upside down. Carl had been pinned between the steering wheel and the roof. Liz was knocked unconscious and had woken up in the dark to find herself bleeding from the head and her husband bleeding to death. She'd used the radio to call for help. It had taken forty minutes for the first person to arrive and another thirty for the ambulance. Roughly four hours had elapsed from the time of the accident to either of them receiving basic medical attention. Not one other car had passed by in all that time.

Nathan had been asleep with Jacqui when the call had come through. She'd made the right sympathetic noises as he'd pulled on his shirt and shoes, while also managing to convey on some level that she was a little pissed off he was leaving her in the middle of the night for a drama involving his own family. It was funny how high and bright the red flags flew in hindsight, Nathan often thought.

Liz was already in the back of the ambulance when he'd finally arrived. A younger Steve Fitzgerald had been on duty, and had taken Nathan aside to explain the situation. Carl was still pinned, but there was no urgency to free him. He was well and truly dead. But it hadn't been quick and wouldn't have been painless, Nathan had later overheard Steve whisper on the radio to dispatch. The bloke might have had a chance if someone had come by to raise the alarm sooner.

Inside the ambulance, with a blanket around her shoulders despite the heat of the night, Liz was almost unrecognisable under the crust of blackened blood.

'She was lucky,' Steve had said. 'She'll heal.'

Nathan had looked at his mum, dazed and battered, and thought she looked far from lucky. Then he had looked inside the twisted metal wreck of the car, and from that day forward had driven a few kilometres per hour slower than was strictly necessary.

Nathan heard Harry grunt and looked over. The man's face hadn't changed.

'You right?'

'Yeah,' Harry said. 'I was just thinking about that time you and Cam ran away to the stockman's grave when you were kids. Remember?'

'Yeah, of course.'

Xander leaned forward. 'What was that?'

Harry looked at him in the mirror. 'You've never heard this story?'

Xander shook his head. Harry glanced at Nathan, who shrugged.

'I wasn't going to tell him, was I? It was a bloody stupid thing to do.'

'Yeah. It was,' Harry said. 'But you were only kids. What were you, twelve?'

'Eleven. Cam was nine.' Nathan felt his insides twist at the memory of his brother, his dusty legs sticking out from below a loaded backpack.

'Why were you running away?' Xander said.

'God knows. I can't remember,' Nathan lied. He could feel Xander watching him, and Bub too, now. 'And for the record, we weren't running away to the stockman's grave. It was a pit stop on the way to town.'

They'd stuffed their backpacks, ridden out well before dawn. Nathan wasn't sure what they'd thought was waiting for them in town. Something better. But they'd had a plan, he knew. They'd discussed it at length, and he could still remember some of the details now. He just didn't want to talk about it.

'So what happened?' Xander asked.

'They didn't get very far, for starters,' Harry said. 'Their dad worked out what they were planning about five minutes after we discovered they'd left. We drove out here, parked by the grave and waited for them to come over the far crest.' He looked at Nathan. 'You remember that?'

'Yeah, I remember.' The feeling of seeing the two men waiting there.

'What happened when you found them?' Xander said.

'We picked them up and drove them back home,' Harry said. 'Held the horses' reins out of the window, let them gallop along beside.'

'Was Dad angry?' Bub's voice came from the back. It was the first time he had spoken since they'd set off.

'Yeah.' Nathan didn't turn to look at him. 'Yeah, he was.'

'I'll bet he was.' The atmosphere in the car felt heavier and they fell silent. Nathan could see the rocky outcrop stretching ahead. Not far to go now.

It hadn't seemed like it at the time, but it was for the best that he and Cam had been found and picked up, Nathan thought. They'd have been lucky to last until morning at that time of year, even with supplies. Danger season. He knew now how stupid it had been. The rules of the outback may seem brutal but they were written in blood. Just ask Cameron. Nathan was jolted from this train of thought as his head jerked forward a little. Harry tapped the brakes as Nathan heard Bub call from the back: 'Right turn here.'

Nathan looked up at the rocks, and the almost invisible gap leading through. They were there. He heard Xander shift in the back and glanced at him in the side mirror. His son was looking at Harry with a strange expression on his face.

The police vehicle came into sight first, parked at the bottom of the slope. Cameron's car was still waiting at the top, exactly where they had left it. Sergeant Glenn McKenna was standing next to it and he raised his hand as they walked up.

'You found it okay, then?' Nathan nodded at the Land Cruiser.

McKenna nodded. 'You can see it briefly if you're coming from town. For a minute or so where the road rises outside your boundary, Nathan.'

'Can you?'

'You didn't see it yourself?'

'I don't use that road.' Nathan looked the sergeant in the eye. 'Only place it goes is town.'

McKenna kept his gaze. 'Fair point. Look, sorry I couldn't be here yesterday. How was the other officer?'

Nathan and Bub exchanged a glance. 'Fine,' Nathan said.

'I've heard good things about him.' McKenna nodded at the car door and frowned. 'I thought he said this was unlocked.'

'It was, when we found it.' Nathan handed over the keys. 'He locked it.'

'Why?'

'In case anyone came by.'

McKenna looked mildly amused, but said nothing as he opened the car and looked inside. He searched thoroughly, checking the same places as his colleague, plus a few more the other guy hadn't thought of. Like Ludlow, he paused at the sight of the food and water in the back. Nathan could smell the sandwiches and fruit starting to turn. Eventually the sergeant slammed the rear door.

'I reckon we've got everything we're going to get, so you're all right to take this when you go.'

Dismay crossed Xander's face. 'You're not going to hold it for – I dunno – investigation or something?'

'No, mate. I'm sorry.' McKenna shook his head. 'Look, I honestly would if I thought it would help. I'd get the CIB boys to fly in from the city, do all their tests, but you have to make a case for it and they won't come for this. There's no sign of a struggle. There's nothing damaged, valuable equipment hasn't been stolen. I'm not sure what was going through Cameron's head but your uncle didn't die in this car.'

No-one spoke for a minute. The crime scene tape tied to the door handles whipped in the wind.

'So what do we know?' McKenna said, looking at the four of them. 'Cameron said he was heading to Lehmann's Hill but for some reason he changed his mind. And it's a fair old hike from here to where he ended up. He would have known what he was getting himself in to, this time of year. On foot with no water. What time did he leave home on Wednesday?'

'About eight,' Harry said. 'Ilse and one of the casuals saw him.'

'I've spoken to Steve at the clinic,' McKenna said. 'The autopsy's been booked but he reckons Cameron was dead by Thursday mid-morning, at the latest. Maybe even a bit earlier given the temperature.' He looked at Bub, his voice gentle. 'You told Sergeant Ludlow you thought Cam had been having a bit of a hard time of it recently, mate. What was that about, do you think?'

'I dunno.'

McKenna waited, but Bub said no more.

'Look.' Harry stepped in. 'Cam ran a tight ship but he kept things close to his chest. You know that. But Bub's right. These last few weeks, there'd been a few things going overlooked.'

'Like what?' McKenna said.

'Nothing big. But stuff he said he was going to do but didn't. Fix the gate to the cattle yard, that kind of thing.'

'He didn't mention falling out with anyone? Someone from town?' McKenna asked and both Bub and Harry shook their heads. 'What about with either of you? His missus?'

There was a tiny bristle at that, Nathan thought, but again both shook their heads.

'Is that a no?' McKenna said. 'Or a don't know?'

'No,' Harry said at the same time as Bub said: 'Don't know.'

The sergeant eyed them each in turn, like a teacher at school, and Nathan started to feel a little guilty himself. Glancing up the line, he suspected he wasn't alone. The only exception was Xander, who was still watching Harry with a curious look.

'Well, I reckon anyone seeing the car standing empty like this would've done the right thing and reported it —' McKenna bit his words short. He glanced at Nathan, who stared back, steady. If he dropped his gaze every time someone mentioned it, he'd never look anyone in the eye again.

'Anyway.' McKenna took a breath and went on. 'No calls came in, so I think we can assume no-one came by.'

'Do you think Uncle Cam might have stopped to help someone and got in trouble?' Xander said. 'A tourist or someone?'

'Look, I won't rule it out,' McKenna said. 'But I haven't heard of anyone coming through.'

It wasn't easy, Nathan knew, for a stranger to make their way across the district without the locals knowing about it. The desert tracks were closed in the summer, leaving exactly two roads in or out. Two choices, leading to two other tiny towns in opposite directions and hundreds of kilometres apart. Everyone was forced to stop for fuel and supplies at some point, and locals tended to stare at strange cars at that time of year. It wasn't easy to sail through unnoticed. But, Nathan thought, it wasn't impossible.

'And things are okay on the property?' McKenna said as Harry nodded. 'And look, there's no point pretending this is a casual question: are your firearms in order over there?'

'Yes,' Harry said, with a slight edge to his voice.

'All accounted for? Locked up properly?'

'Yes.'

'Where's the key kept these days? Locked up securely in line with regulations, no doubt,' McKenna said, deadpan. They all knew it usually hung by the back door.

'I've got it,' Harry said, and Nathan looked over in surprise. 'It's been on my key ring for the past three weeks.'

McKenna looked at him. 'Any reason you're carrying it?'

'No reason,' Harry said. 'Needed it one day and never put it back.'

'Cameron didn't ask for it?'

'He didn't need to ask. He could have just taken it. But no. Didn't ask for it, didn't take it.'

'Right.' McKenna frowned. He looked like he might say something else, then changed his mind. He looked instead at Nathan.

'What about you? Any change on the firearms front?'

'No.' Nathan met his eye. 'All still the same as last time.'

'All right,' McKenna said. 'How's Ilse coping?'

Nathan felt a tiny prickle at her name. 'She's not too good.'

'And your mum?'

'Not too good either.'

'No. Well. Tell them I'll give them a call. And you blokes –' McKenna hesitated. 'How are you all going? Can be hard, this time of year. Lot of pressure from all sides. You all okay?'

Nathan knew what he was asking. *Anyone else feel like walking out into the nothing?*

'We're good, I think,' he said when no-one else answered. 'I mean, considering. Good as can be expected.'

'And you know you can always call me, or Steve at the clinic. If you ever need to just have a yarn or whatever.'

They nodded dutifully.

'Good.' McKenna beckoned to Nathan. 'Come with me. Got some info in the car I need to give you.'

Nathan followed him down the slope and at the police car, McKenna reached into the glove box. He drew out a fistful of cards. 'Cases like these, I'm supposed to give youse these.'

Nathan took them. The cards had the phone numbers and websites for a suicide prevention helpline and a mental health charity.

McKenna was watching him, looking uncomfortable.

'Something else?' Nathan said.

'Look, mate. That wasn't meant to be a dig earlier. About no-one reporting the car. And I wanted to say, I know you generally give town a wide berth –'

'Yeah. Haven't got much choice, have I?'

'Well, that's not true. You do have a choice, mate. You could have come and stirred up trouble over the years but you chose not to, and I appreciate that.'

'Glad someone does.'

'And I know you say you're used to it by now, but in light of all this, if you feel like it's getting a bit much and you think you might . . . ' McKenna trailed off.

'Top myself like Cam?'

'Yeah, pretty much. Look, if you ever feel like things are getting bad, you know you can come into town whenever you need to.'

Nathan nodded. McKenna was an okay guy. What had happened wasn't his fault – it was no-one's fault but Nathan's own – and McKenna had been as even-handed as he could be about the whole incident. It wasn't easy being the only cop. He'd put in a good word for Nathan whenever he could, tried to build bridges. It wasn't his fault it had made no difference.

'Thanks, mate,' Nathan said. 'I'm fine on my own, though.'

'I heard you had your radio switched off when the search call for Cameron went out.'

'So?'

'So I thought we'd talked about that.'

Nathan didn't answer.

'It's not the first time, either.'

'Didn't know there was a law about keeping it on.'

'Good as, around here. Don't be a bloody smartarse,' McKenna said. 'Anyway, look, don't be shy to shout out if you need to.'

'Yep. Okay.'

There seemed to be nothing more to say, so Nathan waited as McKenna got into the police car and drove away. He watched until it was small, then walked back up the slope to the others.

'What are those?' Xander was looking at the cards in Nathan's hand, and Nathan passed them out. Bub rolled his eyes.

Harry was looking out to the west, his expression its usual mask once more. 'I want to go home along the tracks. Stop by the grave on the way.'

'There's nothing to see,' Bub said.

'Still.' Harry slipped the helpline card into his pocket, Nathan noticed.

They all looked at Cameron's car.

'Who wants to drive it back?' Bub asked, and there was a silence.

'We'll do it,' Nathan said with a glance at Xander, who nodded.

'All right.' Harry turned to head down the slope to his car. 'Stick close. Just in case Cam did have some sort of engine trouble.'

'No worries.' It was clear none of them really believed that.

As Bub followed Harry down the slope, Nathan untied the police tape from Cameron's door handles and climbed in. The driver's seat was worn smooth, and he reached down and raked it back and forth until it was the right distance from the pedals. Its contours felt unfamiliar, having been broken in by his brother's lighter frame. Nathan adjusted the rear-view mirror and saw his own eyes reflected back at him. They looked enough like Cam's to make him look away.

'Harry knew where to turn.' Xander's voice was quiet from the passenger seat.

'What?'

'He knew.' He nodded at Harry's car. 'On the way here. He knew which track led through the rocks to Cam's car.'

'Because Bub told him. I heard him.'

'No. Bub said it after Harry had already started the turn.'

'No.' Nathan tried to picture it. 'It was before.' Wasn't it? He'd been lost in his own thoughts at the time, not paying attention. 'Anyway, Harry knew where the car was. He'd been told.'

'I know. But you and I knew yesterday, and we still missed it. We'd even been here once with Bub and we still got it wrong when we drove the other cop out. How did Harry know which gap to take?'

'Because he knows this whole area like the back of his hand. He knows it as well as anyone. He would have been able to guess.'

At the bottom of the slope, Harry's car roared to life. Nathan shook his head and turned Cameron's keys. The car started perfectly, as it had yesterday. Slowly, with his foot poised on the brake, he eased the car into motion and began to follow Harry and Bub towards the grave. Harry stuck to the fence line, retracing the journey they'd made the day before. Nathan could see shadowy heads moving in the car in front as the two men spoke to each other.

'He would've just worked it out,' Nathan said again.

'Yeah,' Xander said finally. He slumped back in his seat. 'Yeah, probably. Sorry. It's been a weird couple of days.'

'I know.'

Harry's car started to pull ahead and Nathan pressed the accelerator to keep up. He couldn't see Harry and Bub moving anymore. Perhaps they'd said everything they wanted to say. Nathan watched the car pull further away and felt a tiny prickle. Like the start of a rash, small and manageable but the wrong side of comfortable. He told himself to damp it down. This was Uncle Harry. Nathan had known the man literally his entire life. If anyone could read the land, it was Harry. It was not unreasonable at all that he could make an educated guess.

Still, a tiny voice whispered in Nathan's ear. It was a big land, and it was a good guess.

Chapter 10

Cameron's abandoned food was starting to smell in the back and Nathan wound down the window a crack.

'We could dump it,' Xander said, clearly thinking the same thing.

'Yeah.' Nathan nodded, but didn't slow down. The stuff in the back was Cameron's survival gear. For reasons he couldn't quite articulate, it felt strangely reckless to discard any of it now.

Xander was still watching the shadows of Harry and Bub in the car in front. Nathan frowned to himself. He trusted Harry, he honestly did. With his life probably, if it ever came to it. Still, as Harry turned his head to say something to Bub, Nathan found himself replaying that minute before they'd reached Cameron's car.

'It's interesting that Glenn could see Cam's car from outside your boundary,' Xander said suddenly. 'It was pretty well hidden otherwise.'

'Yeah. But you could say the same for lots of places. Cam could've dumped it in the middle of the road in broad daylight and there'd be a good chance no-one would find it for ages. How often does anyone come along there? Once a week? And then, it's only us or the Atherton lot.'

'I suppose,' Xander said. 'It's just so flat around here, if I didn't want my car seen, I'd leave it around the rocks, too.' He looked out at the empty land. 'It's shit that no-one drove or flew by earlier. Even if Thursday was too late, Wednesday might not have been.'

Nathan didn't reply, but Xander was right. If the car had been found sooner, the alarm would have been raised immediately and help called to hand. Nathan suddenly wondered − he tried to stop himself, but couldn't − whether the same would be true for himself. If it were his car found abandoned and him in trouble or missing. Would the local passer-by call it in? Or would all those people who still turned their backs on him discover that, actually, when push came to shove, they were no better than he was? He honestly didn't know.

It wasn't Ilse's fault, not even a little bit, but Nathan wouldn't have even been in town that day if it hadn't been for her. It had been his third weekend visit in a row to the pub. He'd stopped pretending to himself that he had business in town that made the trip worthwhile and had gone anyway.

On his second visit, they'd sat across from each other in the empty bar and he had found himself telling Ilse about his divorce and his son living fifteen hundred kilometres away. In turn, she had told him how she'd had to put her degree on hold and become a full-time carer when her mum's cancer prognosis became terminal. She'd been engaged, but the daily grind of end-of-life care had proved a bit too much for him, and by the time her mum died, Ilse wasn't engaged anymore.

They had had another drink and somehow, Nathan wasn't sure how, they'd ended up smiling and finally laughing. Not about what had happened, but about other things, lighter things that made everything else seem more bearable. He couldn't stop staring at her. He liked the way she looked and the way she looked at him. He told her about the sand dunes. She smiled and said she'd love to go with him one day.

On Nathan's third visit, he'd stayed again until closing time and Ilse had reached out for his hand after he helped her lock up. The road had been deserted in both directions. She'd let him lead her away from the only streetlight so they could see the glorious night sky more clearly and he'd found himself, as hoped, in a dark corner pressing her hard against the side of his four-wheel drive, with her mouth warm against his. In a heady mix of delight and disbelief he'd thrown open the rear of his car where his sleeping bag was rolled out and waiting for him. Her skin was soft and hot as he'd reached under her shirt and felt her hands on his jeans. Then he'd held her tight and listened to her fast rhythmic breath as the stars shone down on them through the dusty windows.

Afterwards, he had lain there looking at her, the car doors open to let a breeze in and the sleeping bag kicked aside.

She had smiled, her teeth white in the dark. 'What?'

'Nothing. That was —' He tried to think of the word. Exquisite, revitalising, transformative. 'Great,' he said. It had been the first time since Jacqui had left, but it was more than that. He felt better than he had in years. 'Really great.'

'Thanks.' She'd laughed.

He ran a hand over her. 'So, what now?'

She smiled again. 'I'm pretty sure the backpackers' handbook says this is the part where you disappear into the sunrise and I never hear from you again.'

It was his turn to laugh. 'No way.' He'd pulled her closer, feeling the spark of her skin on his as she rolled onto him. 'That's not what happens.'

She'd been right and he'd been wrong, as it turned out. But he'd really meant it, at the time.

'Why are they stopping?' Xander suddenly leaned forward in the passenger seat and Nathan was brought back to the present. Up ahead, Harry's car was pulling to a halt by the fence. They were nowhere near the stockman's grave yet. They were nowhere near anything that Nathan could see.

They watched as Harry jumped out, leaving the engine running. He crouched and checked the ground, touching his finger to the dust from time to time.

'What's going on?' Xander said.

'I don't know.' Nathan wound down his window and leaned out. 'Harry! What are you doing?'

'Looking!'

'For what?'

'Anything.'

The St Helens cop had said pretty much the same thing, but at least with Harry there was a chance it might actually mean something useful. Nathan wound his window back up and shrugged. 'You heard him. Looking.'

Xander sat back and waited. Minutes ticked by and finally Harry got back into his car. They started moving again.

Ilse had left him just after dawn. The townsfolk may have been few and far between, but they were all early risers. She had kissed him as she buttoned her shirt.

'I'll drive you home,' Nathan had said.

'No need.' She'd pointed to the accommodation block beside the pub. 'That's me.'

'That close? We could have gone there.'

She jumped out of the car and grinned. 'What's wrong? You didn't have enough fun here?'

'Yeah. I did.'

'Me too.'

He was buzzing as he watched her leave. He'd pulled on his clothes and the smile on his face had lasted the whole morning as he'd gone around town getting his jobs done. He was nearly finished, and filling up at the service station ahead of the drive home, when someone pulled in beside him. Nathan clocked the top-of-the-range four-wheel drive and felt his grin fade for the first time.

He'd kept his head down as his father-in-law – *ex*-father-in-law – opened the driver's door and climbed out. Out of the corner of his eye, Nathan thought he saw Keith Walker hesitate. Not for too long though. There were only two pumps, and Nathan was using one. If Keith needed fuel, he had no choice. He picked up the empty one.

'Nathan.'

'G'day, Keith.' Nathan concentrated on the pump. He was going to fill up his tank and drive away. And that was it.

Keith looked over. 'I spoke to Jacqui yesterday.'

Nathan watched the numbers on the dial turn around. 'Oh yeah.' Not a question.

'And look, she's instructing her lawyers to push back.'

'Righto.'

'Nathan, be reasonable. Asking for that level of contact, it's too many calls and visits for a kid Xander's age.'

'My lawyer reckons it's a pretty standard custody split.'

'For divorced couples who live around the corner from each other, maybe. Not with you all the way out here.'

'She's the one who left. Not me.' Nathan shut his mouth, then opened it again. 'Anyway, I would've thought you'd be happy to have Xander around.'

Keith, with four properties, was one of the country's biggest landowners and, in a good year, occasionally troubled the very tail end of the rich list. Now he shook his head, his mouth downturned. 'Kathy and I see Xander in Brisbane. There's no reason for the boy to come out here.'

'I'm his dad, Keith.' The pump clicked off. The tank was full. 'So there's one bloody good reason for you.'

Nathan looked at his father-in-law properly for the first time. He was a bit pale and seemed tired. Probably stayed up too late counting his money, Nathan thought, as he went inside to pay. Through the window, he could see Keith watching him.

Nathan had never been sure what it was about him that the bloke objected to so strongly. Keith hadn't got along with Nathan's dad, but that wasn't exactly unusual. Nathan hadn't got along with his dad either. And Keith had been all right when Nathan and Jacqui had first got together. Although, Nathan wondered, perhaps he'd just been biting his tongue, hoping the romance would run its course and fizzle out.

It got worse the better things got with Jacqui, and by the time the wedding rolled around, Nathan was barely on speaking terms with his new father-in-law. Keith had tried to talk Jacqui out of getting married, more than once, as Nathan learned some time later, when Jacqui screamed it at him across the room.

But the wedding had gone ahead, like it or not, and afterwards Keith had carved off part of his own extensive property and called it a peace offering. It was a relatively small strip directly bordering the Bright family's land, and Keith had presented it to the newlyweds as a gift. Consider it a foothold in Kirrabee Station, he'd explained. If they made it work and outgrew it, they could buy out more from him over time.

Nathan had privately had a few doubts about that bit of land. The strip on that side of the fence had never looked good to him, but Jacqui had been excited, so he hadn't said anything. She'd encouraged him to pour resources into it, set them up properly as a family property with one eye on the future. Nathan took the third of Burley Downs he inherited when his dad died, and sold half his share to Cameron.

His new land swallowed up the money as fast as he could put it in. Jacqui couldn't understand it. She encouraged him to sell the remainder of his Burley Downs stake.

Invest more. Try harder. Her dad made good money from property, why couldn't Nathan? He refused to sell the rest of his inheritance and that was their first big fight as a married couple.

Jacqui went to stay with her parents for a few days. When she came back, Nathan voiced his opinion out loud that the land Keith had given them was a dud. That was their second big fight and Jacqui had climbed straight back in the car and disappeared to her parents' house for another few days. And it occurred to Nathan, as he watched her drive away from the shitty piece of property, that possibly that was exactly what Keith had been hoping for.

Nathan now felt the wheels go over a bump and told himself to focus. The ground was uneven and Cameron's car was unfamiliar. The last thing he needed was to get bogged in a sandbank. Up ahead, Harry's car was slowing again. He had stopped twice more along the way, getting out to examine the ground along the fence line, or turn in a slow circle, taking in the surroundings.

'What does he think he's going to see at the grave?' Xander said as it came into sight.

'I don't know,' Nathan said. 'But he's known Cam since he was born. Maybe he just wants to see for himself.'

'Maybe.' Xander didn't sound convinced.

Nathan had missed Xander even more than he'd expected when Jacqui had finally left for good. She'd been threatening it for so long it was almost a relief when it happened. She was absolutely sick of things. Nathan was a crap husband, crap dad, crap bloody provider and she let him know it. Nathan had thought he would be glad to see the back of her, but the separation from Xander felt like a physical blow.

He had found himself poring over photos. Looking at Xander's happy face, his small hands and his thick hair, already with a bit of a wave. Nathan even missed hearing him cry out in the middle of the night, like an engine warming up. When Xander had been a baby, Nathan used to sit next to the cot in the dark and play his guitar softly. It had been one of the only things that seemed to soothe him for a time and Nathan had been surprised when Jacqui found that more annoying than helpful.

Nathan had refused to fight with her in front of Xander. It wasn't the kid's fault he and Jacqui didn't get along. It probably wasn't all her fault either, Nathan could admit in his more honest moments. It had been a hard few years, both being married and being separated, and since Jacqui had left, he'd found that sometimes he did feel better. Like when he was lying in the back of his car with a nice Dutch barmaid. But he always missed Xander.

Nathan sometimes wondered what would have happened that day if he had ignored Keith at the service station, got in his car and driven straight home. He could have shaken his father-in-law's hand on the way past – he could have punched him full in the face – and things still would have worked out better in the long run.

He hadn't done either of those things. He'd finished

paying for his fuel and Keith called out to him across the forecourt.

'You need to know, Nathan, Kathy and I are going to pay for Jacqui's lawyers.'

'Bullshit.' Nathan stopped mid-stride just metres from his car.

'It's true.'

'I don't bloody doubt it's true.' Nathan changed direction and came close to Keith. 'I mean it's bullshit that you're sticking your oar in.'

'We feel you're being unreasonable –'

'Me?'

'– and we want to make sure Jacqui's well represented. And Xander.'

'Xander's fine, mate. He doesn't need your help. He needs to see his dad from time to time, that's what he needs.'

'Nathan –'

'If your bloody daughter –'

'Hey, watch yourself.' Keith sounded out of breath.

'No, you watch *your*self. If your bloody daughter had her way, I would never see him at all.'

Keith didn't reply, but the answer played out across his face as clearly as if he'd said it. *Yes, ideally.*

Nathan felt a stirring of fear. He'd expected some pushback on the custody arrangements, but he hadn't considered they would go that far. They couldn't cut him off from Xander completely, could they? He thought not, but then Keith had some pretty deep pockets.

Nathan took a step in, raised a finger and pointed at

his former father-in-law. He could see Kylie, the service station attendant, watching them through the window. Later, she would be quick to say that Nathan was behaving aggressively. Right then, he didn't care.

'Keith, mate.' Nathan kept his voice soft and controlled. 'You listen to me carefully, because this is the truest thing you are going to hear all year. You might be able to buy and sell every bloody cow in this district, but you can't keep me away from Xander.'

'It's what Jacqui wants.'

'Tough shit. Jacqui's going to have to live with it.'

Keith jangled his keys, perhaps a touch nervously. 'Not if I can help it. If you'd been a better husband and father in the first place we wouldn't even be in this position.'

'Mate, there's nothing in this world that would keep that woman happy. Maybe if you hadn't always been in her ear telling her what a waste of space I am, then maybe she wouldn't have left.'

'You think it's my fault she saw some sense? I tried my best with you, Nathan. I gave you that land, didn't I? Gave you a chance?'

Nathan laughed. 'Yeah, right, you keep telling yourself that. I never had a bloody chance with that land, and you know it. You wanted me to stuff up and you wanted Jacqui to see it, and you got your wish, mate. Well done. But you're not going to get what you want when it comes to Xander.'

'We'll see.'

'Would you seriously be happy if I abandoned the kid? You think that would be better?'

'Honestly? Yes. I don't think Jacqui or Xander are better off for being around a man like you.'

'Why?' Nathan felt a genuine stirring of curiosity beneath the anger. 'What's so bad about me? You've never even bothered to get to know me, Keith.'

'I know men like you,' Keith said. 'I've lived my whole life in the outback and I know what goes on out here. I know what men like you do.'

'What's that supposed to mean?'

Keith opened his car door. 'This is a waste of time. I'm not getting into this. I've got to go.'

'Wait. Who are you talking about? You mean my dad?'

'For one.'

'Hey. No.' Nathan put his arm out and grabbed the door, blocking Keith's way. He was a lot bigger than the other man. 'That's not fair.'

'You sure about that?' Keith looked pointedly at Nathan's arm until he slowly dropped it. Keith shook his head and climbed into the car. He wound down the window. 'Don't try to call Jacqui. Communication should go through the lawyers.'

'Jesus, Keith.' Nathan had leaned in through the window. Kylie, watching from behind the service station counter, later remembered seeing that too. 'This is between me and Jacqui. Keep your money out of it. You listening? I don't want you messing around with my family.'

'No, Nathan.' Keith had actually laughed. 'You're the one who's not listening. I'm going to keep writing those cheques as long as it takes. Jacqui and Xander aren't your family, they're mine, and I'm going to make sure they're properly looked after. So you listen to me now. I don't give a shit what you want. I care about what I want, and what Jacqui wants.'

'And what exactly is that?'

'Don't bloody come near me or my family again.'

Nathan could have reached through the window and broken the man's nose. To that day, he sometimes wondered if he should have. The whole thing would have been done and dusted a lot quicker, at least. But somewhere, in the midst of it all, he had suddenly thought about Ilse. The magic of the night before had more or less been hosed off thanks to Keith but, for just a moment, the man in front of him seemed a tiny bit less important. He and his money couldn't touch everything.

Nathan had made himself take a long, deep breath. Without another word, and with a level of self-control he had barely demonstrated in all his life, he'd walked to his own car and driven away.

Nathan parked further away from the grave than Harry did. It looked somehow even more lonely than it had the day before. Bub got out this time as well and followed Harry over to the headstone. They stood side by side. The sand and the wind had almost entirely repaired the ground, as Nathan had expected. It was already hard to imagine Cameron lying there. Nathan watched through the windscreen as Bub said something, and the slightest frown crossed Harry's face.

Nathan turned to Xander. 'Do you want to get out?'

'No.' Xander was looking anywhere but at the place where Cameron's body had been. 'Do you?'

'No.' They sat in the car as the smell of rotting food floated through from the back.

Nathan had spotted the expensive four-wheel drive from miles away. He'd left the service station with his hands gripping the steering wheel hard and Keith's words ringing in his ears. Ilse and the night before seemed a long time ago and now Nathan just felt hot and fractious. He'd been planning to drive straight home, but he could feel the lack of sleep catching up with him and that was never good news on the road. He'd pulled over at the bakery and bought a coffee. He still felt tired, but as he sat in his car, sipping coffee and thinking about the reason for his lack of sleep, the smile started to return to his face.

He'd hit the road twenty minutes later and was half an hour out of town when he saw the four-wheel drive parked at an angle on the gravel track. Not even parked, perhaps. Just stopped, half on the road, half off. Nathan had recognised the car well before he'd seen the figure leaning against the hood.

Later, Nathan worked out that he must have had three or four minutes to make the decision. It hadn't been spur of the moment, whichever way you cut it. It had been calculated, and in the end, that made it worse.

Either way, the facts were the same. Nathan had seen Keith's car, parked at an angle, and then he'd seen Keith. One arm waving, one arm clutched by his side and a look of deep disappointment on his face as he realised it was Nathan behind the wheel. Still, Keith had waved a second time, his body bent over slightly. One arm flapping in the air, the other down by his side, near the pocket where he kept his money. Nathan's foot had touched the brake then, without fully letting himself think about it, eased off again. He pictured Xander, miles away from him now, and he'd felt a weight in his chest and a rush of blood to his head. Somewhere beneath it all, he heard Keith's words.

'Don't bloody come near me or my family again.'

'Whatever you say, mate.'

Nathan drove past and did not stop.

Chapter 11

Not that anyone cared, but for the record, Nathan's conscience had got the better of him. He'd turned around after thirty minutes, which became an hour by the time he got back to Keith's car. The bloke's four-wheel drive was still there, still parked at its odd angle, but there was no sign of Keith. Uneasy now, Nathan had called it in on the radio. There had been an unusually long wait before anyone had answered him. Keith had been taken away by ambulance, he was finally told.

'Is he all right?' Nathan had asked. Another long wait. The dead static dragged on into a second minute.

'It's too late, mate,' said a voice at last. It had to be someone he knew, but he didn't recognise the tone.

'Too late for Keith? Shit, seriously?'

'No. For you to pretend you give a fuck. He told us you left him.'

And with that, Nathan's radio had fallen silent.

*

Nathan glanced now over at Xander, who was watching Bub and Harry standing over the stockman's grave. Bub had his back to them as Harry crouched by the headstone, examining what little remained of the small hole at its base. He stayed there for a long time, then finally stood and surveyed the land in every direction. Nathan didn't bother turning his own head. He knew what was out there. Nothing, for miles and miles.

Keith had been having a stroke. He had nearly died. *Nearly.* But not quite, and no thanks at all to Nathan. Even knocking at death's door as he was stretchered into the ambulance, Keith had summoned the energy to drag his oxygen mask from his mouth and tell his rescuers how Nathan had driven past. *Leaving him for dead.*

Keith had, in fact, been discovered within fifteen minutes by a delivery driver. He was bloody lucky, everyone said. Chance in a thousand that anyone came along at all. The story had whipped through the district like a dust storm. The disgust and distrust were palpable. Leaving someone stranded out there was not a matter of manners, it was life and death in the most literal sense. Nathan had single-handedly managed to do the unthinkable and unite the entire town – white, Indigenous, old, young, long-standing rivals, firm friends. Thirty-year grudges were set aside for as long as it took to discuss Nathan's transgression.

On this issue alone, the entire community of Balamara was unwavering. Leaving a fellow man to the mercy of the elements was almost unimaginable and absolutely unforgivable. And if Nathan Bright, outback born and bred, didn't understand that, then the life in that far-flung community was not for him.

Nathan had apologised, sincerely and at length. As had Harry and Liz, on his behalf and, after a beat, Cameron as well. Jacqui had picked up the phone long enough to scream down the line at him from Brisbane, then hung up and called her lawyers. At least she spoke to him, Nathan later thought. She was one of the few who did.

The community punishment was swift. There had been an excruciating town meeting where Nathan had stood up in front of sixty pairs of accusing eyes and read from a prepared apology. He'd been nervous and it had come across as awkward and hollow, even to him. He tried to explain about the custody battle and the pressure he'd been under. It was no excuse. You could be on fire and half-dead yourself and you would still be expected to stop and help. There wasn't a reason in the world that could justify what he had done. If it proved anything, it was that Jacqui's custody concerns were valid. Her lawyers later got a transcript of what Nathan had said and used it against him.

Jacqui herself had taken the trouble to compose an email – to this day Nathan had some very strong feelings about that – which her mother read out loud to the community meeting in a quivering voice, detailing the toll Nathan's actions had taken on the family. That had been exceptionally well received. Nathan had caught even Bub nodding sympathetically in places.

There had been some heated murmurs that Sergeant

McKenna should charge Nathan with attempted man-slaughter, which thankfully came to nothing. So instead, the townsfolk turned their backs and closed ranks. Like a cancerous growth, Nathan was excised and the commu-nity healed without him.

He was banned instantly from every public facility in town. The service station and the post office eventually had to agree to serve him, after Glenn ordered them to, but transactions were completed without eye contact. Pretty soon, words were whispered into the ears of Nathan's casual staff and they handed in their notices, one by one. He was forced to offer higher wages for lower skills and still couldn't find replacements. He wasn't able to handle all his cattle on his own and had to cut back. His usual mustering contractors refused to take his calls, finally admitting they'd been threatened with boycotts if they did business with him. Not that they would anyway. What kind of scumbag leaves a man for dead? He was forced to go further afield, and pay a lot more for a lot less.

One morning, a few months after it happened, Nathan had woken up to a strange stillness on his property. He had lain there, anxious and unsettled, as it dawned on him. He was entirely alone. No staff. Nothing but static on the radio. Nathan stared at the ceiling. There was not a single other person near him for hours in every direction. He had been cast fully and completely adrift.

Xander was avoiding looking at the grave by rifling through the contents of Cameron's glove box. Both cops had had a look, but Nathan hadn't opened it up himself. It appeared well organised and practical. Much like the whole of the property under Cam's dynamic leadership, he thought with a hint of bitterness.

'Anything interesting in there?'

'Not really.' Xander shook his head. 'But it looks like he was planning to go to the repeater at some point. He's got a repair guide here.'

'Really?' Nathan reached out and took it. He turned it over in his hand. 'Maybe just for show? So no-one would realise he was planning to come here instead?'

'Maybe,' Xander said. 'But there's a lot of info here. He's printed out instructions and marked off all the equipment he's packed.'

Nathan frowned. 'I suppose he could have changed his mind on the way?'

Xander said nothing and shrugged, his eyes forward now and fixed on Harry and Bub.

Nathan had tried to call Ilse. He'd left it too long out of fear of what she might have heard, and at a loss himself as to what to say. *Don't believe the worst*, perhaps. But why shouldn't she? It was true.

He'd even looked for her at that terrible town meeting, and felt both giddy with relief and strangely disappointed when she wasn't there. By the time he'd finally worked up the guts to phone the pub during her usual weekend shift, weeks had gone by. The manager had answered. He'd recognised Nathan's voice and told him if he saw or heard from him again, it wouldn't be the police he'd be calling to help solve the problem, if Nathan got his drift.

Nathan had, but still found himself driving towards town the next weekend and the one after that. He had tried to work out which door of the staff accommodation belonged to Ilse and slipped a note underneath. He didn't know if she'd ever got it. If she had, he never heard. He found himself parking in the shadows off the road and watching the lights of the pub from a safe distance. Unable to go in, but unable to stay away.

He'd continued to do that for a while in the following years, maybe once every six months. Just to hear the sound of voices other than his own inside his head. He would park in a dark corner, listening to the muffled chatter and occasional music floating from the pub. He didn't do it anymore. Nearly a decade on, he wasn't sure who would be inside these days, and whether any of the faces would recognise him. They'd remember his name though, he suspected. The story seemed to have been handed down from ear to ear. He had become nothing more than a warning.

One evening, not long after it happened, he'd seen Cameron and Bub come out of the pub, laughing and shaking hands with a few of the same blokes who now looked straight through Nathan. Nathan had kept his distance from his brothers as much as he could since it had all blown up. They hadn't spelled it out, but he knew what he'd done had stained them too. He kept away so they didn't have to ask him to.

He'd watched them outside the pub and his initial flash of betrayal had slowly morphed into something more cautiously optimistic. But the call he'd been hoping for from Cam – 'Come down, mate, I've straightened things out. I've explained. They know you're sorry.' – had never come. A week later, Nathan had driven in again, and this time seen what he realised he'd been waiting for.

Ilse had been illuminated by the single streetlight as she finished her shift. He'd had his hand on the door and a garbled apology ready, when the manager and two stock-hands had followed her out, chatting among themselves as she locked up. They'd lingered in the street after she'd finished and Nathan had had to watch her walk away, the regret sour and sharp inside him. After that, he had swallowed his pride and asked Cameron straight out to put in a good word at the pub.

'Mate, I'm hardly ever in there myself,' Cam had said. It had sounded like he was frowning. 'I only go so Bub has someone to talk to.'

'Please, Cam. Ask if I can come back. There's a girl. A nice one. Working behind the bar.' He was speaking a language his brother would understand.

Cameron had laughed. 'Oh yeah, I've seen her. She's all right.'

'Yeah, listen, so you'll ask them? See if they'll let me back?' Nathan had held his breath until the answer came.

'Mate, I'm sorry. It's too soon. There's nothing I can do, they don't want you there.'

Nathan had hung up. He hadn't spoken to his brother again for three months.

*

Xander returned the papers to the glove box and fidgeted in his seat. Nathan could tell he'd had enough and was anxious to go. Nathan was pretty keen himself. He wondered if they should drive on ahead but felt strangely reluctant to leave Bub and Harry lingering beside the grave. Their heads were down as they spoke in voices Nathan couldn't hear.

'We'll head back in a minute,' he said, and Xander nodded.

Nathan had always been privately gratified that Xander had never really warmed to his grandfather. Jacqui had told Xander her version of the story as soon as he was old enough, so Nathan then hadn't been able to refrain from telling his. Immediately, he'd wished he hadn't bothered. His version hadn't sounded much better. Either way, Keith was dead now. He'd succumbed to a second stroke four years after the first, which was hardly Nathan's fault but did nothing to help lift the finger of blame. Keith's widow had moved to Brisbane to be closer to Jacqui and Xander and now lived in a nursing home. Nathan had hoped for a while that Keith's death might bring an end to his banishment, but if anything, it had seemed to make it worse. As though having suffered the crime, Keith was the only one with the authority to lift the punishment. Now he never could.

It would all blow over, Nathan had told himself daily at the start. Nearly ten years later, he was still waiting. He no longer thought that daily, or at all, in fact. Most days now were spent dwelling on the what ifs. For example, what if Keith had actually died out there on the road that day? If he'd had the bloody decency to fall down quietly with his arm clutched by his side and his mouth shut?

Through the windscreen, Nathan watched Harry kick the toe of his boot in the ground near the grave.

Without Keith around to point the finger, things would have worked out a lot differently for Nathan. Dead men didn't talk, and no-one would have known what he had done. Nathan would have been free and clear.

Finally, Harry said something to Bub, who nodded. Together, they turned their backs on the grave and headed to their car. The engine fired up and Nathan started his own. He took a last look at the ground where Cameron had been found.

Dead men didn't talk.

Nathan must have thought that a hundred times over the years, but as he drove past the grave, the idea slipped slightly, taking on a strange and unfamiliar form. It was uncomfortable as it lodged itself in the darkest corner of his mind.

The wheels juddered over a patch of rough ground as he pulled away. Nathan didn't look back but instead kept his eyes forward. His gaze fell, almost involuntarily, on the car in front. Specifically on the shapes of the two men and on the rear-view mirror, in which Nathan could just make out a pair of eyes. Up ahead, Harry was watching him.

Chapter 12

Even at a distance, Nathan could see his mum react as he pulled up the driveway in Cameron's car. Liz was sitting under the tree by her late husband's grave and stiffened at the sound of the engine. She started to stand, then slumped back down as Nathan, not Cameron, emerged.

He'd parked next to Harry's vehicle, although there was no sign of either him nor Bub. Nathan had fallen so far behind on the drive back that they had eventually pulled almost out of sight.

'I'm going to have a word with your grandma,' Nathan said to Xander as they climbed out.

'No worries. I'll be in my room.' Xander headed off, like he had something on his mind. Nathan watched him go then walked over to see Liz. Duffy was sitting by her feet.

'What did Glenn say?' Liz looked up. She'd been crying again.

'He's going to give you a call. Sends his condolences.'

'Did his condolences include any answers?'

'No.' He sat down on his mum's right side; her hearing wasn't so good on the left. Duffy moved to rest her head on his knee.

Liz stretched out a hand and Nathan took it. He could see an old scar on her arm, its angry mark now faded with age. He ignored it as usual, looking instead at a new one that bloomed below, red and recent. A skin cancer removal, he knew without asking. They all had it, to some degree. Every white adult in the area. Whenever the specialist flew in to town, there was always a queue of people waiting their turn to get the treacherous parts of their flesh cut out or burned off. Then cross their fingers until next time. Nathan had plenty of scars of his own.

'This all clear?' he said, pointing at the red weal.

'I think so, for now.' Liz turned her arm over so he couldn't see it anymore. 'But who ever knows?'

Somewhere close by, Nathan heard a dingo howl and they both turned towards the sound.

'They've been hanging around for a while, those ones,' Liz said. 'They're getting too brave.'

Nathan hesitated. 'You want me to try and get them?'

'Bub'll do it. He likes it. The money,' she added quickly. The council paid thirty dollars for every dingo scalp presented at the cop shop, where Glenn would count them and fill in the paperwork.

Liz sighed. 'Is Bub all right, do you think?'

Nathan thought about his brother standing in the dark with his stream of urine hitting the ground.

'I don't know. Bub's Bub.'

'He doesn't seem worse to you?'

'Honestly, he seems about the same.'

Liz looked at the ground next to Carl's grave. 'I never in my life thought it would be Cameron going here. I can't stop running through things in my mind. What I should have done differently.'

'Don't do that to yourself. There was probably nothing that would have changed anything.'

'That feels worse, somehow.' Liz shook her head. 'I wish I hadn't gone riding that last morning. But someone had to exercise Sophie's horse. It threw her, did she tell you?'

'She mentioned she fell.'

'I wasn't sure if it was her fault or the horse's. She's training for gymkhana again this year, but she'll have trouble if she can't control him. I thought I'd better check how he was travelling, but maybe if I hadn't gone —' Liz stopped. There were tears in her eyes. 'Maybe if I'd sat down with Cameron and talked to him properly. Do you remember what you two talked about last time you spoke?'

Nathan tried to think. 'Mending fences, probably.'

'Really?'

Nathan saw her face and almost laughed when he realised her mistake. 'Not like that. I mean practically. How we were going to split the maintenance costs.'

'Oh. Of course.' She looked down. 'Steve called from the clinic. Unless the autopsy finds it was something other than dehydration, they'll release his body in a couple of days. We can have the funeral on Wednesday if we want.'

'Christmas Eve? That soon?'

'It's either then or we have to wait until the new year. Ilse said she didn't know, so I told them we'd do it then.

Better done, I thought.' She turned her swollen eyes towards the house and the girls' bedroom windows. 'Do you think that was the right decision?'

'I think so. There's no good choice.'

'I suppose I'd better let the neighbours know, then.'

'Will they come? This close to Christmas?'

'Of course they will.' Liz's voice had an edge.

Nathan knew that was probably true. People had liked Cameron, and even if they hadn't, they tended to make the effort for the dead. Funerals were one of the few events that ever drew his mum away from the property. Most were local, within a day's drive, but a few months ago she'd flown all the way to Victoria to see her brother buried.

Nathan had barely listened when Liz had called to tell him his uncle had died. Malcolm Deacon, dead of a coronary, aged seventy-one. Nathan couldn't pretend to care. He hadn't even known the bloke. He'd only met him once, more than twenty years earlier at the funeral for the guy's own daughter. All three brothers had gone to that one, because Liz had made them.

'She was your cousin,' she'd said, and apparently that settled it. Carl had point-blank refused to go, then seemed astounded when that hadn't deterred his wife's plans. Instead, Liz and the boys had flown and driven for hours, trailing all the way out to Kiewarra, some shit-kicker town Nathan had never heard of in the arse-end of Victoria. They'd arrived and Nathan thought he could see why his mum had left practically the day she turned eighteen. It was bigger than Balamara, but there was something that felt off about the place. The soft-cock locals did nothing but bitch about the weather, while the Bright brothers strolled around in long sleeves, enjoying the cool change.

The family had listened to a sermon for a girl they had never met, surrounded by people they didn't know. Nathan knew his cousin had been seventeen, only a few years behind him, but he was surprised by how young that suddenly seemed when he saw the coffin. There were two boys and a girl about her age sitting near the front, visibly shaken, their eyes wide with disbelief. Bub, who had only been eight at the time, had sobbed into his hands as if he'd known her.

After the service, Nathan, Cameron and Bub had held back and watched Liz's frosty reunion with her brother. A cousin on the other side of the family had loitered the whole time, staring at them with the half-glazed eyes of a daytime drinker. He looked like the worst kind of dick-head and Nathan had been glad he kept his distance. Later, the bloke had said something to upset Bub so Nathan and Cam had cornered him in the toilets and roughed him up a little. Not too much – it was still a funeral and they weren't animals – but enough that he'd remember it next time. As they'd left the wake, his mum had shaken her head and muttered something under her breath.

'What was that?' Nathan said.

'Nothing. Just, we should have done better for that poor girl.'

They'd headed out of town the minute it was all done and dusted, Liz apparently not interested in staying even a single night in the farming community she'd grown up in.

That year felt like it was marked by death. Within a few months, they'd prised Nathan's dad from a tangled metal wreckage and buried him in the far corner of the yard.

After that, Liz hadn't set foot on a plane again until three months ago, when she'd announced she was attending her brother's funeral. Nathan had been completely taken aback. He'd felt nothing but vague relief at his uncle's death and had assumed his mum had felt the same.

'Why on earth are you going?' he had asked.

'He was my brother.'

'Yes, but –' he had started, then couldn't think how to continue. She had all the same information that he did. To be honest, Nathan thought it was bloody lucky the heart attack had done the man in before the legal system caught up with him.

Not that the technicalities had mattered to Jacqui. She'd had an absolute field day when she'd heard what his uncle had been accused of and had jumped at the excuse not to send Xander for his visits, citing ongoing legal proceedings and appropriate role model behaviour and all that bullshit. Nathan had been forced to pay a three-figure sum for his lawyer to send a six-sentence letter reminding Jacqui of her court-ordered obligations. So if the bloke was dead in the ground, Nathan – for one – was happy enough about it.

But Liz had seemed determined to go, and Nathan had worried about her doing that absolute slog of a journey on her own. He'd thought about it for longer than he should have, then reluctantly said he'd go with her, only to be told that Cameron had already offered and she'd told him not to bother either.

'For God's sake,' she'd said. 'Mal wasn't worth one airfare, let alone two. Not before and especially not now.'

There had been a long argument and in the end Uncle Harry had gone with her.

'How was it?' Nathan had asked him later.

'Quiet,' Harry said.

'Many there?'

'Pretty much just us. A couple of cops turned up.'

'Officially?'

'I don't think so. One was the local bloke from Kiewarra. Friendly enough but on leave. He was a bit –' Harry had waved at his face, '– damaged. There was another one, tall guy who said he used to live around there but was based in Melbourne now. Didn't say much else, seemed pretty pissed off about the whole thing. I think they were there mainly to check the old bastard was really dead.'

Nathan suspected his mum had gone for much the same reason.

At the thought of Harry, Nathan suddenly remembered the drive earlier. The man finding the hidden track in the rock face on the first attempt.

'Cam never mentioned anything specific that was bothering him?' he said. 'Small stuff, even? Problems with Harry? Or Bub?'

'I don't think so. Like you said, Bub's Bub.'

'And Harry?'

Liz frowned. 'Fine as far as I know. Why?'

'I don't know. Nothing. Just with Harry saying Cam might have been under pressure. I wondered –'

'Wondered what?'

'I don't know. If they'd had a falling out or something.'

'Not that I know of.' Liz's frown deepened. 'Harry's a good man. He's been good to this family.'

'I know.'

'He's been here longer than you have. And he's always done right by us, wouldn't you say?'

'Yeah. I would.'

'So what are you saying now?'

'Nothing. Forget it.'

A pause. 'All right,' Liz said, but Nathan saw her eyes flick towards Harry's four-wheel drive.

'Listen, what happens to Cam's share of the property?' Nathan said, changing the subject. It came out more bluntly than he'd intended but Liz didn't seem to notice.

'It goes to Ilse.' There was a faint stiffness in her voice. 'With the day-to-day stuff, I don't know. We'll have to work out who's going to run the place long term.'

She waited a beat as though half-expecting Nathan to propose something.

'Hire a manager, I suppose,' she said, when he didn't.

'Not Bub then?'

'No.' Liz's answer was quick. 'See what Harry reckons, but I don't think so personally. Make sure you and Ilse include Bub in any conversations, though, would you?'

'Yeah, of course.' Across the yard, Nathan could see a kid's bicycle leaning against the house. 'How are the girls today? This morning they seemed a bit –' He tried to find a better word and failed. 'Strange.'

'God knows. It's hard to tell with Sophie, but Lo's taking it very hard. She was worked up already, even before all this. She's got the idea into her head that the place is haunted.'

'By what?'

'I don't know. The stockman, probably. He's the usual suspect. You all went through that phase as kids yourselves.'

The wind blew across the plain and in the distance Nathan could see a spiral of dust rise like an apparition.

'It's not hard to see why she thinks so.' Liz followed his gaze. 'When I first came to live here we used to have a stockman — a living one — who reckoned this whole area was haunted by the settlers' dead children. The ones who died badly. Childbirth or accidents or illness, I suppose.'

There were plenty to choose from, Nathan thought. The child mortality rate had been sky high. Not a single white baby born in the town had survived until the 1920s.

Liz's eyes shone with tears. 'He used to say the ones who wandered off called the loudest. For the rest of their lives, their mums would hear them crying out in the wind. Do you think that's true?'

'That this place has ghosts?'

'That the mothers would hear their lost children in the wind.'

'Oh.' He reached out and took his mum's hand again. 'No.' He really didn't. If that were true, the outback air would howl so loud the dust would never settle.

Chapter 13

The backpackers were setting the table for dinner when Nathan put his head around the kitchen door. He'd left Liz sitting under the gum tree with her own thoughts and come inside. Simon and Katy both looked up, the clatter of cutlery falling silent as they saw him in the doorway. Nathan had the distinct impression they'd stopped speaking abruptly.

'Sorry,' he said, then wondered why he was apologising. 'Have you seen Bub?'

Simon shook his head. 'I thought he was out with you and Harry.'

'Never mind. Thanks.'

Nathan didn't hear the low murmur of their voices start up until he was completely out of the kitchen.

He found Bub in the living room, sitting on the couch with his feet resting on Nathan's sleeping bag. He was playing a video game, something involving shooting and a masked man. Cameron's painting looked down on them from the wall; a scene of serenity in contrast.

'Hey.' Bub barely glanced up as Nathan came in.

'What are you doing?'

'Nothing. This.' He nodded at the screen. 'You want to do two player?'

'No, it's all right.'

Nathan pulled his sleeping bag out from under Bub's feet. 'That's my bed, you know.'

'It's mainly the couch, mate.'

Katy walked past the open door and returned a second later carrying a clean tea towel. Bub's eyes followed her with raw longing.

'I bloody love her.' He heaved a dramatic sigh.

'Oh yeah? What's her last name?'

Bub grinned. 'I dunno, but I can tell you what it's going to be.'

Nathan had to smile. 'I think you're a bit late, mate. Looks like she's spoken for.'

Bub's face darkened a little. 'It's a bloody crime, great girl like her with a Pommy prick like him. He's not even keeping her happy.'

'How would you know?'

'Does she look happy to you?'

'Hadn't really thought about it.'

'I'd keep her happy,' Bub said, with a meaningful nod in case Nathan had failed to fully grasp his intent.

'Yeah, all right. Never mind that —' Gunfire rang out on screen. 'Listen, can you —' Nathan reached over and paused the game.

'What's your problem?' Then Bub's annoyance faded as quickly as it arrived. 'Is something wrong? Is it about Cam?'

'No. Well, yeah, kind of. I wanted to talk to you. It's –'
Nathan faltered. 'I saw you last night.'

'What? When?' Bub's eyes flicked to the doorway
where Katy had been and his cheeks reddened. Nathan
wondered what he was thinking.

'Outside in the garden,' he prompted.

Bub frowned.

'Taking a slash on the gravesites?'

'Oh, yeah.' Bub actually laughed. 'So?'

'So what do you think you were doing?'

'It was only on Dad's. Like you've never done it.'

Nathan hadn't, in fact. Possibly because he had never
thought of it. 'Do you –?'

'Do I what, mate?'

'Do you do that often?'

'Time to time, whenever I'm passing and can
muster it up.'

'But . . . why?'

'Nate, mate. Come on.' Bub turned back to his game,
nothing more to say.

It might never have occurred to Nathan to piss on a
grave, but he knew Bub maybe had a little more incentive.
The key with Carl Bright that you had to learn quick and
early was to stay out of his way whenever you could and
keep your head well down the rest of the time. Bub, born
late, had never got the hang of it. Being an accidental baby
was hardly his fault, but it hadn't helped his cause. Liz had
never once hinted that Bub's arrival hadn't been entirely
welcome, twelve and ten years after his brothers, but Carl
hadn't bothered to hide it.

It might not have been so bad if Bub had followed Nathan, rather than Cameron, who Carl seemed to find the least offensive by some margin. But Bub's slowness and his difficulty finding the right words had infuriated their dad. And Bub was completely unable to sense when it was happening. Nathan had tried to help him, showing him the signs to watch out for and growing frustrated himself when Bub didn't get it. Cam had tried too, but it was no good. Bub literally couldn't see it to save himself.

Nathan looked at Bub now, older but still the same in some ways. 'Look, Dad's grave is one thing, but Cam's going to be there too, you know.'

'He's not there yet, though.' Bub had restarted the game and his eyes were glued to the screen. 'Anyway, I wouldn't do that to Cam, would I?'

'I don't know,' Nathan said, and Bub looked up sharply.

'Me and Cam got along fine, thanks. Better than you two did.'

Nathan opened his mouth but was saved by a call from the kitchen. Dinner was ready.

'You'll kill the tree if you keep on doing that,' he muttered as they went through, but Bub shrugged.

'Like I give a shit. It's just a tree.'

The atmosphere around the kitchen table already felt subdued. Ilse turned to Nathan as he sat down next to Xander.

'How did it go out there?' she asked neutrally. She was flanked by her two daughters, and seemed to be working hard to maintain a brave face.

'Okay. Glenn's going to call you,' he said. 'He let us bring Cam's car back. It's outside.'

Ilse gave a small nod. 'Thanks.'

Nathan felt a soft hand on his shoulder now and moved his chair to give Liz space to sit down. She looked even worse under artificial light. The skin around her eyes was taut and shiny from crying. Katy put a plate in front of her and Liz stared at it with a faintly puzzled air. The phone in the hallway started ringing and Liz and Harry both pushed their chairs back.

'I'll get it,' Liz said. 'It might be Glenn.'

'What did he say to you all?' Ilse asked as Liz left the room.

'Nothing much we didn't already know,' Harry said. 'He asked a bit about Cam's state of mind. How things were going on the property.'

'And what did you tell him?' Ilse was watching Harry closely.

'What you'd expect. That things were going well here, but Cam had been worried about something.'

'Did he ask what?'

'Of course.'

'And?'

Harry's face barely moved but he kept his eyes on Ilse. 'And none of us were much help. So I reckon he'll be wanting to ask you.'

Ilse shot a look at her daughters, who were watching now. 'Maybe we should talk about this later.'

For a few minutes the only sound was cutlery against plates and the ticking of the kitchen clock. Nathan cleared his throat and turned to Harry.

'I thought I'd go to Lehmann's Hill tomorrow. Try to fix that mast.'

'That'd be good. Bub can give you a hand.' He looked at Bub, who nodded.

'It's fine,' Nathan said. 'Xander'll come.'

Harry shook his head. 'It's a long way and the radio's down. Take Bub too.'

Nathan opened his mouth to reply when Liz appeared at the door, her face strangely fixed. 'Glenn needs to talk to you,' she said to Ilse, who stood up and left the kitchen.

'What's wrong?' Harry said.

'Nothing. Everything's fine.' Liz flashed a rigid smile at the girls. 'But a quick word outside, Harry, if you don't mind.'

Nathan saw his confusion mirrored in Bub and Xander's faces. They heard the slam of the screen door as Harry followed Liz out, and a moment later the hum of low voices on the verandah. The backpackers looked at each other, their meals forgotten on their plates.

A minute passed, then another. No-one came back. Slowly, they all picked up their forks and continued eating. After what felt like a long time, Nathan heard fast footsteps in the hall and the screech of the screen door again. Another murmured voice on the verandah, inaudible but with a new sense of urgency in its tone. *Ilse*, he thought. He waited, but still no-one returned to the kitchen. Finally, he pushed back his chair, six pairs of eyes on him.

'Back in a minute.'

The conversation stopped dead as he stepped outside. Harry cut himself off mid-word and Liz looked up. She had both arms wrapped tightly around herself. Ilse, who

147

appeared to have been looking from one to the other, now fixed her eyes firmly on Nathan. He wasn't sure what she was trying to tell him, if anything. The yellow porch light cast a sickly glow over them all.

'What's going on?'

No-one answered him straight away.

'Anyone?' he tried again. 'What did Glenn say?'

Harry shot a look at Liz. 'He was going through the police records this afternoon for his report and he found a reference to Cameron.'

Nathan frowned. 'Did Cam do something?'

'No,' Liz snapped, and Ilse's jaw tightened.

'Apparently about two months ago someone rang the cop shop asking about Cameron,' Harry said, and looked at Liz. 'You tell him. It was you Glenn spoke to.'

Liz shook her head, a tight jerk of the neck, and glanced at Ilse, who waved her hand impatiently. 'Christ, you just tell him, Harry.'

Harry sighed. 'Someone called the police station, but it wasn't Glenn who took the call. It was when he was on medical leave for that week or so, you remember?'

'Vaguely,' Nathan said. 'Matt covered.' The usual stand-in sergeant from St Helens. He was an okay bloke.

'Right. Well, Glenn noticed a minor entry on the log and asked Matt about it. Matt reckons he got a call at the station from a woman saying she used to know Cameron and asking if he still worked on this property.'

Ilse was now looking out into the night with a thousand-yard stare.

'So Matt says yes,' Harry went on. 'Offers to pass on her

details, but she says something like: "No, it's fine. As long as Cameron's still there, I'll get in touch myself."'

Nathan felt a seed of disquiet unfurl and grow. 'Okay.'

'Matt doesn't think too much of it, but he mentions this woman to Cameron when he sees him in town a few days later. Thinking it's an old girlfriend or whatever.'

Ilse folded her arms firmly across her chest.

'But apparently, Cam wasn't too happy to hear this,' Harry said. 'Told Matt he wasn't interested in hearing from her. Not to pass on his number or email. Get rid of her if she calls again. So Matt thinks fair enough. Old girlfriend.' Harry glanced at Ilse. 'New girlfriend maybe. None of his business. And that's that. Quick note in the log, nothing more to see.'

The creases in Harry's face deepened.

'Until all this, obviously,' he said. 'Glenn saw the log this arvo, got the story from Matt, and thought he'd better call us and see if this woman's name rang any bells.'

'Well, don't bloody keep me in suspense, mate,' Nathan said. Liz was examining the floorboards and Ilse was still staring out into the night.

'It was Jenna Moore.'

Nathan breathed out. 'Shit.' He hadn't heard the name in more than twenty years and he had to dig deep to fully unearth the memory. Dusty and buried, it rose up through the years and clicked into place, and by then it wasn't a bell ringing in Nathan's head, it was an alarm.

149

Chapter 14

They set off for Lehmann's Hill just after dawn. Nathan drove, with Bub next to him and Xander in the back.

He adjusted his mirrors as the sun's reflection rose, blinding red behind them. They were heading west, towards the desert, and the sky loomed huge above the perfect flat horizon. By the time they hit the edge and turned north, they would be able to see the dunes: huge sandy peaks running north to south for hundreds of kilometres.

Xander had helped Nathan collect the mast repair instructions and tools from Cameron's car before they set off. The equipment was all there. If Cameron had never intended to go to the mast, Nathan thought, he'd made an effort to hide the fact.

The house had barely disappeared from view behind them before Xander leaned forward from the back seat. 'So what's the story with this woman that everyone's whispering about?'

He'd clearly been itching to ask and Nathan couldn't

blame him. Dinner the night before had been swiftly abandoned as Nathan had stood out on the verandah with Ilse, Harry and Liz, whispering and talking themselves in circles. It wasn't long before Lo and Sophie had poked their small heads around the screen door to see what was happening, followed by Xander.

Ilse had hastily bundled the girls back inside, ostensibly to put them to bed, and hadn't come back. Nathan had shaken his head at Xander – *Not now, mate* – and the boy had reluctantly retreated. Liz, stiff-limbed and red-eyed, had eventually gone inside without another word. The sound of soft crying had floated out on the night air. Nathan wasn't sure who it was. He and Harry had talked until it was time to turn the generator off, then Nathan had lain awake on the couch for hours. His eyes felt gritty in the morning light, and he rubbed them now with his knuckles. It made them worse.

'Jenna Moore,' Bub said from the passenger seat. 'That's who they're all worried about.'

'Did you hear much about that back then?' Nathan said. It had all been before Bub's time. He would have been – Nathan worked it out – only about seven when it happened.

Bub shrugged. 'This and that.'

Nathan realised both Bub and Xander were looking at him expectantly. Out in front, a cow stepped onto the track and wandered across. He slowed to let it pass, but it stopped dead, turning its head to look at them. Nathan came to a halt and waited, then sounded the horn. The cow didn't move, just blinked slowly.

'Christ. Back in a sec.'

He put the car in park and jumped out, walking slowly towards the animal. That was enough to get it moving, followed by the small herd waiting on the other side of the road. Nathan automatically ran an appraising eye over them. They looked healthy and well fed. Cameron – or Bub, Harry, whoever, he quickly corrected himself – would have no trouble finding a market for them when the time came.

'Anyway,' Xander said impatiently, leaning forward as Nathan got back in. 'Who's Jenna Moore?'

Nathan focused on the road as he drove. He realised he had never actually told the story out loud – he'd never been asked to – and suddenly wasn't sure where to start.

'It was all years ago,' he said eventually. 'I was nineteen, so Cam must have been seventeen. Yeah, he was, actually, because he was still underage.'

Bub gave an amused grunt from the passenger seat at the suggestion that Balamara observed the legal drinking age with any real enthusiasm.

'It was around this time of year,' Nathan went on. 'The week between Christmas and New Year, when everyone who's coming back has come back. All the property kids were home from school or uni or their city jobs or whatever they'd been doing.'

Cameron had been on holidays ahead of his final year of boarding school in Brisbane, while Nathan had been splitting his time between working on Burley Downs and nurturing a hot and heavy mutual flirtation with golden-haired Jacqui Walker next door.

'There was this party in the dunes outside town,' he said. 'I can't even remember who organised it. Some of the Atherton guys, I think. Anyway, we all drove in for it. Some kids we'd done School of the Air with back in the day, a few of the station hands, backpackers, that kind of thing. Most people had left school, so were more my age than Cam's, but he was welcome to come along. Everyone knew him, obviously.'

It had been a good night, Nathan remembered. Warm, but not too hot for once, and the inky sky was heavy with stars as they parked their utes and four-wheel drives in the sand. Someone lit a campfire and cranked up the music as the booze was passed around.

Nathan had driven there with Cameron, and had spotted Jacqui the minute they'd pulled up. She had been sitting by the fire with another girl, who was laughing at something and idly braiding and unbraiding her thick hair in the orange glow of the flames. They were both sipping beer. Jacqui had seen Nathan and given him one of the smiles she'd been giving him lately and Nathan had nearly fallen over himself in his haste to get out of the car. He'd almost forgotten Cameron was even there until his brother appeared at his shoulder, his tall shadow flickering against the ground.

'The girl, Jenna, was working on Jacqui's dad's property,' he said. 'She was English, out here backpacking with her boyfriend. The boyfriend had had to stay behind and work at the station, so she'd come alone to the party with Jacqui.'

It had been a good turnout, for around there. Fresh beers

were cracked open as soon as a bottle ran empty and the sound of laughter and chatter had swelled as mates caught up in person, for the first time in years in some cases. The numbers at the party grew as a handful more people arrived, then dipped occasionally as the booze flowed and the night wore on and couples – some established, some brand new – made the most of rare face-to-face time by disappearing together into the dark of the dunes for half an hour. Nathan was biding his time. Neither he nor Jacqui was expected home that night and they had plans and a mate's empty house waiting for them in town. Cam knew where the back of the car was when he was ready to crash out.

Nathan remembered putting his arms around Jacqui and seeing her hair shine in the light of the campfire as she smiled at him. He knew what was in store later and was feeling pretty great about life in general. He wasn't sure when he'd first noticed Cameron and Jenna together. Maybe when Jenna had stood up to get them both another beer, stretching her arms high above her head and exposing a flash of taut skin as Cam gazed up at her. She had definitely been watching Cam watching her, as she'd walked slowly all the way over to the coolbox, then slowly all the way back, and sat down again right beside him. Nathan could picture that clearly.

'Jenna was older, I remember,' Nathan said. 'I think she was about twenty at the time.'

Cameron had been at that awkward in-between stage. In his school uniform, face scrubbed and hair combed, he looked like a teenager. In his work clothes, on the property, with his back and shoulders and forearms honed from physical work, he could be mistaken for a man. In the uneven firelight through the hazy film of alcohol, he could have been either.

'And it was obvious Cam was interested,' Nathan said. 'A couple of people said Jenna had this boyfriend back on the station, but it didn't seem to bother her, so it didn't bother any of us. I didn't see her even talking to anyone else much, it was mainly her and Cam together for most of the night.'

Nathan had had a few drinks himself by the time he'd next looked over and seen Jenna sitting in the sand by the campfire, leaning against Cameron's legs. Cam said something and she laughed. He said something else and her face tilted up so it was close to his. They were each holding a beer bottle. Their free hands were entwined.

When Nathan had looked over next, they were kissing and Cameron's hand was now stroking Jenna's semi-braided hair. Nathan had fleetingly wondered if he should have a quick man-to-man word with his younger brother, but suspected Cam wouldn't thank him for it. Then Jacqui had stretched up on tiptoe and whispered something in Nathan's ear and all at once it was time to go.

They'd tossed Nathan's car keys at Cameron and told him to give Jenna a lift back to town later, or make sure someone else did, then driven to their mate's empty house as fast as Jacqui's red four-wheel drive could take them.

Nathan glanced at Xander now in his rear-view mirror.

'So I left the party with your mum to make sure she got back to town safely –'

155

Bub smirked and Xander pretended not to notice.

'– and the next morning, we ran into a few people from the party. A girl Jacqui knew and a couple of the blokes from Atherton, and everyone was talking about how after we'd left, Cam and Jenna had –' He saw his son's reflection and hesitated.

'Had a root?' Bub supplied from the passenger seat.

'Yeah. Thanks Bub.'

It had actually seemed pretty funny, Nathan remembered. They'd all laughed about it. Cameron Bright, home on his school holidays, managing to nail a backpacker behind the dunes.

'So that was it. Bit of gossip floating around. Pretty standard morning after,' Nathan said. 'I found Cam sleeping it off in my car behind the servo with a pretty pleased look on his face. Jacqui went to track down Jenna, and me and Cam came home.'

Jenna had slept in the staff accommodation at the pub along with a few of the other casual workers. She had been fine on the drive back to their property, Jacqui had told him later. A bit quiet perhaps. Embarrassed, maybe. Hungover, definitely. But fine. She hadn't offered a word about Cameron and Jacqui hadn't asked.

'And that was that, for about a day,' Nathan said.

Cam had been grinning like an idiot out of Nathan's passenger-side window the whole way home. He'd still been grinning when the call came through the next afternoon.

'Then what?' Xander leaned further forward.

'Then Jenna said she wasn't fine anymore.'

Chapter 15

When he'd hung up the phone, Carl Bright had been the worst type of furious. The kind of stone-cold anger that made him particularly unpredictable and made Nathan particularly wary. He had summoned his eldest sons.

'You two. In here.'

Nathan and Cameron had jostled not to be last. They had stood with their backs against the wall as Carl had pointed at the phone. When he spoke, his voice was all the worse for its softness.

'What's this bullshit I'm hearing about some girl, then?'

Nathan stared now at the road ahead. Bub was watching him from the passenger seat as Xander leant forward. He tried to shake the old feeling creeping through him, but couldn't entirely.

'The stories from the party started to spread, obviously,' Nathan said. 'Apparently Jenna's boyfriend found out what had happened with Cam, and was less than happy, as you can imagine.' He was quiet for a minute. 'Then, next thing, Jenna and her boyfriend were back in town and had turned up at the medical centre –'

At the clinic, Jenna had spoken to a younger Steve Fitzgerald, fresher-faced back then as he found his feet during his first posting in Balamara. After that, she and her boyfriend had crossed the street and walked into the police station. Over a cup of tea, they had sat down with the sergeant at the time. It hadn't been Glenn back then, but a cop not unlike him. When they'd left, the sergeant had phoned the Bright household as a courtesy from one local to another. Nathan could still picture the look on Liz's face when she learned what was being said. Variations of the same two emotions: horror and disbelief.

'What did Jenna tell the police?' Xander asked.

'That she hadn't wanted to have sex with Cameron, but she'd been too drunk to stop him,' Nathan said.

There was a stunned silence in the car.

'She said *Uncle Cam* raped her?' Xander sounded bewildered.

'I think technically that word was never used,' Nathan said. 'The cop at the time reckoned she never actually said that exactly.'

Liz had wanted to immediately drive Cameron into town and speak to Steve Fitzgerald and the sergeant – maybe even speak to Jenna herself if they could – and get all this mess straightened out. Carl wouldn't let her. *That boy is not going to be jumping through hoops because some uppity bitch has woken up and changed her fucken mind, right?* Cameron had hovered, white-faced. No-one had asked him what he wanted to do.

'So what Jenna was saying spread around town in about five minutes flat. But –' Nathan stopped, his eyes on the dusty track. 'But loads of us had been at that party and they'd been all over each other all night. Everyone saw it. I saw it, your mum saw it, Xander. Everyone who was there said the same thing.'

Even people who hadn't been there reckoned they'd seen it, by the end of the day. Jenna was a full three years older than Cameron, who was on his bloody school holidays, for Christ's sake. And she was the one who'd been putting alcohol in the kid's hand all night, even though he was technically too young to be drinking. Plus there were plenty of girls at that party – sensible outback girls who didn't take any shit from the local idiot blokes – so if Jenna hadn't wanted something to happen with Cameron behind the dunes, all she'd had to do was call out and she'd have been right. She'd let him drive her back to town afterwards. If it had been some of the other blokes in town, then yeah, maybe you'd give her the benefit of the doubt. But not Cam Bright. He was only a kid, and a good one too. He was barely even old enough to know what he was doing down there.

Nathan came to the turning in the track and the car juddered as the wheels went over a rougher patch.

'Watch out,' Bub said. 'It was somewhere here that I wrecked those tyres the other day.'

'Along here?' Nathan could make out the peak of Lehmann's Hill in the far distance. He glanced at Bub. 'I thought you were coming from the north paddock to meet Cam?'

They went over a pothole and Nathan's eyes were forced back to the road as the whole car lurched.

'Track was too sandy,' Bub said. 'I had to loop around. Danger spot's further up, I'll shout out if I see it in time.'

Nathan was trying to work out where Bub would have joined the track when Xander interrupted.

'So what happened after Jenna spoke to the police?'

Nathan thought for a moment. 'Nothing, actually.'

'Nothing?'

'No. I mean, it was all pretty bloody tense for a day or two. Dad wasn't happy.' It was one thing for Carl Bright to bag his own sons, but it was quite another for someone else to talk shit about one of them in public. Especially if that one was Cameron. 'But it blew over before it really got started.'

'What, just like that?' Xander frowned.

'Yeah. Jenna's boyfriend calmed down, apparently. Jacqui said they both went to her dad, told him they'd thought better of it and wanted to move on. Handed in their notice. Next day, they packed up and left. And that was the end of it.'

Cameron's colour had slowly returned to normal over the following week. No formal complaint had been made, leaving his police record unblemished, which was more than a lot of people in town could say for themselves. And fair enough too, had been the general consensus. It wasn't fair that a good kid like Cam should have his life ruined by some drunk backpacker with a few hungover regrets.

Xander sat back in his seat. 'And he never heard from Jenna again?'

'Not as far as I know.'

'So why now?'

'Yeah. Good question.'

Cameron had been over-prepared, as usual, Nathan thought as he stood on top of Lehmann's Hill. They had managed to arrive with all four tyres intact. As the ground had grown sandier, Nathan and Bub had got out and deflated them to avoid getting bogged. They'd driven up to the peak and got out to examine the repeater mast, squinting in the sun.

Nathan could tell almost immediately that they wouldn't need the repair instructions Cameron had carefully printed out before he'd left home on the second-last morning of his life, or most of the tools and equipment he had gathered. The mast on the top of Lehmann's Hill was suffering from nothing more serious than the wear and tear of constant exposure. A good clean-out of clogged sand and grit and a couple of replacement wires and it would be good to go. It wasn't really a two-man job, let alone three, so Nathan worked while the others watched.

'Pass me that small screwdriver, Bub,' Nathan said, an hour later.

There was no reaction. Bub was standing with his back to the desert and his arms folded, staring out at their own land. Xander was in the car a short distance away, awaiting an instruction to try the radio.

'Bub? That screwdriver there.'

'Sorry.' Bub handed it to him. 'I was just thinking about some stuff.'

'Oh yeah?' Nathan grimaced as a gust of wind blew some grit into his mouth.

'I should've gone down earlier.'

'What's that, mate?' Nathan straightened up.

Bub picked up a small rock and fiddled with it before tossing it down the hill. It rolled for a long way. There was nothing in its path. Lehmann's Hill was not particularly high but it was tall enough to offer a view. The paddocks glowed red and green from up there and Nathan could see distant shadows as the odd herd of cattle wandered along. They were tiny. The other way, to the west, all was still. The desert looked pristine and untouched, with perfect ripples in the sand. Nathan had seen the landscape so often and in so many ways, he was almost blind to it at times, but sometimes, in the right light, it was still breathtaking.

'I shouldn't have waited for Cam for so bloody long. I sat up here in the car for ages.' Bub squinted out into the distance. Apart from the odd ripple of shadow, there was almost no movement. 'I dunno why. You can see there's no-one bloody coming.'

It was true, Nathan knew. A moving car was usually easy to spot.

'This wasn't your fault, mate,' Nathan said finally. 'He could have been parked somewhere. Or coming from a different direction.'

'Yeah, maybe. But even when you can't see it, you can kind of feel it sometimes, don't you reckon?' Bub said. 'When there's someone near?'

Nathan nodded. Sometimes. Kind of.

'Yeah, well, I felt bugger all. If I'd left then, got to the track before dark, I might've been able to raise the alarm earlier. It might not have been too late then.' Bub dropped his gaze. Xander was watching them, out of earshot, from the car.

'I would've waited too,' Nathan said finally.

'Would you?' Bub looked up at that.

'Yep.' It was true. 'You arranged to meet him here, you waited here. Nothing wrong with that.'

Bub didn't reply straight away. 'I was pissed off with him. That's why I left it so long.' He didn't meet Nathan's eye. 'I thought he'd got bogged or got a flat himself. Decided I'd let him sweat it out on his own for a while.'

'Why?'

'It's stupid. It was over bloody nothing.' He sighed. 'I was half thinking about heading to Dulsterville next year. Become a roo shooter.'

'Were you?' Nathan was surprised. It had never occurred to him that Bub might want to leave the property one day.

'Yeah, I thought, maybe. Why not?' Bub sounded defensive.

No reason at all, really, Nathan thought. Kangaroo shooting probably wouldn't be a bad option for him, and it was the main industry in Dulsterville so there'd be plenty of work. Nathan had driven through the small outback town a few times on his way east. He'd seen the modified utes parked and ready for the night's work. With their spotlights and their rifle rests mounted on the doors so shots could be taken through the open windows. Large spiked cages on the back to hang the carcasses. The collection point at the edge of town where the tagged ones

163

were turned into cash for the shooters and pet food and fur products for consumers. It was a living.

'So you going to do it?' Nathan said.

Bub shook his head. 'Cam thought it was stupid. Said I should stay and focus on things here.'

'So? You don't need Cam's permission.'

'Need money though. Cash, I mean. Not all tied up in bloody long-term property investment stuff. I need to get the equipment, fix up the Land Cruiser. Find somewhere to live, that kind of thing.' Bub squinted into the sun. It was hard to read his expression. 'I wasn't asking for anything that wasn't mine. I just wanted to free up some of the money – *my money* – in this place.'

'Cameron said no?'

'Not straight out. But he wanted me to think about it. Talk to him again next year. Make sure I was doing the right thing.'

'Sounds sensible.'

'But what do you think of the idea?' Bub seemed genuinely interested.

'Me? I dunno, mate.' Cameron's and Bub's interests may not have aligned exactly, but Cam was probably right to suggest Bub think things through. 'It depends. You don't want to be too hasty. I mean, I only sold out in part and I still ended up in the shit.'

'Yeah, I suppose.'

Bub looked dejected and Nathan felt a bit bad. In all honesty, his brother would probably make a pretty decent roo shooter. 'Look,' he said. 'It doesn't sound like the worst plan.'

'Yeah, well, tell that to Cam.' There was an awkward moment, then Bub shrugged. 'It'd be good, though. You ever thought of doing it? Money for nothing.'

'No, not for me.'

'Haven't got the balls for it?'

'Something like that.' Nathan tried to keep his tone casual. 'Haven't got the licence for it anymore, either.'

'Wait.' Bub stared, incredulous. 'You haven't got your gun licence anymore?'

'No.'

'Why not?'

'Expired.'

'Are you bloody joking, mate? When?'

'Dunno. Few months.'

Just over six, actually. Nathan had felt something start to change in him last year after his dog, Kelly, had died. Steve had called him on the phone from the clinic and made him do this questionnaire all about how Nathan was feeling and things like that. Nathan had toned down his answers, but after that either Glenn or Steve had seemed to coincidentally find themselves in the region of Nathan's property every couple of weeks.

He'd started to feel a bit sorry for them, trailing all the way out to his place to check up on him with fabricated excuses so threadbare they were transparent. So when his licence renewal had rolled around, he'd let it lapse partly to put their minds at rest, he told himself.

Nathan knew there must be some sort of watch list in their desk drawers, and he knew his name had to be on there. Probably high up, possibly even right at the top.

Either way, ready access to firearms was unlikely to be on the recommended treatment plan and he could tell it was making them nervous. So he'd surrendered his weapons to Glenn. Now, Nathan's rifle cabinet door swung open, unlocked, and every once in a while, when he found himself somehow standing in front of it, there was just an empty shelf.

Nathan glanced at his son in the car. 'Listen, don't tell Xander. He gets funny about things sometimes.'

Bub was still staring at Nathan as though he'd admitted to chopping off his right arm and losing it somewhere. Xander caught the expression and called something out of the window. The words got lost in the wind.

'What's that, mate?' Nathan shouted back.

The car door opened and Xander walked over. 'What's wrong?'

'Nothing. You okay?'

'I suppose. Hey, listen, why didn't Jenna say anything to Mum?' Xander said, in a way that suggested he'd been dwelling on the subject for the past hour. 'When they were driving home together?'

He looked upset. When he was five years old, Uncle Cam had given him a pony called Mr Tupps. The pony arrived wearing a straw hat with holes cut for its ears, and Xander had been pink-faced with delight. He had phoned Cam every week for months to regale him with tales of what Mr Tupps had been up to now.

'Yeah,' Nathan said. 'People wondered that at the time too.'

Jenna and Jacqui had been alone in the car for nearly

three hours. Jenna had been quiet, apparently, but then so had Jacqui, who would've been more than a little bit tired and hungover if Nathan remembered rightly.

'Mum would have helped her.'

'Anyone would have helped her, mate. We're not monsters.'

'I didn't mean –'

'No, I know. Of course your mum would have helped her. If she'd said something.'

It hadn't only been that, Nathan knew. After whatever had happened in the dunes, Cameron had offered to drive Jenna back to town and she'd accepted. She possibly didn't have many other options at that time of night, Nathan realised, but as Cam had pulled up outside the pub, the landlord had seen two people leaning towards each other in the front seats, their kiss illuminated by the dull yellow of the interior light. Jenna had then climbed out of the car and walked away in the dark to the staff accommodation block.

'Looked completely normal, mate,' the landlord had told people later. 'No worries at all there.'

'And she didn't tell anyone that morning while she was still in town?' Xander sounded uncertain.

'No.'

More than anything else – more than Cameron's good nature, more than what anyone had or hadn't seen at the party – it was the delay that swayed public opinion. The morning after the party, Jenna had sat in the bakery, drinking a coffee while waiting for Jacqui. The police station was fully visible through the bakery windows and the medical centre was at the end of the road. She had visited neither.

'As far as I know, she didn't say a word about it until her boyfriend heard the stories from the party.' Nathan dusted his hands on his shirt and nodded at the car. 'Go and check the radio. See if this is working.'

'It's so weird that Jenna would suddenly contact Uncle Cam now, though,' Xander said.

'Yeah. Try the radio.'

'Because if it's a coincidence, the timing –'

'I know. The timing's shit. Radio.'

'So –' Xander didn't move. 'Do you think it's possible that something bad actually did happen at that party?'

'If I did, I would have said so at the time.' Nathan walked past him, pulled open the car door and tried the radio himself.

'But even if you didn't think so at the time, now –' He heard Xander follow him.

'But nothing, mate.' A bleep on the airwaves. The mast was working. 'This is fixed. We can go.'

'What if –'

'Look –' Nathan's voice was louder than he'd intended and he took a breath, made himself lower it. 'This is your Uncle Cam we're talking about. He's family. You know him.' *Knew him*.

'Yeah. I know.' Xander looked down.

'He was shocked when he heard what she was saying.'

It was true. Cameron had sat on the verandah steps and cried, his shoulders shaking as Liz sat next to him. She'd rubbed his back with one hand and pinched the bridge of her nose with the other, her eyes squeezed shut.

'And he was always really clear about what happened.'
Nathan looked at his son. 'He was asked about it loads
of times over those few days – by our dad, by your
grandma, the town cop at the time – and he always said
the same thing.'

Cam had met Jenna at the party. They had talked, they
had been drinking, they had gone behind the sand dunes
and they had had sex. Yes, they had both wanted to. No,
she hadn't told him she had a boyfriend. Yes, of course she
had gone with him willingly. No, she hadn't said anything
that made him worried. Nothing at all. Not during, not
afterwards.

Nathan started packing up around the mast.

'How does anyone know what actually happened,
though?' Xander said in a way that made Nathan look
up. Bub had abandoned loading the car and was watching, his arms folded across his chest. Xander blinked,
suddenly looking a little nervous.

'Just, the way you're telling it, it sounds like it's impossible for anyone to say for sure what really went on.'

'Then I've told it wrong.'

'It's not that –' Xander stopped. 'But two people can
remember different versions of something and both think
it's the truth.'

'Can they?'

'Yeah. Of course. You and mum do it all the time.'

'Hardly the same thing, mate.'

'I know. I'm just saying it doesn't matter what anyone
else thinks they saw, or what Jenna should've done. Only
two people were actually there and –'

169

Xander stopped. He didn't finish his thought out loud but he didn't have to. Nathan knew what he was thinking. Only two people were there that night, and now one of them was dead.

Chapter 16

They blew a tyre an hour into the journey back.

'Yep,' Bub said, surveying the landscape with his hands on his hips as Nathan sweated over the jack with the afternoon sun searing his back. 'It was near here that I got stuck, too. I remember those big rocks.'

'Great. Would've been good if you'd seen them earlier,' Nathan grunted as Xander hovered, trying to help but mostly getting in the way.

'Yeah. Would've been. Didn't though.'

'Nope.'

In the heat, it took Nathan forty-five minutes and two litres of water to get them back on the road. They didn't talk and the rest of the drive seemed longer for the silence. Whenever Nathan checked the rear-view mirror, Xander was staring out of the window, deep in thought.

The daylight was bleeding into evening by the time they pulled up outside the house. Dinner wasn't far off and Nathan could hear the backpackers in the kitchen as he scrubbed the oil and grit from under his nails in the small bathroom off the hall. His hands as clean as he could get them, he wandered out, pausing when he saw a light under the door on his left. The office. Ilse's office, now.

He heard a high voice and pushed the door open. Sophie and Lo were sprawled on the floor, with toys and books scattered around them. Lo was lying on her front, her sandy-blonde hair hiding her face as she made firm marks in a sketchbook. Sophie was cross-legged, struggling to play a handheld video game with one arm in her sling. They reminded Nathan suddenly of him and Cameron. They'd been best friends at that age, perhaps only through lack of choice, but nevertheless the outcome was the same. Both girls jumped when they saw Nathan.

'You scared me,' Sophie said. She hesitated. 'I thought you were Mummy.'

'No. Why? Are you not supposed to be in here?'

Nathan came into the office. It was well organised, with neat files and stacked paperwork on the desk. The year's employment record lay on top, with Simon and Katy's names the most recent additions. A large full-year wall calendar for the twelve months ahead was already carefully marked with dates for deliveries and crucial invoices and everything essential to a smooth-running operation. He ran his eyes over it.

'Sophie's supposed to be reading, not playing her game,' Lo said, without looking up. 'That's why she was worried.'

'I see.' Something had been marked on the wall planner in red on a number of different dates. The words were written tentatively, and all had later been crossed off, with a black line scored through them.

'Anyway, we have Mummy's permission, so we are allowed in here,' Sophie said, with authority. 'Are you allowed?'

'Hmm, I don't know,' Nathan said, still looking at the planner. In fact, the room did feel a bit off limits. Nathan and his brothers had never set foot in here when it had been their dad running the show.

'He's allowed.' Ilse's voice came from the doorway. She gave him a tired smile. 'Dinner's nearly ready. Start tidying up, girls.'

His hands might be clean, but as Ilse came into the room, Nathan felt suddenly very aware of his shirt dried stiff with sweat and the dust in his hair. He didn't react, other than to move a subtle half-step away as she stopped next to him in front of the wall planner. Over the years, he'd found it was easier on himself if he maintained some physical space between them.

From time to time, Nathan had wondered if Cameron knew what had happened that once between him and Ilse. If so, he hadn't heard about it from Nathan. Although Nathan had been tempted to tell him once or twice when Cam was being a dickhead. Cam might well have asked Ilse – he'd known Nathan had been interested back then – but the fact Nathan had never heard a word about it made him pretty sure his and Ilse's shared secret had stayed a secret.

Nathan had done his part, keeping his mouth shut and keeping his distance ever since that first time he'd run into her in the kitchen of this house. It had been the first Christmas after his public banishment. There was no sign the festive season had put anyone in a forgiving mood, and Jacqui had dug her heels in and refused to send Xander for even a few days. Nathan would have been happy enough to lie in a dark room with a sheet over his head, but Liz had insisted he come to stay. In the end, she had worn him down until it was easier to give in than to argue. Weary from the effort and dusty from the drive over, he had gone into the kitchen in search of a beer and instead found Ilse.

When she had turned, water jug in hand, Nathan had honestly thought for one crazy and exhilarating moment that she was there to see him. The sight of Cameron walking through the kitchen door and right up to her had been like a gut punch that had taken Nathan's breath away.

'You two have introduced yourselves?' Cameron had said, and Nathan thought his brother had actually winked at him. Head reeling, Nathan had barely been able to nod. He had sat mute during dinner as the rest of the family chatted to Cameron's new girlfriend. Attempts to draw Nathan into the conversation had been met with grunts. He hadn't trusted himself to speak.

Afterwards, he had been hovering in the hall and debating whether he could simply leave, when Ilse had found him. They were alone, standing close, but not too close. An appropriate gap between them.

'It's good to see you again,' she'd said.

'You too.' He'd both truly meant it and truly hadn't at the same time.

'You never came back to the pub.'

'No.' He'd rubbed a hand over his chin and had the sudden overwhelming urge to sit down and tell her everything. All the things that were weighing so heavy on his mind. How hard the last few months had been, how deeply he regretted what he'd done to Keith, how scared he felt about the future. How he'd missed seeing her. Then from somewhere outside, very faint, Cameron's voice had floated into the hall. Nathan had taken a shallow breath. 'I had a few things going on.'

'So I heard.' Ilse had waited. Then, when he didn't say any more: 'You look like you've been having a difficult time.'

'I'm fine.' His voice had cracked and he'd swallowed. 'It'll be fine.' He'd looked down at her and known what he should say. The apology was already forming on his tongue when a door slammed somewhere along the hall and they'd both jumped. Ilse had taken a small step away, then another. The appropriate distance was now a little too far to speak easily.

'I actually didn't expect to see you here.' She looked uncomfortable now.

'Yeah, well, Cameron's my brother.'

'I know, but he said –' She stopped. 'Nathan, I didn't know that when I met him.' She held his gaze. 'I'm sorry.'

He made himself look her straight in the eye, and shrugged. 'Really doesn't bother me.'

Her face had hardened, and her smile was a fraction late. 'Good.'

Maybe Ilse hadn't known they were brothers, Nathan thought, but Cameron obviously had. And fine, Ilse was a grown woman and it wasn't like Nathan owned her after one roll around in the back of his car. And maybe he was

175

dead wrong, but Cameron hadn't even seemed that interested until Nathan had called up begging.

*'Please, Cam. There's a girl. A nice one. Working behind
the bar.'*

'Oh yeah. She's all right.'

Sophie had been born ten months later and Cameron
and Ilse had got married four months after that. Nathan
hadn't gone. Instead he'd driven eighteen hours to
Brisbane. He'd turned up on Jacqui's doorstep with his
custody agreement in hand and they'd screamed at each
other until someone called the cops.

Now, he watched as Ilse directed the girls to pick up
their toys. She seemed distracted and he got the sense that
she wanted to talk about something – Jenna Moore, he
guessed – but couldn't with her daughters in the room.
Instead, he pointed at the wall planner and the crossed-
out markings.

'What's all this? Was Cam going to change the mustering times next year?'

'Oh.' Ilse stood up and joined him in front of the calendar. 'No. I mean, it was a thought.'

Nathan frowned as he deciphered the notes. 'What
would it involve? Move them here, and here?'

'Yes, and same thing again, later.'

She took a thick diary from her desk and opened it so
he could see.

'Move the dates like this –' She pointed and her hand
brushed his arm. 'Avoid the bottlenecks, and that contractor clash with Atherton that happens every year. I
also thought if we coordinated with you – if you were

interested, obviously – but then we'd get the scale benefits.'

Nathan frowned, flipping through the pages of her neat writing. 'Yeah, maybe.'

'You think it could work?'

'I'd have to go through it properly. But it could be worth a try.'

'It was Bub's idea, actually. I just worked out the dates and the logistics.'

'Bub thought of this?' Nathan said, surprised.

'I think he was getting fed up with the same issues year after year and wanted to try something else. He's quite good at things like that. Cameron said it was because he was lazy, but if it makes things more efficient, who cares?'

Nathan could hear footsteps in the hall. The girls had gathered up the last toys. Lo appeared to be counting them carefully, checking each one, and Ilse frowned a little at the sight. The office door opened and they all looked up as Bub put his head in.

'Mum says come for dinner.'

He saw Nathan and Ilse examining the planner and a shadow crossed his face as the girls clattered past him into the hall.

'What are you talking about?' Bub came into the office. 'Something about this place?' *Without me?* went unsaid.

'I was telling Nathan about your mustering idea,' Ilse said and Bub looked slightly mollified.

'Oh. Yeah. Not bad, hey?'

Nathan nodded at the wall planner. 'Why is it all crossed off?'

'There were some kinks in the plan,' Ilse said. 'Cam wanted to work them out before making any big changes. He thought maybe leave it a year, make sure everything would work.'

'Yeah, right.' Bub made a noise. 'Look, Cam's not here now so I'm not going to bag the bloke, but we all know if Cam had thought of it first, we'd be doing it. Sorry, but that's how it was. The only thing wrong with the idea is that it wasn't Cam's bloody idea.'

Bub stepped closer to the planner, reading what Ilse had written. The office was quiet for a moment.

'We could do it now, though.' Bub's tone was too casual. 'Us three.'

Bub had been thinking about this, Nathan realised, as he turned to face them. There was something in the air as they stood there. Something almost complicit, Nathan thought, and not entirely comfortable. He wasn't sure what to say, so he didn't say anything and finally Bub shrugged.

'Whatever. Think about it.' He walked to the door. 'But there's nothing to stop us.'

They watched him go and Ilse shook her head, a strange expression on her face.

'Listen, what Bub said about it not being Cameron's idea. That wasn't the only reason. Bub knows that. Anyway –' She tossed the diary back on her desk. 'I don't know. I can't think about this now. The details are all in there if you want a better look.'

She headed out and Nathan followed her, turning off the light and plunging the office into darkness behind them. The kitchen was far too hot, and Nathan immediately felt frazzled.

'How'd you get on at Lehmann's?' Harry said as he sat down.

'Yeah, fixed it,' Nathan said. 'Nothing too serious.'

'You have to be careful at Lehmann's Hill.' The tiny voice seemed to come out of nowhere and it took Nathan a moment to realise it was Lo speaking. She was ignoring her dinner as she scrawled furiously on a piece of paper.

'What's that?' Ilse reached out and stroked her hair.

'Daddy was supposed to go to Lehmann's Hill and he never came back.'

Ilse's hand stilled on her daughter's head. 'Daddy didn't go to the hill, Lo. That has nothing to do with why he didn't come back.'

'I know that. I know why Daddy didn't come back.'

No-one said anything for a long moment.

'Why is that, Lo?' Harry's voice cut through the silence.

The girl raised her eyes and, realising everyone was watching her, looked straight down again.

'Lois? I asked you a question.'

'Nothing. It doesn't matter.' Lo's voice was barely audible.

Ilse put an arm around her. 'That's okay, sweetheart.'

'Let her talk, Ilse,' Harry said.

'She doesn't want to.'

'She did a second ago.'

'She's a child, Harry.'

'I want to know what she meant –'

'Ilse's right.' It was the first time Liz had spoken since they sat down. She had been crying again, Nathan

179

could tell. She had lost weight in the past few days, and the skin on her face looked slack. 'You're scaring her, Harry.'

Lo sat very still, her eyes on the table, then finally picked up her pencil and continued drawing.

'Daddy didn't come back because he was sad,' Lo said to the paper. 'About all those things going missing.'

There was an audible collective sigh of relief around the table.

'Oh God, this again. It's okay, Lo.' Ilse took her daughter's free hand and held it between her own. She saw Nathan and Xander's confusion. 'Lo was a bit scared for a while that there was a burglar –'

'There is!' Lo snatched her hand away. Her scribbling became more furious.

'Sweetheart, there's not –'

'Or a ghost, then.'

'No ghost either,' Ilse said. She gave a tiny shake of her head and looked at Nathan. 'She thought a few things had got lost. Some of your toys and bits and pieces went walkabout, didn't they, Lo?'

'They didn't go walkabout! Someone was here and took them.'

At the other end of the table, Simon gave an awkward laugh. 'Maybe it was Santa,' he said, trying to lighten the mood.

Lo gave him a look that could kill a cow. 'Not Santa.' She left the *dickhead* implied. 'Someone else. Someone bad.'

She was getting upset now and Ilse took the pencil from her hand.

'Lo, if someone was on the property, we would know. No-one has been here.' But as Ilse glanced at the night sky darkening in the window, Nathan caught a hesitation in her voice. 'We thought a few things had gone missing but we found them again, didn't we?'

'What kinds of things?' Xander shifted in his seat.

'My toys and clothes,' Lo said.

'But we found them,' Ilse replied firmly.

'Not all of them, and not straight away. Anyway,' Lo pushed her mother's hand away, 'Daddy never found his things.'

'What do you mean?' Harry said.

Lo didn't answer. She looked nervous. Her hand inched towards her confiscated pencil and she hid her face behind her hair.

'No,' Harry said, his voice unusually sharp. 'Answer please, Lo.'

'Sweetheart.' Ilse leaned in. 'What things?'

'Money, I think,' Lo whispered. Nathan was struggling to hear her. 'And other things. I don't know what. Daddy was searching but he couldn't find them.'

'How much money are we talking?' Harry said, and Ilse glared at him.

'For God's sake, she struggles to count to a hundred, she's not going to know that. Anyway, Cam wasn't missing money. Or anything else. Don't make things worse.'

Lo's eyebrows shot up. 'He was! He was, Mummy. He was looking everywhere. Someone has been here –'

'Jenna.'

The name floated out under someone's breath. Nathan wasn't sure who had spoken until Liz pointed sharply across the table.

'Shut it, Bub. I mean it.'

'– And Daddy *had* lost things.' Lo's voice was rising. 'I know, I saw him. He was looking in the sheds and the stables and everywhere. I knew you wouldn't believe me, Mummy.'

'It's not that.' Ilse's protest was almost drowned out by her daughter. 'If Daddy was missing something why didn't he say so?'

'Because he knew you wouldn't believe him either, like you don't believe me.' Lo was shouting now. 'That's probably why he said to keep it a secret.'

There was a sharp silence and Lo put her hand over her mouth as though trying to claw back the words. Her tiny face was flushed an ugly red.

Ilse was very still. Her eyes flicked to her older daughter, who looked shocked. Sophie shook her head. *No idea.* Ilse turned Lo around in her seat so they were facing each other. 'Lo, this is very important, what exactly did Daddy say?'

Lo shook her head, silent once more.

'For God's sake –' Harry sounded frustrated.

'Harry.' The warning note in Liz's tone was clear. Outside, the dingoes had started howling again. They sounded close.

'Lo, it's okay.' Ilse leaned in so her face was level with her daughter's. 'You're not in any trouble. Just tell the truth. You're sure Daddy was looking for something?'

The little girl's face was pinched and anxious. 'Yes, I saw him.'

'And Daddy told you to keep it a secret from everyone?'

'Not everyone.' Lo looked at her mother. 'Just you.'

Chapter 17

Nathan sat on the porch watching the night creep in. The red from the ground and the sky bled into one until they both deepened to black. Lo had been unable – or unwilling – to offer any more useful information, and Ilse had eventually taken her off to bed.

Nathan had been putting Cameron's instruction manuals away when he'd discovered a guitar in the hall cupboard. Xander was reading in his room, so Nathan took Duffy and sat on the verandah. The guitar was out of tune and the discordant notes jarred as he tightened the pegs. Across the yard, the lights were still on in the back-packers' caravan and he could hear the murmur of voices. He couldn't make out the words, but from the tone it sounded like an argument. Beyond the caravan, he could see nothing. He played softly, trying to get an ending right when he heard the screen door open and looked up.

'That's my guitar.'

Sophie was leaning against the door, her head haloed by the yellow light.

'Sorry. I found it.'

'It's okay. Did you write that song?' She sat down opposite as he started playing again.

'Yeah. Nearly ten years ago.'

'Does it have a name?'

He'd written it for Ilse. 'No,' he said. 'Untitled. What do you think?'

'I don't know. It sounds kind of sad. But hopeful. Kind of. You could call it "Sunrise" or something.'

'Good name.' More appropriate than 'For Ilse' at any rate. He played some more.

'It's nice. The ending's not right, though.'

'No. I know. I've never been able to work it out exactly.'

'If you haven't got it after ten years, maybe you should give up.'

'I think you're probably right.' Nathan smiled at her. 'So you play?'

'When I don't have this.' Sophie held up her sling, then listened for a bit longer. 'You're really good.'

'I have a lot of time to practise.' He tried not to sound bitter.

'Do you play every day?'

'If I can. Since I was your age, probably.'

'That's such a long time.' She looked so staggered he had to laugh. 'Every day?'

'Pretty much. Except for a couple of years when I didn't have a guitar anymore.'

'Why didn't you?'

Nathan's smile faded. 'It got damaged.'

It was actually his clearest memory of his dad, which was

surprising because it was far from the worst. It had been the day Nathan and Cam had tried to run away and Carl Bright had rounded them up at the stockman's grave. Nathan could still remember sitting in the truck, looking at the back of his dad's head and wishing he would just start shouting. It was the stillness that scared him. They did not see another car or person the whole drive home, Nathan remembered clearly. That wasn't at all unusual, but that day he had noticed. There was no-one else around.

Nathan had been sure he'd known what was waiting for them when they got back, but to his surprise Carl had got out of the car without a word, leaving his sons looking at each other. They'd walked on eggshells all day, waiting. It was only late that evening, after Harry finally said good night and headed off to his own cabin away from the house, that Carl had at last looked their way. It was almost a relief when he'd murmured under his breath: 'Outside, both of you.'

Nathan had braced himself, trying to control his reaction. Carl didn't like it when his sons looked afraid. He had told them to build a fire and both boys had gaped at him until he'd said it louder, grabbing Nathan by the shoulder and pushing him towards the woodpile. They'd staggered over, bewildered.

Carl hadn't spoken again until they'd got a decent bonfire going. His face flickered in the light as he instructed them in a disturbingly soft voice to go inside and each bring out their favourite possession. Nathan had a tight, hot knot in his chest as he'd eventually wheeled out his bike.

'Nice try.' His dad had gripped his arm so hard he could already feel the bruise forming. 'Get it right next time or I'll burn everything you bring until you do.'

Nathan had gone inside for a long time, and finally come out with his beloved guitar. His hand had sweated and slipped against its wooden neck and, despite knowing it would make things worse, he had cried and begged his dad not to do it.

Liz had been there as well, tears in her own eyes. 'Please, Carl,' she had tried. 'Can't he keep his guitar?'

Her husband had ignored her and she'd tried again, until he'd finally turned from his sons to look at her.

'You want me to teach them this a different way?' he'd said in a way that made Nathan glad Liz didn't ask again.

Nathan had held out the guitar, barely able to see though his tears, but his dad had made him throw it on the fire himself. Nathan had finally done so, then reflexively tried to snatch it out. He'd burned his arm and still had a scar.

Cameron had got his selection right first time, of course. He had brought out an illustrated history of stories from World War II. Nathan thought it was bloody boring but Cam had been fascinated by it. Cameron had actually looked Carl in the eye, craning his neck upwards to do so, as he'd thrown the book on the fire. Then he'd said something, under his breath. The words were almost, but not quite, lost in the crackle of the flames.

Carl had gone very still. 'Say that again.'

Cameron hesitated, then opened his mouth. When he spoke, he actually raised his voice a fraction. 'Nazis burned books.'

Liz had sucked in a breath so sharp it squeaked, her shoulders high. There had been a terrible silence, then to Nathan's astonishment, Carl had very nearly smiled. A hard, toothy twitch of his lips. He had seemed almost amused as he stared at Cameron. He had clenched and unclenched his fist, just once, then opened his mouth.

'Get the rest.'

Cameron had obeyed without flinching. He disappeared inside, returning a few minutes later with his books piled in his arms. Nathan sat on the steps with Liz and watched as Cam threw them into the flames one at a time. Cameron's eyes had been completely dry as he watched them burn.

'Apologise to your dad,' Liz said after the first five. Cameron ignored her, tossing another book on the pyre while Carl watched his son with an expression that Nathan had never seen before. He was struck by the sense that on some level, they were both getting a strange enjoyment out of the stand-off.

The whole thing took more than an hour. Finally, as the last book was burning and Nathan was nervously glancing at the house, wondering what would happen next, Cameron had looked Carl in the eye.

'Sorry, Dad.' He'd dropped his gaze, finally contrite.

Nathan felt Liz go slack. Even Carl had seemed a little relieved, as the embers glowed in the hot night air. He had looked at Cameron, as though trying to work something out, then turned to Nathan with a far more familiar look.

'Either of you ever try this bullshit again, I promise you it will be ten times worse. And not just for you two.'

Nathan had felt Liz tense again, and after that, for a

long time, both he and Cameron had done exactly what they were told.

On the verandah now, sitting opposite Sophie, Nathan's fingers stopped moving on the strings. He didn't feel like playing anymore. Sophie didn't notice straight away. She was glancing back at the house, towards her sister's darkened bedroom window.

'Any idea what Lo was talking about at dinner?' Nathan said.

'No.' Sophie picked at her sling. 'She probably doesn't know herself. She has trouble with make-believe stuff.'

'She seemed scared,' Nathan said.

'She is. She thinks someone's coming to get her.'

'Someone imaginary? Like the stockman? Or does she actually believe someone's out there?'

'I don't know. I've told her that she doesn't have to worry. She still does, though.'

'It must be hard for you two, after what's happened with your dad.'

Sophie nodded but said nothing.

'Did your dad ever mention the stockman's grave to you?' Nathan said. 'Talk about it being somewhere special to him?'

'I don't think so. There was his picture, I suppose. But I never knew why he painted it, he thought the stockman was stupid. And he was.'

'Oh yeah?'

'He shot himself by mistake. Climbing through a fence and not paying attention. His foot slipped and he accidentally blew his own head off with his gun.'

'Who told you that?

'Daddy.'

'Right.' It wasn't true, but Nathan thought now wasn't the time to correct her. Her memories of her dad would be confused enough, without him pulling minor ones apart.

Sophie sighed and looked at the guitar. 'Can you play something else?'

'Happy to take requests.'

She named a song he didn't know by a band he'd never heard of, so she hummed it and he managed to pick it up. By the end, she was smiling a little, mostly at his mistakes.

'I'm going to practise when my arm's better,' she said. 'While there's no school.'

She meant School of the Air, Nathan knew. He had gone through all that himself, mucking around while he was supposed to be listening in to some faraway teacher crackling on the radio. Much of the teaching burden fell to whoever was supervising at home though and he remembered poor Liz trying her best and pleading with him to concentrate the way Cameron did. It was all done online now, mirroring the term times and lesson structures of a physical school as closely as possible. The teachers could at least video chat with students for a couple of contact hours a day, which had to be better than the radio, he guessed. He thought of something and frowned. 'So Katy supervises your home learning?'

'Yeah. It used to be Mummy, but now Katy does it. She's supposed to look after us during the day when we're on holiday.'

He saw her face. 'No good?'

'It's boring. She doesn't have any fun ideas. The day Daddy went missing she just made us sit in the classroom and watch movies the whole time.'

'Was she with you?'

'Yeah, she was there, but she didn't do anything. She kept going on breaks and she's always kind of moody.'

'Is she any better at supervising the school stuff?'

Sophie wrinkled her nose. 'Not really. She doesn't know what we're supposed to be doing and she doesn't always make sure we keep up. I heard Mum tell Daddy he shouldn't have hired her, that she's –' she lowered her voice to a whisper and looked left and right, '– crap.'

Nathan suppressed a smile. 'That's what your mum said?'

'That's one of the things. But I think Mummy's right, she is . . . crap.' Sophie leaned in. 'I don't think she's even really a teacher.'

'No?' The light was still glowing in the caravan. 'What makes you say that?'

'She cut our hair,' Sophie said. 'Nicely. I think she's a hairdresser.'

Nathan looked at Sophie's hair. It was a shoulder-length bob, with crisp edges all the way around. Nathan did not claim to be an expert; his own routine involved waiting until his hair grew too thick and shaggy to cope with, then shaving it all off over his bathroom sink. But even to him, the cut looked pretty professional.

Nathan eyed the caravan again. Behind the thin curtain, he could see someone moving in the glow of the lamplight. The faint sound of voices drifted over. They were still arguing. A hairdresser, not a teacher, Nathan

wondered. It wasn't uncommon for travellers to embroi-
der their resumes. In fact, it was unusual for them not to.
But it always posed the obvious question: If they weren't
who they claimed to be, then who were they?

'We came back from a ride one day and they were both
here,' Sophie said. 'Daddy didn't even tell us they were
coming. I think that's why Mum was annoyed.'

'Why was I annoyed?' There was a gentle screech from
the screen door and Ilse appeared.

'About Simon and Katy coming here,' Sophie said.

'Oh.' Ilse frowned. 'No. It was a surprise, that's all.
Don't go around saying that please, Sophie. They'll feel
unwelcome.'

'How's Lo?' Nathan asked.

'Asleep in your mum's room.' Ilse beckoned to her
daughter. 'Your turn now.'

'But –'

'Sophie. Please. Not tonight.'

Grudgingly, Sophie stood up. 'Good night.' She
looked at her mother, belligerent. 'Are you coming to
tuck me in?'

'In a minute,' Ilse said. 'Go and get ready.'

The screen door slammed. Even lit from behind, Ilse
looked exhausted as she came out and leaned against the
railing. She opened her mouth but said nothing, as though
unsure where to start.

'What do you make of what Lo said earlier?' asked
Nathan, by way of an opening.

'I don't even know what to think. Cameron never
said anything to me. Obviously.' There was a sour note

in her voice as she stared out into the darkness. 'Not to mention that whole thing with that woman trying to contact him.'

'Cam told you about Jenna, though?'

'Of course.' Ilse's face clouded. 'He said she was a girl he met at a party once whose boyfriend got jealous. He made it sound funny. Like a misunderstanding.'

Nathan didn't say anything. It had been a lot of things, but funny wasn't one of them.

'He'd been so stressed lately. He was –' Ilse stared into the dark. 'Something had changed these past few weeks. Probably around the time she tried to get in touch, I realise now.'

'It would have been a bit of a shock, I suppose.'

'Yes. I imagine it was.'

Ilse looked at Nathan. He could hear the gentle rush of the night wind. A small voice floated out from inside the house.

'Mummy. I'm ready.'

'In a minute,' Ilse called, then turned back to Nathan, more urgent now. 'Listen, no-one actually believed what that girl said about Cameron, did they?'

'No. Of course not.' He opened his mouth again, then stopped.

'What? Tell me.'

'It's nothing, really. I was just going to say –' He wavered. 'Maybe Steve did, for a while.'

'Steve Fitzgerald? At the clinic?'

'Yeah. Maybe. Not believed her exactly,' Nathan said, trying to remember. 'I mean, he took it seriously, I suppose. That's his job though, isn't it? As a nurse. And he's that type as well.'

He was put in mind of Steve's constant nagging. His unannounced visits and constant questions and his insistence that Nathan come to the clinic. He was persistent to the point of intrusion.

'Not seriously enough for it to turn into a formal issue, though,' Ilse said.

'No. It didn't go anything like that far.'

Ilse exhaled slowly. 'Cameron never really got on with Steve.'

'No. Well, I guess you tend to remember things like that.'

Sophie's voice called out again. 'Mummy!'

Ilse ignored it this time, keeping her eyes on Nathan. 'You always believed Cam?'

'Yes. Absolutely.'

'No doubt at all?'

There was a strange note in the air that Nathan couldn't quite place. Her face was hard to read in the weak porch light, and he squirmed a little as he felt a long-buried guilt resurface. Cameron may not have told his wife everything, but looking at her now, Nathan could bet he had told her some things.

'No,' he said firmly. 'No doubt.'

Ilse's face altered a fraction into another expression he couldn't interpret. Sophie's voice rang out again.

'For God's sake. I'd better go.' She opened the door and paused for a moment. 'Good night, Nathan.'

'Good night.'

She disappeared inside and Nathan looked down at Duffy, who wagged her tail and offered no comment. Nathan sat there for a minute longer, then put Sophie's guitar down and wandered down the verandah steps and out into the dark of the yard, Duffy at his heels. He waited for his eyes to adjust. All was quiet from the back-packers' caravan. They must have made their peace, for now at least.

When he could see well enough to make out Carl Bright's grave underneath the gum tree, he walked over and stood at the edge, unable to shake the feeling that he'd stuffed up. He'd meant to reassure Ilse, but could tell he'd missed the mark. He had fallen short in defending Cameron, and not for the first time. Nathan looked down at where his dad lay.

'What's this bullshit I hear about some girl?' Carl had said. He'd hung up his call from the sergeant and summoned his two eldest sons.

Nathan remembered hovering, his back against the wall, as Cameron stuttered through an explanation. After a minute, Carl had cut him short and turned to Nathan.

'Where were you when this was going on? Sniffing after that little bitch next door?'

'Jacqui, you mean.'

The back of Nathan's head bounced against the wall with a sharp smack. Carl hadn't even bothered to look at him properly as he'd lifted an arm and taken a swipe, his attention focused on Cameron. The blow had come too fast for Nathan to defend himself; not that he necessarily would have anyway. Sometimes it was easier not to. He realised Carl was still waiting for an answer and this time Nathan just nodded. *Yeah, I was with Jacqui.*

'Why weren't you looking out for your brother?'

Nathan had no idea what to say to that.

'You saw them, though?' Carl was pointing at Cam, but shouting at Nathan. 'Go on, then. Tell me. Has he done something I need to worry about?'

Carl's eyes were on him now. Their gazes drew level these days, and Nathan wondered why he was still flooded with the same terror he'd felt his whole life. The feeling that came whenever Carl raised his voice or his hands or both. When Nathan had been forced to burn his guitar.

It would never change, Nathan realised with a terrible flash of clarity. Carl wouldn't stop and Nathan didn't seem to be able to make him, so perhaps they were stuck like this for the rest of their lives. He was exhausted by the thought. His head hurt from the blow. He looked at Cameron, and whatever his brother had or hadn't done, Nathan was suddenly sick of it all.

He didn't want any of this. It wasn't him bringing that kind of trouble home. He at least had the bloody sense to check he had the nod from Jacqui before he took her pants off. Nathan's head was still ringing as he looked from Carl to Cameron and all at once he didn't want to be near either of these men. He wanted to be all alone, somewhere far away. He was still thinking about that when Cameron brushed his arm lightly with his elbow, and brought him back with a jolt. Nathan realised his mistake and opened his mouth and did what he would expect Cam to do for him. Have his back.

'No,' he said. 'Cam didn't do anything.'

In reality, the answer had come only a beat late. Not even that; half a beat. A delay so slight it was barely discernible. But Carl had noticed it, as his eyes slid from one son to the other.

'Right,' he said, in a voice that suggested that, for once, he understood his boys perfectly. 'Leave. I need to talk to your brother.' And with that, Nathan was dismissed.

He had sat in his car with the doors shut so he couldn't hear anything coming from the house. He saw Bub sneak out and opened the passenger door to let him climb in. He could tell Bub wanted to ask questions, and Nathan felt he should try to answer, but when neither found the words they simply sat together in shamed silence.

Nathan, already guilt-ridden, used the time to rehearse in his head what he would say to Cameron. *I didn't mean to hesitate. It meant nothing.* He'd learned a long time ago to think first and talk second, because Carl did not like getting the wrong answer. *I was scared, Cam. I was scared of Dad. I'm sorry. I know you didn't do anything wrong.* Nathan wanted to say all that and more to Cameron, and he did, later, several times. It made no difference.

It took a long time for Cameron to look Nathan in the eye again. When he did, it was through a shadow of betrayal that never, in twenty years, fully went away.

Chapter 18

Xander's room was empty when Nathan went back inside, but he could hear the shower running in the bathroom. A half-read book lay open on Xander's bed. It was the same book Nathan had bought to give his son for Christmas, he noticed with annoyance. The card being used as a bookmark indicated it was a gift from Xander's stepfather, Martin, an architect whose work with dazzling reflective polished metal surfaces was occasionally described in newspapers as 'polarising'. Nathan took a deep breath, closed the door and walked back to the living room.

Through the window, he could still make out the dark outline of the backpackers' caravan. He watched it for a minute, thinking about what Sophie said, then turned and fired up the family computer on the desk in the corner. Ten minutes later he had managed to access the wheezing internet and was waiting for a social media site to flicker to life. When it finally loaded, he clicked on the search bar and typed in Katy's name.

The computer grunted as Nathan scrolled through the search results slowly the first time, then twice more. Nothing. Nothing that he could see, anyway. There were plenty of people with the same name as Katy, but none with a profile or picture that seemed to match. He checked his watch. Not long until the generator went down for the night. He tapped in Simon's name next, scrolling as fast as the groaning technology would let him. He was on the third page when the floorboards in the hall creaked. Harry appeared in the doorway. He glanced at the computer but couldn't see the screen from where he stood.

'I've been talking to Bub,' he said.

'Oh yeah?' From his face, Nathan could guess what this was about.

'And we both know Bub gets things wrong from time to time,' Harry said.

'Sometimes.'

'So I'm seriously hoping he's wrong about you not having your gun licence anymore.'

'I didn't get around to renewing it.'

'Bullshit. What, for the first time in your life it slipped your mind, did it?'

Nathan said nothing.

'You've surrendered all your weapons to Glenn?'

'Those are the rules, Harry.'

'It's basic equipment, mate —'

'I'll get it renewed.'

'You're all the way out there on your own. You turn your radio off for days at a time —'

'Jesus, Harry, I said I'll renew it.'

'Does your mum know that's how you're living?'

'I'm sure you'll tell her.'

'Does Xander?'

The question hung in the air.

'Did you want something else, Harry?' Nathan said at last, his voice cold.

Harry gazed back, unmoved, until Nathan was the one to look away. 'Generator's going off in ten.'

He disappeared from the doorway and Nathan stared at the computer screen until the glow made his eyes water. He blinked, then checked the time again. Progress had been slow, but he'd seen enough to know that there wasn't much to be found of the backpackers online.

That wasn't unheard of. But it was unusual. Nathan could count on one hand the number of backpackers he'd known to resist the temptation to upload a string of identical photos of rocks and sky and cows for the folks back home. He looked at the clock once more, then, as fast as the computer would allow, opened a fresh search window and typed in a new name. There were a lot of results for Jenna Moores in the UK. He might have been sifting through them for hours if someone hadn't already beaten him to it.

A link came up right at the top, the different-coloured font showing it had already been clicked on at least once before on that computer. Nathan had no idea if it was possible to find out when. Maybe Xander would know. For now, he clicked on the link again.

She had become a florist. She ran her own business and there was a photo of her planting something tall and green into a pot. The braid was gone and the twenty-odd years were visible on her face, but it was her.

Her photographic smile was wide but slightly stilted and Nathan got the impression several attempts had been made to get the shot right. Jenna's fingers were partly buried in soil, but he could see no wedding ring. He wondered what Jenna's boyfriend from the time was up to these days but he couldn't remember the guy's name. He wasn't sure he'd ever known it. He looked at Jenna's face. There was a phone number at the top of the screen. Nathan reached for a pen, wrote it down and stood up.

The hallway was empty and the kitchen and Ilse's office were both dark as he picked up the phone and dialled. He listened to the ringtone, and was just realising he had no idea what time it was in England, when someone answered.

'Good morning, Northern Blooms.' The voice was chirpy.

'Is Jenna Moore there, please?'

'She's on leave, I'm afraid. Can I help you with something?'

Nathan hesitated. 'She was trying to get in touch with my brother.' He waited, but there was no discernible reaction down the line. 'I wanted to pass on some information. Does she have another number I can try?'

'Oh. No, I'm sorry.' The girl sounded genuinely apologetic. 'Not one I can give out, unfortunately. But it wouldn't be much help anyway, she's abroad and out of mobile range.'

Nathan looked at the landline cord in his hand. 'Really.'

'I can take your number if you like.'

'I'm actually out of mobile range myself, as a matter of fact.'

'Are you?' The girl sounded amused by the novelty. 'I don't suppose you're on a yoga retreat in Bali, by any chance?'

'No,' Nathan said. 'No, I'm not.'

'I suppose that would be too much of a coincidence.' She laughed. In his other ear, Nathan heard a soft electronic *whump* and he was plunged into darkness. The generator was off. The vanished light from the hall left a ghostly glow in his eyes. He blinked, temporarily blind.

'Where are you based?' he said, as the grey outlines of furniture slowly started to take shape.

'At the end of Bell Street.'

'Sorry, I meant which city?'

'Oh. Manchester.'

Nathan wasn't sure where that was. Somewhere northern, he guessed.

'Anyway,' the voice was saying, 'she'll be back in the store in – bear with me – eleven days, if you'd like to try her again?'

It was then that Nathan heard the noise. Not on the phone. Something at his end, faint in the night's stillness. Harry, maybe? The window beside him was a black square. He could see nothing but his own reflection in the glass.

'Jenna's definitely still in Bali?' he said. He heard the noise again and looked over his shoulder. Had it come from inside the house? He held his breath. Another soft thud. No, it was outside. He turned back to the window. Still nothing.

'Yes. Not looking forward to coming back to the freezing weather. She says it's almost *too* hot, if you can imagine.'

'Is that right?' Nathan looked out into the inky darkness. 'Well, thanks for your help.'

'You're welcome. And thank you for your interest in Northern Blooms!'

Nathan hung up. Outside the yard was black. There was no movement at all. He waited a minute, then two. Nothing. He was about to turn away when he heard the noise again.

Chapter 19

Nathan stepped into the dark and waited for his eyes to adjust to the sliver of moonlight. The back door creaked behind him and he pulled it shut. He stood patiently and listened.

A muffled thump.

He followed the noise around the side of the house. A glow seeped out from under the garage door, soft, but enough to ruin his night vision. He walked over slowly, telling himself not to be ridiculous while still treading quietly. He recognised the back of the head immediately. It was half-in, half-out of a low cupboard, the shadows stark under a battery-powered hurricane lamp.

'And here I am, thinking this is my big chance to catch Lo's burglar red-handed,' Nathan said, leaning against the door. The head turned and Xander looked up.

'What's going on?' Nathan nodded at the cupboard Xander was searching through. 'Couldn't sleep?'

'No.' Xander stood up and wiped his hands on his

jeans. 'I keep thinking about what Lo said about Uncle Cam looking for something.'

'Sophie thought she might be confused.'

Xander ran the back of his hand across his forehead, leaving a dusty smear. 'What did Ilse say about it?'

'I don't know. She hasn't really talked to me about it.'

'Oh, right. I just thought she might have.'

Nathan pulled up a cracked plastic chair and sat down. The garage had doubled as a bolthole for Cameron, by the look of things, with benchtop space and a battered desk in the corner.

'You found anything, then?'

'No. Doesn't help not knowing what to search for. Could be anything. Or nothing, I suppose.'

Nathan looked at Xander. Every time he saw his son these days he seemed more grown-up. But now, standing there with his shoulders and back broadening out and dust on his hands, he looked like a man.

'Where have you looked?'

'Around here, so far.' Xander waved a hand at one side of the garage.

'Think you'll be out here much longer?'

'I don't know. Till I find something, I guess. Or get too tired.' He shrugged.

'I'd better give you a hand then.' Nathan pulled himself up. He opened the nearest storage cupboard and came face to face with neatly stacked tools.

'I've already checked there. Maybe try that one.' Xander pointed.

'Okay.' Nathan moved across. He didn't expect to find

anything — he had no idea whether Lo was right about Cam's missing items, but even if she was, he couldn't imagine that his brother hadn't thought to look in his own garage. He suspected Xander felt the same, but he knew that sometimes there was value in doing something, anything, even if that something was rifling through dusty drawers. They worked side by side, developing a sort of rhythm as they moved through the garage. Open, check, close. He kept an eye on where he was putting his hands and feet, though. There were plenty of snakes around those parts that he really did not want to catch by surprise.

The work might seem pointless, but Nathan was happy to do it if it made Xander feel better. When Nathan and Jacqui had got married, she'd had to insist on a baby. He'd never actually agreed, but he hadn't exercised his options to resist either, so it had happened. Whatever their differences, he was still grateful to Jacqui for that. He sometimes thought he wouldn't have minded another couple of kids, if things had turned out differently.

Nathan had felt pretty detached during her pregnancy, only wading in when he'd had to save the kid from some of her bullshit name suggestions. He hadn't been crash hot about Xander, and still wasn't, to be honest. It wasn't even Alex, which at least sounded okay shouted across a paddock. Only when Jacqui had started musing about the potential of Jasper had Nathan thrown his wholehearted support behind naming their son Alexander.

She'd been right in the end, Nathan thought. Xander was a good fit for the lifestyle his kid had ended up leading.

'So, you're planning on going to uni, hey?' Nathan

said, and Xander looked up from the box he was sifting through. 'That's great.'

'Oh. Yeah. Thanks.'

'Need to get good marks for that, I suppose.'

'Yeah.'

'Listen, your mum said you'd probably need to stay in Brisbane during the holidays now. Have time to study a bit more, do your homework properly.'

There was a pause. 'I might do.'

'Because if you do –' Nathan made himself say it. 'That's fine, mate. Whatever you need to do is fine with me. I mean, you're always welcome to bring your books here. Nice and quiet. I wouldn't get in your way –'

'It's mostly online. I need fast internet.'

'Oh, right. Yeah. Better in Brisbane. Makes sense.'

'I'm sorry.'

'It's fine. Honestly, mate.'

'It's not that I don't like visiting –'

'I know.'

'– because I do. It's –'

'Mate, I know. You've got things you need to focus on. I get it. And you should do it. Get the marks. Go to uni. You're smart enough for it.'

'Thanks.' Xander gave a small smile. 'You never wanted to go?'

Nathan shook his head. 'Not for me.'

In fact, he had never considered it, always assuming he would end up back on the property, where the cattle didn't ask to see your qualifications. Then Cameron had surprised him by applying to a uni course in Adelaide. He'd come back three years later with a degree in agribusiness, a lot of big ideas, and a handful of new friends who occasionally came to get dust on their inappropriate city shoes and look around in wide-eyed amusement. When they spoke to Nathan at all, it was in voices a little louder and slower than normal.

'It's weird,' Xander said, his hands in an open box. 'Going through someone's stuff after they're gone. All these things that were important to Uncle Cam, and now someone else has to get rid of it all, or whatever.'

'Yeah. They'll still need a lot of this, though,' Nathan said. 'Property still needs to be run.'

'By you?'

'I have enough trouble with my own place.'

'Who then? Bub?'

'They'll hire a manager, probably. I guess Ilse will decide. She gets Cam's half.'

Xander ran his finger through the thin layer of dust on the lid of a battered storage box. 'Cam didn't give Bub a bigger share? Or leave anything for Harry?'

'Doesn't sound like it. Bub still has his third, though.'

'Yeah, but you and Ilse have the rest.'

Something in the way he said it made Nathan look over in surprise. 'So?'

'So nothing, I suppose. But her half plus your sixth makes a majority. I wonder how Bub feels about that?'

'He shouldn't feel anything, it's exactly the same split as it was with Cam.'

'But it's not the same, is it? When Cam was alive, it was him and Bub controlling the place –'

'I'm not sure Bub saw it like that.' Nathan thought about his brother scowling at the calendar in the study.

'Well, either way, it was clearly you in the minority. Now it'll be more like you and Ilse in control. It's a different dynamic.'

'It's not. There's nothing –'

'Dad, mate,' Xander said, a half-smile on his face. 'It is.'

Nathan felt a flush creep up his neck. He didn't reply.

'Don't worry,' Xander said, reading his mind. 'I don't think anyone else has noticed. You should think about it, though. When it comes to decisions, who would you side with? Ilse or Bub?'

'Neither. I'd do what's best for the property.' Nathan saw his son's expression. 'I would.'

'All right. Does Bub know that, though? Or Ilse?'

'Yeah, of course.' Nathan frowned. Of course they knew, because it was the truth.

'Well, that's okay then.' Xander opened another cupboard.

Nathan pulled a new box off a shelf. It seemed to hold nothing more than old electrical wiring. He stifled a yawn. He was getting tired now, but didn't want to be the one to pull the pin. He sifted through it half-heartedly, looking at the black square of night outside the door. There was nothing to see, but Nathan knew he was facing south. Somewhere in the distance lay the stockman's grave and beyond that, his own property.

His house would be empty, over the invisible horizon, but he could almost feel it sucking him in. It was actually a pretty decent house, with nice enough furniture. Jacqui hadn't bothered taking a single thing other than Xander when she'd left. It was the land around the house that was the problem. It was a constant headache, but it was Nathan's livelihood and he simply could not afford to let it slide, not even a bit. But sometimes, all the time really, he wished he had somewhere else to go. He hated that house. The place felt like a black hole that extinguished all the light in his life.

He had seriously considered abandoning the property, several times. Downing tools, leaving the door swinging open and driving away. Maybe try to get some work in the mines out west, but he worried he was getting a bit old for that now. And while Nathan could abandon the land, he couldn't abandon the debts on it. They stayed on the bank's balance sheets and would still need to be paid off somehow. Thank God that Liz and Harry had convinced him to keep his sixth of Burley Downs. After expenses, the income from that wasn't enough to keep him afloat, but at least it was something.

'Sell your place to Cam,' Harry had said two Christmases ago, after a particularly bad year had left Nathan white-faced with stress. 'You're always going to struggle on your own. Let him buy you out, mate. Get the scale.'

Nathan had said he'd think about it. By that point, he had already privately asked his brother three times. Cam would dutifully pore over the spreadsheet Nathan had prepared, asking questions and stroking his chin as Nathan tried to find positive answers where none existed. Cam always responded in the same way, whether Nathan was asking him to look at a spreadsheet or begging him years earlier to put in a good word in town.

Cam would pause, for a fraction of a beat. Just as Nathan had done, once, under their dad's hard stare when the tables were turned and it was a teenage Cameron who needed the help. It still surprised Nathan how much could be conveyed in such a thin slice of silence.

Cameron's answer was always no.

Now, though, as Nathan looked out to the south, a new thought edged to the surface. Xander was right. And Bub, for that matter. Without Cam, things were different. Without Cam, Nathan realised, he could probably push the sale through, if he could get Ilse or Bub to agree. He let himself imagine for a moment what that might mean and suddenly, for the first time since he had driven over the crest and seen Cameron's body under the tarp, Nathan could breathe a little more easily.

'Dad.'

He dragged his attention back to the garage. Xander was holding something square and heavy-looking and partially covered by bubble wrap. A large paper bag lay discarded by his feet.

'What's that?' Nathan dusted off his hands and walked over. He could see Cameron had written Ilse's name on the bag in neat capital letters.

Xander moved into the light so Nathan could see what he was holding. It was one of Lo's paintings, and it had been professionally framed. It showed a family of four, with Cameron fully recognisable alongside his wife and two daughters. Everyone in Lo's picture was smiling, for once.

'There's a card as well.' Xander held it out.

It was a small square with a picture of lilies on the front. Nathan could tell from Xander's face that he'd already read what was inside. Nathan opened it and read the words in Cameron's distinctive handwriting.

Forgive me.

Chapter 20

In the morning, Ilse was already gone.

Nathan had woken far later than usual, opening his eyes to find daylight creeping through the curtains in the living room. He and Xander had stayed up too long, the hurricane lamp burning in the garage as they sat and stared at Cameron's words.

Forgive me.

Eventually, Nathan had taken the card and put it in his pocket.

'You going to show it to Ilse?' Xander had said.

'Yeah. Tomorrow.'

But the house was quiet as Nathan dressed. From the window, he could make out the small shapes of Sophie and Lo playing some sort of game in the garden, while Liz watched. Even from that distance, Nathan could see the slump to her shoulders, and the exhausted curve of her spine. There was no sign of Ilse with them.

Neither was she in the kitchen, where Katy was cleaning up alone, or in her office. Nathan walked back down the hall and checked on Xander, who was still sleeping. Relaxed against the pillow, his face looked younger than it had the night before. Nathan closed the door. Across the hallway was the girls' bedroom. It had been Cameron's room when they were kids. Nathan stood, remembering all those bleary-eyed pre-dawn mornings when he had opened his door and come face to face with his brother. Since taking over the property, Cameron had slept in the master bedroom at the end of the hall. Cameron and Ilse, anyway. Liz had moved to the smaller bedroom along from the girls, where she'd said she was happier.

The door of the master bedroom was open, and Nathan wandered up and peered inside. The big items of furniture didn't look like they had been replaced since the room had belonged to his mum and dad, but the space was unfamiliar beyond that. Someone, Ilse presumably, had painted the walls and added photos of the girls and a few other personal touches.

The room looked cared for but now felt – Nathan tried to put his finger on it – disturbed. The bed was made, but badly, and the deep dents in the pillows hinted at a poor night's sleep. Old coffee cups left clusters of rings on the bedside table, on Ilse's side, he guessed. A bottle of pain-killers stood among them with its cap off. A few pills were scattered loose beside the cups.

Nathan glanced back at the girls' room, then at the bottle on the table. He hesitated, then walked in, the floorboards creaking loudly under his boots. He gathered up the loose pills, tipped them into the bottle and clicked the safety cap on. He checked the label. It was only over-the-counter paracetamol, but there were a lot of tablets in the bottle. He stood there for a while, then returned the bottle to where he'd found it.

He stepped out into the hall and grunted as he collided heavily with someone in the shadows. They both stumbled. It took Nathan a beat to place the man in front of him in the dim light.

Simon.

Simon's gaze flicked past Nathan to the bedroom behind him, then settled with an expression that was hard to read.

'I've been trying to find you,' he said.

'I was looking for Ilse.' Nathan could hear the defensive note in his tone and cleared his throat. He didn't have to explain.

'She went riding along the drive about an hour ago.'

'Oh. Thanks. And what did you want?'

'Phone call for you.'

'For me?' Nathan couldn't think of a single person who would want to speak to him. 'Who is it?'

Simon shrugged. 'Someone you've been trying to reach, apparently.'

It was the electrical contractor.

'Dave,' Nathan said, as he heard the man's voice. 'How's my coolroom?'

'I couldn't tell you, mate. I was out at your place on Friday like we arranged, but I couldn't get in.'

'To the coolroom?'

'To your house. It was locked.'

'But –' Nathan squeezed his eyes shut. 'Shit.'

215

The only time he ever bothered to lock his doors was when Xander was staying. The chance of the kid's laptop getting stolen was zero, but it seemed to make Xander feel better. Dave's voice was crystal clear down the line. That didn't bode well. He must be somewhere well populated. 'Please tell me you're still in the area,' Nathan said anyway.

'Nup, sorry. Had to head home. Christmas with the kids.'

'Christ.' Nathan had been waiting three weeks for the contractor to get enough jobs to make the trip from St Helens worth his while. 'You couldn't have broken in?'

'Well, I could have.' Dave sounded mildly offended. 'But I didn't know how you'd feel about that.'

'I would have felt fine about it. I need the bloody thing working.'

Dave allowed a brief silence to convey his displeasure with Nathan's tone. Nathan took a breath.

'Sorry, mate. Not your fault. When are you coming back?'

'Not 'til the first week of Feb.'

'February!'

'And only if another couple of jobs come in.'

'I can't wait until then. I need it fixed now. Harry reckons the water might be coming.'

'If it floods, I'll be even longer.'

'So what am I supposed to do?'

'Look, I can talk you through a few ideas,' Dave said. 'Got a pen?'

Nathan scrabbled about and found one under the phone. The battered family log book lay open on the side table and he flipped to a fresh page near the back. He started making notes.

'I've already tried that,' he said a few minutes in.

'All right, well, in that case,' Dave started talking again. Nathan stopped writing after a few words. He'd tried that too. He was pretty sure the coolroom needed a part. He started to close the log book, then stopped. As Dave continued speaking in his ear, Nathan flicked back a few pages.

Anyone going further than the homestead fence was supposed to make a note of where they were going and when they expected to return. In theory, the log book was filled in every time. In practice, it was clearly done only as often as anyone remembered.

Only half listening now, Nathan read over the most recent entries. Harry was presently out inspecting a water bore, apparently, while Ilse – Nathan traced his finger over her writing – was indeed riding in the paddock bordering the driveway. As Simon had said. It was the same place she'd been the morning Cameron disappeared, Nathan remembered. When her husband had stopped to talk to her for the final time before he drove away.

'I'm sorry, mate,' Dave was saying, and Nathan tuned into the phone conversation again. The man was clearly waiting for a response.

'Thanks anyway, I'll have another crack at fixing it myself,' Nathan said.

'I wasn't talking about the coolroom.' Dave's frown was almost audible down the line. 'I said I was sorry to hear what happened to Cameron.'

'Oh. Right. Thanks.'

'I liked him a lot. He was a good bloke.'

'Yeah.'

'What a bloody shock it must have been.'

'It was.'

'Any idea what, you know, made him do it?'

Nathan flicked the log book back to the date that Cam had gone missing. He saw his brother's firm capital letters: LEHMANN'S HILL. Nathan felt something hard in his chest. Cameron had expected to return the following day by dinner time, if not before, according to the book. Nathan pulled Cameron's card out of his back pocket. Two words in the same handwriting. *Forgive me.*

'No,' Nathan said. 'No idea.'

The line above Cameron's entry was filled with Liz's cursive letters, noting that she'd taken Sophie's horse for a hack, due back that afternoon. On the line above that, Harry had written that he and Simon would be out checking the bores, with an expected return by dinner. Bub's misspelled scrawl the previous day noted that he would be staying out in the north paddock before driving to Lehmann's Hill to meet his brother. Nathan ran a finger down the surrounding lines. There were no other entries for the day Cameron had gone missing. He flipped back and forward a few pages, then closed the book.

'Anyway, mate,' Dave was saying. There was an awkward note in his voice. 'I realise this isn't a great time for you, but I'm still going to have to invoice you.'

'Right.' It came out more bitter than he intended.

'No choice, I'm afraid. It costs me a hundred in fuel to come up that north road.'

'I know.' Nathan's heart sank, as it always did these days when money was involved.

'Look, seeing as it's Christmas, I'll knock a bit off the call-out fee.'

'Yeah? Thank you.'

'No worries. I had to be at Atherton anyway on Thursday so it wasn't a totally wasted trip.'

'You were out at Atherton?' Something snagged in Nathan's mind. He reached out but the thought dissolved before he could grasp it.

'Yeah, generator problems. And sorry again to hear about Cam. Bloody shame no-one saw him in time to help.'

That tug again. Sharper this time but gone as quickly.

'Thanks, Dave.'

'Good luck with the coolroom.'

Nathan would need it. He hung up and stared at the phone for a long minute. Finally, he turned to head outside and jumped as he saw someone leaning against the door to Ilse's office, watching him. Simon, again. Nathan wondered how long he'd been standing there.

'Did you want something else?' Nathan started to walk past him but Simon took a dithery half-step at the same time and they came to an awkward halt.

'Have the police said any more about what they think happened to Cameron?'

'No. Why?'

'Just interested. I liked him a lot. But the police are taking it seriously?'

'I suppose. But it's pretty much only the one cop around here anyway.'

'I know. That's so weird.' Simon gave a half-laugh. 'Is he coming out here to talk to us all?'

'To the house?' The guy hummed with a nervous energy that made Nathan itch. 'Is it a problem if he does?'

'No. Of course not.' Simon opened his mouth, then seemed to think better of it and closed it again. They stared at each other.

'How did you say you met Cam again?'

'In the pub. When we arrived in town.'

'From out west.'

'That's right.'

'Quite hard to get here from out west this time of year,' Nathan said. 'Desert routes are mostly closed.'

'Tell me about it. We had to take the scenic route. Looped south.'

'Right.' There were always more jobs than backpackers willing to do them in the outback, but Nathan wondered why Cam had picked this pair. There wasn't even much to do that time of year. He thought about his phone call the night before. *Thank you for thinking of Northern Blooms!* 'Where did you say you guys were from again?'

'In England? Hampshire.'

'Is that in the north?'

'No. South. Why?'

'Doesn't matter.'

'Is it something to do with that woman you're all talking about? Jenna?' Simon's voice was low and made Nathan turn his head.

'Do you know something about that? Or about her?'

Simon caught his tone. 'No. Of course not. Why would I?'

'You're the one who brought her up.'

'Look –' Simon glanced at the kitchen where they could hear Katy clattering dishes. 'I've approached this all wrong. You don't know us, I get that. But whatever's happened with your brother –' Simon lowered his voice another notch. 'It's not me or Katy you need to be worrying about.'

Nathan frowned. The guy was so skittish he was hard to read. 'What do you mean? Should I be worried about someone else?'

'Maybe not worried, exactly –'

'That's what you said.'

'– I know, I meant, if you *were* –'

'For God's sake, say it or don't, mate.'

Simon swallowed, his Adam's apple bobbing. 'I heard Cameron having an argument. With Harry. The week before he died.'

'So?' Nathan said, because he couldn't think how else to respond.

From outside, he heard the faint sound of someone calling his name. 'Nathan?'

Ilse. He turned towards her voice, then made himself look back and focus on Simon.

'I thought you'd want to know,' Simon was saying. 'One night when Harry was going to turn the generator off. I heard them from the caravan. Not the specifics, I wasn't trying to listen in, but there were definitely words exchanged.'

'Nathan?' Outside, Ilse's boots clattered up the wooden steps of the verandah.

Simon took half a step closer. 'Listen, Cameron sounded pissed off. More than I'd heard him before. And Harry was getting angry, saying that he'd lived here for more than forty years, been around longer than Cameron had. Something like: "I know more about what's going on here than you think."'

'What's that supposed to mean?'

'I don't know.' Simon shrugged. 'And that was pretty much it. I think Harry walked away then. And I might not have thought too much of it, but —'

He stopped as the screen door opened at the end of the hall. Ilse appeared in the light of the doorway.

'Oh, good. There you are,' she said. She sounded a little breathless. 'Harry's not around. Are you free? I need your help.'

'Yep. Give me a sec.' Nathan turned back to Simon. 'But what? Quick.'

'But then Harry has never mentioned it.'

Chapter 21

They had left the track three kilometres earlier and the wheels of Nathan's car bumped over the uneven ground.

'Hopefully it's still stuck,' Ilse said as the holding pen came into sight in the distance.

'Yeah.' Nathan hoped so too. A calf tangled in the fence wire was one thing; trying to catch a calf running free with wire wrapped around it was an absolute pain in the arse.

'There it is. I can see it.' Ilse pointed through the dusty windscreen. They were the first words they'd exchanged in fifteen minutes.

Cameron's card lay open and discarded on the seat between them. *Forgive me.*

Nathan scanned the herd of cattle. The cows bristled at the sound of the car engine and began walking almost as one, in a wave of movement. A single animal remained, watching her calf wrestle with the wire that trapped its hind leg.

'I saw it while I was riding,' Ilse had told him earlier in the hallway. 'I didn't have anything to cut it loose.'

'Right,' Nathan had said. Something like that was ideally a two-person job anyway. 'Give me a minute. I'll meet you at your car.'

There had been a slight hesitation. 'Mine's not working. Take yours?'

'No worries. Keys are on the seat.'

Actually, where was Ilse's four-wheel drive? Nathan had wondered as he'd watched her leave. He hadn't seen it since he'd got there.

Nathan had written their destination in the log book by the phone, then ripped out an empty page and scribbled a message for Xander. He'd looked back at Simon, who was still hovering.

'You're sure that's what you heard with Cam and Harry?' Nathan said. 'You're not trying to cause trouble?'

'No. *No.* Why would I?'

'Have you told anyone else? Bub or anyone?'

'No.'

'Why not?'

'Bub and Harry seem pretty close.'

'Harry's close to everyone here.'

'Not you as much. You're kind of –' Simon shrugged. 'Anyway. Look, I didn't know Cameron well, but he was good to us. And I like to think I'm a good guy.' He looked at Nathan. 'I suppose I'm taking a punt that you are too.'

Nathan hadn't known what to say to that. Finally, he had turned and followed Ilse outside, leaving Simon staring after him.

Ilse had already been sitting in the passenger's seat with the engine running. The air conditioning was a relief as Nathan climbed in. They pulled away, heading down the long driveway. The house was far behind them before they'd opened their mouths.

'Ilse, I found something from Cam —'

'What was up with Simon —?'

They had spoken in unison. Ilse frowned.

'What did you say?' she said. 'Something from Cameron?'

Nathan pulled the card from his back pocket and she had practically snatched it from him. He had kept his eyes on the road as he explained where he and Xander had found it, along with the framed family drawing. Long minutes ticked by as Ilse sat and stared, her head bowed and her hair falling into her eyes.

'Ilse —' Nathan said finally.

She cleared her throat and dropped the card on the seat as though she suddenly couldn't bear to touch it anymore.

'It's okay. I'm okay. I don't know what to tell you. Every day —' She gave a tight shake of her head. 'Every day, I feel like I understand my husband even less.'

They hadn't spoken again until they reached the herd.

Nathan stopped the car a fair distance away to avoid causing more stress than necessary to the calf and its waiting mother. They got out and Nathan threw open the rear door, rummaging through his equipment bag. He found a couple of pairs of different-sized wire snippers and turned to find Ilse standing a short distance away, watching. From the way her eyes flicked to the side, he could tell she hadn't been looking at him, but past him.

Into the back of his four-wheel drive, where they had been together, once upon a time, a million years ago. Nathan slammed the door and started towards the calf. The animal watched warily as they approached. The mother stiffened and flicked her tail. The rest of the herd eyeballed them.

'I heard that was how the stockman died,' Ilse said quietly. 'Trampled in a stampede.'

'Really? No –' Nathan started, then stopped as the calf started to bellow. Its mother swished her tail, her muscles quivering. 'Keep an eye on her, though. She's not going to like this.' He handed the wire snippers to Ilse. 'Are you right with this?'

'I've done it before. Just tell me when.'

Nathan approached slowly, letting the animals get a good look at him. For all the use that was. The cattle were so free range they were almost feral. They never got used to seeing people. The mother eyed him up as Nathan got closer to the calf. He could see that the wire was not too tight around its leg. A bit longer and it might well have pulled itself free. For now, though, it was stuck. Behind him, he heard the mother snort.

'She okay back there?' he called.

'Yes,' Ilse said. 'Keeping her distance still.'

In the dust a few metres away, Nathan could see the telltale tracks of a passing snake. Almost certainly long gone now, but he still took a good long minute to check around nonetheless. Antivenin was expensive and had a short shelf life, so the medical centre in town did not keep supplies.

'What happens if you get a bite?' Nathan had heard more than one backpacker demand in disbelief.

Nothing good, was the answer, not with the kind of snakes that called the area home. Nathan liked to live by the rule of thumb that if he got bitten, he would die. End of story. As satisfied as he could be with that, he stepped towards the calf.

'I'm going for it now.'

'Okay. Say when you're ready.'

In a single movement, Nathan put his arms under the calf and heaved. Before the animal knew what had happened, he had flipped it on its side and wrestled it down, lying across it and using his weight to pin it to the ground. It was stunned, then opened its mouth and bellowed its outrage into his face. It kicked and struggled, and he leaned into its body, using his knees and elbows to pin it so it could barely move.

'Got it,' he grunted, but Ilse was already there, crouched by the rear legs with the wire snippers in hand.

He could feel the heat coming from the calf and hear its heart pounding in its ribcage. It struggled and kicked out.

'Shit,' he heard Ilse say.

'Did it get you?' He leaned in hard until the animal was subdued again.

'I'm okay –' He heard her move. 'I'm going to try the smaller cutters. I don't want to catch its skin.'

Nathan was straining a little to hold the calf. It was only a couple of months old but it was strong. It would weigh in heavier than Ilse, and Nathan reckoned he might only have about twenty kilograms on it. It didn't matter, though. He was stronger and that was enough to make it do what he wanted. It lay still. Nathan listened to the frightened thump of the beast's heart. And all at once, before he could stop himself, he thought of Cameron.

'Ilse?' he called.

'Yeah?' She was back by the hind legs.

'I tried to ring Jenna Moore. In England.'

He couldn't see her, but sensed her stiffen.

'And?'

Nathan shook his head as best he could. 'She wasn't around.'

'Where is she?' He could hear the tension in her voice. Beneath that, a soft snipping sound.

'Bali, according to her colleague.' The calf strained, its eyes rolling in its head. He checked to see the mother was still keeping her distance, and leaned in. 'Wherever she is, she's out of phone range apparently.'

Neither said anything for a minute. *Snip. Snip.*

'Why did you call her?' He still couldn't see Ilse but she sounded closer. He tried to lift his head to look and the calf sensed its opportunity. He gripped it harder.

'I don't know,' he grunted.

'Are you having second thoughts? About what she said about Cam?'

'No,' he said, too quickly. 'It wasn't that.'

She didn't reply. Finally, he felt her stand up.

'I've finished,' she said.

Nathan rolled off the calf, which immediately righted itself and bounded away to its cross-looking mother. She threw Nathan an ungrateful sneer and the pair ran off together without as much as a backwards glance, happy to be at liberty once more.

He sat on the ground, breathing heavily. His muscles ached from the effort of holding the calf down. Above him, Ilse was clutching the strands of cut wire in her hands. She had tears in her eyes.

'Shit. Ilse –' He stood up. 'I don't know why I called. I just wondered what she had to say.'

Ilse fiddled with the wires. 'Bali.'

'Apparently.'

She said nothing for a long minute, then lifted her eyes to look at the horizon. 'Lots of flights between Bali and Brisbane.'

Nathan didn't reply. He walked over to his Land Cruiser to get a length of wire to repair the fence.

'You think you'd always see someone out here,' Ilse said when he got back. Her eyes were dry now. 'But you can't always, can you? If someone is standing still, or parked a long way away. It's only when they start moving you even know they were there.'

Nathan thought about Lehmann's Hill. 'Bub was saying pretty much the same thing the other day.'

Ilse nodded. 'I've heard Bub talk about that. Being able to tell when someone else is around.'

'Yeah.' Nathan crouched and used pliers to twist the snapped ends together with the new wire. 'I reckon he's right.'

'Do you?' Ilse sounded surprised. 'Cameron always said that was ridiculous.'

'Oh.'

'You can feel it, though?'

'I dunno,' Nathan said. 'Sometimes. Maybe. It's like –'

He couldn't quite explain it. Like a pulse over the empty land. The strange heaviness that indicated you were sharing the air with someone else. He knew realistically there would be some sort of explanation. Subconscious recognition of something amiss on the landscape. It was nothing more than that, and it wasn't even accurate. He'd been getting false positives out at his own property lately. And there could have been hundreds of times over the years that there had been someone unknown over the horizon.

'Cam was probably right,' he said finally.

Ilse stood very still, only her eyes moving as she looked out. 'What about now?'

'Do I think there's someone else here now?'

'Yes.' Her face was serious.

'Ilse, it's not a science. It's not even a thing.'

'I know, but can you feel anyone?'

Her looked up at her. He could hear her breathing and see the wind catch the ends of her hair. He could not hear her heartbeat, but he could feel his own.

'Only us,' he said truthfully. He turned back to the wire. He could feel Ilse watching him but he didn't look back. He focused on his work for a while before opening his mouth again.

'Look, there's no way that Jenna is out here,' he said. 'We'd have heard something if she'd come through town.'

'Unless she didn't go through town.'

'She'd have had to. You know that. She couldn't stay entirely under the radar. You'd have to have all your supplies, keep completely off-road.'

'It can be done, though. You do it. Bub's done it. And Cameron.'

'And how many tourists have died in their cars trying to take a short cut?' Nathan twisted the last piece of wire and checked the tension. Satisfied, he stood up and stopped when he saw the look on Ilse's face. 'What is it? Why are you so fixed on this?'

'Cameron tried to call Jenna as well,' Ilse said. 'Three times.'

Nathan stared. 'When?'

'Once two weeks ago, then twice more in the week before he died. He used the office line, not the main house one. I can see the number on the bill online. She's a florist in England, isn't she? I looked her up.'

Nathan nodded.

'I don't think he spoke to her,' Ilse said. 'The calls are very short, all less than thirty seconds.'

'Why would he wait so long to call her? He'd known for a few weeks she was thinking about contacting him.'

'Maybe it took her that long to actually reach him,' Ilse said. 'He might have got an email or something. I don't know. I don't have his password.' She stopped. 'Or maybe she didn't get in touch at all and the waiting was driving him crazy. Looking back now, he'd been worried since he heard she'd rung the police station, but it had been getting worse. And he made some other calls in his last week as well.'

'To who?'

'To St Helens. The medical centre up there, for one.'

'Was he sick?'

'Not that he said. And he wasn't a patient there, as far as they would tell me. But then Cameron didn't like to go and see Steve at the clinic either, so who knows? He called one of the hotels in St Helens too.'

'Which one?' There were exactly three accommodation options in St Helens.

'The cheap one.'

'Did he make a booking?'

'If he did, it wasn't under his own name.' There was something hard in Ilse's face now. 'They had nothing under Jenna's name either. Neither did the other places.'

Nathan felt an unpleasant sensation creep through him and he had the sudden urge to check over his shoulder. There was nothing there but cattle and stubby grass and the horizon. All was quiet. Ilse was watching him closely.

'You really don't think Cameron had anything to worry about with that woman?' she said.

Nathan hesitated. For real, this time. A long and disloyal silence that stretched on and spoke volumes.

Ilse nodded. 'Because Cameron was acting like he did.'

Chapter 22

They barely spoke on the way back. Nathan drove while Ilse stared out of the window, chewing her nails and occasionally turning Cameron's card over in her fingers.

'You need to tell Glenn,' Nathan said. 'About Cameron trying to call Jenna.'

'I already tried.' Ilse didn't look over. 'He wasn't at the police station when I called last night.'

'Did you leave a message?'

'No. I got diverted to the Brisbane switchboard. I didn't want to –' Ilse sighed, still staring out at the passing landscape. 'I'll try him again.'

She didn't say anything else until the homestead came into sight up ahead.

'I'll get out here,' she said, as they passed the stables. 'I put away the horse quickly earlier. I want to check on her.'

Nathan pulled to a stop. 'Ilse –' he said as she climbed out. She waited. He wanted to tell her it would all be okay. Instead, he shook his head. 'Nothing.'

She slammed the door and Nathan watched her walk away. When he pulled up outside the house he could see the girls riding in the far exercise yard. Liz was looking on while Xander sat nearby in the shade, flipping through a sketchbook in his lap.

Nathan walked over and leaned on the railing next to his mum. He waited for her to tell Lo to keep her heels down, but she didn't. Her eyes were dull.

'Everything all right?' he said.

'Steve called from the clinic. The –' Liz stumbled over the word, '– autopsy has been completed. We're right to go ahead with the funeral.'

Nathan thought about Cameron's call to the medical centre in St Helens. 'They didn't find any other health problems?'

Liz shook her head vaguely and didn't ask why. Xander looked up, though.

'Do you want to have a rest?' Nathan said. 'I'll help the girls with the horses.'

He waited for Liz to argue, but she just nodded. With visible effort, she pushed herself away from the railing and trudged towards the house.

'She's been bad all morning,' Xander said. His voice was a little cool. 'Lo nearly fell off earlier and she didn't even notice.'

'Right,' Nathan said. 'Mate, listen, I'm sorry about going without you just now –'

'It's fine.'

It wasn't, Nathan suspected, but Xander seemed distracted as he looked up from the sketchbook. 'Did you show Ilse the card from Uncle Cam?'

'Yeah.' Nathan told him what Ilse had said. He hesitated, then told him what else she'd said, about the phone calls to St Helens.

Xander frowned. 'Did Cam think Jenna might be in St Helens?'

'I don't know. Maybe he did.'

Xander's eyes fell again at the sketchbook in his lap. It was full of Lo's paintings.

'What're you looking at?' Nathan said.

Xander handed him the book, open to the page he'd been examining. Nathan flicked his eyes across the painting. It showed two girls, one smaller than the other and both with dirty-blonde hair. It was hard to tell how old they were, but the bigger one had her arm encased in a colourful sling.

The two girls stood in the foreground of the picture, with bright orange earth under their feet. Behind them, looming large, was a big dark shape that blocked the line of the horizon. It had been drawn by someone young but skilled, and was entirely recognisable.

'The stockman's grave, isn't it?' Nathan said. Beside the headstone, Lo had painted another shape. It was shadowy and unfinished, but had a strangely human quality. A woman, Nathan thought, for reasons he couldn't quite qualify. While the girls were clearly identifiable, the woman's features were formless and elusive. Nathan looked up from the picture. Cameron's daughters were riding now over by the far fence.

'I didn't know they'd been out to the grave.' Xander pointed at the sling on the painted girl's arm. 'Not recently, anyway.'

235

'Me neither.' Nathan raised his voice and called out, 'Girls.' His tone made them pull up their horses immediately. 'Come here. I need to talk to you.'

'Are we in trouble?' Sophie said, as she cantered over and drew to a halt in front of him in a swirl of dust.

'No. I wanted to ask about this picture, Lo.'

Lo leaned in, but as he held it up her face changed. She didn't reach out to take it. Behind her, Sophie craned her neck to see. Her horse was disturbed, turning in tight circles. Nathan could see the reins wrapped tight around Sophie's good hand, the leather biting into her knuckles.

'What's this painting of, Lo?' Nathan prompted.

'It's obviously the stockman's grave,' Sophie snapped. The chatty girl from the previous evening was gone. Her expression was wary, and Nathan could see her good hand grip the reins even more tightly.

'I didn't know you'd been out there.'

'Once. With Mummy.'

Nathan pointed at the shadowy woman. 'That's your mum there?'

'Of course,' Sophie cut in before Lo could answer. 'Who else would it be?'

'I don't know,' Nathan said, truthfully. 'Maybe a friend of hers?'

'Mummy doesn't have any friends. What?' Lo said as Sophie scowled at her. 'None of us do.'

'So you went out there with your mum?' Xander said. 'When?'

'Ages ago,' Lo said.

'No, not ages ago. Just after I hurt my arm.' Sophie's

236

horse twisted again and she was forced to whip her head around to look at Nathan.

'What did you do there?'

The sisters glanced at each other, but Nathan had the sense they were not being deliberately evasive.

'Nothing. We got there but then –' Sophie frowned. 'We just drove home again. Mum said it was supposed to be a picnic.'

'But we didn't have any food,' Lo said.

'We did. Later, remember? We had it by the stables instead.'

Lo frowned, her tiny face creasing.

'We only stayed at the grave for a few minutes,' Sophie said.

'Yeah.' Lo nodded. 'I didn't like it.'

'And nothing else happened? At all?' Nathan watched his nieces shake their heads. 'All right. Thanks, girls.'

Sophie's horse was still straining and Nathan could see the whites of its eyes as they rolled. She loosened the reins and shot off across the yard.

Lo remained behind, her pony more docile. 'Is Mummy going to be in trouble?'

'No. Why would she be?'

'Because you look sad.'

Did he? 'Sorry.' Nathan rearranged his face into what he hoped was a more neutral expression. He started to close the sketchbook, then stopped. 'Why didn't you finish drawing your mum in the picture?'

Lo, suddenly unsure, looked for her sister, who was out of earshot across the yard. She faltered, then leaned in on her pony.

'Daddy didn't like it,' she whispered.

'What do you mean?'

'He saw my picture and was cross with Mummy. I didn't want to make it worse.'

Ilse was no longer in the stables by the time Nathan had walked the girls' horses back. Lo had been distracted, losing concentration and control of her pony a couple of times. She didn't know why Daddy was upset, she'd said, she just thought that he was. Nathan and Xander had exchanged a look as Lo grew increasingly worried, and hadn't pushed it. After Lo nearly fell off for a second time, Nathan asked Xander to take the girls inside and find something safer to do. He had led the horses to the stables and taken his time settling them in as he thought about things.

It was as he was walking the long way back that he heard the sound. He was under a window outside one of the cabins and stopped. The soft catch of breath. Someone was crying. He walked around the front and up the steps.

The inside of the cabin was a surprise. It had been converted into a proper schoolroom, with a whiteboard and small desks, and alphabet posters covering the walls. A lot of it appeared homemade, and Nathan thought he recognised Ilse's handiwork on much of it.

Katy was sitting in a large beanbag in the reading corner. She wiped her eyes as Nathan came in.

'Sorry,' he said. 'I heard you outside.'

'It's okay.' Katy blew her nose on a shredded tissue. With

a little difficulty she pulled herself out of the beanbag and stood up. 'I should be getting back anyway.'

'What's wrong?'

'Nothing.'

'Do you want me to get Simon?'

'No. I'm fine.'

Nathan found a roll of paper towel by the art station and handed her a sheet. 'Just take a minute.'

'Thanks.' Katy took it gratefully and wiped her eyes.

Nathan wandered around while she gathered herself. The classroom was a lot nicer than anything he and Cam and Bub had had when they were kids. Their schoolwork was mostly done at the kitchen table or not at all. On the teacher's desk was a laptop with some post-it notes written in what he presumed was Katy's handwriting.

A thick teaching folder supplied by School of the Air lay open and Nathan remembered his conversation with Sophie on the verandah.

I don't think she's a real teacher.

He looked up. Katy was blowing her nose again. He flicked through a few pages in the folder. The lessons were all laid out for the home supervisor to follow.

Introduce the unit, he read. *Hold up the book and say to students: 'Today we will be exploring picture books. We will be learning about characters in this story.' Show students the front cover. Ask them to read the title out loud.*

Nathan frowned. He read on. The instructions were all there. It didn't seem too hard to supervise if you followed them. He thought he could have a crack at it himself, at a push. He closed the folder and saw Katy watching him.

'Better?' he said.

'Yes.' Her voice was a touch too bright and her makeup had smudged slightly, making her eyes look strangely dramatic. 'I'm just a bit homesick. I'll be okay.'

'Are you going back to the house?' he said. 'I'll walk with you.'

She opened the cabin door, and he followed her down the steps into the blinding daylight.

'Are you in charge here now?' Katy said as they walked.

'Me? No.'

'Who is then?'

It was a good question. 'Ilse, I suppose. It depends what you want.' Nathan looked over in time to see something flicker across the woman's face.

'Simon and I need to move on soon. Not because of what's happened,' Katy added quickly. 'I'd actually discussed it with Cameron but –' She stopped.

'Right,' Nathan said. 'When were you thinking?'

'I'm not sure. Soon. Next week maybe. I have to check with Simon.'

'Just make sure you say goodbye to someone before you go. If a worker goes missing we're required to report it, in case they're –' He stopped. *Lying dead in the middle of nowhere.* 'For their own safety.'

'It's not that we're not grateful for the work,' Katy said quickly.

'It's fine. No-one stays forever. Will you go back to England?'

'I want to but –' Katy shook her head. 'Simon isn't ready yet. He likes it out here.'

240

'Right,' Nathan said again. He had the distinct sense he was missing something. 'You two been together long?'

'Three years.' Her voice was completely flat. 'We're engaged.'

That may be so, but Bub was right for once, Nathan thought with some surprise. She wasn't happy.

'If you need to talk to someone,' he said eventually. 'Someone not on the property, I mean, there's always Steve at the clinic.'

'Why do you say that?' Katy said, a sudden sharpness in her face.

'No reason. Sometimes workers have stuff they don't want to discuss with their employers. That's all.'

'Oh.' She nodded. 'Sorry. I'm not usually like this, I promise. I'm struggling a bit with everything that's happened.'

'It's okay. I don't blame you.'

'My head's all over the place,' Katy said. 'I know Cameron was your brother and I'd only known him a few months but I can't stop thinking about what happened.'

Across the yard, the windows of the house were dark against the daylight. There was no-one else around and it felt like they were all alone. Harry's car was still absent from the driveway.

Nathan hesitated, feeling a little treacherous. 'Simon said he heard Cameron and Harry arguing one night.'

'Oh. Yeah,' Katy said. 'He mentioned that. It can't have been too much of an argument, though. I slept through it.'

'Do you think Simon might have got the wrong end of the stick?'

'I don't know. Simon liked Cameron a lot. He thought he was a good boss and he liked working here. It's possible he read more into it than there was. Having said that –'

She slowed her pace, then stopped entirely.

'What?' he said.

'Listen, I just work here,' Katy said finally. She gazed out across the yard. 'I didn't take this job looking to make friends or get involved, definitely not in anything like this. I'm just trying to earn some money.' She turned to look at him. 'And I don't know what's going on, but there's something really messed up about what happened to Cameron.'

Nathan waited, the silence pressing in on them.

'When I saw Cam that last morning, he told me he'd be back the next day,' Katy said. 'And I can't explain, so don't ask, but I'm sure that he meant it. I don't know what happened in between, but that morning Cameron was planning on coming home. I wish someone else had been there to see him. Simon, or the girls even. They'd tell you.'

'Well, there was Ilse.' Nathan hesitated. 'She saw him.'

'Yeah. I suppose she did.' Katy started walking towards the house again.

'And she reckons he said much the same as he said to you. That he'd be back the next day.'

'Well.' A small shrug. 'I was too far away to hear, so we'll have to take Ilse's word for it.'

'And yours.'

Katy looked up at his tone, then gave a hard half-smile. 'That's true. Although –'

She broke off suddenly, looking at the house. Nathan followed her gaze and could see a shadow in one of the windows that had previously been empty. Simon. He was looking out at them, his eyes hidden by the reflection of the glass.

Katy started walking faster and Nathan jogged a couple of paces to catch up with her.

'Although what?' he said. 'What were you about to say?'

'It's nothing. It doesn't matter.'

'It does.'

'Honestly, I'm not looking to cause trouble. I'm trying to mind my own business.'

'Come on, Katy.' Nathan stopped walking. 'Please. He's dead.'

'I know that.' But she stopped. 'All right. It's just, if that's the only thing Cameron and Ilse said to each other that morning, they took their time getting it out.' She seemed to debate for a moment. 'Plus, Ilse didn't wave him off as he drove away.'

'So? That doesn't mean anything.'

'Maybe not.' Katy's dark, smudged eyes gave him a look he couldn't decipher. 'But when you leave, she waves to you.'

They stared at each other, then Katy shrugged.

'I told you it was nothing.' She shoved the tissue into her jeans pocket. 'Thanks for before, by the way. I feel better now.'

He watched her walk away. When Nathan next looked back towards the house, Simon was gone, and every window was dark again.

Chapter 23

Up close, Nathan thought, it was interesting how things could appear so different. He stood alone in the living room, his nose near to Cameron's painting. The image of the stockman's grave hung on the wall at eye level. Outside, the night was drawing in, and it was hard to see the detail properly under the artificial glow of the ceiling light. Still, it was mildly hypnotic, examining the lines of the brushwork and the way two colours bled together into something new. He was about to move away when his gaze snagged on the left edge of the painting. There was a dark smudge on the horizon that he'd never noticed before. It was a muted grey mark, and faint to the point of transparency.

Nathan frowned and leaned in. What on earth was that supposed to be? A person? A shadow? Just a dirty mark? He reached out and lightly ran his thumb over it. No, definitely paint. Deliberate and permanent on Cam's part, then.

'Cameron would kill you for that.' Ilse's voice came

from the doorway and he turned. 'Don't touch the picture. Golden rule in this house.'

Nathan put his hands up and took a step back.

'That's probably safer.' She gave him a weary smile. He could hear the sounds of dinner being cleared away in the kitchen. The meal had been mostly silent and entirely subdued.

'Ilse –' he said as she turned to leave.

She stopped, waiting.

'I was talking to the girls earlier. They said you'd taken them out there.' Nathan nodded at the picture.

'To the grave?' Ilse said. 'How did that come up?'

'Lo drew a picture of it.'

A ghost of a smile crossed her face. 'Right. Of course.' She came into the room and joined him in front of the painting. 'It was a stupid idea. I took them there for a picnic a few weeks ago, after Sophie hurt her arm. I was trying to come up with something to take her mind off it, and I thought seeing the grave in person might help Lo. Remove the mystery, I guess.'

'Sophie said you didn't stay long.'

'No.' Ilse gave a half-laugh. 'I knew it was a bad plan the minute we got there. It was too hot. Lo was scared. I pretty much bundled them back into the car and drove home. It was a long way to go for five minutes, but it was for the best. We ended up having a picnic by the stables instead. I should've done that in the first place.'

Ilse was staring at Cameron's painting, then slowly, she took another step in, until she was as close to the canvas as Nathan had been.

'Cameron wasn't happy when he heard we'd been out there,' she said. Nathan couldn't see her face now.

'Why not?'

'He didn't like it that I took the girls so far. He said it was too isolated and exposed for this time of year.' Ilse leaned in, examining the solid dark paint of the grave. She raised a hand slowly and extended her index finger. 'He said it was dangerous.'

Her finger hovered, an inch from the canvas. 'It's kind of funny,' she said in a voice that suggested it wasn't funny at all, 'how it turned out he was right.'

Half an inch.

'No! Don't touch the painting, Mummy!'

The voice at the doorway sounded horrified. Nathan turned to see Sophie, open-mouthed. Ilse immediately curled her fingers into a fist and dropped her hand.

'Daddy's painting is *off limits*,' Sophie recited.

'I know.' Ilse stepped away and relief and confusion crossed Sophie's face. She caught sight of the beer in Nathan's hand.

'No food or drinks near the picture, either.'

'Yes, we both know, Soph,' Ilse said. 'No-one was touching it, we were just looking.'

'It's bad luck. The stockman will get upset.'

Ilse appeared to be fighting not to roll her eyes. She succeeded, barely. 'Sweetheart, the only person who got upset about fingerprints on the painting was Dad. Come on, it's time for bed anyway.'

Sophie threw a final warning look at Nathan then reluctantly disappeared back into the hall. Ilse went to follow, pausing at the door.

'She's right, though,' she said. 'Cam really hated anyone touching the painting.'

'I'd better leave it alone then.'

She nodded as she left. By himself once more, Nathan collapsed onto the couch. As he took a mouthful of beer, his eye was drawn to the darkened window. He paused, bottle halfway to his mouth. Something was different. The night was somehow not as black as it had been.

Nathan hauled himself to his feet and looked out through the glass. His reflection stared back at him, with an expression he didn't quite recognise. He gazed beyond it, into the night. From the angle of the window, it took him a moment to process what he was seeing.

A pair of headlights, their beams piercing through the dark. He could hear a soft hum. In the otherwise empty driveway, Cameron's car was running.

The white light was blinding. Nathan put his arm up to shield his eyes from the headlights, but it made no difference. His night vision was shot. He stood alone on the driveway. He couldn't see into the car. He could see nothing, in fact, but the brilliant cones of light.

He made himself walk straight to the driver's side and his hand was on the door when it clicked open. The interior light went on. It was no match for the headlights and it still took Nathan's eyes a minute to adjust.

Xander sat behind the wheel.

'Jesus.' Nathan dropped his hand. 'You scared me.'

Xander said nothing, just stared out through the

windscreen. Nathan walked around the front of the car, his shadow slicing through the perfect beams of light. He tried to open the passenger-side door. It was locked. For a split second, Nathan realised he wasn't sure what his son was going to do next. A beat passed. Then Xander leaned over, lifted the old manual door lock and let him in.

'You couldn't have turned the lights down?' Nathan blinked. 'I can't see a thing.'

No apology. That was new. His vision still a little dazzled, Nathan looked at his teenage son slumped in the seat, and possibly for the first time ever, found himself wondering what his ex-wife would advise.

'What are you doing?' he said.

'Nothing.' That was probably partly true. Xander wasn't wearing a seatbelt and the car was in neutral with the air conditioner running. It didn't look like he'd been planning on going anywhere.

'Okay.' Nathan sat back. In the ghostly glow of the headlights, he could see the smear of dead insects and baked-on dust on the glass. A large part of his reluctance around fatherhood, he had realised after Xander was born, had been fear. It had been deep and ingrained in a way that Nathan tried to keep buried. He had not told Jacqui. Instead, he had stumbled his way through by thinking about how his own father would react to any given situation and then – with sustained effort at times – doing exactly the opposite. A lot of the time, that meant simply shutting his mouth, so that's what he did now.

He settled in, making himself comfortable against the

worn car seat. Xander turned his head but didn't say any-thing as Nathan closed his eyes. Nathan wasn't worried; he could do silence better than anyone he knew. He could literally go weeks without speaking, and had done, several times. Xander, raised amid city bustle and constant noise, would talk first.

'I really liked Uncle Cam.'

Nathan opened his eyes. Not even three minutes, he could see from the clock on the dashboard.

'It's strange without him.' Xander's voice was quiet.

'I know.' Nathan did understand. Sometimes he felt that everywhere he looked here, he was reminded of Cameron. The pair of them practising cricket in the yard as kids, pushing themselves to outdo each other on horses as teenagers, trying to make a living from the land as men. Cameron had always been methodical in his approach to life. He had thought through what he needed to do to achieve his desired outcome, then he'd done exactly that. Nathan leaned more towards having a crack and hoping for the best. Cameron's way proved better, time after time.

'I came out to search a bit more.' Xander nodded at the nearest shed. 'See if I could work out what Uncle Cam might have lost.'

'If Lo was right.'

'Well, yeah, exactly. Who knows?' Xander shook his head. 'And it's pointless anyway. You could search for something until you died out here and never find it. There's too much bloody space.'

'I suppose.'

'It's true.' Xander turned to Nathan, his voice more urgent. 'I've been thinking. You should leave here.'

Nathan blinked. 'What do you mean?'

'Leave your property. Move away. Do something completely different.'

'Like *what*? What are you talking about?'

'Come to Brisbane.'

'I can't come to Brisbane. What would I do in Brisbane?' Nathan tried to imagine himself. Concrete under his boots. Walls everywhere. Cars all over the place.

'Do anything,' Xander was saying. 'There must be some other job you could do. Work in a park or something. It doesn't have to be in an office.'

'What about the property?'

'Abandon it.'

'I can't, mate.' Nathan lowered his voice, even though they were the only ones around. 'I can't afford to. I owe the bank. I'd need to sell.'

'Then sell!'

'Jesus, Xander. Who to?'

'I don't know. Just get rid of it somehow. Please, Dad. You need to leave. It's not good out here.'

'What's wrong, mate? Why are you suddenly saying this?' He knew exactly why.

'Because.'

Nathan waited. Less than thirty seconds this time.

'Because I don't want you to end up like Uncle Cameron.'

'Xander –'

'What?' Xander snapped. 'It's not going to happen? Is

that what you're going to say? Let me guess, you're absolutely fine and there's no way you would consider doing what Uncle Cam did.'

Nathan didn't reply.

'Because everyone thought Cam was fine,' Xander went on. 'Okay, maybe not completely fine, these past couple of weeks. But way better than you.'

Nathan had never seen his son like this and it scared him a little.

'No-one ever says you're fine, Dad. When I come to visit, or talk to Grandma on the phone. No-one ever says you're doing well.'

Nathan was quiet.

'Harry said you got rid of your gun licence.'

'For Christ's sake. Harry should mind his own business.'

'Are you going to get it back?'

'Yeah, I can do, seeing as it's causing everyone so much concern.' Nathan tried to make his voice light. 'I thought you'd be happy, anyway. You're always off marching in those bloody rallies.'

'You don't trust yourself around them. Why would that make me happy?' Xander sounded suddenly exhausted.

'That's not the reason, mate.'

'Isn't it?'

'No.' Nathan looked over. 'No. I mean, there's a whole rifle cabinet here, isn't there? I don't have any problem with that.'

'You're not all alone here.'

Nathan made himself breathe in and out, deep and long, until he felt a little calmer. 'Listen. I'm sorry. It's not your job to worry –'

'Don't be sorry,' Xander cut in. 'Do something about it. Move away. Somewhere where there are other people. Make a fresh start. Maybe Mum could lend you some money. I know she left you but –'

'The split was mutual, thanks, mate.'

'– but she's a lot happier since she's been with Martin. I bet they'd help if I asked –'

'Don't ask. I mean it, Xander. Do not ask your mum.'

'Jesus, Dad, then *you* have to do something. Are you listening?' Xander ran a hand through his hair. 'I'm afraid, all right? That the property, and all this –' he gestured at the void outside the window, '– all this bloody *outback* – is going to get to you, like it did to Uncle Cam.'

The silence between them was almost louder than the thrum of the engine. Nathan hadn't realised it was possible to feel worse about his situation. 'You don't need to be scared. What can I do to make you feel better?'

'You can turn your own radio on, for starters.'

'Okay. Easy.'

'And use it once in a while. Let people know you're alive.'

'I already do that. I have that system.' A year ago, after Nathan had been flooded and unreachable by phone for two weeks, Harry had driven over and presented him with a simple GPS satellite tracker.

'I've been sent to give you this,' he said. 'You press this button for okay; this button for not okay. It sends a signal to Burley Downs. Press it every night, Nathan, no excuses.' So Nathan did.

'You should get another dog as well,' Xander said.

'I don't want another one.'

'I bet no-one would mind if you took Cam's dog. She seems to like you.'

'I don't want her.'

'Why?'

'Because I don't want someone to bait her like they did with Kelly.'

Xander was quiet. 'I thought Kelly wasn't actually baited, in the end?'

'She was.' Nathan shook his head. 'You think I don't know what I'm talking about?'

'No, I do. I believe you. Just, I thought Glenn said there was no bait found and she must have been sick or something.'

'How do you know what Glenn said?'

'He told me last time I was here.'

'Right. Good.' Nathan stared straight ahead. There was a sharpness between them that he wasn't used to.

'Look, Dad, people are only worried because it doesn't take much for things to go wrong out here. And everyone knows you have it harder than anybody. Harder than Uncle Cam, and –' Xander sighed. 'I mean, even he couldn't cope with it in the end.'

'I know things haven't been great lately. But honestly, the problem's not the property, mate. Not just that, anyway.'

'What then?'

Nathan didn't answer immediately. 'I don't know. Lots of things. I've made some bad choices. Done some stupid things. That thing with bloody Kei– with your granddad.'

He didn't go on, but it was such a well-worn path he could navigate it with his eyes closed. All those *what ifs*.

253

What if he hadn't been in town that day? What if he had filled up with fuel the night before, and hadn't run into his father-in-law? What if he'd driven home an hour earlier or later and never seen Keith stopped by the side of the road? What if he hadn't driven past a man in need of help? What if he had been a better man?

That brought Nathan's thoughts to a halt, in the same place, every time. The answers swirled lazily in the air above the shining, shimmering road not taken.

'It's not just the property, Xander,' he said again. That was true, he thought as he listened to the purr of his brother's car beneath them. It was also a silent radio, and the fact he couldn't get decent workers, and a sea of red bank statements and a broken coolroom and now, he remembered with a flash of irritation at his son as he recalled his locked house, an invoice from an electrical contractor who he had to pay for doing bloody nothing but drive in and drive out again. It was Ilse –

Nathan's mind caught on something again and his train of thought screeched to a halt. He frowned. What had made him stop? Ilse. No, not her, for once. His property? Partly, but that wasn't it. The contractor. Maybe. Yes. What about him? Nathan tried to cast his mind back to their phone conversation earlier that day.

'So you won't even think about leaving?' Xander's voice was cold in a way Nathan didn't recognise.

'It's not that I haven't thought about it –' Nathan forced himself to focus. In the back of his mind, he could feel something lying just out of reach. What had the contractor said? He hadn't been able to fix the room. He would have to charge Nathan anyway. But he would knock some off the bill because he'd had to drive to Atherton that day anyway –

'What then?' Xander was looking at him. 'What's keeping you here? Is it Ilse? Is that it?'

'No, mate.'

'Whatever it is,' Xander said. 'Is it more important than me?'

'Nothing is more important than you, Xander.'

'Then will you at least think about it? Please, Dad? Whatever happened to Cam, to make him drive out there –'

There it was again. That loose thought again. Nathan tried to grasp it and separate out the strand. It was lost in a murky tangle.

'– I don't want that to happen to you. Dad, okay?'

A pause. 'Okay.' The answer came too late.

Xander stared at him. 'You're not even listening to me.'

'I am. Xander, mate, I am. I promise.'

'You're not. I can see you're not.'

'I am. I was just thinking –'

'This is bullshit.' Xander opened his door.

'Come on. Please –'

'Forget it.' Xander turned the keys and cut the engine dead. The headlights flickered and disappeared, plunging them both into darkness. 'I don't care. Do whatever you want. I'm going to bed.'

He tossed the car keys at Nathan and slammed the door. Cameron's keys landed on the vinyl seat. Nathan reached down and felt the warm jagged metal and the coil of the lanyard wrapped tight around his fingers. He was sitting there alone in the dark with his mind freewheeling when he caught it. The thought he had been chasing. It slid up against him, cold and disturbing and fully formed.

'Hey –' he called out into the dark, but it was too late. No-one was there to hear him. Xander was gone.

Chapter 24

Nathan's passenger seat was empty and, for once, that felt strange. He had got used to Xander filling it out the last week or so. Duffy jumped up from the footwell and wagged her tail as she looked out of the window, but it wasn't the same.

As Nathan approached the rocky outcrop, the road was completely deserted and the morning sun was climbing in the sky. He glanced again at the empty seat and couldn't help thinking about the way Xander had looked at him in the pre-dawn light when Nathan had woken him to explain his plan.

'Do you want to come?'

Xander had just stared at him, then slowly shaken his head. 'No.'

That was fine, Nathan thought, as he slowed and pulled off the road at the hidden track. He didn't need anyone else. It wasn't a two-man job anyway. He'd found the right gap in the rocks straight away, this time, and drove through. At the top of the gentle slope was an empty space where Cameron's car had stood four days earlier.

Nathan had managed to catch the contractor on the phone before the sun was up. Dave hadn't sounded happy about either the hour or the call.

'Mate, it's my day off. Look, I'm sorry about the cool-room, all right, but I was there like we arranged –'

'Dave, it's not about that. Listen, you said you drove out to Atherton on Thursday. So you went along the north road, right? Past my boundary?'

'Yeah –'

'What time?'

'I dunno, I set off usual time so would have been about eight, I suppose. Just after.'

'So it was light then. Light enough to see?'

'Of course. I'm not driving that bloody road in the dark.'

'You see anything from around my place?'

'Like what?'

'Anything. Up on the rocks?'

A frustrated laugh. 'Not that I remember, but I'm not sure what you're asking, mate.'

'No, it's all right. Me neither. Just trying to get a few things straight.'

'That invoice is coming your way, I'm afraid.'

'Yep. Looking forward to it.'

Nathan had hung up and immediately dialled Glenn's number at the cop shop. He had heard the blip in the ringtone, the telltale sign he was being diverted. Glenn McKenna had been called out to the north of his patch, the officer who answered informed him. A road train had hit a tour bus. Multiple casualties, the voice said. He was not expected back to Balamara for a couple of days.

'What about the other one? The St Helens cop. Sergeant Ludlow.'

A tap of a keyboard. Multiple casualties, the voice had repeated. Ludlow had been called out to the job as well. 'Can I help?' the voice said.

'Where are you based?' Nathan asked.

'Brisbane.'

'So you're not exactly in a position to be much help.'

'I'm in a position to take a message, mate.'

Nathan had sensed movement in the hall behind him but when he'd turned, no-one was there.

'Tell Sergeant McKenna that Jenna Moore isn't in the UK. I don't know if he can check where she is, but –' Nathan hesitated. 'Just tell him I need to speak to him.'

Nathan drove to the top of the slope this time and climbed out. He left the engine and air-con running for Duffy as he opened the back of his Land Cruiser, pulling out a shovel and the marker flags he used around his own property. He looked at the ground. There was no sign that Cameron's car had ever been there, so Nathan made his best guess, driving the flagpoles in at the points where he thought the wheels had stood.

Twenty minutes later, Nathan was sweating hard and still unable to get the fourth post securely into the ground. Frustrated, he finally propped it up against one of the others and hoped they would hold. He climbed into his driver's seat, and was hit by a sudden sense of déjà vu as he remembered doing exactly the same in Cameron's abandoned car on that very spot. *Not exactly the same.*

Nathan's hands stilled on his steering wheel. He and Cameron had almost the same car, and he was parked in almost the same place, but something was different this time. He tried to picture himself a few days earlier, out here with Bub and Harry and Xander. He'd offered to drive Cam's car home, climbed into the worn driver's seat, reached down and adjusted the distance from the pedals –

Nathan stopped. He and Cameron were the same height. They had been since they were teenagers. Why had he had to adjust the seat? Had either of the cops moved it during their search? Nathan didn't think so, but he wasn't sure. By how much had he had to correct it? Backwards first, or forwards? He sat there for a long while, trying to think. He couldn't remember.

Finally, he started his engine and drove slowly down and out through the gap. He was back on the road in minutes, heading towards the boundary where his property bordered the gravel track. He drove along the deserted road until he was sure he had gone far enough, then did a U-turn and headed back the way he'd come. He kept the speed steady, not too fast, not too slow, trying to guess what pace a contractor with only a couple of jobs lying between him and his Christmas break would do.

He kept his eyes facing front, deliberately not scouring the rock face out of the driver's side window. Three minutes later he saw them.

The flags caught his eye immediately, the poles tall against the sky and completely visible. They stayed in sight for as long as it took Nathan to breathe in and out a couple of times, then the angle of the rocks shifted in the window and the flags disappeared from view.

Nathan exchanged a look with Duffy, who appeared thrilled just to be there. He turned the car around and drove back. He tried again and nearly missed them this time, turning his head barely in time to see them slip out of sight. The third time, he knew he was on alert, but he saw them clearly once again. He counted as he passed. The flags were exposed for nearly four seconds. And these were only flags, he thought. Cam's white Land Cruiser would have been clearer.

Nathan slowed the car as he approached the hidden gap and drove back in. He parked on the slope, thinking again about the position of Cameron's seat as he climbed out. The poles were far easier to pull out of the ground than they'd been to put in and he was driving away in less than a minute.

'I was right, mate,' he supposed he would be able to say to Xander when he got back to the house. Although he wasn't sure he would say it. Xander hadn't been too impressed by Nathan's theory that morning as he'd sat in bed and listened.

'Look,' Nathan had whispered, not wanting to wake the whole household. 'If Dave drove to Atherton on Thursday morning, he should have spotted Cam's car on the rocks.'

Xander had rubbed some sleep from the corner of his eye and said nothing.

'But Dave didn't see the car,' Nathan continued.

'He says he didn't.'

'Why would a contractor lie about that? He's not even from around here. He only knew Cam to say hello to when he's out on a job. If he'd seen the car when he was driving past, he'd say so.'

'I suppose, but –' Xander had propped himself up on his pillow, his chest bare and his hair messy.

'What, mate?'

'Maybe he just missed it.'

'Why would he miss it? Glenn saw the car from the road. He told us.'

'Glenn's a cop. He's trained to look for stuff like that. And he was coming to meet us, so he knew Cam's car was somewhere around here.'

'That's why we should go and check,' Nathan said. 'See how visible it would have been from the road.'

'And what if it was visible?' Xander sounded worried. 'If it was too obvious for the contractor to miss when he drove by, but he reckons he didn't see it, then what are you saying? That the car wasn't there on Thursday morning?'

'I don't know. Maybe. I suppose so.'

'But Steve said Uncle Cam was already dead by then, or nearly. So if his car wasn't where we found it, then what? Someone moved it?'

Nathan didn't say anything.

'Who would do that? Jenna?'

Nathan still didn't reply.

'Someone else?' Xander said. 'One of us here on the property? Someone in this family?'

'Come on, mate.'

'Then what?' Xander's voice was rising.

'Look, I don't know,' Nathan heard himself snap. 'That's why I want to check it out before jumping to conclusions.'

'Don't, Dad. It sounds –' Xander looked at him. 'Crazy.'

Nathan blinked now, seeing the track in front of him properly for the first time, and put his foot on the brake.

'Shit.'

He was going the wrong way. He had started driving blindly towards the stockman's grave rather than back to the road. He hadn't even realised he was doing it, and a tiny part of him wondered if he should be worried about that. He listened to the engine tick over and tried to gather his thoughts. They felt loose and disconnected, as though floating through his fingers.

Duffy scratched the seat impatiently and Nathan put his foot on the accelerator. He was approaching a gentle crest where the land rose enough to hide the track ahead. He gunned the Land Cruiser up the mild slope, turning the wheel for a wide U-turn. From the peak, the grave would be visible somewhere below.

Instead, he saw a dust cloud.

Nathan stopped, the tip of the Land Cruiser at the peak of the crest. The small haze billowed along in the distance for half a minute before he caught the first glint of metal. He sat with his foot on the brake, watching the movement. It was coming along the dirt track and from the direction of travel, there was only one place it could be headed.

Nathan turned off his engine and heard the hum of the distant vehicle. He reached out and scrabbled in the glove box for his battered binoculars. Next to him,

Duffy whined. Without the air conditioning, the car was getting warm.

He looked through the binoculars until he found the moving vehicle. He recognised it immediately. He had seen it parked around Cameron's property for years. It was a general-use four-wheel drive, used mostly by casual workers and, most recently, by Simon.

The car slowed a few metres from the stockman's grave, its windscreen reflecting nothing but sky. Nathan steadied the binoculars. The vehicle came to a stop, its angle now turning the windscreen dark rather than opaque.

Nathan watched, unblinking. There was a movement inside, as the driver reached for something in the passenger seat. From a distance, through the glass, Nathan could see a wrist and a sweep of long hair falling over a shoulder. It definitely wasn't Simon behind the wheel. It was a woman.

Chapter 25

The driver's door opened and a jean-clad leg stepped out. The woman was hidden by the open door and Nathan's binoculars slipped a little, sending the scene out of focus. He steadied himself in time to see the door slam and in the red dirt beside the stockman's grave stood a wholly familiar figure.

Ilse.

Nathan realised he was holding his breath and blew it out, long and heavy. The window of opportunity to announce himself came and went almost immediately. He didn't beep the horn, or wind down the window and shout out. By the time he wondered whether he should, it was already too late.

Ilse stood with her back to him, looking small and isolated. A black shape lay at her feet. Some sort of bag, Nathan thought, hoping she wouldn't suddenly turn around. He was a fair distance away, and his car was filthy, almost the same colour as the ground. He was parked nose-forward on the edge of the rise and the sun was working mostly in his favour. It would be at least partly in her eyes if she turned his way. If she looked directly at him, she would probably see the car, though. If not, the ground and the distance and the stillness might be enough of a cover.

Nathan lowered the binoculars, feeling uncomfortable. Below, he could just about make out the sight of Ilse kneeling and reaching for the bag. Duffy whined and he poured some water into a plastic cup and pushed it towards her. A bead of sweat ran down his temple and into his eye. The interior of the car was heating up fast without the air con. Nathan shifted again, his back damp against the seat. His hand hovered over the car keys. He couldn't start the engine now. There was no way Ilse wouldn't hear it. Nathan picked up the binoculars again.

Ilse took something from her bag, but at that angle Nathan couldn't tell what. She was bending forward, close to the earth where her husband had been found, and was partly hidden by the headstone. Nathan breathed out a lungful of hot air, and tipped the last of his water bottle into Duffy's cup. The rest of his water was packed out of reach in the back. The interior of car was stifling now. He let himself open the window a crack. It made no difference.

Glenn had told him a story a few years earlier, about James Buchanan from town who'd got into an argument with his wife. Worse than an argument, really, and as things escalated she'd managed to lock James out of the house. He'd knocked on the door, then, when she wouldn't answer, gone around the outside of the family home and smashed the air conditioner with a cricket bat. Then he'd sat down and waited, bat in hand. His wife had been too scared to open the doors and windows, Glenn had said. Eventually she passed out from heat exhaustion. She had nearly died, there on her kitchen floor. Nathan thought Glenn had been trying to make him feel better. *See? Other people do shitty things too.* It had not made him feel better at the time – at all – and now as his skin stuck to the seat, he couldn't stop thinking about it. He glanced at Duffy and wound down the window some more.

He wondered how long Ilse was planning to stay. She must be feeling the temperature herself, down there. When he looked again, he thought he could see her shoulders moving. Was she crying? he wondered.

She knelt for another minute, while he sweated, and then finally, at long last, she stood up. Nathan breathed out. She ran her hand over the headstone, before picking up her bag from the ground. With a last look at the grave, she opened the car door.

Nathan wiped a hand over his face, freezing mid-motion as Ilse suddenly stopped. She was scanning the land, her head turning slowly. As her gaze reached Nathan's direction, it seemed to settle. He held his breath. Down the binocular lenses, it was as though they were looking straight at each other.

Can you feel anyone now?

Only us.

Nathan didn't dare move. He held the binoculars in place, staring back as his heartbeat thumped in his ears. Had she seen him? He wasn't sure, but there was something unfocused in her face that made him think perhaps not. At last Ilse dropped her eyes. She climbed into the car and he heard it start.

Nathan sat watching the dust trail as she drove away, back in the direction she'd come from. He made himself wait until she'd fully disappeared from sight before finally turning on his own engine.

The air came through lukewarm at first but he gasped with relief, gulping in huge lungfuls. He got out and grabbed water bottles from the back, and while both he and Duffy drank deeply, Nathan checked his watch. Ilse had been at the gravesite less than fifteen minutes from start to finish. It felt longer, but it hadn't been. He frowned. All that way for fifteen minutes. Sophie's voice popped into his head. *We didn't do anything at the grave. We got out of the car, then we went home again.*

Nathan drank another mouthful of water, watched the horizon and listened. No dust, no noise. She was gone. He put the car into gear and slowly made his way down, over the crest and towards the grave. He parked a short distance away and got out. The dust circle around the headstone was long gone, but had been replaced with Ilse's footprints. He could see the soft dents in the ground where she had knelt. Could she have been praying? he wondered. She had never seemed the type, but death did funny things to people. Nathan touched the headstone, warm in the sun. Something felt wrong, but he couldn't tell what. Finally, he knelt down himself and all of a sudden, he could see it.

The hole they'd exposed beneath Cameron's body was disturbed. It had nearly refilled itself the last time he'd

been there with Bub and Harry, but now it looked different again. Nathan reached out and touched the ground.
The earth was freshly turned. He ran a hand through it,
looking to see if Ilse had left anything here, but all he
could feel was sandy soil. There were a few small things
that could possibly be seeds and Nathan thought of his
own dad's grave. He and his brothers hadn't even liked
the bloke and they'd still planted a tree for him. Had Ilse
been doing something like that for Cameron?

The sun was beating down on him and he shifted on
his knees until he was in the shadow of the headstone.
His movement left a mark in the dust that was familiar in
a way that made Nathan feel slightly ill. He stood up so
fast he was dizzy.

Back in the safety of his car, Nathan turned up the air
conditioner. It was a physical relief to be back in the cool,
and he sat back, feeling the fibres in his body respond as
his temperature crept back down towards normal.

Cameron would have fought for his life to stay with his car.

The thought came out of nowhere. Nathan reached for
his water bottle and took a long sip. Cameron knew what
it was like to be out there with no shelter and no supplies.
It was a death sentence. If Cam had been forcibly separated
from his car, he would have fought. Nathan stared at the
grave. He pictured his brother's body as the tarp slipped
away. There had been no injuries to his hands or face.

Nathan took another slow sip of water and thought
about that. An hour later, he was still not sure what to
think. He knew he should go home. It was Cameron's
funeral tomorrow. Another one for the land. Nathan

should drive back and speak to his son. Speak to Ilse. Instead, Nathan sat in his car beside the grave until the sun moved the shadow almost all the way around the base of the headstone.

No-one else came by.

Chapter 26

Nathan left it almost too late to make it home before nightfall and as he pulled up the windows of the house were glowing. He slammed his car door and stopped as his eyes fell on the large gum tree across the yard. Beneath it, hard to see in the growing dark but impossible to miss, was a gaping black hole.

Nathan walked over and stood at the edge. Cameron's grave lay deep and empty, ready for tomorrow. There were no howls from the dingoes that night and the air felt hot and thick as Nathan turned his back and trudged to the house. The voices coming from the kitchen were muffled but urgent as he closed the screen door behind him.

'You said – no, don't give me that bullshit – you said we could try it –'

'For God's sake, I know, Bub, but I have a thousand other things to –'

Three faces looked up as Nathan walked in.

'Great. Here comes your reinforcements,' Bub snapped at Ilse, who was sitting at the kitchen table. She was wearing the same clothes Nathan had seen her in earlier at the stockman's grave, and was staring firmly into a glass of wine. Bub looked to have been pacing, his face set, while Liz hovered in the no-man's-land between them.

'Bub, just calm down. Please.' Liz shot a glance at Nathan. 'You've been a very long time.'

'I was checking something at the fence line. What's going on here?'

'Nothing,' Ilse said.

'It's not bloody nothing.' Bub sounded like he'd been drinking. 'I'm not bloody taking orders –'

'No-one's asking you to, Bub!'

Bub looked at Nathan. 'You tell her. You thought my mustering plan was a good idea, didn't you?'

'Wait –' Nathan felt lost. 'That's what this is about?'

'Tell her.' Bub's voice was rising. 'Tell her that I'm right about this.'

Nathan frowned. 'I haven't even had a chance –'

'No. Of course not. Jesus, I bloody knew it would be like this.' Bub closed his eyes. 'This is bullshit.'

'Why are you doing this now, mate?' Nathan said. 'Let's talk about it later. We're burying him tomorrow.'

'Yeah.' Bub opened his eyes and looked at Ilse. 'Still, silver lining for some, isn't it?'

'Bub!' Liz said. 'Enough!'

Ilse sat completely still as Bub walked out, slamming the kitchen door. They all stared after him as the sound reverberated in his wake.

'What's his –?' Nathan barely started before Liz turned on him.

'You're no better. Have you spoken to your son yet? He's been worrying all day about you. He wanted Harry to take him out to search.'

Nathan opened his mouth. 'I told him where I was going.'

'You've been gone for hours.'

'Well –'

'Your radio was off. Again.'

'Shit. Yeah, okay. Sorry –'

'It's not me you should apologise to.' Before Nathan could answer, Liz looked at Ilse. 'Are you all right, at least?'

Ilse, still sitting at the table, didn't move and didn't look up. 'Yes.'

'Good.' Liz sounded defeated. 'Then I'm going to see to Bub.'

The door swung shut behind her. Ilse was still staring at the glass in front of her. Nathan opened the fridge and got a beer, leaning against the counter as he opened it and took a sip. He could see traces of the red dust in the creases of Ilse's shirt and jeans. He had the same on his own. *Just ask her.* Instead he nodded at the door.

'I didn't realise Bub was so serious about the mustering thing.'

'I think it's less about the mustering and more about who makes the decisions around here now.'

Nathan didn't reply.

'He called Cameron's lawyer,' Ilse said.

'Bub did?'

'Asking about the property split and what happens now.'

'What did the lawyer say?'

'That Cam's share goes to the girls.'

'Not you?'

'Not technically. I'm just the guardian until they're old enough. But the point is, it doesn't go to Bub. Or you.' Ilse looked at him properly now. 'Please tell me you already knew that?'

'Yeah. It's okay.'

She looked relieved. She lifted her foot under the table, and kicked a chair out a little way. Nathan wavered, then pulled it over and sat down.

'I'm surprised Bub even knew who Cam's lawyer was,' he said. 'Let alone think to call him.'

'Your mum said that too. I told you, though. Bub's more switched on than you all give him credit for. Especially about property work. Either way –' She sighed. 'I guess he was really keen to know.'

'Had Cameron promised him something different?'

'I don't know. But with the way it's split now between you and me and him, I think Bub feels –' She hesitated and took a sip from her glass. 'Left out, or something.'

'Maybe he's worried about what you're planning to do with the place.'

'God, I haven't even thought about it. I mean, it's not like I asked for this. I'd probably sell it to him, if he'd let me get a word in edgeways.'

'I doubt he could afford it,' Nathan said.

'Or to you, then.'

'I definitely couldn't afford it.'

'Not even at mates' rates?'

'We'd have to be bloody good mates.'

The silence was laced with something at the edges. They were both too old to be embarrassed and Nathan thought he saw the very corner of her mouth twitch. Ilse looked at the empty beer in Nathan's hand, then looked at him.

'Will you have another one?'

He hesitated. He tried to avoid drinking too much around her, preferring to keep a clear head. Still. She sat opposite, looking over at him. He could.

He would pay for it later though, he knew, in a few days' time when he was back in his empty, silent house. Over the years, Nathan had discovered that his isolation was strangely easier to cope with when he was on his own for long stretches. Then, the loneliness became routine, sometimes fading to barely more than a dull background ache. His early desperation for human contact had changed too. Other people's company should have been a relief but now just stirred up complicated emotions that he later had to deal with all on his own, long after they were gone. It was getting harder for him to recover each time and taking far longer to get back to normal, if he could even call it that. But if spending time with other people was bad enough, spending time with Ilse was worse. As much as he wanted to, and the biggest and deepest part of Nathan really wanted to, he simply couldn't do it to himself.

He looked at her now as the kitchen clock ticked loudly, and took a breath. 'No. Thanks, though.'

Her eyes followed him as he stood up and all of a sudden, she looked very alone. He pushed in his chair.

'I'd better go and talk to Xander.' That was true, actually.

Ilse looked down at the table for a moment, then nodded. 'It sounds like he was worried.'

'Did he say something to you?'

'No. But I wasn't here most of the day. I've barely seen him.'

'Oh yeah?' Nathan tried to keep his voice light. 'What were you doing?'

Ilse shrugged, and the red dust settled deeper into the fabric creases. 'I needed to get out of here so I took the workers' vehicle and went for a drive.'

He frowned. 'What's wrong with yours?'

Strangely, Ilse looked almost amused. 'It's very unreliable. I've got stuck a couple of times.'

'Cam and Harry couldn't get it going?'

'Sometimes, but then there'd be something else.'

'You want me to take a look? Although if they couldn't fix it, I can't make any promises.'

He thought he heard a movement in the hall and they both looked over at the empty doorway. No-one appeared. Ilse looked back, a slightly odd expression on her face.

'Why not?' she said. 'Thanks. It's in the small garage.'

'No worries.' Nathan stepped back from the table. *Ask her.* 'Where did you drive to today?'

Ilse's gaze flicked once more to the doorway. It was still empty. 'Don't tell the others.'

'Okay.'

'I went out to the stockman's grave. I wanted some time alone to think about Cameron. With the funeral tomorrow, everyone's going to be talking about him –' She looked down. 'I feel like Cam – the Cameron

276

that I knew – could get lost in all this. Do you know what I mean?'

Nathan nodded. They might be burying Cameron tomorrow, but he realised part of him still half expected his brother to appear around the corner. It was almost unbelievable that the man he had grown up with and fought with and loved in his own way wasn't there anymore. That the deep hole outside could be for Cameron.

'Yeah,' he said finally. He looked at Ilse, with her eyes heavy above her dust-stained collar. 'I know what you mean.'

Chapter 27

Xander's bedroom door was shut.

Nathan knocked. 'Can I come in?'

No response. He waited, then opened the door anyway. His son was lying on the bed, reading. Xander barely looked up.

'You're back.'

Nathan sat on the end of the bed. 'Sorry I was so long.'

Xander stared at the page, his eyes unmoving, then dropped his book on his chest. 'Did you do your test?' His voice was not friendly.

'Yes.'

'And could you see the flags from the road?'

Two out of three. 'Not every time.'

'So what does that mean?'

'I don't know.'

Xander flopped back and picked up his book again.

'Grandma said you were worried.'

No answer.

'I really am sorry, mate.'

Xander stared at the page. Nathan waited as long as he could, but this time he broke the silence himself.

'I didn't mean to –'

'It's fine.' Xander turned a page.

'It's not, though, is it? Not if you're unhappy.'

No response.

'Xand –'

Xander made a frustrated noise. 'What do you want me to say? I'm trying to read.'

'I want to –'

'What?'

'I don't know. Fix things.'

Xander turned another page. 'Don't worry about it. There's no point arguing with you. Mum was right. You're always like this.'

'Like what?'

Xander shook his head. 'Forget it.'

'Mate, you can tell me –'

'No.' Xander's face was hidden behind the book. 'Do whatever you want. I don't care anymore.'

Nathan waited. Long minutes ticked by. Finally, Xander turned another page and Nathan got up and left the room.

Ilse's four-wheel drive was covered in the requisite layer of dust. It was the only vehicle parked in the small garage, and someone had dumped a load of empty crates in front of it. They looked like they'd been there for some time. How long had the car been out of action? Nathan wondered as he fished the keys out of the footwell.

He had to adjust the driver's seat as he climbed in and was again reminded of doing the same in Cameron's abandoned car. No clearer what to make of that, he pushed the thought to one side and tried the engine. It stuttered a little from lack of use, but turned over and came to life. Nathan listened to the hum. It was clear and steady.

He switched on a lamp so he could see better in the evening gloom, and opened the bonnet. He leaned inside and began checking it over, starting with the typical trouble spots and moving through to the less obvious problem areas. An hour later he was on his back under the chassis, a torch in his hand and none the wiser.

As he worked, his mind drifted to Xander. Specifically to a faded memory from years earlier, when his son had been about eight. They'd been camping out during one of his first solo visits, and Nathan had woken up in the back of his Land Cruiser to find Xander's sleeping bag empty beside him. He had lain there, listening for the sound of urine hitting the hard ground outside or the rustle of a cereal packet. When he hadn't heard either of those things, or anything in fact, he'd called out. There had been no answer.

Nathan had sat up, the air already stifling and his clothes sticking to him with sweat. He'd called again, this time hearing the alarm in his own voice. No reply.

The fear had been immediate and absolute. Nathan had clambered to his feet and stood by his car, his pulse pounding as he scanned the surroundings, almost blinded by terror. It would be over forty degrees by noon. A child

Xander's size might last half a day, depending on water and luck. How long had he been gone? Nathan didn't know. Kids far younger than Xander, toddlers even, had been known to walk for kilometres. Some had been found miles from their home. Some were lucky, for some it was too late.

Nathan had felt the sun beating down. When he was sure there was no sign of his son in any direction, he'd had to fight the overwhelming urge to pick one at random and start running. Instead, he had made himself get into the car and drive in increasing circles.

He had found Xander within fifteen minutes, over a slight rise, and looking bewildered after following a cow and her calf too far. He was fine, if bemused by his dad's flush-faced panic. But it had been the worst fifteen minutes of Nathan's life. He had hugged Xander hard and then, shaking with relief, yelled at him in a way he never had before or since.

Nathan lay staring at the underside of Ilse's four-wheel drive now. He frowned, then clicked off his torch. He'd started to slide out when he heard the soft tread of footsteps outside the garage. He sat up and looked at the door, blinking into the night. Harry appeared.

'Here you are. Your mum was looking for you.' He looked past Nathan at the dusty vehicle. 'What are you doing?'

'Ilse said the car was playing up.'

'Again?'

'Apparently.' Nathan stood up and wiped the grease off his hands.

Harry stepped into the light. A wire hook swung from his hand, its point threaded through two bloodied dingo scalps. He peered beneath the open bonnet for so long Nathan began to get irritated. It was late and he was getting tired.

'What did Mum want?' he said.

'Wanted to make sure you were okay.' Harry was standing at an awkward angle, almost blocking the way. 'You're feeling all right about tomorrow?'

'I suppose.' Outside, the fresh grave was well hidden from sight. 'Who dug the hole for Cam?'

'Me and Bub mainly. Xander and Simon helped as well.'

The thought of the backpacker taking Nathan's place on a job like that riled him. 'I should have been here to help.'

'Yeah. You should have.' The thin streaks of blood on the scalps looked black in the dim light. 'He was still your brother, whatever problems you two had.'

It was the note of judgement that made Nathan turn.

'Me? What about you? I hear you were arguing with Cam not long before he died.'

Harry looked at him sharply. 'What are you talking about?'

'Simon heard you. One night when you were turning the generator off.'

Harry's features creased more deeply into a frown. 'I wouldn't call it an argument.' His thumb ran over the end of the wire hook. 'Cam and I exchanged words from time to time. Same as you two did. You know that.'

'What was it about?'

'Same as always. Running this place.' Harry looked down,

his features lost in shadow. 'I told you something was up with Cam, and it had been affecting his work. His concentration had gone to shit, I was having to chase after him, double-checking everything.'

'Simon thought you sounded angry.'

'That's a bit strong. It was late. I was probably just a bit pissed off.'

'And you were saying something about knowing what was going on around here.'

'Yeah.' Harry flashed a humourless grin. 'Well, that's fair enough, isn't it? Don't think anyone would argue with that.'

They wouldn't, Nathan knew. Harry probably understood this property better than he or his brothers ever had. But despite that, and whatever went right or wrong with the place, it was their names on the title. Harry's was a strangely insecure existence, Nathan realised, now he thought about it. This might be his home and he might seem like family, but Sergeant Ludlow had been right, Harry was an employee. And Cameron – or Ilse now – just had to say the word and an employee would be gone.

'Harry,' Nathan said. 'Did Cam threaten to get rid of you?'

'No, mate.'

It had been a shot in the dark, but the answer was so breezily dismissive that Nathan felt a seed of doubt form. He thought about Cameron, who ran this place so efficiently. Kept a tight ship, as Harry had said himself. Would Cameron let himself be challenged by a worker, even if that worker was Harry?

Nathan looked at him now. 'You sure?'

'I'm sure,' Harry said. 'Look, he reminded me who was in charge when I needed reminding. And he liked me to mind my own business. But when he takes his eye off the ball and that means more work around here, it becomes my business, whether I like it or not. There's nothing I can do but bring it up, so that's what I did.'

'Is that why you didn't say anything to us?'

'I didn't say anything,' Harry said, 'because I felt bad – I still feel bad – about it. I thought Cam needed to hear what I had to say, but I dunno. Maybe I should have been listening more. I didn't know that Jenna woman had tried to get in touch, or how bloody stressed he was about it. I wish he'd said.'

Nathan was quiet for a minute. 'Why do you think he was so worried about her?'

'I don't know. Cam said at the time he'd done nothing wrong, and I believed him.' He looked at Nathan. 'Believed you when you said the same.'

'She's not in England. Hasn't been for a couple of weeks. Bali, apparently.'

Harry was very still. 'Is that right?'

The silence stretched out.

'Look,' Harry said, his voice was gentle now. 'This whole thing with Cam. It feels complicated, but when it comes down to it, I think it's actually pretty bloody simple.'

'Is it?'

'Yeah. He was not a happy man, mate. Not at all. And I'm starting to think that had been the case for a long time.'

Harry sighed. 'We need to get this funeral out of the way. Everything will look better after that.'

'I suppose.'

'It will. Always the way. Trust me.' Harry frowned at Ilse's car. 'You planning to stay out here much longer? I'll leave the generator on, if you want.'

Nathan shook his head. 'I'll stop now.'

'You worked out what's wrong with it?'

'No.' Nathan had done everything he could think of. It seemed to be in good shape to him.

'Yeah, I always had trouble finding the problem too.' Harry stared again at the exposed engine. 'I had one idea, though.'

'I'm all ears, mate.'

Harry hesitated as out in the blackness, they heard footsteps on the verandah and Liz's voice called out, 'Harry?'

'Never mind.' He tapped the car. 'I should take another look myself first. There'll be no rush anyway. Ilse hates driving that thing, she's not going anywhere in that.'

'Harry?' Liz's voice again.

'I'll tell her you're fine.' Harry nodded at the bloodied scalps at the end of the hook in his hand. 'Better do something with these as well.'

'You got them, then?'

'Yeah. Wanted to get it done before everyone arrives tomorrow. They were getting too comfortable.'

'I thought Bub was going to do it.'

A look flitted across Harry's face that suggested Bub might also be getting a little too comfortable.

'I had the chance, got it done,' he said. 'If you're

finished out here, generator's going off in ten. I need to get some sleep.' He swung the hook gently. The matted fur and skin was already curling at the edges. 'Big day tomorrow.'

Chapter 28

Nathan awoke to the ache of dehydration pulsing in his temples. He squinted into the early-morning light and reached for his water glass beside the couch. It was empty. He must have drunk it during the night, but he couldn't remember doing so. It felt like a hangover with none of the fun. He tried to remember how much water he'd drunk yesterday. Not enough, clearly.

He stood up too fast, and had to steady himself briefly against the wall as his head spun. He waited, blinking slowly, until the sensation passed. He looked around. Something felt off.

Nathan frowned as his gaze was dragged once more to Cameron's painting. It hung there in front of him, looking the same as ever. Not quite though, somehow. He stepped closer, his head still pounding. The scene was fully familiar, with the same colours and shapes. The dark grave and bright sky swam in front of his eyes. The translucent smudge was still there, as unclear as ever. What was different? Was the horizon slightly tilted? He wasn't sure, and reached out, instantly making things worse as the frame slid at an alarming angle too far the other way. He corrected it hastily, trying to judge a straight line.

'Be careful.' Liz was at the doorway. She was entirely in black, except her eyes, which were bloodshot red. 'Cameron loved that.'

'Maybe we should take it down for today? I can put it somewhere.'

'What? No. Why would we?' She came over, gently reaching out and straightening the frame. Much better, Nathan could tell immediately.

'Stop it getting damaged,' he said.

'But everyone will want to see it. It belongs here on the wall. Cameron would have wanted that.'

'I suppose. I just thought, you know, with the subject matter.'

'It's still a beautiful painting.' Liz wiped her cheek with the back of her hand. Nathan hadn't even realised she was crying. 'And whatever was wrong with Cameron, he was always a beautiful painter. It reminds me of all the best things about him. I don't want to hide that away.'

'Yeah, all right.' Nathan shrugged. 'It was only a thought.'

Liz looked over. 'How's Xander coping?'

'I haven't spoken to him since last night. He's still pissed off with me for being gone so long yesterday.'

'Are you surprised?'

Nathan considered. He was, actually, a little. It wasn't like Xander to hold a grudge. Or get pissed off in the first place, for that matter. 'There was nothing for him to panic about. When I'm back at my place, I'm out on my own all the time.'

'That's exactly part of the problem, Nathan.' Liz turned to him. 'Listen, I want you to have a chat with Steve today. Get him to make you an appointment at the clinic.'

'Why? What for?'

'See if he can give you something to get your head straight.'

'I don't need –'

'You do. Because if you think it's all right to disappear like that, to the point where your son is scared about what you might be up to, then there's something seriously wrong.' Liz lifted her head to look at him properly. 'Please, Nathan. Losing one of you is bad enough. Today is going to be the worst day of my life. I can't go through this twice.'

He couldn't bear the look in her eyes so he nodded. 'All right.'

There was a noise in the hall and they both turned to see Bub in the doorway. He had a slightly unstable air that made Nathan suspect he'd already started drinking. Or perhaps not long stopped from the night before.

'What are we doing?' Bub leaned a supporting hand against the doorjamb. 'Admiring Cam's masterpiece?'

Liz flinched at the sarcasm. Definitely been drinking, Nathan thought.

'We were talking about whether to take it down or not,' he said.

'Shit, no. You don't mess with Cam's picture. He'd

289

bloody come back and haunt you for that.' Bub almost laughed and Nathan felt Liz tense.

'What do you want, Bub?' he said.

'Oh, yeah. Funeral guy just called.'

'And?'

'Body's on its way.'

Nathan had to wear his dad's old suit. Liz had dragged it out from somewhere and handed it to him without a word. It was twenty-five years old but had the stiffness of rarely worn fabric. It was black and fit well. Nathan put his hand in the jacket pocket and found a faded supply list written in his dad's handwriting. He crumpled the paper without reading it and fought the urge to rip off the jacket.

Bub walked into the living room and dropped his beer when he saw Nathan.

'Shit. I thought for a second –' Bub took a step back before recovering. He bent down and picked up his bottle, swiping at the floor with a dirty tissue while he avoided looking at Nathan. 'You seen yourself, mate? You look just like him.'

Nathan turned and stared at his dark and distorted reflection in the TV screen. He didn't recognise himself. Carl Bright's jacket was suddenly too tight and Nathan couldn't breathe properly. He pulled it off and kicked it under the couch.

Xander wandered in dressed in Cameron's only suit, then stalled in the doorway as Nathan and Bub both stared at him. The suit fit like it had been made to measure and

Xander looked taller and broader and older than Nathan had ever seen him.

'Grandma told me to wear it,' Xander said, looking down. 'But maybe –'

'It's fine,' Nathan said. 'Looks good, mate.'

Xander helped first Bub, then Nathan, fix their ties properly. Nathan stood face to face with his son, watching him looping the fabric around. Nathan could hear him breathe and see a tiny patch of dark stubble where he'd missed a spot shaving. He could see the small scar on his hairline where he had fallen off a horse when he was five. He watched the slight narrowing of eyes that had been blue like Jacqui's when he was born, but had turned brown like Nathan's within a year. Nathan suddenly wanted Xander to be small enough again that he could pick him up and hold him. Instead he stood there, feeling uncomfortable in his borrowed suit.

'Xander, listen, about yesterday –'

'Finished. Better.' Xander pulled the tie tight and stepped away. He looked over at Bub, who was staring at Cameron's painting. 'Hey, do you think the painting might upset people today? With that story about the stockman wandering off?'

'No-one believes that shit,' Bub said, not turning around. He took a sip of his beer and pointed the bottle neck at the grave. 'He raped an Aboriginal girl and got himself killed for it, everyone knows that. Don't know why he gets so much bloody glory.'

'Is that true?' Xander said, looking to Nathan, who shook his head. It was true there were plenty of white blokes who had done all that, and worse, but not in this case. He opened his mouth but was cut short by a noise outside.

Bub turned to the window. 'It's here,' he said.

Nathan and Xander joined him at the glass. Out on the driveway, the funeral director's black four-wheel drive was pulling up. It had been modified to carry six-foot-long cargo in the back. The vehicle may have been shiny when it set off from St Helens, but the journey had branded it with the same grit and grime as everything else. At the homestead fence, Ilse stood watching its arrival, flanked on either side by her daughters' small figures. Together, they looked like a flock of birds, all in black, the edges of their skirts catching feather-like in the wind.

Far beyond them, Nathan could just make out a distant billow of dust. The neighbours were arriving.

The service was brisk and to the point, conducted by a chaplain from St Helens who at least seemed to understand that however much Cameron Bright might be missed, it didn't make the sun any less hot. The freshly turned soil around the grave was already dry and flaky, and the shade of the gum tree wasn't enough for those sweltering in their once-a-year outfits. Nathan stood in his shirtsleeves and his fancy knotted tie and looked around the crowd with a strangely detached interest.

There were maybe forty there, he counted, as they all fidgeted in their town clothes and best hats. A good turn-out. Excellent, in fact. He hadn't seen most of them in years but he recognised about two-thirds. Old Tom, young Tom, Kylie from the service station – with a couple of kids in tow now – and Geoff who used to be her boyfriend and now looked to be her husband. That dickhead engineer who'd been based out at Atherton for years – Nathan couldn't remember his name, there were so many dickheads over at Atherton. Steve from the clinic, of course. No Glenn, but no surprise there.

Nathan had phoned the police station that morning and been diverted again. Sergeant McKenna was still clearing up from that tour bus spill in the north. Did Nathan want to leave another message? 'Just ask him to call me,' he'd said finally, and hung up.

Nathan didn't know the chaplain, and from the generalised phrases he was leaning on, felt sure the guy had never actually met Cameron. Nathan mostly tuned out the service and stared at his neighbours, taking in the greying hair and the extra kilos. Most of them stared back, curious and with a slightly bewildered air, like they'd almost forgotten that he really existed.

Liz nearly made it through. The dreadful keening started in her throat as the chaplain neared the end, and grew to an eerie crescendo by the time Sophie and Lo were invited forward to plant a small sapling at the head of the grave. Liz's shoulders heaved and her cries were muffled as she buried her face in her sleeve. Harry whispered something, taking her arm and attempting to lead her away, but she shook him off violently.

Lo, eyes wide and trowel quivering in her hand, took one look and started to wail herself, followed quickly by

Sophie. Ilse took a swift step forward, scooping them close to her and ushering them towards the house.

'But what about the tree?' Lo's voice floated back, high-pitched through her sobs. 'We're supposed to plant the tree.'

Without a word, Liz picked up the discarded trowel and dropped to her knees. She dug, hard and fast, stabbing the blade into the loose soil as the dust flew up and clung to the dark fabric of her dress. Her grief was the raw and messy kind, and Nathan could see people glancing away, uncomfortable. The act of memorial had taken a voyeuristic turn and eventually he couldn't stand it any longer. He stepped forward, picked up the other trowel and dug with her. As soon as the hole was big enough, Liz grabbed the sapling and shoved it in, covering it loosely with the grainy earth. It wouldn't survive, Nathan thought – it wasn't deep enough – but at least it was done. He stood up and helped Liz towards the house, ignoring the gawping eyes of his neighbours as they watched him leave.

Chapter 29

An hour later, Liz had been tucked up in her darkened bedroom with a mild sedative supplied by Steve, and Nathan found himself standing alone by the lounge room door. The room was fuller than he had ever seen it and despite the heat, some of the crowd had spilled into the hall and out onto the verandah. They left a self-conscious clearing around Cameron's painting though, Nathan noticed.

'At least no-one's touching it.' Nathan heard the voice by his side. Ilse was looking past him at the picture.

'I thought we should take it down.'

She frowned. 'No, not at his funeral. People would ask about it. It's Cam's legacy. He would've wanted it there for everyone to see.' There was a faint note in her tone he couldn't quite make out over the noise.

'That's what Bub said too.'

'Did he?'

'Pretty much. And Mum.'

'They're right.'

They probably were, Nathan thought now. The guests may have been keeping a respectful distance but they all threw snatched glances towards the painting. Curious but reluctant to appear ghoulish. He saw Katy squeeze through the doorway and into the crowd, holding a tray of sandwiches. Instead of passing them around, she dumped the tray on a table and walked straight back out.

Ilse watched her with narrowed eyes. 'God, they're useless. Both of them.' A pause. 'I could sack them,' she added suddenly, realisation dawning in her voice.

'You might not have to. I think they're planning to leave.'

'Still. I could. If I wanted to.'

'Yeah. I suppose so.'

A woman with shoulder-length strawberry-blonde hair caught Ilse's eye across the room and raised her hand in a small wave.

'Who's that?' Nathan said.

'I don't know. I thought she was waving at you.'

'I don't think so.'

The woman waved again, a little hesitant now, and Ilse sighed. 'I'd better go and speak to a few people anyway. I'll talk to you later.'

Nathan sipped his beer and watched her make her way over to the woman in the corner. Ilse offered her hand and they exchanged a few words, their heads tilted close to hear each other over the chatter. Then Ilse turned and pointed to Nathan. She said something else, and the woman thanked her and threaded her way through the crowd towards him.

'Nathan. Hello. It was actually you I was waving at,' the woman said, once she was in front of him. She gave an embarrassed smile. 'You don't remember me. That's okay. It's Melanie. Birch? From Atherton.'

'Melanie.' He was struggling.

'From Atherton? Or I was, anyway, for a few years. And now, I'm back.' She gave a self-conscious laugh. 'Don't worry, I was a couple of years behind you so I don't think you even noticed me then. But I was friends with Jacqui when you two were dating.'

'Oh. Right. I don't –' He was still struggling, but at least she was still smiling. 'Jacqui and I have been divorced a while, so –'

'Oh. Me too.' She shrugged. 'City bloke. Didn't work out, surprise surprise, so after that I went travelling for a while. Was out west for a couple of years, and now I've ended up here again. Still working with the horses.'

'Right.' Nathan could now just about picture the girl he sometimes saw around at the gymkhanas, part of Jacqui's loose circle. A strawberry-blonde ponytail and freckles in the summer. There weren't loads of young people around, but they came and went with surprising frequency, to schools and jobs and other places. He wasn't sure he'd ever known her name was Melanie, having only really had eyes for Jacqui. Melanie was pretty, though. Both then and now.

'I'm sorry to hear about you and Jacqui. That's a shame, I thought you'd work out. You were so good together.' She hesitated, as if deciding how much to say, then gave him a small sideways smile. 'We were all horribly jealous of her because there were so many arseholes and never any good guys and she grabbed you so quickly. She was always telling us how much fun you two were having and how you made her laugh.'

'Really?' Didn't sound like Jacqui. Not at the end, anyway. Although — the memories were buried pretty deep — perhaps at the start. At the start, Nathan might have said the same about her. He looked at Melanie, properly this time. 'So, how do you like being back?'

'It's very quiet. I'd forgotten.'

'Yeah. It is. Quite quiet.' Nathan's mind was utterly blank. He couldn't think of a single thing to say. Across the room, he saw Ilse glance towards them, then immediately look away. She was being talked at by an older woman who Nathan didn't recognise.

'Anyway,' Melanie said. 'Listen, I'm so sorry about Cameron, and I completely realise this isn't an ideal time, but I wasn't sure when I might run into you again so I wanted to say hi. I mean, I don't know if you're ever in town —'

'I'm not. Hardly ever.'

'Oh.' She blinked, then recovered. 'Well, if you ever were and wanted to catch up for a drink or something, let me know.'

'Oh. Okay.'

'You can call me over at Atherton. And it's Melanie.'

'Melanie. Yeah, I know. Got it.'

'Good. Okay then.' She smiled, and as she turned to move away, she touched his arm lightly in a way that no-one had touched Nathan for a very long time. The heat of her fingertips lingered on his skin, so clear and sharp it was almost painful. He watched her blend back into the crowd, then jumped as Harry suddenly appeared at his side.

'I'm going to be honest, mate, I'm not sure you're in any position to play hard to get.' Harry handed him a fresh beer.

'Jesus, Harry. I don't even think that's what she was —'

'Well, you'll never know if you don't try, will you? You should give her a call. Start showing your face in town a bit.'

'She's been away. She won't know —'

'About all that business with Keith? She will. If she's based at Atherton, they'll have said something. No question.'

'Still. I dunno. I'll think about it.'

'Do. Because you're not making it easy, mate.'

'Easy for who?'

'Anyone. Them. You.' Harry nodded at the crowd. 'At least give them a chance to forgive you.'

'I did my begging ten years ago. It didn't work out well.'

'No-one's asking you to do that. Just meet them half-way. Or a bit more, maybe. A lot of time has gone by.'

'Same faces.'

'Some. Some not.' Harry dropped his voice. 'And a couple of them have been asking about you. Young Tom. Geoff. Asking what you've been up to. Look at them. They know that could've easily been you we buried out there. Still could be one day soon, if they're not careful. And that'd be something they'd all have to live with. This kind of thing brings things into perspective, puts people in a forgiving mood.'

'Yeah? Well, good on them.'

'I'm just saying, mate.'

Nathan shrugged. Across the room, he could see Bub chatting to a group of blokes about his age. Over in the corner, Ilse had escaped the older woman and was now talking to Steve.

They were standing apart from the other mourners, in the no-man's-land under the painting. Ilse had her head close to Steve's and looked to be speaking in a low voice. She was saying something, her face unusually agitated, while Steve pursed his lips. When Ilse stopped, the nurse shook his head. He opened his mouth to respond but she cut him off and started whispering again, more urgently this time. The crowd shifted and resettled and Nathan lost sight of them.

He leaned back against the wall. It was hot in the room and the chatter suddenly sounded loud. Nathan put down his beer and reached for the water jug on the nearest table. It was empty, as were two others he could see.

'I'm going to fill these up,' he said to Harry.

Harry shrugged. 'I'm telling you, mate. You're not doing yourself any favours, hiding away today.'

Nathan didn't reply.

The kitchen was no cooler, but at least it was quiet. Katy was standing alone by the sink, staring out of the window. She started as Nathan clattered the jugs on the draining board.

'Oh. Sorry,' she said. 'I thought you were Simon.'

'No. Where is he, anyway?'

'I don't know.'

Nathan checked the fridge. No cold water in there. He went back to the sink. The water ran hot from both taps, but it would have to do.

'Listen —' He held the jug under the stream. 'You two might be planning to hit the road soon but you're still on the payroll today.'

'I know. I'm sorry. I don't feel a hundred percent.' Katy leaned against the counter and Nathan saw that her face was in fact a little pale. Maybe it wasn't a great idea to have her serving food, he thought.

'Are you all right?'

'It's probably the heat.'

'The nurse is around. Do you want me to get him?'

'No. Thanks.' She went over to the table and picked up another tray of sandwiches.

Nathan watched as she put it straight back down again, a pained look on her face. 'Look,' he said. 'We'll manage. Go and lie down if you're ill —'

'Who's ill?' Simon stood at the door with an empty tray in his hand.

'No-one,' Katy said. 'I'm just a bit hot. Let's get back to work.' She swapped Simon's empty tray for the full one. 'You take that, and I'll take these.' She picked up the water jugs and flashed a smile. It looked almost real. 'And everyone's happy.'

She walked out of the kitchen and, after a beat, Simon followed. Nathan watched them go. Out in the hallway himself, he could hear the sound of chatter, louder now as more people spilled out from the cramped living room.

Nathan could see a few faces he recognised. Maybe he should go and try to talk to them. Go and find Melanie, even. Try to think of something to say this time. It was possible that Harry was right. Maybe people would forgive him.

Or maybe, Nathan's thoughts darkened fast these days, maybe not. It had taken Nathan a long time – years – to get used to his life as it was. The swift cut of rejection had hurt enough at the time when it was sharp and fresh, but it was the way the wound had festered that had been the killer. He had got through it once, barely. He knew with whole-hearted certainty that he could not do it again. A group of men jostled out of the living room and down the hall in his direction. Quickly, Nathan opened the nearest door and stepped inside. Ilse's office.

He shut the door behind him and breathed out. It was peaceful in there, the noise from the lounge and the hallway nothing more than a muffled hum. He stood for a minute, enjoying the peace, then walked over to the window. On the verandah, Sophie was playing some game with Kylie's kids, while Lo looked on. Xander was nearby, leaning against a post and chatting to a girl who looked around his age. She was smiling.

At the other side of the yard, someone was standing alone by the graves. Bub. He seemed to have his flies done up at least, Nathan thought, so that was something. His brother wasn't even looking at the earth. He was standing at the fence, with his back to the house, staring out into the beyond. Nathan watched for a minute more, then turned and looked at the wall calendar. Bub's mustering plans. Written on and then firmly crossed off.

Nathan sat down in the spare office chair and reached for the day planner on the desk. He flicked to the section Ilse had pointed out to him, and began to read the mustering notes. They were detailed, laying out what a change in the schedule would involve. The pros and cons, risks and rewards. He read it through, twice, then leaned back, thinking. Bub and Cameron had both been right, in their own ways. It was a good plan, but there were snags that needed to be ironed out before anything should happen. Just because Bub was the only one left to argue his case didn't mean Cam hadn't had a point.

Nathan started to close the diary, then stopped. Idly, he flipped the pages to the present week. There was almost nothing listed. The activity had been halted by a combination of Christmas and Cameron's death. The days were mostly empty and whatever was written there looked as though it had been added some weeks earlier.

He turned back another page, to the day Cameron had gone missing. There were quite a few items written down, listed in Ilse's handwriting. Reminders of several phone calls to be made, and a handful of invoices to chase before the end of the year. The weeks before showed more of the same. The day Ilse's husband had died looked to have been just another busy day for her in a busy six months.

He turned back and forth a few more pages. Everything she had written down appeared to be fairly standard stuff. He made similar phone calls and orders himself, he just didn't record them as efficiently. Ilse may not have asked for this, Nathan thought, and Bub may not like it, but she would probably be pretty good at running this place if she had to. Now she did have to, he supposed. He was about to close the book again when something at the bottom of a page caught his eye.

In the corner was a single tick with a time written next to it. Nathan frowned and turned back a few pages, then a few more. The same mark had been made every day for the whole year as far as he could see. There was no other information, just the checkmark and the numbers. The time recorded varied over two hours, coming in anywhere between 7 pm and 9 pm. Nathan stared at it. Somewhere, deep inside, he felt a stirring of recognition.

He was still trying to work it out when he heard a noise outside. He looked up as Ilse came through the door, Duffy at her feet. She jumped when she saw him.

'My God.' She put a hand to her chest. 'You scared me.'

'Sorry,' he said. 'I was –' He held up the planner.

'Oh, right. Fine.' She shut the door behind her and leaned against it, her face flushed.

'What's wrong?'

'It's my husband's funeral,' she snapped.

Nathan blinked. He'd never heard that tone from her before. 'What else?'

Ilse paced across the room, dropping into the chair behind her desk. 'How long have you been hiding in here?'

'Not that long.'

She nodded. 'It's strange out there, isn't it? Listening to

304

all those people go on about what a great guy Cameron was and how much they'll miss him.' She shook her head. 'I don't recognise some of them, and a lot of the others I haven't seen in years. They never come around, they never call. They barely knew him, really.'

'No. I suppose not.'

Duffy, who had been sniffing around the desk, ran over to Nathan and he bent down to her. He could feel Ilse's eyes on him. He still felt a touch light-headed and dehydrated. How many beers had he had? Not many, but more than he felt comfortable having when he was alone with Ilse.

'Sorry.' He started to stand. 'I'll get out of your way.'

'Yeah. That sounds about right.'

The sharp edge in her tone made him stop for a second time. He stared at her and she stared back.

'Go on, then. Don't let me keep you.' She jerked her head towards the door. 'You must have been here with me for – what? – two whole minutes already? Well past your normal cue to leave.'

Nathan stood there. 'Do you want me to stay?' he said, finally.

He waited. Ilse said nothing for a long time. At last she took a breath.

'I was talking to Steve. About Cameron and –' She dropped her eyes. 'And about Jenna.'

'Did he say something that upset you?'

Ilse made a bitter noise. 'No. The opposite, actually. He didn't say anything. I wanted to know what he thought happened back then, but he wouldn't tell me anything.'

She looked at Nathan now. 'You said he took her seriously. So why is he being so secretive now?'

'Well, you said it.' Nathan shrugged. 'It's your husband's funeral. Maybe he's trying to protect you.'

'Me?' The flush in her face grew angrier. 'It's not about protecting me. It's about Cameron. It always is. He's dead and we're all still dancing around him. Don't touch his painting. Don't do Bub's plan. Don't talk about –' She stopped. 'I'm sorry. I'm finding today very hard.'

'I know. It's all been hard.'

She took a deep breath. 'Listen, ignore me. Of course you can leave if you want.'

'Ilse, it's not –'

'No, I know. I get it. It's fine.' She waved a hand. 'Anyway, you probably should be out there. It's a good time to let people see you.'

'Harry said that too.'

'You should listen to him.' A pause. 'Who knows? Your friend might be looking for you.'

'Melanie?'

'Is that her name?'

'Apparently. I don't remember her very well.'

'She remembers you.'

'Well.' He smiled and shrugged. 'Can you blame her?'

At last, Ilse smiled back.

Nathan pushed his chair aside. 'I should probably go back, though,' he said. 'Otherwise Harry and Xander will notice I'm missing and read something into it.'

'Well, good luck,' she said. 'You might not need it as much as you think.'

'Maybe. But –' He could still hear the chatter through the door. 'It's what you said. I haven't seen most of those people in years. And maybe they can forget what I did, but now I'm supposed to just forget what *they* did? It's been ten years. Xander's suffered, my livestock, someone poisoned my dog –'

Ilse looked up at that. 'Really? That's how Kelly died? I didn't know that.'

'Yeah.' Nathan said. 'Not that anyone believes me.'

'Why not?'

'Because there were no other reports of baiting. Glenn and Xander think I'm paranoid.'

Ilse swung a little in her chair. She was frowning. 'Wait. Remind me. When was this?'

'About eighteen months ago.'

'Bub went through a phase of baiting dingoes last year.' Nathan stilled. 'Did he?'

'For the bounties. He was talking about moving away and trying to save his money. Cam told him not to do it around our own stock, of course. But Bub was still bringing home a lot of scalps so it was obvious he was doing it somewhere. I thought –' She stopped. 'Cam said he was going to warn you.'

'Well, he didn't.'

There was a silence. Nathan could feel pressure building in his temples and his neck and shoulder muscles were tight.

'I thought I was losing my bloody mind,' he said. 'I thought I'd imagined it.'

'No.' Ilse looked at him and slowly shook her head. 'No, I don't think so. I'm sorry, Nathan.'

'And before you try to tell me Cam wouldn't have for-gotten on purpose –'

'I wasn't going to say that.'

'Oh.'

'No, actually, I expect Cam probably did do it on pur-pose.' Ilse's gaze was clear and steady. 'He could be a bit funny about you. And he wouldn't overlook something like that by accident.'

Nathan couldn't think what to say to that.

'But listen.' Ilse sat forward in her seat. 'Try not to be too angry with Bub, okay? For what it's worth, he must have felt bad about it because he suddenly stopped baiting overnight. He didn't say why, but it was like he wouldn't touch it anymore.'

Nathan felt the tightness spread from his shoulders to his chest. Out of the window, Bub was no longer anywhere in sight. The fence by the graves stood empty. He didn't trust himself to speak.

'I'd better go.'

'Stay,' she said. 'If you want.'

'No, it's okay. Thanks.'

'Just –'

'What?'

'Whatever you're thinking of doing, please don't do it now. Not with all these people here.'

Nathan stood at the door.

'Please, Nathan. Leave it for now. For me.'

He stepped out. The hallway was quiet and he shut the door behind him and bent down. As Duffy licked his face, Nathan thought about the day that Kelly had died. It had felt like the beginning of the end in a lot of ways. It was after that that he'd let his gun licence lapse, and he'd turned off his radio for good, and he'd stopped answering his phone to the point where Harry had put the satellite tracker into his hands and ordered him to check in daily. *I'm okay; I'm not okay.*

Nathan definitely did not feel okay right then. After Kelly died, he had felt his fingertips starting to slip. He had been holding on for so long and it was too hard and he was just tired. He had felt himself, for the first time, simply giving up. Not all at once, and not entirely willingly, but a little at a time, slipping away, day after day.

And while this was going on, his bloody brothers had known all along what had happened. Nathan looked left towards the busy living room and right towards the yard outside. He'd well and truly missed his chance with bloody Cam, but where would Bub be? Behind him, the office door was still shut. He took a deep breath and made himself think about what Ilse had said. *For me.*

He pictured her, still sitting at her desk, and the bell in Nathan's head rang again, suddenly so close and clear that it took him by surprise. Ilse at her desk, working late into the evening after all those long and busy days laid out in her planner. And suddenly Nathan knew what the daily checkmarks were in the bottom corner of her diary.

Nathan had always assumed it had been Liz who had sent Harry over with the satellite tracker. Two buttons. *I'm okay; I'm not okay.* Each night he pressed the same one, no matter how strong the urge was to do otherwise. He didn't think it was even monitored anymore; no-one had ever mentioned it again. But he pressed the same button every night anyway, if only for himself. *I'm okay.* The same message, sent up by a fragile beam into the night sky. Shooting up to a satellite, then falling all the way back down to Earth. A connection through thousands of kilometres of space. He stood outside the office door, with Ilse on the other side, and for the first time in as long as he could remember, he didn't feel so alone.

Chapter 30

Nathan stood outside the office, one hand on the door, debating whether to go back in. He wasn't sure what he would say to Ilse, but he wanted to say something. Thank you, maybe.

He was still hovering when he heard a familiar cough in the gloom. He looked up the hallway. Liz was standing outside her bedroom. Her feet were bare and she was leaning against the doorway for support. She started as she saw Nathan watching her.

'You looked like your dad for a second.' Her gaze was unfocused as he walked over. 'Everyone's still here.' She sounded surprised.

'You haven't been asleep long.'

'Oh. I thought it would all be over.'

'No. Not yet,' he said, wondering vaguely what medication Steve had given her. 'Maybe you should lie down again.'

'I can't. I close my eyes and I think about Cameron. I wake up and I think about Cameron. I may as well be up.'

Someone passed by at the other end of the hall, their shadow long. Old Tom. He saw Liz and raised a hand.

'I should go and say hello to people.' She didn't move.

'I don't think anyone would mind if you didn't.'

'Cameron would mind.' Liz turned to him, her eyes suddenly clearer. 'Have you spoken to Steve yet? Made an appointment?'

'Not yet.'

'You promised me, Nathan.' Liz took his arm, her fingers surprisingly strong.

'I know. I will.'

'Let's go now and –'

'Grandma?' Xander stood at the end of the hall with the girl Nathan had seen him talking to outside. He touched her elbow. 'I'll catch up with you in a minute.'

The girl looked a little disappointed, but nodded. As she wandered away, Xander turned back. 'Are you okay, Grandma?'

'We're going to find Steve.'

'He's outside.'

'Is Bub out there too?' Nathan said, feeling a few certain words about a certain dog brewing inside him.

'No.' Xander hesitated. 'He was a bit drunk. Uncle Harry brought him inside for a rest.'

'Let's go and find Steve, Nathan.'

'Grandma, you haven't even got shoes on,' Xander said, with a note of accusation that Nathan felt was directed his way.

'Oh.' Liz looked down. 'I don't know –' She scanned the floor, flustered, as though they might appear.

'They're probably in your bedroom,' Nathan said. 'Xander, you help your grandma. I'll go and have a word with Steve.'

'Are you actually going to talk to him?' Xander said, as Liz stumbled back into her room. 'Or are you just saying that to shut her up?'

'No, I'll talk to him. Good enough?'

'Not really.' Xander was looking past him.

Nathan sighed. 'You planning to carry on like this until you leave? Because I'm not sure I'm up for another three days of it.'

'Are you going to think about what I said?'

'About what? About me moving away? Mate, we've been through this –'

'No, we haven't. You haven't even thought about it. But, yeah, whatever. Like you said, I'll be gone in three days and you'll be back on your own again and can do whatever you like. Everything back to how you want it.'

'Mate, this is not how I want it.'

'Bullshit, you –'

There was a soft tumble from the bedroom that sounded like shoes being dropped and they both looked over. Nathan started for the bedroom door.

'I'll go.' Xander stopped him. 'You're supposed to be getting your head straight.'

He disappeared into the bedroom and Nathan stood in the hall alone for a moment.

He was lucky, Nathan thought as he turned away. For years, Xander had never given him a moment's grief. He went to school, he was polite to old people, he didn't drink or take drugs, as far as Nathan knew, anyway. He was naturally good-hearted in a way that Nathan was surprised had come from he and Jacqui. If the kid was pushing back now, it wasn't before time.

Still, it had felt easier when he was younger. He could still clearly remember that day more than sixteen years ago now, when Jacqui had told him she was pregnant. Her eyes had gleamed with delight and they'd both managed to pretend for a while that their marriage wasn't already on shaky ground.

Nathan heard the toilet flush in the small bathroom down the hall. The chatter still coming from the living room had taken on a slightly different tone. Things were starting to wrap up, Nathan thought. People would be leaving soon. A tray of half-eaten sandwiches had been abandoned precariously on the table by the phone, threatening to topple off. He picked it up and headed for the kitchen.

Jacqui hadn't been smiling for long though. It had been a hard pregnancy. She'd had severe morning sickness, gagging at the sight of anything but plain rice. It had lasted most of the day and far past the week when the books had promised it would stop. She had lain on the couch in the heat with a bucket by her side, waving away anything Nathan could think to offer.

As Nathan passed the toilet, he heard the lock turn on the door and Katy came out, pale-faced and clutching a balled-up tissue.

'How are you feeling —?' He stopped as her bloodshot gaze fell on the sandwich tray in his hands, and she gagged in a way he had last seen more than sixteen years earlier. 'Oh.' He breathed out. They stared at each other for a long moment, and he knew by the look in her eyes that he had guessed right. 'Congratulations?'

She didn't say anything, just pressed the tissue to her lips.

'Go and sit down,' he said. 'I'll find Simon for you.'

'Wait. No.' Her hand shot out and clutched him above the wrist. Her grip was so firm it was nearly painful. 'Don't get Simon.'

'Why not?'

Katy wiped the corners of her mouth with the back of her hand. 'For God's sake. Why do you think?'

For a moment, Nathan tried to convince himself that it could be Bub or even Harry, at a push.

'Cameron?' he said, finally.

She nodded.

'Definitely?'

'Yes.'

'No chance at all it could be Simon?'

Her mouth twitched. 'Simon and I haven't been getting along for a while now.' A fresh sheen of sweat had broken out across her forehead.

'Did Cameron know?'

'Yes.'

Through the door to the living room, the crowd shifted and Nathan could see the top of the backpacker's dark head. The sound of laughter and chatter rose and fell.

'Do you want to speak to the nurse?' he said finally.

Katy shook her head.

'Someone else?'

She gave a dry laugh. 'Like who? Who else is there to talk to around here? There's no-one.'

Nathan hesitated, then took Katy's arm and swiftly led her up the hall.

'Come in here.' He opened the door to Xander's bedroom. 'Tell me.'

She sat on the bed, and he leaned against the wall. He waited while she picked at the faded floral bedspread.

'Simon's in debt,' she said finally. 'He has a plumbing business back home and I knew things were tough, but it turns out it was worse than I thought. Worse than he'd told me, anyway. He owes quite a lot to quite a lot of people, and I don't know what he's going to do about it.' She shook her head in frustration. 'The point is, we really need the money. Or he does, anyway.'

'Okay.'

'I didn't want to come and work here.' Katy's fingers were still plucking at the quilt. 'I'm sorry, but it's too lonely and I'd had enough of that on the properties out west. I wanted to go home, but Simon said we needed to save as much money as we could, otherwise we'd have nothing at all when we got back.' She paused. 'I don't know if that's true or not. I don't know what to believe from him anymore.'

'So Simon wanted to take the work here?'

'Yeah. We met Cameron in the pub in town, like we said, but –' Katy looked at her hands, still picking. 'I'm sorry, I know he's your brother. But I didn't have a good feeling about it.'

'In what way?'

'Just —' Katy frowned. 'I knew that it wasn't Simon that he was hiring. Something about the way he looked at me. I'm not even a teacher.' She looked up. 'And I told Cameron that. Simon was annoyed with me later, he said I should have lied to get the job. But Cameron didn't mind. He said the work was easy, that it was hard to find people and they needed the help for his girls, and if anyone asked — his wife, whoever — he'd say I was qualified.' She balled her hands into fists, trying to still them. 'So I owed him a favour before I even started.'

Nathan thought about his brother and what it felt like to need something from him.

'Simon didn't have a problem with this, though?' he said.

'Simon really needs the money. And Cam was offering good wages. More than we were making before, and cash in hand. So we agreed, and I thought maybe it would be okay. I mean, I'm thinking, it's a family property, and he's got his wife and his kids running around. And it *was* fine, for about three weeks. Which was longer than I'd expected, actually.'

'Then what?' Nathan frowned. 'Cam came on to you?'

'No. Not exactly. He was smart about it, I'll give him that. He was always friendly. Asking me questions and actually listening to the answers. I wondered if maybe I'd got him wrong, but it meant he ended up knowing all kinds of things about me. What I liked, what I found funny. My weak spots, like missing home. I was alone with him a lot. There'd always be some legit reason, and nothing exactly happened. I just felt a bit weird about it.'

'Did you tell anyone?'

'Simon, obviously. But Simon –'

'Really needs the money. Yeah, I'm getting that.'

'He said I should try not to be alone with Cameron. Keep things strictly professional, and there'd be no problem. Something had happened at our last place out west. Something –' Katy paused, '– a bit worse than this, I guess. A guy out there who was a bit too keen. I complained, and me and Simon both got sacked, so he wanted me to keep quiet this time. He couldn't really see what the problem was, and I couldn't really explain. I stopped telling him, and he never asked.'

'Right.'

'Cameron started flirting. Making comments. Kind of sexual stuff, you know? If I got uncomfortable he would act surprised, like I'd imagined it. Or seen something I wanted to see.' She shook her head. 'But I didn't imagine it. Or want it.'

Katy's fingers started plucking again at the bedcover. A long way from home, Nathan thought. Few local connections, if any. Backpackers might enjoy the flexibility of casual postings, but it left them vulnerable in other ways. Everyone knew that. Cameron knew that. And Nathan found himself thinking again of that other backpacker, more than twenty years ago, with her messy braid glowing orange by the flickering light of the campfire. The blunted edges of the memory had suddenly become cut-throat sharp, threatening to slip and slice him if not handled with care.

'When I told Cameron that I wasn't interested, he

laughed,' Katy was saying. 'Like I was overreacting and couldn't take a joke. Or we were both playing a game, and knew how it would end.'

The sharp edges did slip now, just a little. *You've seen this before.* A campfire. A flirtation. The air pungent with possibility.

'I told Simon we should leave,' Katy said. 'But he didn't want to. I thought about just heading off myself, but the car and the caravan belong to him. I couldn't just leave him stranded. We've been together three years. And he loves me, he just couldn't understand what the big deal was. He thought Cam was a great boss. It was good that he was friendly. Why couldn't I take it as a compliment?' She shook her head. 'He doesn't know what it was like, though. It was exhausting. Cameron was around every day. And he wasn't finding it fun anymore. He still joked around but I could tell he was getting frustrated. Like he'd brought us here and now I wasn't keeping up my end of the deal.'

You have seen this before. Not exactly, Nathan told himself. He stopped. Not exactly, but a version of it. More immature, far less refined, but the basic elements. An intense campfire flirtation. Patient persistence. A backpacker grateful for someone to talk to among a crowd of strangers. The gentle manipulation and focused attention that meant when she looked up, hours later, she had spoken to no-one else and made only one connection all night. The groaning weight of expectation. *You have seen this before.*

'I'm sorry.' Nathan was not sure who he was talking to.

319

Katy looked down and he realised there were tears in her eyes. 'I was homesick and lonely and miles from any-where. I felt completely worn down. Everyone wanted something from me. Simon wanted me to keep Cameron happy, Cameron wanted me to keep him happy. I was so sick of it, and eventually –' She dragged the back of her hand across her face. 'Eventually, it was just easier to say yes than no. So I did. I let him fuck me on the beanbag in his daughters' schoolroom. Six times in total.'

The room was quiet for a long time, and Nathan could hear muffled voices in the hall.

'I'm sorry,' he said again, definitely talking to Katy this time.

'It's not your fault. It's my fault. I'm the one who gave in.' Her shoulders slouched. 'And after all that, it didn't even help things. Cameron seemed disgusted with me, or with himself. It didn't stop him coming back for more, but I think he felt ashamed for five minutes and he blamed me for that. And then –' She gestured down at her flat stomach and shook her head. 'If he wasn't happy before, he definitely wasn't happy about this.'

'When did you tell him?'

'As soon as I realised myself. About two weeks before he –' She swallowed. 'Before he died. He was angry. Told me I had to get rid of it. Which was fine by me, there's no way I wanted this either. That's what he was talking to me about on the morning he went missing. He'd got me an appointment at the big medical centre next week.' Her eyes were clear now. 'That's why I'm sure he was plan-ning to come back, though. He was telling me I had to go through with the appointment. I was going to anyway, but if he was about to disappear, why would he care?'

It was a good question, Nathan thought, although it at least answered another one. 'The medical centre is the one in St Helens?'

'Yeah.'

'And you had somewhere to stay up there?'

'A couple of nights in one of the hotels.'

'And Cameron called to arrange that?' She nodded and Nathan pictured the office phone bill. Two calls to St Helens, the week before Cameron died.

'And Simon definitely doesn't know?' he said.

'Not yet.' She pressed her lips into a line. 'Not at all, I hope.'

'What will you tell him about the appointment?'

'Nothing. I'll make something up. He's squeamish. He won't ask for details. But I need to get it done. He's not a complete idiot, either. If he finds out, he'll finish with me.'

Nathan opened his mouth, then shut it again. The despair on Katy's face made him open it again.

'Would that be so bad?' He shrugged when she looked surprised. 'Your call, but I'm not sure you owe Simon anything.'

'We've been together for three years.' She held up her left hand. 'We're engaged.'

'So what? People can change their minds. My ex-wife and I were married for longer than that before she left.' He gave her a small smile. 'She's doing great, by all accounts. Never been happier.'

Katy hesitated. 'I don't know. I'll think about it.'

Nathan pushed himself away from the wall. 'Anyway, look, take it easy from here. We'll cope without you.'

'Thank you. Really. I honestly don't know how it came to this. I was just so confused and lonely.' She breathed out. 'Thank you for believing me.'

He might not have, Nathan knew in the most honest part of himself as he opened the bedroom door. He might very well not have, had it not felt so unnervingly familiar. Maybe he should have paid more attention to the warning signs back when he had the chance. There was nothing he could do about that, but he could heed them now.

It was time to find Steve.

Chapter 31

'Mate, what do you want me to tell you? That Cameron attacked a backpacker on the sand dunes after they both got drunk at a party?'

Steve's gaze was firm and steady and Nathan had trouble meeting it.

'No. Jesus. I don't know.'

Nathan ran his hand through his hair and took a breath. The air was cloying. He had found the nurse in the living room and gripped his arm. He'd seen Liz notice, with a spark of hope in her eye, as Nathan wordlessly led Steve out onto the verandah and around the side of the house, where they could talk in peace. Now, though, he was finding the conversation exceptionally difficult.

'I just want to know what really happened,' Nathan said.

'I can't tell you that, mate. No, listen –' Steve raised a finger to cut him off. 'I'll tell you exactly what I told Ilse earlier – I'm guessing it's no coincidence you're both asking about this – I don't know what happened that night any more than you do.'

Nathan made a frustrated noise. 'But at the time –'

'Yeah, at the time, I had an opinion, same as everyone else.'

'That's what I'm asking.'

'But it's important that you understand –'

'Understood. Get to the point.'

Steve squinted into the fierce afternoon light. They could see the graves in the distance. One old, one brand new. He ran his tongue over his teeth.

'There was some light bruising on Jenna's inner thighs. And a mark on her upper arm. Here.' Steve touched the soft flesh below his own armpit. 'No tearing or bleeding to speak of, but that doesn't necessarily tell you anything either way.'

'But it looked like it had been, what –?' Nathan's mouth felt dry and gritty. 'Rough?'

'Possibly. Or possibly just clumsy. Inexperienced, even. Some people bruise in situations where others might not.' Steve pressed his lips together. 'But that's what I'm trying to tell you. Physically, I would say it wasn't possible to draw a conclusion. The benefit of the doubt would probably fall Cameron's way, in fact.'

Nathan waited for a trickle of relief that never came. He shifted his weight. He could see some movement around the front of the house. The odd person wandering out, making a move to leave. He turned back to Steve.

'So what else was there?'

'Honestly, nothing. It came down to what she said.' Steve watched as a few more people came out into the open air, shielding their eyes against the sun. 'Her boyfriend – this real soft-spoken English boy – had convinced her to come in, and I know most people thought that was because he was angry, but that wasn't the case as far as I saw. He was worried about her, a bit scared even. Like he didn't have a clue what to do. He probably didn't, I think he was doing a degree in botany or something. I remember he kept blinking at me behind his glasses like I was going to be able to fix everything.' Steve shook his head. 'I don't think they'd been together very long. Anyway, he waited outside while Jenna and I talked, so whatever she told me wasn't for his benefit.'

'And what did she tell you?'

'You already know,' Steve said. 'You've heard the story. That she'd been drinking, and she'd started flirting with this kid because she was bored and didn't know anyone and she was annoyed her boyfriend had stayed behind at the station rather than come to the party. Cameron was young.' Steve frowned as he remembered. 'She told me she'd thought he was harmless. It was all just a bit of fun to pass the time. And there were a lot of other people around, so she said she'd felt safe. I remember her saying that.'

The crowd at the front of the house was growing. Nathan could hear car doors slamming and engines starting up, but didn't look over. He stayed focused on Steve.

'Then Cameron offered to drive her back to town.' The nurse's voice had a darker note now. 'She'd been drinking, she said. And was feeling a bit unsteady. Apparently, she'd thought she was following him to the car, but realised she was actually alone with him on the dunes. He started kissing her, picking up where they'd left off around the

325

campfire. Jenna told him she'd had enough and asked him to stop.'

Steve looked at Nathan.

'Cameron didn't want to. And I know he was only seventeen, but he wasn't a child, physically at least.'

Nathan thought of the calf, struggling underneath him. A knee in the right place, an elbow. A little bit of pressure. The struggling could be managed.

'Jenna couldn't get away from him?'

'Honestly, she might not even have tried. She said she froze. I think she felt a bit ashamed about that but it's actually a very common response. Either way, she was out there on her own in the dark with this big, insistent bloke.' He looked at Nathan. 'Someone can decide it's in their best interests to agree to something, but a choice is only really a choice if there's a genuine alternative. Otherwise it's manipulation and it's taking advantage.' He shrugged. 'It's rape.'

Nathan thought of Katy. It was easier to say yes than no.

Steve was watching him. 'I'm sorry. I know that's hard to hear.'

A burst of laughter caught on the breeze, raucous and deep. Nathan looked over this time. Whole groups of guests were spilling out now. He saw Melanie, her hair glowing red-gold in the sunshine. She caught his eye and waved.

'I'm heading off now,' she called, pointing to a nice-looking Land Cruiser where a couple of the Atherton crowd were already climbing aboard. 'It was good to see you.'

'Yeah. You too.'

She smiled at him and he had a sudden image of her, younger, and smiling just like that as she sipped a drink under a night sky. Had she been at the party by the sand dunes that night? Nathan wondered. He honestly couldn't remember. He realised she was still waiting and he cleared his throat. 'Maybe see you again.'

'I hope so.' She looked pleased and with another wave, jogged towards the waiting vehicle.

Nathan turned his attention back to Steve, who was still watching her leave.

'You should call her,' Steve said. 'She'd do you far more good than anything I could prescribe.'

'So I keep getting told.' Nathan waved an impatient hand. 'Listen, if Jenna was so scared, why did she let Cam drive her back to town afterwards?'

'How many kilometres from the dunes to town?'

'Twelve.'

'Long way to walk at night when you're shaken up and alone.'

'She could have asked someone else.'

'I thought she didn't know anyone else there.'

Nathan said nothing. She hadn't. Only Jacqui, who had left earlier, with him. He imagined Cam and Jenna driving back into town. Pulling up outside the pub, where they were seen by Rob, the owner.

'Rob saw Jenna kissing Cam in the car back in town,' he said, finally.

'Did he?' Steve's eyes were watchful. 'Or did he see Cameron kiss Jenna, and her allow it so she'd be let out of the car?'

'Jesus, Steve, how am I supposed to know that?'

'You're not. Just like I don't know. And Rob looking out of his pub window doesn't know either. Like I said, an opinion is the best I can offer.'

Nathan frowned. He could see Harry among the crowd now, alongside Liz. She was clinging to him like a lifeboat as people reached out to grip her hand and pull her towards them in an embrace. There were waves and calls of farewell. Harry caught Nathan's eye and beckoned him over. Nathan ignored him.

'Jenna took her time telling anyone.' He turned back to Steve, surprised by the defensive note in his tone. 'She didn't help herself there by pretending everything was fine.'

Steve almost smiled, but caught himself.

'What?' Nathan demanded.

'Just that that's bloody rich coming from you,' Steve said. 'Nathan, people pretend to themselves that they are fine *all the time*. Every day, and for years on end.'

He gestured at the departing crowd, sweating in their dusty funeral clothes and with hours of driving ahead of them. 'Life out here is hard. We all try to get through the best way we can. But trust me, there's not a single person here who isn't lying to themselves about something.'

Ilse's head appeared amid the group, loose strands of hair plastered to the sides of her hot face. Steve's eyes fell on her for a second and he took a breath as if to say something, then appeared to change his mind, releasing the air from his lungs. He turned back to Nathan.

'You are one of the worst around here for that kind

of thing by an absolute mile. You're so far from fine that you're terrified to admit to yourself how bad things have got. Let alone admit it to your mum or your son. They've both asked me to get you in for a chat and a check-up, by the way.'

'I know. Okay.'

'Really? You'll come in? No argument?'

Nathan shook his head. He knew he had crossed a line somewhere – maybe in the last few hours, maybe in the past few years – and suddenly that line seemed a very long way away. He didn't want to be alone on this side of it anymore. He just hoped he could still find his way back.

More people came out of the house, Simon among them. Katy followed a few paces behind. They stood slightly apart, both from the crowd and each other, Katy occasionally glancing at Simon with a faintly confused look, as though she was trying to work something out. She did not turn once towards Ilse, who was wandering from group to group, looking overwhelmed.

'If this had all been dealt with at the time, it would have been better for everyone,' Nathan said. Across the yard, the graves lay silent and lonely. There was no-one around them now. All the activity was with the living. 'Including Cam.'

Steve nodded. 'I sometimes think I should've encouraged Jenna to make things formal straight away. But it was my first posting out here. I was younger; I hadn't been qualified for long. I'd do things differently now, but at the time, I did my best. Jenna said she needed to think about it, and I felt I should respect that. Then, of course, she'd left town a couple of days later, so the problem went with her.' Steve shrugged. 'But you'd know the reasons for that better than I would, anyway.'

Nathan frowned. 'What are you taking about? I don't know why she decided to leave.'

It was Steve's turn to frown. 'Don't you?'

'Of course not. How would I?'

The last of the crowd were climbing into their cars now. Cameron's farewell was coming to an end.

'You might not think you know, Nathan.' Steve shot a pointed look across the yard to the two graves under the gum tree. 'But can you really not take a guess?'

Nathan opened his mouth to protest, then stopped as he heard the distant thud of a car door. And another one. He shut his mouth slowly.

He'd been in that same yard, twenty-three years ago, not far from the spot Steve was looking at now. Nathan and seven-year-old Bub had been messing around with a cricket bat over by the fence there, back when the ground was still clear and undisturbed. Bub had been practising his bowling as Nathan tapped the ball back in his direction.

It had been a full day since the terrible phone call from the town's sergeant had come through and Nathan had stood sullenly with Cameron in the hall while their dad demanded answers. A day since Nathan had been a fraction late coming to his brother's defence, and since Cam had last spoken to him.

Nathan had let the cricket ball sail past him as Carl Bright's dirty four-wheel drive had roared up the driveway and shuddered to a halt outside the house. Nathan lingered, keeping his distance, as he always did when he had a choice in the matter. Carl had been gone most of the day. That was not unusual. Nor was the fact that he'd failed to write down where he was going. He was bristling as he slammed his car door shut with a force that shook the vehicle.

Cameron had come out of the house.

Nathan had had the urge to whistle sharply, the way they'd always used to warn each other over the years. *Watch out, Dad's coming.* He didn't, though. He wasn't sure what was going to happen and, if possible, he didn't want Bub to see. Instead, Nathan tossed the cricket ball in the air and lobbed the bat at it, sending the ball a fair distance in the other direction. Bub scampered after it, swearing and complaining.

Anyway, it was too late for a warning, Nathan could tell as he turned back. Cameron had seen their dad, pounding across the driveway towards him. And their dad had clearly seen Cam. Cameron had paused. And then, instead of wheeling around and disappearing into the warren of the house, he walked down the wooden steps and waited at the bottom. As Carl Bright approached his middle son, he barely broke stride. He brushed past him, turning his head just once. And before disappearing into the house, Carl gave Cameron a single sharp nod.

It's done.

Chapter 32

It's done.

Of course it was.

Carl Bright never nodded at his sons. Not in greeting, certainly not in approval. He had disappeared from the property for a few hours, and the very next morning Jenna and her boyfriend had gone to their employer and told him they were leaving. No reason and no notice, they just wanted to be on their way.

Keith had tried to talk them out of it, Jacqui told Nathan later. Keith had, of course, heard about the events at the party, and had asked if that had anything to do with anything. No, Jenna had said. It was a misunderstanding. She had been embarrassed and had blown things out of proportion.

Nathan sat on the couch in the living room now, staring at the Christmas tree bulbs glowing weakly in the dying afternoon light. The debris of the wake lay scattered around, empty plates and cups cluttering every surface. Steve had been among the very last to leave, pressing an appointment card into Nathan's palm. By the time he'd driven off, the rest of the family had drifted their separate ways, rattling around a house that suddenly felt too big and empty.

Keith's attitude towards Nathan had markedly changed after Jenna left in such a hurry. Nathan didn't see Keith that often, so it took a while for him to fully notice. But where Keith had always been civil, if a little cold, he suddenly became hard and unpleasant. Nathan's visits were greeted with increasing hostility, until eventually he and Jacqui stopped meeting at her house. They still met, though, and had laughed with the intoxication of forbidden intimacy at Keith's disapproval.

Nathan could still remember Keith's face all those years ago at the service station.

I know what men like you do.

Maybe, Nathan thought as he sat on the couch now, the bloke had actually had a point. The thought was deeply depressing.

There was a noise in the hall and Bub appeared in the doorway. His shirt was creased and he was squinting into the low light.

'Where is everybody?'

'Gone. It's over.'

'Already?'

'You've been asleep for a while.'

'Oh.' Bub flopped down on the couch and Nathan could smell the alcohol coming off him. Bub rubbed a hand over his face then peered at Nathan with bloodshot eyes. 'What's wrong with you?'

Nathan, who couldn't think where to start, looked at his brother and immediately pictured his dog Kelly lying dead in his hands. It had slipped to the back of his mind in the last couple of hours but now jostled its way forward once more. He opened his mouth, then with an effort, took a breath. 'Nothing.'

'Doesn't look like nothing.'

Nathan shrugged.

Bub yawned and slid his eyes around the room. 'Lots of people came, hey?'

'Yeah.'

'Do you think that many would come out for us?'

'Nope.'

'Me neither.' Bub sounded resigned. 'Bloody Cam. I don't know how he did it. He was as much of a dickhead as the rest of us, he was just better at hiding it.'

'That's what you think?'

'Yeah, of course.' Bub stared at the wall for a minute. His voice was rough and his words still a little slurred. 'It's the truth, isn't it? I mean, Dad was a dickhead, Cam was a dickhead. I am. You are.'

Nathan almost laughed. 'I'm not arguing that, mate. But some things are a lot worse than other things.'

'If you say so.' Bub suppressed a small burp.

'I do.'

'Well, you would know.' Bub hauled himself off the couch and over to the TV. 'I mean, Cam could be an arsehole, but you left a bloke for dead.'

'That was ten years ago. And he didn't actually die.'

'No thanks to you. But maybe that's not your fault. Like

I said: family of dickheads. Not much you can do about
that.' Bub stood over the TV, untangling the wires for his
computer game.

'People can change, mate.'

'Okay.'

'No. Listen. I am nowhere near as bad as Cam.'

'Righto.' Bub didn't look up. 'Try to remember that
when you and Ilse are screwing me over with this place.'

'Jesus, Bub, no-one's trying to screw you over.'

'We'll see.'

'Hey.' Nathan lowered his voice. 'What exactly is
your problem?'

'I dunno. Not knowing what's going on with my own
property for one thing. Never having a say, for another.
Having you and Cam for brothers, for a third.'

'Well, you've only got me now, so there's at least some
good news for you.' Nathan could feel the anger building
in him. He stood to leave. 'By the way, you got anything
you want to tell me about my dog?'

'Which dog?'

'You know which bloody dog. Kelly.'

Bub's hands went still on the computer wires. 'No. I
dunno what you're talking about.'

'No?'

'No.'

'Nothing to say about some baiting happening around
my place? Not ringing any bells in there?' Nathan reached
out and tapped Bub on the side of the head. Bub swiped
his arm away.

'Get fucked.'

'No, you get fucked. Kelly was in a lot of pain at the end. I had to watch it happen. There was nothing I could do to help her.' Nathan could feel the tears prickling behind his eyes and he blinked hard.

'She was only a dog.'

'I loved her. She was my best friend.'

'Then you need to get out more.'

Nathan made himself take a breath. He felt a rage building that he knew wasn't all about Bub. Still. Bub was right in front of him.

'All right,' he said. 'That's fine. But when you and me and Ilse sit down to talk about this place, I'm going to look at you and think about what you did to Kelly and then I'm going to think long and hard about how I can best repay you for that.' He stepped closer to his brother. 'You're wondering why Cam didn't bloody trust you with this place or money or anything else? Take a look at yourself. He might have been an arsehole – worse than that – but he didn't have rocks in his head.'

Nathan didn't see the blow coming until it was almost too late. It caught the side of his head and sent him stumbling backwards. He felt another hard jab under his ribs and Bub's arm was suddenly tight around his neck.

'Fuck you, mate. And Cam.' Bub's breath was alcoholic on his face. 'You think you can turn up here and push me around and start acting like you know what's best for everyone?'

Nathan felt the air knocked from him as they banged against the wall and lost their balance, hitting the floor with a thud. A loose fist connected with his cheek and Nathan put his hand up too late as another blow sailed through.

'You and Cam always bloody think you're better than me, but you're not, are you? He's dead and you're a total fuck-up.'

Bub landed a sharp punch over Nathan's eye, and his face was angry and slick with sweat. There was something reckless in his eyes as he pulled his fist back again.

'You think if you take Cam's place and start behaving like him people will respect you?' Bub was saying.

'No.' Nathan tried to push him off, banging his head against the floorboards. He could see movement at the doorway.

'You think they'll suddenly talk to you in town?'

'Get off.' Nathan shoved back and they rolled over, hitting the couch and the coffee table. Something fell off and shattered against the floor.

'Hey!' A shout from Harry, as Liz's voice also cried out from somewhere.

'They don't ignore you because you're not Cam, mate.' Bub's words were hot in his ear. 'It's not even because you left whatshisname for dead. They don't talk to you because you've got a bit weird, mate. You're a weird, lonely loser and no-one wants to be around y–'

Nathan got in a punch that time, a hard one, and they rolled again, colliding with something. Nathan felt the tremble at the same time as a gasp came from the doorway. The Christmas tree tilted, then fell in a shimmering jangle of decorations and plastic pine needles and tinsel. It caught the corner of Cameron's painting as it fell, sending the frame rocking at an alarming angle on its twine.

'Oh, shit,' Bub said, his voice nearly drowned out as Liz shrieked and darted across the room. Harry got there first, smacking the frame hard against the wall as he caught the picture just in time.

'Christ,' he said. 'That was close.'

Liz was already at his side, running both hands over the frame as she checked for damage. Nathan could see her shoulders move as she breathed heavily and could tell she was trying not to cry. Finally, she straightened the painting against the wall.

'Jesus, of all days,' Harry was shouting. 'You realise your brother's gone, don't you? You can't respect his memory for five bloody minutes?'

'Sorry.' Nathan pushed Bub off him and stood up. He reached out for the painting. 'Is it all right?'

Harry slapped his arm away. 'Don't you bloody touch it.'

'Hey! I was just trying to –'

'Well, don't! You've done enough damage.'

'Stop it!' Liz turned, tears in her eyes now. She looked from Nathan to Bub, who was still sprawled on the floor, shimmering gently with a dusting of loose tinsel particles.

'Isn't today already bad enough for you two?' she said. 'What's wrong with you both? Not enough misery here? You have to turn on each other as well?'

'Sorry, Mum,' Nathan said.

She didn't answer. She was wiping her eyes.

'I'm sorry,' he tried again. He ignored Bub, who was clambering to his feet. 'I'll fix it.'

Liz took a breath. 'I don't want you to fix anything. I have had it up to here, Nathan. I don't want to see you – either of you – again tonight.'

'But –'

'Nathan. Bub. Please. Just go away and leave me alone.'

She turned back to the painting and didn't move again as her sons left the room.

Chapter 33

It was dark as Nathan sat on the porch, playing Sophie's guitar. He didn't know where Bub had gone, and he didn't care. Xander was crashed out, asleep on top of his bed when Nathan had checked on him. A light was still on in the backpackers' caravan. Nathan watched the shadows flicker in the windows as he sat on the steps and messed around with some chords.

'That's nice.'

He looked up, his fingers stopped on the strings. 'Thanks.'

Ilse was holding two beers. 'Can I sit down?'

'Of course.' He paused. 'Always.'

She put one bottle next to him. Condensation had already started to form as she clinked it with her own and sat down opposite. 'Merry Christmas, I suppose.'

'Yeah. You too.'

Ilse leaned against the verandah post and tilted her head back, watching him. She'd had a shower and swapped her dark dress for shorts and a shirt. Her hair was wet and shone dark and sleek in the porch light. Nathan had changed back into his jeans earlier, and immediately felt dusty and gritty.

'I didn't mean to put you off.' She nodded at the guitar. 'Don't stop.'

He drew a blank, scrabbling around for something to play. In the end, he settled on an old bush song his mum had used to sing when they were kids. It reminded him of Cameron when they were young. Playing cricket in the midday sun until Liz had yelled at them to get into the shade. It reminded him of the Cameron that he used to know, a long time ago.

Ilse stretched her legs out along the step, her feet bare against the wood. She took a sip of her beer.

'How are you feeling?' he said.

'It's been a terrible day. But now it's over, I feel –' She considered. 'A bit better, I think. How about you?'

'Yeah,' Nathan said, realising it was true. 'Me too. Are the girls asleep?'

'In your mum's room. Everyone's having an early night.'

'Yeah. Right.'

They sat as he played softly. She did seem better, he thought, in a way he couldn't quite put his finger on. There was a lightness in her face that hadn't been there before.

Ilse was looking at the bruise forming around his eye. 'So you spoke to Bub after all?'

'Oh.' He touched it. It hurt quite a bit, actually. 'He kind of spoke to me.'

'Did you sort things out?'

'Not really. I'll catch him tomorrow.'

'Well, it is Christmas. He might be more willing to make up.'

'I suppose. Either way, my dog's still dead.'

'I know.' She stretched out and touched his boot gently with her toes. 'But that'll still be the case whether you forgive your brother or not.'

'Yeah. Maybe.'

'Definitely, I think, Nathan. Unfortunately,' she said, and he felt himself smile.

Ilse settled a little on the step and the wood creaked. 'How much longer are you here for?'

'Until the day after tomorrow. Xander's getting the plane on the twenty-seventh.'

'Before you go home, we'll have to talk over what to do about this place. With Bub, of course.'

'Of course.'

She leaned back, her eyes half-closed. 'Not now, though.'

'No,' he said. 'We don't have to do it now.'

'Now, I'm going to sit here and listen to the music.'

'Sounds good.'

The light flicked off in the backpackers' caravan and they both looked over. It was pitch black out there now. Above, Nathan could make out the evening stars.

'So they're thinking about leaving?' Ilse said.

'Yeah. Well, Katy anyway. But, listen –' He hesitated. He didn't really want to have this conversation. Not now. 'I was talking to her –'

'I think she's pregnant,' Ilse said suddenly. 'She seems it.'

Nathan stared at her, then nodded.

A long silence as Ilse stared out into the night. 'Is it someone's other than Simon's?'

'Apparently so.'

'Ah.' The word was like an exhalation and Ilse's face twisted. She might have suspected, but Nathan could tell she hadn't known for sure.

'I don't think she's planning to keep it,' he said. 'If that makes a difference. But that's why Cam made those calls to St Helens.'

'That's what it was about?'

'I think so.'

Ilse stared at the darkened caravan for a long time. 'I'm pretty sure she's not even the first,' she said eventually.

'Really?'

'I don't mean the pregnancy, although –' She shook her head. 'What do I know? But do you remember Magda?'

Nathan did, actually. A gentle Polish girl with a soft accent who had been there one Christmas a few years ago. Not long after, he heard she'd gone, two months before her contract was up.

'And there was a girl over here from Perth. I think her, maybe. For a while. Maybe others.'

'Cam was –' Nathan struggled to put it into words. 'Not good enough. In a lot of ways.'

Ilse had a look on her face he couldn't quite read. She twisted the beer bottle in her hands, her fingertips leaving streaks in the condensation.

'Is that what the card with your present was about? Katy?' he said.

Forgive me.

'I'm honestly not sure. Maybe.' She examined her hands. 'Maybe not. With Cameron, it could have been a few things.'

'Yeah. I'm starting to realise that.' The dark felt thick and heavy. 'I spoke to Steve earlier. About Jenna.'

'Oh, yes?' Ilse's eyes flicked to him.

'He said he told me the same as you.'

She leaned back, disappointed. 'So nothing definite. No physical evidence, he told me.'

'I don't know. It sounded pretty definite to me.'

'Did it?'

'I thought so. Especially in hindsight, for whatever that's worth. I should have, I don't know, at the time –' Nathan was quiet. 'But Cam's my brother. I believed him.'

'I know.' Her eyes were on him. 'What do you think now?'

He looked up. The night sky was huge.

'I think Cameron forced her.'

'I do, too.'

They looked at each other for a long time.

Nathan had finally opened his mouth to say something when he heard footsteps on the other side of the yard. 'Sounds like Harry doing the generator. Do you want to get inside before the lights go out?'

Ilse took a sip of beer, not quite looking at him now. 'Do you?'

'No.'

Her eyes turned back to him just before the familiar electrical thump plunged them into darkness. The

344

generator fell silent and there was the sound of Harry climbing the stairs to his own cabin.

Nathan put the guitar down. He could hear nothing now but the distant rush of wind and Ilse breathing. Against the inky night sky, he watched as her shadow tilted its head back and looked up at the stars.

'I was trying to leave him.'

Nathan felt something stir deep inside him. 'Were you?'

'I've been planning it for a while. Leave with Sophie and Lo. It's not that easy around here, though. Practically, I mean. You can't just pick up and go. I mean you can, physically, but –' She waved a hand at the hundreds of kilometres of space all around them. 'Go where?'

To me, Nathan wanted to say. *You could have come to me.* He stopped himself. 'Were you leaving because of Katy and the others?'

'No, actually. Although that obviously didn't help. There were other reasons.' She was quiet for a long time. 'It's hard being married to someone who really doesn't love you.'

Nathan thought of Jacqui, and felt a sudden flash of sympathy for her. Their marriage hadn't been easy on him, but it hadn't been easy on her either. He looked at Ilse. 'I'm sorry you were unhappy.'

She gave a small laugh, and he saw her take another sip from her bottle. 'That's not your fault, Nathan. I just wish –' She stopped.

'What?'

They sat across from each other in the dark, the

constellations brilliant above, their drinks warming in the air, the guitar lying on the step.

'I honestly didn't know Cameron was your brother when he first started talking to me,' she said, finally.

'Ilse, it's okay. It doesn't matter now.'

'No, listen to me. I could have guessed, though. It wasn't hard to work out. But I was all by myself in this strange town. I didn't have any friends. I don't know exactly what I was hoping for with you, but when you disappeared –' She paused and Nathan felt a familiar painful twist at the sheer missed opportunity. Ilse sighed. 'I was feeling sorry for myself, and suddenly Cameron was there. And he was good-looking, and so *charming*.' She said the word like it was a fault. 'He laughed at my jokes. I was flattered, I suppose. I'd never had anyone like him interested in me. And I was so young and stupid.'

'Yeah, well,' Nathan said. 'I know what that's like. I wasn't even that young when I stuffed everything up, so I've got no excuse.'

He saw the flash of a smile in the dark, quick but real. The step creaked gently. He didn't see her move but all of a sudden she felt a little closer.

'Cameron said he loved me. And then I was pregnant and then we were married and then ten years later, here I am. It's just, sometimes I stand on this verandah and I look out and I wonder –' Her voice was soft. 'How things might have turned out if I hadn't been quite so young and dumb. If I'd only done one or two things differently.'

'I wonder that all the time.'

'Do you?'

346

'Every day.'

Her hand was inches from his own in the dark. He could feel the ends of his fingertips tingle against the dusty porch.

'Ilse.' He said her name softly.

The step creaked again. Definitely a little closer. Her clean damp hair smelled like the ocean.

'Ilse, I wanted to say —'

'Nathan.' Her voice was quiet. 'It's honestly okay.'

'No. Please —'

'It's okay, truly.'

'I am so sorry.'

'I know.' Her fingertips brushed his.

'I tried to come back to see you, more than once. I was ashamed of what I'd done. And I was worried what you'd say, but I should have tried harder. I really wanted to talk to you.' The words were tumbling out, falling over each other in relief at being finally spoken. 'I regret that more than —'

'You don't have to.'

'I do, though. I'm sorry that I didn't tell you that when I could have. And if I hurt you.' Her eyes were bright in the darkness and he could feel the warmth of her fingertips against his. 'I'm sorry about so much. Everything, really. And I'm sorry for me. For having it all in front of me and letting you go like that. For missing my chance.'

Her voice was close. 'That was all a long time ago.'

'I know, but I've been wanting to tell you that ever since.'

'You've been waiting ten years to tell me that?'

'Yes.'

'Nathan.' He could feel her breath soft on his lips. 'What are you waiting for now?'

He leaned in.

Chapter 34

They broke apart for air, half standing, half stumbling up the darkened steps with her skin warm against his, and Nathan felt Ilse pull him towards the sleeping house. His hand was tight in hers and his mind leaped and bounded ahead, up the steps, past his sleeping bag on the couch and to her room – Cameron's room – and he felt her hesitate at the same time.

'Wait. Not there,' he said into her hair.

'Where then?' she whispered.

'This way.'

He took her by the hand, moving as fast as the dark would let him around the side of the house and towards the driveway, and suddenly it was ten years ago and he was pressing her up against the side of his four-wheel drive and he could feel her mouth hot and sweet on his, and her hands fumbling at his waistband. He threw open the rear door of the car, shoving equipment and supplies aside as he dragged a blanket onto the floor.

The suspension creaked as they stretched out and he

could hear their breath as the moon shone through the windows. She reached for him and he could feel the weight of the years falling away, and for the first time in as long as he could remember, he could breathe properly. She was warm and steady and suddenly it was all flooding back: the way he had felt that first night, lying close to her with the years laid out ahead of him and the choices still there to be made. And he felt as though in this moment, for once in his life, he was exactly where he should be, with his arms around her as the Christmas stars burned hot and bright in the night sky above them. It felt right. It felt like a second chance.

Later, in the dark blue pre-dawn of Christmas morning, they lay side by side. A warm breeze blew through the open car doors as they watched the giant sky move through its nightly rotation. Neither had spoken for a while.

'I don't believe Sophie hurt her arm riding,' Ilse whispered. Her eyes were still on the stars.

'Don't you?'

'Cameron did it. I'm sure.' They didn't look at each other. 'He scared himself. I could tell from his face.'

Nathan continued to stare at the sky.

'He was the only one out at the stables with Sophie when it happened.' Ilse propped herself up on her elbow, facing him now. 'She can be lazy cleaning them out, and she hadn't done it properly. And Cam had been in this terrible mood all day. Worse than usual. I didn't realise he was alone with her or I would have –' She stopped. 'I don't know what.

Anyway. They came into the house, with Sophie crying her eyes out and Cameron with this story about her horse throwing her off. I suppose it could have happened. But she's a good little rider, and when she falls she knows what to do. It was Cameron who gave himself away, though. I could see it. He was scared by how far he'd gone.'

Nathan still said nothing, just looked out at the endless stars instead.

'It's true,' she said. 'I promise.'

Slowly he reached out a hand and rested it on hers.

'I believe you. I'm just –' He thought about his brothers and himself. And their dad and the years growing up under him. What they'd all become. 'Very sad.'

The sky was a whole shade lighter when they spoke again. He ran his thumb along her forearm, stopping at a deep purple bruise near her elbow.

'That wasn't him,' Ilse said. 'That was from the calf the other day.'

He moved his thumb instead to the back of her hand, where there was an old burn mark shaped like the tip of an iron. They looked at each other for a long time, then, in the dusky half-light, she nodded. She twisted gently and showed him her shoulder and another scar, older and differently shaped. She twisted again. And again. Secrets written on patches of skin.

Nathan pictured the large bottle of paracetamol on her bedside table. 'I'm sorry.'

'He didn't do it all the time. Not every day. Nothing like that. Sometimes months could go by. Sometimes he wasn't –'

'What?'

'As bad.'

Nathan made himself ask. 'Did anyone else notice?'

'I don't think so.'

'Really?'

She looked at him. 'Did you?'

The impulse to ignore the question was so strong it was an almost physical reaction. But he made himself lie there and look at her. He thought about leaving rooms as she entered, avoiding anything but the most superficial conversation. Looking at her only through the veil of his own suffocating self-pity and regret. Finally, he shook his head. 'No,' he said honestly. 'I didn't.'

'You're not alone. I did wonder if maybe Harry suspected, but there's so much to do here so he's always so busy. Bub −' She shrugged. 'Cam bullied him as well in his own way. I don't think Bub even realised it anymore. He's so used to being pushed around he thinks it's completely normal.'

'What about Mum?'

Ilse's face hardened.

'What?' he said.

'I tried to talk to her once. It didn't go well.'

'What did she say?'

'Nothing at first. She seemed to think I was talking about typical marriage spats. I don't know if she honestly didn't get it, or if she deliberately wouldn't. So I tried again. And that time −' Ilse stopped. 'That time, she got annoyed. Told me this property was hard enough to run and I should be supporting Cameron, not picking fights. I was scared she would tell him what I'd said, and that would've made it so much worse. I never brought it up again.'

Nathan was quiet again, for longer this time as his mind ran back through the years, remembering all sorts of things. Finally, he took a breath.

'Our dad —' he started, then stopped, not sure how to go on.

Ilse waited. 'I know,' she said when he didn't continue. 'Cameron told me how bad he was.'

'Did he?' Nathan was genuinely surprised. He had never told anyone. Not Jacqui, not Xander. Not Bub and not Cameron. He and his brothers had never talked about it, not once in their whole adult lives.

'Cameron thought he could be different,' Ilse said. 'I do think he wanted to be a good dad and a good husband. And he could be great, he really could, but then he would turn. It could be over nothing. He became someone else. For a long time, I was worried about him and then one day I woke up and realised I was scared of him.'

Nathan looked at her.

'The funny thing is, I think he knew it before I did.' She shook her head. 'I was already too late. He'd chipped away at everything over the years. I have nothing of my own out here. Our bank account isn't even in my name, did you know that? He checked all the statements, had to approve every transaction.' She glanced in the direction of the garages. 'Did you find anything wrong with my car?'

'No. Nothing.'

'I think Cameron used to sabotage it.'

'Seriously?'

'Not often, but getting stuck out there once or twice was enough. He knew how to do it too, so I'd get a few kilometres before it would drop out. Like last year, I was stuck for nearly five hours, waiting for him to come and drag me home like an animal. I couldn't trust the car, and if I couldn't trust it, he knew I couldn't drive it. And I couldn't take the girls away in it.'

Ilse lay back again. The stars were growing fainter now.

'Not that we'd get far anyway,' she said. 'My passport has expired. Neither of the girls even has one. He'd taken my driving licence and residency documents, in theory to file away, but when I wanted them, I couldn't find them. I haven't had a paid job since I worked in the pub. I don't have any family in this country, no real friends. And people around here liked Cameron. If they had to choose a side, it wouldn't be mine.' Ilse turned her head. 'Just ask Jenna Moore.'

'What about Glenn? He's a good bloke. He could have protected you.'

'How?' Ilse's gaze was serious and Nathan realised she was really asking. 'How is he going to protect me from my husband in the next room? He's three hours away in the police station on a good day. Do you know what an angry person can do in three hours?'

Nathan said nothing. He did, actually.

'There are accidents just waiting to happen around here,' she said. 'Maybe next time it's me who falls from my horse, but instead of breaking my arm, I break my neck. Or I get my hand ripped off in machinery. Or get backed over by one of the cars. Or Sophie does, or Lo.'

354

Nathan thought about that, then had to stop thinking about it.

'Things had been getting worse these last few months,' Ilse went on. 'Since he found out that Jenna called, in hindsight. I'd made an emergency plan, in case I had to leave in a hurry. I started collecting cash, anything small I could get my hands on. I put aside some things for the girls, clothes and toys. Not enough that Cameron would notice, but then Lo made a fuss and I had to put most of them back. So I concentrated on trying to find some of the most important documents, the girls' birth certificates, my proof of residency, things like that. When I had a few things together I'd drive out and hide them.'

Nathan pictured her kneeling under the blazing sun by the headstone at the stockman's grave, turning the soil.

'You hid them at the grave?'

'It's on the way to town, but far enough away from here that I felt a bit safer. If Cameron had found out —' She stopped. 'Anyway. I wrapped everything in a plastic envelope and buried it.'

'So what happened?'

'Cameron hurt Sophie. That was the final straw. Or I thought it was, at least. I'd always told myself it was one thing when it was between me and him, but when it came to the girls —' She sat up. 'The next morning, I put Sophie and Lo in the workers' car. I didn't tell anyone we were going, didn't pack anything. But reality sank in on the way. I hadn't saved nearly enough money. The fuel alone to get anywhere from here is bad enough, and I'd have to pay for accommodation, food, clothes for the girls to replace what we'd left. Legal fees, maybe? I didn't have anything like enough for long-term survival.' She looked out at the far horizon, visible now against the encroaching dawn.

'So you came back?'

'It was terrible. I hated myself for it. I just stood beside that stupid grave. I didn't even bother to dig up the envelope in the end. I put the girls back in the car. It was the longest drive of my life. The girls were confused. I couldn't think what to tell them.' She shook her head. 'After that I started grabbing whatever I needed as fast as I could.'

She shook her head.

'Cameron noticed. I'm sure of it. He was always around, I couldn't get out of his sight. Harry had to practically order him to go and fix that mast on Lehmann's Hill, Cam had been putting it off so long. On that last morning, when Cam pulled over on the driveway before he left –'

She frowned, remembering.

'He was tense, like something was going to happen. I asked if he was going to the mast with Bub, and he said he was. But he looked at me in this strange way, and I knew he was lying.' She lay back down. 'He'd been looking through Lo's sketchbook the night before. I think he saw that painting again, the one of me and the girls at the grave, and put two and two together. When I heard he'd been found dead out there, I kept waiting for someone to ask me about the envelope.'

Nathan pictured Cameron's body under the tarp and the shallow hole in the ground. 'He didn't have anything with him when he was found.' Certainly not a plastic envelope full of cash and documents.

'I know. I thought it must still be buried there. I was scared someone would stumble across it. I didn't want anyone to think that I —'

'What?'

'Had anything to do with what happened to him.'

The faint tan lines and freckles on her skin were visible in the early-morning glow. The sky was almost fully light now. The household would be waking up.

'The day before yesterday was the first chance I had. I went out there and dug, same spot as always.'

Nathan remembered her kneeling at the grave, bent over in the sun, the small movement in her shoulders. 'So you got it back?'

Ilse shook her head. 'No. That's just it. The envelope wasn't there anymore.'

Nathan stared at her. 'Are you sure?'

'Completely.'

'But if it's not there, and it wasn't with Cameron,' he said. 'Then where is it?'

The shadows of the dawn light stretched across her face. 'I don't know.'

Chapter 35

Nathan stared at Cameron's painting. The house was still quiet, but only just. He and Ilse had stayed tangled in the blanket in the back of his car as long as they could, whispering as the sky grew lighter. Finally, they'd had to prise themselves apart. It was Christmas morning. The girls would be on the move.

'It could have been a dingo,' Nathan said, his voice low as he zipped up his jeans. Despite everything, he still felt a warm buzz when he looked at her.

'I know.' Ilse ran a hand through her hair. 'That's what I wondered too. I'd always been a bit worried about that happening. A dingo could dig up that hole, couldn't it? Take the envelope?'

'Yeah.' Dropped it somewhere when it lost interest. It was probably under a pile of sand by now. 'And Bub said there were dingoes sniffing around.'

'Oh, right. Well, then.'

They both fell quiet at the same time.

'I know Bub was out there by himself for a bit, but —'

Nathan pictured the rumpled tarp, and Bub's face after Cameron's body was moved. 'He was as surprised to see that hole as anyone.'

That didn't necessarily mean he couldn't have taken something from Cameron's pockets, though, Nathan thought. He didn't say that out loud.

'I feel like Bub would have said something to me by now if he'd found it.' Ilse was whispering now, as they approached the house. 'Especially with him being so annoyed about the property.'

They hesitated at the foot of the verandah steps. Nathan took a breath.

'There's no way Jenna might —'

'Realistically, she couldn't —'

They both started and stopped at the same time. Neither said anything.

'I really don't think —' Nathan said.

'No.' Ilse shook her head firmly. 'I don't either. I don't.'

They stood for a moment longer, just looking at each other, then turned to go inside. As he held open the screen door, she brushed his fingertips with her own as she passed.

'Thank you, Nathan,' she said, politely.

'You're welcome, Ilse.'

He could see her smiling to herself as she disappeared down the hall.

Nathan sat now on the couch, looking at Cameron's artwork. He could pinpoint the spot beneath the head-stone where the earth had been dug up in real life. In the painting, that piece of ground was smooth and untouched. In the corner of the room, the Christmas tree shivered in a draught of air. Someone had put it back up since yesterday.

The pounding of small footsteps filled the hallway and the girls piled into the room. They were holding presents under their arms, and even Lo seemed interested for once. Liz followed, carrying a tray of coffee mugs. There was the sound of a toilet flushing along the hall and a minute later Bub appeared. He hovered at the edge, leaning against the door. He had a beer in his hand.

'What? It's Christmas,' he said, as Liz frowned.

She turned to Nathan. 'Where's Xander?'

'I'll get him.'

'We're not waiting to start opening, Uncle Nathan.' Sophie's voice floated behind him as he got up.

'I wouldn't dream of asking you to.'

Xander was fast asleep in bed, his hair dark against the pillow, and Nathan felt a pang of nostalgia. It had always been Xander who had woken him up on Christmas morning, every second year. This could realistically be the last Christmas they would spend together, Nathan thought. And either way, his son would be fully grown up next time. The room felt a little bare and Nathan realised Xander had already started packing a few things. He stared at his backpack and sighed.

'What are you doing?'

Nathan looked over to see Xander awake. 'Watching you sleep, my son and heir.'

Xander smiled. 'That's weird.'

'Then you should have got up earlier. Happy Christmas.'

'You too.' Xander seemed in a better mood than

yesterday, at least. He nodded at Nathan's bruise. 'Your eye looks bad.'

'It's all right. You should see the other guy.'

'I did, last night. Bub was fine.' Xander was watching Nathan with a bemused look. 'What's up with you anyway?'

'What do you mean?'

'I don't know. You seem sort of . . . happier.'

'Oh. Well. It's Christmas, isn't it?'

'Yeah. I suppose.'

'There you go. The girls are opening their presents.'

Xander pulled himself up to sit against the pillow. 'So we're really doing this? Christmas like nothing has happened?'

'They're just kids, mate. You were excited at that age too.' Nathan started towards the door. 'Get dressed and come through when you're ready.'

'Dad –' Xander took a breath. 'I don't think Sophie hurt her arm riding.'

Nathan sat back down.

'I was talking to her yesterday and when I mentioned it, she seemed to kind of . . . forget. Then she got this weird look on her face, like she'd said something she wasn't supposed to.'

The funeral had opened the floodgates, Nathan thought. With Cam safely in the ground, it seemed everyone felt more able to say what they couldn't when he was walking around. Nathan looked now at his son. He was nearly grown up in so many ways now. Not a child anymore. And there had already been too many secrets kept for too long in that house.

'Cameron hurt her,' Nathan said. 'Ilse told me last night.'

Xander didn't reply for a long time. 'Sophie's just a kid,' he said finally. 'How could he do that?'

'I don't know, mate.'

'Do you think Cameron felt bad about it?'

'I hope so.'

'Maybe that explains why he left his car.'

'Yeah. Maybe it does.'

'Are the girls okay?'

Nathan could hear voices down the hall and thought about Cameron buried outside. 'I think so, right now, anyway. Why don't you come and join in?'

He stood up.

'Dad —?'

'Yeah.'

'Sorry about the past couple of days.' Xander threaded the bedcover between his fingers, the way he used to when he was young. 'I was just worried.'

'I know. I'm sorry too,' Nathan said. 'And look, you're right. I've got an appointment with Steve. And I'll have a think — a proper one — about some changes. I can't promise I'm going to move away, mate —'

Xander looked disappointed, but Nathan wanted to be honest. And it was true. He couldn't simply leave, for lots of reasons. Financial. Practical. And not least because sometimes, quite a lot of the time, he felt connected to the outback in a way that he loved. There was something about the brutal heat when the sun was high in the sky and he was watching the slow meandering movement of the herds. Looking out over the wide-open plains and seeing the changing colours in the dust. It was the only time when he felt something close to happiness. If Xander couldn't feel it himself, and Nathan knew not everyone could, then he couldn't explain it. It was harsh and unforgiving, but it felt like home.

'Things will be better, though, I promise.' Nathan reached out and put his arms around his boy. Xander hugged him back. 'You can trust me.'

'Yeah. I know.'

They pulled apart and Nathan left Xander to get up and dressed. Out in the hall, he could still hear chatter coming from the living room. It was a nice sound. He started towards it, then stopped at the sight of the landline phone. He glanced back at Xander's room, then without thinking too hard about it, he walked over and dialled a number. It had been a while and he got it wrong the first time. He tried again.

'Hello?' The voice was both familiar and that of a stranger.

'Jacqui? It's Nathan.'

There was a confused pause, then: 'Has something happened to Xander?'

'No, he's fine.' He heard her breathe out in relief. 'I wanted to talk to you, actually.'

'Oh.' Another pause. 'Okay.' She sounded surprised, but not nearly as hostile as he remembered. She sounded different from the way she did in her emails or through her lawyer.

'Listen, Jacqui, I wanted to tell you that I'm sorry for abandoning your dad. Whatever had happened between me and you, it was a terrible thing to do and if I could go back and change it, I would.'

'Oh.' An even longer pause. 'Thank you.'

'And I'm sorry I wasn't what you needed, for you or for Xander.'

He expected the silence this time and waited.

'You've always given Xander what he needed,' Jacqui said finally. He heard her take a breath. 'Sorry, Nathan, I have to ask, is it skin cancer? Have you had a bad result?'

'What? No.'

'Then what's brought this on?'

'I just –' He stopped. 'It felt like it was time.'

It was true, he realised. It was hard work staying angry for ten years. Jacqui sounded tired too. They spoke for a bit longer. It was awkward and rusty, but it was like an old piece of machinery. He could imagine it being functional once again. She sent her condolences about Cameron. Nathan gritted his teeth and asked politely after Martin. He was doing very well, apparently, his star continuing its ascendance in the field of metal-centric architecture. Nathan's gaze wandered as Jacqui made awkward small talk about some renovation work they were planning for Xander's bedroom. His eyes landed on the key rack above the family log book. Cameron's car keys hung from their lanyard, exactly where Nathan had put them himself a couple of days earlier.

It was the silence on the other end of the phone that told him he'd missed something. 'Sorry, what was that?'

A small sigh of disappointment. That brought back a few memories, but he pushed them aside. 'I was saying thanks for understanding about Xander's exams and him needing to be at home more.' Jacqui paused. 'I know you miss him.'

'Yeah.'

'He misses you too.'

'Does he?'

'Of course. You're his dad.'

Nathan felt a flicker of warmth between them and for a moment he could remember what he'd once loved about that golden-haired girl on the other side of the fence.

'Seeing Xander's the best part of my year. He's really great, you should be proud.'

'Well. As should you, Nathan.'

Nathan heard movement and saw their son in the hallway. He waved him over. 'He's here now. I'll put him on. Happy Christmas, Jacqui.'

Xander took the phone, mouth agape in a way that made Nathan feel both a bit better and a bit guilty. He should have tried to do this years ago.

As he turned away, his eye caught once more on the key rack and he reached out and unhooked Cameron's keys. He wandered down the hall, running the lanyard through his fingers. It still had a little red dust on it, and he couldn't help picturing it, dumped on the front seat of Cam's car on that terrible day when they'd found him. *Not dumped*, a small voice whispered in his head. Neatly coiled, in a way he had never seen from his brother.

Nathan's thoughts were scattered by shrieks as Sophie and Lo careered out of the living room and ran past him. Ilse followed with a smile and a rubbish bag full of torn wrapping paper. Nathan slipped the keys into his pocket and smiled back. Liz came out, looking better than she had the day before, Nathan was relieved to see. She headed towards the kitchen and squeezed his arm as she passed. She seemed to have forgiven him at least.

'I'd better get lunch on. I've given the backpackers the day off, so feel free to help.' She turned and called out: 'Sophie!'

'Yeah?' a voice shouted back.

'Can you please run out and tell Simon and Katy that lunch is at twelve?'

'Okay.' More pounding of feet. Sophie appeared and drew to a brief halt. 'Can I whip the cream for the pav?'

'No! I want to!' Lo shouted.

'You both can.' Liz rolled her eyes. 'We're not there yet, anyway.'

She headed into the kitchen as Sophie ran outside. There was a silence, then the verandah boards rumbled again. Sophie reappeared at the door, and Nathan could see by her face that something was wrong.

'It's gone.' She sounded confused.

Harry appeared at Nathan's shoulder. 'What has?' he said.

'The backpackers' car.'

'They've gone?'

'The caravan's still there. But their car is gone!'

Harry frowned and Nathan followed him outside.

Sure enough, the backpackers' battered car – their own private vehicle that they'd driven into town – was no longer there. It had been parked last night, and every night before, right next to the caravan. Now there was just an empty patch of ground in its place. Sophie ran up to it and spread her arms wide.

'See?' she shouted. 'I told you.'

The caravan door opened and Simon poked his head out, surprised to see Nathan and Harry and the girls staring at him. Over his shoulder, Nathan saw Ilse and Bub wander out onto the verandah to see what the fuss was about.

Simon blinked in the sunlight. He looked like he'd just woken up.

'Is Katy already in the house?' he said. It took him another moment to realise what they were all looking at. His eyes widened, any last traces of sleep gone. 'Where's the bloody car?'

He ran out, hitching up his shorts. He stood on the bare patch of land and circled around one way, and then the other. The car did not reappear.

'Where were the keys, mate?' Harry said.

Simon stopped turning and dashed back into the caravan. He re-emerged looking, if possible, even more perplexed.

'They were right there in the cupboard, but now they're gone!'

He ran down to the empty space again.

'And no sign of Katy in there with you?' Harry said quickly, before Simon could start circling once more.

'No! She's gone too! And her bag!' Simon stopped dead still and stared at them. 'Wait. Katy took my car?'

'I would say, mate, that's the way it's looking.'

'But – why?' Simon's eyes widened, then with a speed that surprised Nathan, his expression darkened. 'It was *my* car. How could she do this to me?'

Nathan cleared his throat. 'She did mention she was quite keen to head off,' he said, neutrally.

'So, what? She just gets to make the decisions, does she?' Simon's eyes flashed and he paced up and down the empty space. 'Shit. *Shit*. I can't believe this.'

'Did you not hear her leave?' Harry said. He looked mildly entertained.

'I take sleeping tablets at night,' Simon snapped back. 'I've been very stressed lately. Shit.' More pacing. 'No-one else heard her go?'

Nathan resisted the urge to glance around at Ilse. Now Simon mentioned it, he had vaguely registered the faint thrum of an engine at one point. He'd been dozing and dreamed it was the generator. By the time he'd opened his eyes, he'd looked at Ilse sleeping next to him and instantly forgotten all about it.

He watched Simon pacing and mumble something that sounded suspiciously like 'stupid bitch' and felt a certain warm glow at the idea of Katy buggering off under the cover of darkness. She deserved better, all things considered, but it was a start.

'How am I supposed to get out of this shithole without the car?' Simon was shouting now. His tone was bordering on screechy. Nathan heard Bub on the verandah, failing to suppress a laugh.

Harry caught Nathan's eye. A flicker of a smile caused his craggy features to move a fraction.

'I can tow you into town tomorrow, mate,' Harry said, not unkindly.

'And then bloody what?' Simon snapped.

'I dunno, mate. I reckon you'll be able to work something out from there, though.'

Simon took one more look at them, one more look at the empty space, then turned and stomped back into the empty caravan where his girlfriend used to be and slammed the door, hard.

Nathan could still hear Bub laughing as he disappeared with Ilse and the girls back into the house. He and Harry exchanged an amused glance.

'On that note.' Harry started towards the house. 'You coming back in?'

Nathan felt Cameron's car keys weighing down his pocket.

'Harry.' He felt his smile dim. 'There was nothing wrong with Ilse's car.'

Harry turned at that. 'No?'

'She reckons Cam was messing around with it, so it was too unreliable to use.' Nathan watched his face. 'Is that what you'd thought?'

Harry said nothing for a moment, then nodded. 'Yeah. I wondered. Eventually. There's not a lot that stumps me on those vehicles, but that bloody car –' He shook his head.

'She reckons he was doing other things as well.'

'Like what?' Harry said.

'Things like Dad,' Nathan said. He waited. 'You don't look surprised.'

'It's not that.' Harry glanced towards the house. 'Look,

Cameron was a smart bloke. A lot smarter than Carl, but you know that. Carl was a violent aggressive bastard and didn't care who knew it. But Cam was never like that. He wanted people to like him and respect him. And they did, didn't they? Underneath, though –' Harry said nothing for so long that Nathan thought he might not continue. 'I'd started to wonder if Cam was more like your dad than he let on. Maybe worse even, because he was clever. He could hide it better.'

'You never saw him do anything?'

'No, but I felt like I'd seen some of the signs before. Lo's bloody sad drawings. Sophie's arm sounded like bullshit to me as well, but she swore that was what happened.'

'Jesus, Harry, you should have done something.'

'Hey.' Harry pointed a callused finger at Nathan. 'You haven't shown your face here in a year, mate. Don't tell me what I should or shouldn't have been doing. I kept that key to the rifle cabinet close, in case he started getting any ideas. I sent Cam away from here on any job I could think of. I tried to talk to him. When that didn't work, I argued with him, like your bloody backpacker mate overheard.'

'You could have called the police.'

'So could you,' Harry said suddenly. He stared at Nathan with a clear gaze. 'All those times with your dad, and you and your brothers and your mum. You were all old enough to pick up the phone and call someone. Why didn't you?'

Nathan opened his mouth, then shut it. 'I don't know,' he said finally.

He did though, he realised. He hadn't called anyone for help because it simply hadn't occurred to him that he could. He knew the unspoken rules: don't tell anyone, not even each other. And even if he'd thought to ask for help, there had seemed no point asking for something that simply wasn't there. Nathan may not know much, but in his heart he had always held on to a single ingrained truth. Out there, he was on his own.

'I did call the police once,' Harry said, his features again inscrutable. 'When things got bad between your mum and dad. You and Cam were away at boarding school. But ask Bub, I guarantee you he'll remember it. Afterwards, your mum made me promise never to do it again. It caused a lot of problems that a visit from the sergeant didn't stop, and it didn't turn out well.'

'For Mum?'

'For Bub.'

They both stared out across the yard at the graves for a long while.

'I know Bub can be hard work when he wants to be,' Harry said. 'But he did it even worse than you and Cam growing up. Just bear that in mind, all right? You and Cam weren't the only ones who had a bad time.'

Nathan was quiet for a minute. 'Yeah. I know.'

Harry was looking back at the house now and Nathan followed his gaze, catching a glimpse of Liz in the kitchen window. She was smiling and looking down, probably talking to one of the girls. As Harry looked on, his features relaxed and for once his eyes were as open and unguarded as Nathan had ever seen them. Nathan looked at Harry looking at his mother and suddenly wondered, for the first time, if there was something other than the land and lifestyle that had made Harry want to stay on the property for so many years. Then Liz moved away from the window and the shutters behind Harry's eyes snapped closed so fast Nathan thought he might have imagined it.

The gum tree bristled in the hot air and they both turned back towards the graves.

'I spoke to Steve at the funeral,' Nathan said. 'He thinks Cameron did attack Jenna that night.'

Harry just nodded.

Nathan felt the car keys in his pocket, sharp and jagged. 'What do you think she wanted to say to him when she called?'

'Dunno. Could have been anything.'

'But do you think –'

'Look, I'll tell you what I think, mate.' Harry cut him short. 'Sometimes – whether by accident, or whatever – I reckon sometimes things turn out for the best. And when you end up in the right place, it's not always helpful to go digging up the road that got you there, you know?'

His eyes flicked over to the graves one last time as the wind lifted dust all around them.

'Now.' Harry turned firmly back to the house. 'You coming in to join everyone?'

The metal of the keys bit into Nathan's skin.

Ilse's envelope had been taken by a dingo.

Jenna Moore was not around.

The lanyard, uncoiled now, was still gritty in his fingers.

Cameron's car stood lonely on the driveway.

Nathan shook his head.

'Not just yet.'

Chapter 36

Cameron's Land Cruiser was still parked where Nathan and Xander had left it all those days ago.

Duffy followed at Nathan's heels, excited to be in the familiar car once again as they climbed in. Nathan sat in the driver's seat, feeling where the contours had worn exactly to his brother's frame. It was the right distance from the pedals now. He fished the keys out of his pocket. The engine started immediately, as it had every other time. No car trouble for Cameron, Nathan thought with a sour note as he pictured Ilse's neglected vehicle. He waited until the air conditioner was running nice and high, then got out and started at the back while the dog watched.

Nathan pulled out the bottles of water, the tinned food, the cooler. He took out the first aid kit and then removed the contents, checking the edges of the bag for anything envelope-shaped. He unhooked the spare tyres and felt around the inside rims. The car had already been searched, twice, by the police. But, Nathan thought as he worked through methodically, they hadn't known then what they were looking for.

He ran his hands over the floor mats, feeling in the cracks for anything slipped between. He checked the fabric of the roof and the car seats for any hidden seams. He went through the tool kit, then slid down on the ground and examined the underneath of the chassis with a torch. He opened the bonnet and checked for anything taped to the sides or underneath.

An hour later, he was down to opening the packets of food and peering inside the water bottles. After another thirty minutes, he opened one of Cam's beers, climbed into the front seat and let the air conditioner blow on his face as he fed Duffy biscuits from Cameron's stash.

Nathan looked at the mess around him. Nothing. If an envelope had ever been dug up from the stockman's grave and dumped in this car, it was beyond him to find it. And if anyone other than Cameron had been in the vehicle at that time, they hadn't revealed themselves to Nathan. Maybe – Nathan took a sip of beer and grimaced; it was as hot as coffee. Maybe there never was anything to be found.

He was still sitting there, sipping and thinking, when he heard footsteps and a figure appeared through the dusty windscreen. Bub.

'I heard the engine.' Bub climbed into the passenger seat. 'Been looking for you.'

'Have you?' Nathan offered him one of the five remaining cans in their brother's six-pack.

'Twist my arm.' Bub took one, his gaze flicking over the car. 'What are you doing in here?'

'I honestly don't know.'

'Right. Anyway –' He cracked open the warm beer and barely winced as he took a sip. 'Mate, listen. I wanted to say sorry.'

Nathan looked over in surprise. 'Oh yeah?'

'About Kelly. I know it was my fault, but I promise you it was an accident. You have to believe me. I seriously never meant for that to happen. Kelly was an awesome dog. I was gutted when I heard that she'd died. I'd never have done that to her on purpose.'

'I know,' Nathan said and meant it.

Bub looked down at the can in his hand. 'I felt bloody awful. I shouldn't have been baiting, but I didn't know you'd be in that area. I thought I'd picked them all up. When I heard about Kelly, I wanted to explain, but Cam said he'd do it. Make it all right. He told me he'd talked to you, and that you were pissed off. But he said you knew it was an accident and with you being so, you know –' Bub tapped his head. 'It was best to let you get over it and not bring it up.'

Nathan took a long, warm sip from his can. 'He never spoke to me.'

'No. Well, yeah. I'd started to wonder. Then when you said all that yesterday, I just panicked. I'm sorry, mate. I don't know what to tell you. It was a shit thing to do, and I've felt shit about it ever since. I should've come to talk to you instead of trusting bloody Cam.'

Ilse was right, Nathan thought. Whether or not he forgave his brother, it wouldn't bring Kelly back.

'Thanks for telling me, Bub.' Nathan sighed. 'Listen,

though, it's me who should be sorry. I should have said this years ago, but I'm really sorry, mate, for not doing a lot more to help you with Dad –'

'No. Christ, Nathan, it's not your fault. You tried. Cam as well, to be fair.'

'Still, we should've –'

'What? What could anyone do with a bloke like him?' Bub looked over. 'Anyway, it was as bad for you.'

'It wasn't, though. Not really,' Nathan said. 'Me and Cam always had each other.'

They sat and drank and stared out together through the windscreen for a while. It was so dusty by now that it was hard to see through.

'I don't like living here,' Bub said eventually. 'It reminds me too much of some stuff. That's why I was baiting those dingoes. Trying to get some money to go to Dulsterville, after Cam wouldn't help. That's why I've been such an arsehole about this place as well.' He sighed. 'It's nothing personal, mate, but the thought of staying here and answering to another one of my bloody brothers for the next ten years does my head in. I just need to be somewhere else.'

'Roo shooting in Dulsterville, hey?'

'Yeah.' Bub had a faraway look in his eye. 'It'd be so great there. Get my own place, meet some people. There's chicks living in Dulsterville, you know? Heaps more than here.'

'Yeah.' Nathan gave Bub a small smile. 'I've heard.'

'And then when Cam died, I thought that was my chance. If I couldn't leave, then maybe running this place wouldn't be so bad. Could make some changes, but then –' Bub broke the ring pull off his can. 'It was bloody obvious that no-one thought I could do it. They're all flat out hoping you're going to come back and help Ilse, and it pissed me off.'

Nathan frowned. 'I don't think that's what they want. Ilse will get a manager or someone.'

'Mate,' Bub said, 'that's exactly what they want. I've heard Harry say it, and Mum. Ilse as well, I reckon. They're waiting for you to say you're interested.'

'Seriously, no-one's mentioned it.'

'I know, because they're all shitting themselves about putting too much pressure on you after, you know, what happened to Cam. And the fact you can be a bit . . . '

'What?'

'Like I said.' Bub tapped his head.

'I'm not.' Nathan suddenly felt very aware of the ransacked car. 'Not always. Anyway, I can barely run my own property.'

'Yeah, 'cause it's complete shit. No-one could make money running that place. Harry says that all the time. Even Cam used to say that. You're doing well to have kept going as long as you have.'

Nathan said nothing for a long time. He reached over and opened another beer. It was a little cooler this time thanks to the air con. Slightly above room temperature. 'What about you?' he said finally.

'Nate, I don't want to run things. Too much paperwork. Don't get me wrong, I wouldn't have minded being asked, that would have been the bloody polite thing to do, but never mind. I just want to free up some cash and go to Dulsterville.'

'Roos and chicks, hey?'

'Exactly, mate. Exactly.'

Nathan smiled. 'Well. It's good to have a dream.'

'Yeah. So you'll talk to Ilse for me? See if she'll buy me out? At least partly?'

'You could talk to her. She wants to know what you think.'

'Yeah, I know. But when I walked past the living room at about three this morning, it looked to me like that sleeping bag of yours wasn't getting much use.' Bub shot Nathan a sideways glance and grinned. 'So, I reckon it's fair to say you know how to talk to Ilse better than me.'

Nathan suppressed a smile and said nothing.

'Or hey,' Bub went on. 'Maybe you could buy me out? Slowly would be okay, I don't need that much at first. If you ever get off your arse and work out what you want.'

Nathan looked through the dusty windscreen. He could barely make out what lay ahead. 'Yeah,' he said. 'Maybe. Look, either way, we'll work something out for you.'

'That's great. Thanks, mate.' Bub glanced over. 'I'm sorry about your face too, by the way.'

'Don't worry about it. Are you all right?'

'Yeah.' Bub laughed. 'You didn't even graze me. And I was pretty hammered.'

'Good to know.'

'So, are we okay?'

'Yeah. We're okay.'

'Awesome. Thanks, mate.' Bub opened the door to get out. 'I'm heading back in. You all done here?'

Nathan looked around at the interior of the car. There was nothing to be found.

'Yeah.' He opened the door. 'I'm done.'

Chapter 37

'I can't get it.'

'It's like this.'

Nathan repositioned Sophie's hand on the neck of the guitar and moved one of her fingers on the string. She tried again and the chord rang out, a little disharmonious still, but closer. Sophie's sling lay by her side on the verandah step. Steve had given her permission to take it off for a couple of hours a day, she'd said, and she was making the most of it. Nathan shifted, the late-morning sun warm on his back, and adjusted her hand on the strings once more.

'Try again. Yeah, better that time.'

He saw Lo grimace at the sound, but she said nothing, just concentrated on her painting. From the aroma floating from the kitchen, the lunch preparation was coming along well, and Nathan could hear Liz rattling pots and pans inside. He and Bub had gone in to help, only to be shooed out by an exasperated Liz twenty minutes later for getting underfoot. Bub had been happy enough. He'd got a new cricket bat for Christmas and had roped Harry into bowling for him around the front of the house. Nathan couldn't see them from where he sat, but could hear the occasional *thwack* and cheer.

The screen door slammed and Xander appeared. He was holding a folded piece of paper as he sat down next to Nathan. 'Sounding good, Sophie.'

'Thanks.' She smiled, focusing on the strings. It wasn't only the absence of her sling. It was like a cloud had lifted after the funeral.

'Here.' Xander handed the sheet of paper to Nathan. 'It's not exactly a Christmas present but I wanted to give you this.'

'What is it?' Nathan unfolded it. Inside was a handwritten list of dates.

'So these are the term dates and the exam weeks for this year.' Xander pointed. 'And here are all the potential holidays, here and here. Here, too. So we can plan something.'

'Oh.' The writing blurred a tiny bit as Nathan looked at it. 'Thanks, mate. But seriously, you should stay in Brisbane, focus on your work, if you need to.' He smiled. 'Who knows? If your marks are good enough you might be able to follow Martin into the world of blinding metallic buildings.'

'Yeah, I'm not going to be doing that.' Xander grinned back. 'But look, I probably will have to stay home most of the time, so that's why you should come and visit me in Brisbane.'

Nathan hesitated.

'It was Mum's idea,' Xander said, reading his mind.

'Really?'

'Yeah. Maybe I could ask her if you could stay with us. Martin built a guest house in the garden.'

'*Really?*'

'Well, he drew it and then paid someone else to build it.' Xander laughed. 'He can't do the practical stuff as well as you can. Anyway, you should come. I'd really like it.'

'Yeah. Well, thanks. I'd really like it too.'

'Good.' Xander stood up. 'If you need help packing up the car at any point, just yell.'

'You're keen. We're not leaving until tomorrow.'

'I know.' Xander smiled. 'I just don't want to miss the flight. New Year's Eve in Brisbane has the edge on here somehow.'

Nathan caught a glimpse of Ilse passing by her office window. She gave him a little wave. 'I struggle to believe that.'

'Believe it,' Xander said, and Nathan watched the screen door slam behind him.

He heard the thud and clip of the cricket ball as he turned back to the girls. Sophie was still fiddling with her chords and Lo had her head down over her latest artwork.

'Do you want to have a go on the guitar, Lo?' he asked.

'I'm doing this.'

Nathan moved over to look at her pictures. They had been laid out across the porch, weighed down with rocks. She had been painting the same scene over and over again, he saw now. Every one was a variation of her dad's painting.

'You're trying to paint the grave?' he said.

'I can't get it right.'

'They look pretty good to me.'

Lo threw him a look that implied his artistic opinion was of questionable value, but Nathan could tell she was pleased. He wasn't making it up, either. The images were all imitations of Cameron's theme and were unavoidably childish, but they were strangely expressive. Where Cameron had been heavy-handed with the shadow, she had managed to capture corners of light.

'Are you missing your dad?' he said, and Lo exchanged a glance with her sister.

'Do you think Daddy was scared out there at the grave by himself?' Lo said, finally.

'No,' Nathan lied. He thought for a minute. 'He liked being out on the property.' More truthful. 'But I think he found some things in his life very hard.'

The girls mulled that over.

'I don't like the stockman's grave,' Sophie said, eventually. 'It's scary.'

Nathan shook his head. 'It doesn't have to be. There are a lot of stupid stories about the stockman. None of them are true.'

'How do you know?'

'I went to the State Library once and looked it up.'

He'd spent a few hours there, years ago, in Brisbane, when Xander was still young and Nathan had found it particularly hard to pass him back into Jacqui's arms. It had been a difficult handover and Nathan had missed the flight home. Adrift, he'd found himself walking the city streets until he'd ended up outside the library, with the sudden urge to find out more about the only person he could think of who was more alone than him. A librarian had helped him search, and as he'd read the old newspaper article in the cool air conditioning surrounded by the discreet hum of company, he had felt more at peace than he had in a long time.

'So what happened to the man?' Sophie said.

'It was this bloke called William Carlisle and he actually lived on this property with his wife and kids. Two boys about seven and ten, I think.'

'Did they live in this house?' Lo said.

'No, it wasn't built then. They were somewhere closer to where the grave is now. Anyway, they'd gone out riding together one day and had got off their horses to have lunch or whatever, and suddenly they realised a dust storm was coming.'

'Oh no,' Sophie said. 'I really hate them.'

'Me too,' Nathan said. The sight of the sky turning red as a towering wall of dust bore down. The storms engulfed everything in their path, sucking away the oxygen and filling the air with missiles. They sent the cattle stampeding and reduced visibility to nothing.

'You know how fast they come in,' he said. 'So the stockman put his wife and the littlest kid back on their horses and told them to ride home. But the older boy had gone exploring. Over the crest or somewhere. Out of sight, anyway. The stockman went looking for him, yelling out I guess, while the storm would have been coming closer.'

Nathan thought for a minute. He remembered himself driving in desperate circles as he searched for eight-year-old Xander, and the way his heart had pounded in his ears and the fear had run pure and cold. *Please let him be okay.* It would have been worse for the stockman, alone on horseback, on the brink of a natural nightmare.

'Did he find his little boy?' Sophie asked.

'Yeah, he did, eventually.' Nathan hesitated. 'But the kid's horse had panicked and thrown him off. The kid was okay but the horse was gone.'

'So what did the man do?'

'He must have decided one horse wouldn't be able to outrun the storm carrying both of them, because he gave his own horse to his little boy.'

Nathan imagined the man telling, *ordering*, his son to go on without him. Promising him he would find the other horse and be right behind. Saying it, and knowing that wasn't true.

'Did the little boy get home safely?' Sophie asked.

'He did.'

'But not the stockman?'

'No. He would have known he wouldn't.'

'That's sad.'

'Yeah, it is. Although.' Nathan paused. 'I like to think that maybe he wasn't sad, right at the end. Knowing that at least his kids were safe.'

'He'd done it to save his family,' Sophie said.

'Exactly.' Nathan turned to Lo. 'So I know it can be a bit creepy out there, but it doesn't have to be. You don't have to be scared of him.'

Lo thought it over. Finally, she leaned in. Nathan could

feel her breath on his face and see the specks of paint on her skin.

'I wasn't scared of the stockman,' she whispered. 'I was scared of Daddy.'

'Oh.' Nathan took her hand.

'He's not coming back, though, is he?'

'No. He's not, Lo.' He put his arms out and she hugged him. She was small and warm. 'It's going to be okay. You're safe here and we all love you.' He pointed at her artwork. 'And you know what else? I reckon you're a better painter than your dad.'

He got a small smile at that. 'No,' she said with something that sounded suspiciously like false modesty. 'Daddy's painting won a prize.'

'That doesn't mean anything. Yours are just as good.'

'No, they're not. Stop being silly.'

'It's true.' He got up. 'Hang on.'

Nathan went inside, his vision poor as his eyes adjusted to the light. Lunch smelled great as he passed the kitchen. Through the hall window, he could see Bub and Harry out on the grass. Bub was bowling now, letting Harry have a go of his bat. The door to Ilse's office was ajar, and Nathan toyed briefly with the idea of going in to see her. Say hello. Say he'd missed her. He hesitated, but kept moving. The girls were waiting.

In the living room, Nathan stood in front of Cameron's painting. He raised his hands, feeling the buzz of an outlaw as he lifted the frame from the wall. It was surprisingly light for something that seemed to take up so much space in the house. Nathan waited a moment, but nothing happened. Cameron's spirit did not, in fact, rise from its otherworldly slumber to warn against the perils of leaving fingerprints on the brushwork.

Nathan grinned to himself as he carried the painting down the hall, looking at the colours of the land and the sky and the grave. He realised that what he had said to Lo was absolutely true. There was nothing special about this painting. There was no life in it. It was the flat uninspired work of a man who was too blind to see all the good things he had.

He stepped out onto the porch, the screen door slamming behind him, and was greeted by a stunned silence. Lo's mouth actually dropped open. No-one said anything for a long moment and Nathan was vaguely aware that even the sounds of cricket ball against bat had stopped.

'Oh my God,' Sophie gasped. 'What have you done?' But beneath her horror, her eyes gleamed with delight at the sheer scandal of it.

'Yep.' Nathan nodded. 'I touched the painting.'

'You'll be in so much trouble,' she breathed. Lo was giggling, her hands over her mouth.

'I won't. Because it's just a painting, Soph. That's all. And yeah, it's pretty good, I suppose. But my question right now is, is it better than Lo's?'

Lo was hopping from foot to foot, equal parts thrilled and horrified.

'Okay,' Nathan said. 'Lo, you hold up your best picture. Let's compare.'

With a grin, she chose one.

'Sophie, you be the judge. Which is better?'

Nathan flipped Cameron's painting over in his hands. He held it up in front of his face, the painted side facing away from him. And all at once, the world tilted. Sophie's laughter was muffled by the pounding in his ears.

'I judge that Lo's is better,' Sophie was saying. 'Ten out of ten.'

Her voice seemed very far away and when Lo cheered, it sounded like she was underwater. Nathan tried to nod, but his head felt heavy and unbalanced. He realised the girls were watching him.

'I agree,' he said, his tongue thick in his mouth. He saw Lo smile, but only in his peripheral vision. His gaze was trained on the back of the painting. Specifically, on something taped there. Something worn and opaque with fine red dust in the plastic creases. Nathan felt the ground sway a little.

'It's hot out here, girls,' he managed to say. 'Go inside and grab a drink of water.'

'Okay.' He heard their footsteps and the door slam behind them.

Nathan's hands were shaking as he laid the painting face down on the verandah. The plastic envelope was taped carefully in the centre of the frame. He fumbled at it, not caring about any damage to the front of the picture, and wrenched it free. He stood up.

Beneath the dust, he could see the coloured edges of banknotes, the etched lettering of a passport cover and several folded official-looking certificates. Nathan felt his heart skip, as though there was a sudden hollow in his chest. He had not actually expected to find it, he knew in that instant. Not really.

Don't touch the painting.

Nathan shot a glance around the deserted yard. There were no sounds of cricket ball against bat any more from the other side of the house. He couldn't hear Bub cheering now.

Shit, no. You don't mess with Cam's masterpiece.

In the distance, Harry's cabin stood dark and secluded, its door firmly closed.

Don't you bloody touch it. You've done enough damage.

Behind Nathan, the house loomed over him, as though holding its breath. He could not hear Liz or Ilse moving around. The windows to the kitchen and office were still and blank.

It belongs on the wall.

Somewhere behind him, Nathan felt rather than heard the creak and tread of footsteps on the hall floorboards. A moment later the screen door gave its soft shriek. He didn't move. He couldn't bring himself to look around.

Golden rule in this house.

Who had warned him?

Don't touch the painting.

Everyone. Everyone had.

The footsteps were close now.

'I tried to tell you,' a voice said. 'You never listen, Nathan.'

He turned.

Chapter 38

'I tried to tell you.'

Nathan knew the voice as well as his own. He turned around. A few steps away, face partly shrouded by the shade of the verandah, stood his mother.

Liz's eyes darted from the painting on the ground to the plastic envelope in Nathan's hands. She looked up at him. Her gaze was steadier than he had seen it in days.

'That was nice.' Her voice was low. 'What you told the girls about the stockman. I could hear from the kitchen.'

Nathan's hands felt numb, like the envelope could slip through his fingers. 'True story.' His voice broke a little on the words.

Liz met her son's eye. 'Can I tell you another one?'

The rattle of a girl's footsteps rang out from the hall, and immediately Liz took a quick step forward and plucked the plastic envelope from his hands.

'Not here. Walk with me, Nathan.'

She took his arm, her grip firm, as she propped the

painting against the house and slipped the envelope into her apron pocket.

In the midday light, Liz's shadow had shrunk to a tight dark spot beneath her feet as they crossed the yard. They walked towards the gum tree and stood under the gentle sway of its branches. At their feet, the graves lay side by side.

Nathan could hear the blood rushing in his ears as he looked at the ground. Old dirt next to freshly turned earth. He had so many questions, he couldn't find just one to ask.

'I'd gone out riding,' Liz said, finally. 'After Sophie hurt her arm, and told us all that her horse threw her. We couldn't have that happening. Not with her wanting to do gymkhana. So I wanted to take her horse out myself.'

Nathan suddenly didn't want to hear. But he closed his eyes and made himself listen as she spoke. On the day Cameron would fail to come home, Liz told him, she had done what she did every day. She saddled up. It was a habit she'd formed during her marriage. On a horse, she was taller and faster and for a few hours at least, no-one could touch her.

That day, she was on Sophie's horse. It needed the exercise while Sophie's arm healed. Liz had ridden for longer than usual, feeling for any problems with the animal. The riding seemed fine, and the horse was responding well. Liz thought about Sophie's arm and rode on, trying harder now to sense the faults. She'd already gone further than she meant to when the thought first crept in, slick and dark.

'There was nothing wrong with that horse,' Liz said,

391

the shadows of the eucalyptus leaves playing across her features. 'I couldn't work it out. It didn't make any sense.'

Nathan thought of Ilse's car sitting neglected in the garage. That hadn't made any sense either, until it had.

'So I just kept riding,' Liz went on.

She had pushed ahead, growing more uneasy with every step. Sophie had been pale and shaking as she had clutched her injured arm, Liz remembered. She had cried, and said she was scared. But she'd wanted to jump back on her horse the minute she was allowed. They'd all praised her for being so brave. Sophie had barely responded to that.

The feeling in the pit of Liz's stomach had already started to take on a familiar shape when she saw the man standing by the stockman's grave. She slowed the horse. Her eyesight wasn't as good these days, and for a long minute, under the blinding sun, the man looked very much like someone else.

Liz had stopped to watch, then walked the horse closer. She recognised the four-wheel drive nearby and breathed out. Of course it wasn't the man she'd first thought, there was no possible way it could have been. It was her son, Cameron.

'What was he doing?' Nathan asked. He'd opened his eyes and was staring at the ground.

'He was digging.'

Cameron had had a shovel in his hand, and was slicing it into the soft soil. Liz rode up, taking her time. Cameron had not been right lately, and even now he dug with a restless energy that set her teeth on edge. Liz dismounted and hooked the reins around the wing mirror of his car.

Cameron had straightened then, wielding the spade in both hands. The metal glinted in the sun and she was reminded, once again, of a different man. Something about the look in his eyes. He wasn't pleased to see her.

Can I get some water for the horse? She walked to the rear of his vehicle, where he kept his supplies.

Cameron had waved a hand, his attention already back to the soft ground at his feet, as Liz found a bucket and filled it with water. She looked over as the horse drank.

What are you doing?

He bent down. *Checking something.*

Checking what?

Why my bloody wife's been dragging my kids out here.

Liz hesitated. *I thought you were going to the repeater tower?*

I am.

Bub'll be waiting.

I'm doing this first.

Cameron ploughed the spade into the sand once more, then stopped. He made a noise in the back of his throat.

'He'd found something.' Liz's voice was hard to hear.

The noise Cameron made was not quite one of triumph; the undertone was too hollow for that. Liz suddenly wished she had ridden in the other direction that morning. The horse had finished drinking, she saw with relief. She put the empty bucket back in the rear and turned in time to see Cameron stoop and dig his hands through the sand. When he stood up, he was holding a plastic envelope, opaque with red dust.

What's that?

Cameron smiled in a way that made Liz's stomach clench. *Buried treasure.*

'I knew what it was.' Liz rubbed a hand over her arm and Nathan could see both the recent skin cancer wound, and the other, older, scar that they never talked about. One of many. They all had those kinds of marks: Liz, Nathan, Bub. Cameron, as well. Marks they kept hidden and never acknowledged.

'I knew straight away what Cameron had found,' Liz said. 'I used to have something just like that myself.'

Liz's version had been an old biscuit tin and she'd hidden it in the middle of a bucket of horse feed. Or at least she had until Carl had found it. The blow had burst her left eardrum and her hearing had never recovered. But she'd learned her lesson, and she'd never tried that again. The boys had still been small and she had been too scared of the consequences.

But as Liz had stood by the stockman's grave, watching her middle son, she wondered how much worse the consequences were for her not having tried.

You should leave that alone. She had surprised herself by speaking.

Cameron was surprised too, and his eyes hardened. *You don't even know what this is.*

I do, Cameron. I know.

Then you'll know it has nothing to do with you.

He straightened then, up to his full height. The shovel was hanging by his side, and his hands were gently gripping the handle. It hung loose. He hadn't lifted it, not even a little. He wasn't threatening her, he wasn't, but as Cameron stood there, with the metal blade catching the light as it swayed gently, Liz knew exactly who he reminded her of. He wasn't her little boy anymore. Or at least, he wasn't just her boy. He was his father's son as well.

And she knew, as she had always known in some part of her, what Ilse had tried to tell her. And what Harry had been so worried about. And why Lo's pictures were so sad. And why Sophie's arm was in a sling. And why it would be again. Or worse.

Liz flinched involuntarily as Cameron stepped past her towards his car. He tossed the shovel into the rear and slammed the door before dropping the envelope through the passenger's side window and onto the car seat. Liz's horse bristled, tugging at the reins hooked over the mirror, and she whispered something to calm it.

I've got to get going. Cameron didn't look at her. *Things to do.*

Are you driving to the repeater tower? Liz's voice sounded odd to her own ears.

Cameron walked back to the grave and started kicking dirt back into the hole.

I was going to but – His anger shimmered like the heat. *I might go home first. Have a word with Ilse.*

Cameron. Please. The trickle of fear was now a fast-running flood. *The girls are at home.*

He said nothing, then at last, he looked up. *So? Maybe they need to hear this too.*

And with the tone of his voice and the sun in her eyes, it was suddenly thirty years ago and Liz knew, without a shadow of a doubt, what happened when men like that came home.

She felt her hand reach out before she was quite aware

what she was reaching for. She had done the calculation in her mind without realising it. Calculations that had become an ingrained instinct years ago. Fight or flight. He was five metres away, six maybe. And he was looking down, distracted, kicking the sand to paper over the damage he had done.

Liz was behind the driver's seat in the time it took her to draw a first breath, and she had turned the key by the time she drew the second.

Cameron had looked up, but by then her foot was already on the accelerator. She wound down the window and unhooked the reins from the wing mirror. The horse followed obediently as she pulled away. Not too fast. There was no need; a cantering horse can outrun a man.

'Cameron tried, though.' Liz's voice was hollow with horror. 'He really tried.'

And he had, screaming as he chased her. He had known what was happening and he knew what it meant. It had taken every shred of self-control for Liz not to put her foot down and tear away from that terrible sound. But she kept a steady pace, with her ears shut tight and her eyes straight ahead. And eventually, much later, when at last she slowed and looked in the mirror, there was no-one else around. She was all alone.

Chapter 39

Nathan stared down at the graves for a long time before he finally spoke.

'Cameron's car wasn't at the rocks on Thursday morning.'

Liz looked surprised. 'You knew that?'

'I thought someone had moved it. Or that I was going crazy. I wasn't sure which.'

'I made a mistake,' Liz said. 'I'd hidden it off the track near home. But I realised that night that it was too far away. He couldn't have walked that distance. When they found the car, they'd know someone else had been there.'

'So you moved it?'

She nodded. 'Next day. I rode out early, led the horse on the reins again and drove to the rocks. I thought that was possible, for someone like Cameron. About ten kilometres.'

'It's nine, actually.'

Liz didn't argue. 'I just didn't want it to be seen too quickly.'

Nathan said nothing for a while. He didn't want to think about it.

'I didn't know what to do with Ilse's documents,' Liz said. 'I wanted to give them back to her, but I couldn't think how. The girls are always in and out of everywhere – my bedroom, the stables. Then Xander started pulling things apart in the sheds as well.' She shook her head. 'But everyone knows not to touch that bloody painting.'

Nathan stared out across the property. At Cameron's car parked on the driveway and at the house where they'd grown up.

'The way Cam died never felt right,' he said. 'I really thought for a while that Jenna Moore had something to do with it.' He was quiet. The sun was approaching its peak in the sky, the horizon was a flat line in the distance. 'I wonder what she wanted with him.'

When Liz didn't respond, he looked over.

'What?'

Liz hesitated, then reached into her pocket.

'Caroline from the post office brought our mail with her yesterday. She thought we might not get into town to collect it for a while.'

She handed something to Nathan and he turned the slightly rumpled letter over in his fingers. Cameron Bright's name had been written on the front of the envelope. There was no return address, but in the top right-hand corner was a stamp from the UK. It had already been torn open and Nathan pulled out the contents. The letter was folded into thirds and felt slightly worn at the creases, like it had been opened and read several times. He took a breath and looked at the words.

Cameron, it started. Nathan did not recognise the handwriting, but it was neat and firm. *Please read this letter to the end. I am aware that you may not even remember me, Cameron, but I need to tell you one thing:*

I forgive you.

You may not want my forgiveness, or feel like you have done anything that needs to be forgiven. I truly hope, however, that is not the case. Regardless of what you might tell yourself, or what threats your father made on your behalf when he had me cornered and alone, you and I know what happened the night we met. You know what you did, and I do too.

I used to hope that you would be living your life with the same sense of regret and shame that I have for years. That is no longer important to me.

I have wasted years feeling guilty about something that wasn't my fault, and I have given you a power over me that you do not deserve. With the support of my therapist and the love of my beautiful family, I am proud to say that this is no longer the case.

In so many ways, I have built a happy life. I wish the same for you, Cameron. Those in great pain cause others great pain, and I hope, for your sake and for those around you, that you have found some peace.

Jenna Moore

Nathan read the letter three times, then refolded it. He handed it back to Liz.

'What are you going to do with it?' he said.

'I'll show it to Glenn, I suppose.'

'It doesn't excuse you, you know.' Nathan's voice was harsh even to his own ears. 'That doesn't make what you did any better.'

'I know.'

'I saw what Cameron looked like at the end, when Steve took him away in the ambulance. All the damage.' Nathan saw Liz flinch at that but he went on. She needed to hear it. 'He didn't go easily. You should know that. He suffered a lot.'

She didn't answer and he realised she was crying. He didn't move. Finally, she took a breath. 'I'm not asking you to forgive me —'

'Good.'

Liz was still for a long time.

'Nathan, I was eighteen when I left home,' she said at last. 'And when I did that, I promised myself things would be different.'

She had travelled north, she explained, and then west, going wherever she wanted and feeling free for the first time in her life. She had stopped in Balamara only when it became apparent she was running out of road before the desert. Within a couple of days, she'd found herself a job in the post office and was earning her own money for once. Work was enjoyable and the locals were friendly. They always had time for a smile and a chat and when Carl Bright had grinned at her over his mail and insisted on buying her a drink, she'd said yes.

'And for a while, it was great. He was a lot of fun, believe it or not, and I thought he was so good-looking.

And he was nice to me. And for a while my life really was different.' Liz's face darkened. 'Then we got married and things started to change, and suddenly one day I realised my life wasn't so different anymore. Your dad had told me he'd had a bad time himself when he was young and we both wanted something better. But it wasn't better. It was the same as what I'd left behind. And I was so disappointed, Nathan, and I was just so tired. I'd come all this way only to end up in exactly the same place. I didn't have the energy to fight it. What was the point?'

She shook her head.

'But then I was pregnant, and I told myself that whatever went on between me and him, I wasn't going to stand for it with you kids.' Liz wiped her eyes. She couldn't look at her son. 'And I tried my best, Nathan. Please believe me. I made plans, I thought about it every day. But I was scared and I felt so alone and trapped. I'm so sorry. It wasn't good enough, I know, not at all. But it was the best I could do.'

Liz was quiet for a long moment.

'And then your dad had that accident. And I believe that saved my life. Bub's too, possibly.'

Suddenly Nathan was back, years ago, on that hot dark night, looking through torn metal at the sight of Carl Bright pinned between the roof and the steering wheel. The nurse's comment.

It hadn't been quick.

Liz's face had been frozen as she'd sat in the back of the ambulance with the blood congealing around her wound. It was the shock, Nathan had thought at the time. Maybe though, a dark thought unfurled now, maybe it was something else. He looked at the two graves at his feet for a long time. Old earth and new earth. Maybe, he thought, some lines were easier to cross the second time.

'How long –?' he started, then stopped. *How long were you unconscious after the accident? How long did you leave it before you called for help?*

He wanted to ask, but he didn't, because he could tell from his mother's face that she would tell him the truth.

Liz was watching him closely.

'I'm sorry for a lot of things,' she said, at last. 'But I am not sorry he's gone.'

Nathan didn't ask who she meant. The gum tree rustled and Nathan felt the sand in the air and the grit on his skin. The screen door slammed in the distance and they both turned towards the house. Ilse was walking over, shielding her eyes.

'Phone for you, Nathan,' she called.

'For me?' His voice sounded strange. He cleared his throat.

'It's Glenn. He says you left a message with the police switchboard.'

'Oh. Yeah.'

He still didn't move. Then suddenly Liz reached up and pulled him to her. He could feel her hands, gentle on his back as she held him close, and smell the familiar scent of her hair. She had tears in her eyes.

'I never meant for you to have to deal with this,' she said quietly. 'I did what I felt was right in my heart. But you're a good man, Nathan. And you have to do what you think is right.' She drew back and looked up at him. 'Either way, you should come home.'

Liz held him a moment longer, then let him go and turned towards the house.

'Bub's got everyone playing cricket around the front if you want to join them,' Ilse said and Liz gave her a sad smile as she passed.

'Thanks, I think I will. Lunch will be ready soon.'

Ilse watched her walk away, then turned back to Nathan. She saw his face and frowned. 'Is everything all right? Glenn's waiting.'

'Yeah.'

'Are you sure?'

He turned his back on both graves, and immediately felt a bit better. 'Yeah.'

'Come on, then.' Ilse waited until Liz had disappeared into the house, then slid her hand into his. Her palm was warm and dry as they walked.

'Listen,' she said. 'Harry was talking about driving over and helping you with your flood prep, but —' Her words came out in a rush. 'I was thinking he should stay and make sure everything's ready here, and I could drive over and help you for a couple of days. If you want.'

Nathan stopped walking and looked at her. 'I would absolutely love that.'

'Are you sure? Because if you actually need Harry's help, or Bub's —'

'No. God, no.'

'Is there much to do?'

'No.'

'But I should still come?'

'Definitely.'

'Okay.' She smiled. 'Good. So maybe Thursday and Friday next week?'

'New year.'

'Yes.' She smiled. 'I suppose it is.'

They reached the verandah. Lo's pictures were still pinned by rocks, the edges flapping in the breeze. Cameron's painting was propped up against the railings where Liz had left it.

'Oh God, what is this doing out here?' Ilse said as she climbed the steps.

'I brought it out.'

'Oh.' Ilse picked up the painting and held it out. The colours were already dulled by a light coating of dust. Ilse frowned for a minute then, without warning, licked her thumb and wiped a long smudge from the top corner. It removed the mark, but left a smeared wet thumbprint. The edge of her mouth turned up a little. 'Better.'

She put the painting back down with the clatter of wood against the floorboards. 'Anyway, I'll see you outside after your call.'

'Ilse –'

'Yes?'

'Just –' Nathan took her hand, her fingertips light against his. 'Are you happy? Now, I mean?'

Ilse's face clouded as she considered.

'I don't know,' she said finally. 'It's been a bad week. A bad year, really. But if you're asking me if I feel better than I did last week, or last year, then the answer is yes.'

They looked at each other and slowly she took a step forward, leaned in and kissed him. Nathan closed his eyes, and warmth that had nothing to do with the sun spread through his body and he felt himself smile.

'I suppose when I think about the future now,' she said as they broke apart, 'I can imagine being happy again. And I haven't felt that way in a long time. Do you know what I mean?'

'Yeah,' he said. 'I do.'

She opened the screen door and pointed at the phone, off its cradle. 'I'll see you afterwards.'

Nathan watched her disappear around the side of the house, then let the door slam behind him. He walked down the darkened hall and picked up the phone.

'Hello?' he said. Through the window, the cricket game was in full swing. The girls were taking turns bowling while Bub called out instructions.

'Nathan,' Glenn's voice came down the line. 'Sorry, mate, I only got back late yesterday and got your messages. So we've looked into it, and this Jenna woman has been in Bali for nearly three weeks. Flights and passport movement all add up, and I called the retreat she's staying at and had a brief word with her. She said she was sorry to hear about Cameron, mate. Apparently she just wanted to send him some letter.'

Xander spotted Nathan through the window and waved as Lo somehow managed to bowl Bub out. Bub fell to his knees in mock humiliation as the girls celebrated to a loud chorus of laughter. Bub pointed at Nathan through the glass, and gestured. *Come and help me.*

'Nathan, mate? You still there?' Glenn's voice sounded far away.

'Yeah.'

'Was there something else you wanted to talk about?'

'Sorry,' Nathan said. 'It was –'

Ilse was laughing as the girls ran victory laps.

Nathan took a breath. 'You know what, mate? It was nothing.'

'You sure? Message made it sound urgent.'

Lo was at the wicket now, struggling with a bat that was almost as big as her. Harry bowled underarm and she made contact and everyone cheered.

'No, I wanted to say –' Nathan stopped. 'I wanted to tell you that I'm going to be coming into town more often from now on. I'm not looking to make any trouble, but I'm going to show my face when I want to. So tell whoever you need to tell, but that's what's going to be happening.'

'Righto,' Glenn said. 'I wouldn't say that was particularly urgent myself, but it doesn't sound like a bad idea at all to me.'

'Thanks, Glenn.'

'No worries.' The cop gave a polite cough. 'If that's all –?'

Through the window, Nathan could see Liz standing to one side, a little in the shade, a little unnoticeable, watching over her family. She looked at peace. Harry was giving the girls batting tips while Bub said something to Xander that made him laugh. Ilse was smiling, her hair shining in the sunlight.

'That's all,' Nathan said.

'Merry Christmas, then.'

'And you.' He hung up.

Outside, the light was dazzling as he opened the door and went to join his family.

Acknowledgements

I have loved writing this book and I'm so grateful to the many people who helped me bring this story to life.

Once again, I am indebted to my outstanding editors Cate Paterson and Mathilda Imlah at Pan Macmillan, Christine Kopprasch and Amy Einhorn at Flatiron Books, and Clare Smith at Little, Brown. Thank you so much for your wise advice, insights and encouragement throughout.

I am constantly grateful for the tireless work of my wonderful agents: Clare Forster at Curtis Brown Australia, Alice Lutyens and Kate Cooper at Curtis Brown UK, Daniel Lazar at Writers House and Jerry Kalajian at the Intellectual Property Group.

I would never have been able to write this book without the goodwill of so many people who took the time to speak to me and share their lives and their stories.

A huge thank you to retired Birdsville police officer Neale McShane and his wife Sandra, who invited me into their home. Not everyone would be willing to drive a stranger 900 kilometres across the outback and answer questions the entire way, and I'm so lucky that Neale was one of the few who would. It was a once-in-a-lifetime road trip and I'll never forget it.

It was an honour to spend time in Birdsville with Aboriginal elder and Munga-Thirri National Park ranger Don Rowlands and his wife Lyn. Their insights and experiences opened my eyes to many things I had never before considered, and I am truly grateful they were willing to share their thoughts with me.

A big thank you to Birdsville nurse Andrew Cameron for all the fun and fascinating conversations and trips around the area. I learned a huge amount and his help with the factual research for this book was invaluable.

I am also very grateful to David Brook for kindly sharing his extensive knowledge and expertise of property management, and patiently answering a long string of questions about cows, radios and everything in between.

Thank you to cattle farmer Sue Cudmore for telling me her stories about calves, and to author Evan McHugh for introducing me to his friends and contacts and talking to me about his own experience of the outback. His books *Birdsville* and *Outback Cop* (co-authored with Neale McShane) were both useful in my research.

I am grateful to everyone who helped me along the way, and any mistakes or artistic liberties are fully my own.

Last but not least, thank you to my dad Mike Harper for the idea that eventually became *The Lost Man*, and as always to Helen Harper, Ellie Harper, Michael Harper, Susan Davenport, Ivy and Ava Harper, and Peter and Annette Strachan.

And of course, the biggest thanks must go to my lovely husband Peter Strachan and our beautiful daughter Charlotte Strachan. You give me so much and I couldn't write these books without you.

Jane Harper

Force of Nature

Five women reluctantly pick up their backpacks
and start walking along the muddy track.
Only four come out the other side.

The hike through the rugged landscape is meant to take them
out of their air-conditioned comfort zone of the office and
teach resilience and team-building. At least that's what
the corporate retreat website advertises.

Police officer Aaron Falk has a particularly keen interest
in the whereabouts of the missing walker. Alice Russell
is the whistleblower in his latest case – and Alice knew
secrets. About the company she worked for and the
people she worked with . . .

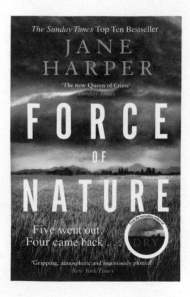

Jane Harper
The Dry

WHO REALLY KILLED THE HADLER FAMILY?

It hasn't rained in Kiewarra for two years. Tensions in the farming community become unbearable when three members of the Hadler family are discovered shot to death on their property. Everyone assumes Luke Hadler committed suicide after slaughtering his wife and six-year-old son.

Federal Police investigator Aaron Falk returns to his hometown for the funeral and is unwillingly drawn into the investigation. As suspicion spreads through the town, Falk is forced to confront the community that rejected him twenty years earlier. Because Falk and his childhood friend Luke Hadler shared a secret, one which Luke's death threatens to unearth . . .

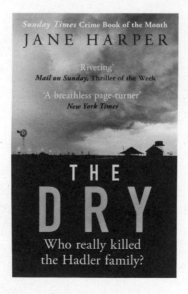

Continue reading
for an extract from *The Dry* . . .

Prologue

It wasn't as though the farm hadn't seen death before, and the blowflies didn't discriminate. To them there was little difference between a carcass and a corpse.

The drought had left the flies spoiled for choice that summer. They sought out unblinking eyes and sticky wounds as the farmers of Kiewarra levelled their rifles at skinny livestock. No rain meant no feed. And no feed made for difficult decisions, as the tiny town shimmered under day after day of burning blue sky.

'It'll break,' the farmers said as the months ticked over into a second year. They repeated the words out loud to each other like a mantra, and under their breath to themselves like a prayer.

But the weathermen in Melbourne disagreed. Besuited and sympathetic in air-conditioned studios, they made a passing reference most nights at six. Officially the worst conditions in a century. The weather pattern had a name, the pronunciation of which was never quite settled. *El Niño.*

At least the blowflies were happy. The finds that day were unusual, though. Smaller and with a smoothness to the flesh. Not that it mattered. They were the same where it counted. The glassy eyes. The wet wounds.

The body in the clearing was the freshest. It took the flies slightly longer to discover the two in the farmhouse, despite the front door swinging open like an invitation. Those that ventured beyond the initial offering in the hallway were rewarded with another, this time in the bedroom. This one was smaller, but less engulfed by competition.

First on the scene, the flies swarmed contentedly in the heat as the blood pooled black over tiles and carpet. Outside, washing hung still on the rotary line, bone dry and stiff from the sun. A child's scooter lay abandoned on the stepping stone path. Just one human heart beat within a kilometre radius of the farm.

So nothing reacted when deep inside the house, the baby started crying.

Chapter One

Even those who didn't darken the door of the church from one Christmas to the next could tell there would be more mourners than seats. A bottleneck of black and grey was already forming at the entrance as Aaron Falk drove up, trailing a cloud of dust and cracked leaves.

Neighbours, determined but trying not to appear so, jostled each other for the advantage as the scrum trickled through the doors. Across the road the media circled.

Falk parked his sedan next to a ute that had also seen better days and killed the engine. The air conditioner rattled into silence and the interior began to warm immediately. He allowed himself a moment to scan the crowd, although he didn't really have time. He'd dragged his heels the whole way from Melbourne, blowing out the five-hour drive to more than six. Satisfied no-one looked familiar, he stepped out of the car.

The late afternoon heat draped itself around him like a blanket. He snatched opened the back-seat door to get his jacket, searing his hand in the process. After the briefest hesitation, he grabbed his hat from the seat. Wide-brimmed in stiff brown canvas, it didn't go with his funeral suit. But with skin the blue hue of skimmed milk for half the year and a cancerous-looking cluster of freckles the rest, Falk was prepared to risk the fashion faux pas.

Pale from birth with close-cropped white-blond hair and invisible eyelashes, he'd often felt during his thirty-six years that the Australian sun was trying to tell him something. It was a message easier to ignore in the tall shadows of Melbourne than in Kiewarra, where shade was a fleeting commodity.

Falk glanced once at the road leading back out of town, then at his watch. The funeral, the wake, one night and he was gone. *Eighteen hours*, he calculated. No more. Keeping that firmly in mind, he loped towards the crowd, one hand on his hat as a sudden hot gust sent hems flying.